Surviving Through the Night

Emilee King

ISBN-10: 1966173014
ISBN-13: 978-1966173014

To my brightest stars—Nan and Court—
for continuing to shine even through my darkest nights

1

I'm alive.

I silently crept down the winding road, acutely aware of my shoes pressing against the asphalt. The street was deserted; I was the only one in sight. I kept reminding myself that I was alone and concealed. In the night, the inky black sky created almost total darkness, which I knew kept me perfectly hidden in the shadows, but I did not feel hidden. I felt hideously exposed, naked, and unprotected. The starless sky seemed to be reaching down, mouth agape as if to swallow me whole. There was too much space to move in, too much air to breathe, too many sounds to hear.

I can't handle this. I hadn't been outside since May. Since Florida. It was January now. After eight months of dark walls in square rooms, the world felt disgustingly huge and foreign, making my compulsion to curl up in a ball and close my eyes almost impossible to fight.

Of course, that wasn't really an option at the moment. For all I knew, Dalton was following me right now. It had been a few days since I'd escaped and he probably had guessed where I would go first. I knew it was stupid to be this predictable—especially since I wasn't sure this would work or end well—but I didn't know what else to do. This was what I would've done eight months ago and that old judgment was the only thing I had to go on. I was just going to have to trust myself.

Or trust who I used to be, I guess.

Finally, my destination came into view. The one-story building looked vacant and forgotten, hallways spreading out from the main entrance like lifeless fingers. I stopped at the set of concrete stairs that led to a glass door secured with metal bars.

Office of Cultist Intelligence—Colorado Division, the sign read. The capital 'O' had fallen off and Colorado had only half of its 'C'.

This is it.

I pulled out two narrow plastic pieces from my hoodie pocket and tiptoed up the stairs. My fingers fumbled as I began to work on the lock. For a second I wondered if I would be unable to get the door open—it had never taken me this long before—but I finally heard a click. Both relief and disappointment hit because I almost wanted the excuse of not being able to get in. Brushing the thought aside, I pulled the heavy door open. It gave a piercing creak and the sudden intrusion of sound made me jump. I lost my grip on the door and it slammed shut. Automatically, I froze and glanced around, sure that I had just compromised everything, but I was still alone.

Calm down, I told myself, *before you ruin your only chance.*

Taking a deep breath, I opened the door again and slipped inside. The reception area smelled musty and stale, the walls painted in ugly shades of green. All lights were off except one in a long hallway, so I clenched my fists and went in that direction.

I passed by all of the closed doors and kept moving until I heard the buzz of voices. An urgency exploded inside me, overtaking all fear. I needed this *now,* despite any consequences.

I didn't stop as I turned a corner and walked straight into a conference room. At a lengthy table, two men— an early thirties guy and an older fifties one—were sitting across from each other, bouncing a small red ball back and forth as they argued. A younger woman sat at the head, drumming her fingers against the table in frustration, her shoulder length brown hair swept to the side and her chin in her hands. All three of them gaped at me when I appeared in the doorway.

"Who are you?" the finger drummer asked as she stood up from her chair. Her voice had more power and authority to it than her appearance suggested. "How did you get in here?" The two men gave me questioning stares, the silver-haired one dropping the red ball. It bounced three times on the floor before rolling out of sight.

The woman started toward me, and my instant reaction was to retreat. As she came closer I automatically started to walk backwards. She stopped when she saw my sudden fear, folding her arms across her chest, studying me. Her face softened slightly.

"How did you get in here?" she asked again, less harshly.

You're going to have to answer, I tried to tell myself. *You're going to have to talk to her. You can't blow this.*

The anticipation of wanting to and not wanting to was eating me away, making me dizzy but resolute: this was my only chance. I hadn't risked everything to find this place just so I could screw it all up.

"Are you Lindsey Carter?" I blurted, my voice hoarse.

She nodded once, a fleck of surprise in her eyes.

I cleared my throat and it sounded like a dying engine. "So you're in charge of this place, right?"

She sighed. "Unfortunately, yes."

"You have a prisoner here, right? That's why you're here in the middle of the night."

A faint gasp went through her teeth as the two men stood up from their chairs—apparently they'd been expecting something else from me. Instantly, any molecule of friendliness that might've existed toward me was replaced with suspicion.

"How do you know that?" Lindsey asked, taking a step forward. I stepped backward again, wrapping my arms around myself, trying to stay calm.

Keep it together. You can't blow this.

"Look, uh, Lindsey, or, um, Ms. Carter…" How was I supposed to explain this? "I know that you don't know me, but…I, uh, need you to do me a favor."

"A favor?" She narrowed her eyes. "How about you do *me* a favor and tell me who sent you here?"

"Sent me? No, nobody…" I shook my head. "I mean, I'm here by myself. I'm on my own and I need your help. Please."

Her body relaxed slightly, but the two men weren't convinced, leaning forward slightly as if at the ready to neutralize me at any moment.

Just pretend they aren't there. They aren't. It's just you and this nice Lindsey lady.

"And how can I help you?" she asked, her tone a bit more resigned.

"I need to see him." The words came out faster than I meant to.

She raised an eyebrow. "You want to see Sark?"

My heart ached at the name, both in longing and anxiety.

"Yes. I need to see Sark right now."

2

I shifted in my chair as I avoided Lindsey's gaze. She had taken me into what looked like an interrogation room and was waiting for answers. Answers that I was not going to give.

"Let's try this again," she said, polite and commanding at the same time. "How do you know Sark?"

"I told you." I kept my voice was quiet in case it would shake. "I'm his sister."

"We have been after Sark for quite some time," she said for the hundredth time, her tone still patient but almost annoyed. "We know he has no living family, and he has admitted that himself."

"He…" I was going to have to tread carefully here. "He...doesn't really know about me."

"So you've never met him?"

My hands fidgeted in my lap. "No, no, I've met him...I mean, he knows me, he just…we haven't seen each other in a long time."

Lindsey took this in with a calculating expression. I stared at a small chip in the table.

"Do you owe Sark something?" she asked.

I shook my head, not understanding what she meant.

"Sark is high up in an organization that is extremely dangerous. If you got mixed up in that, then I understand. I see that quite a bit. They'll resort to anything: kidnapping, blackmail, extortion, forcing people into—"

"No. Nothing like that."

"You aren't affiliated with it at all? Are you aware of Sark's crimes? There's plenty to tell."

Fully aware. "I know."

She leaned back in her chair, clearly confused. "Then why—"

A knock at the door interrupted whatever she was going to say. The silver-haired agent opened it and motioned at Lindsey. She gave me one more glance before getting up and following him out the door, shutting it behind her.

I looked around the empty room, a pit in my stomach. This was taking too long. Not that I expected to be able to walk in and get what I wanted immediately, but I couldn't stay much longer. Dalton could be close. I shuddered, pulling my knees to my chest and burying my face in my hands. I had no way of knowing if Dalton found out I had hacked into his computer before I escaped a couple days ago. But if he did…

My body started shaking, my breathing speeding up. He would be so mad, for so many different reasons. He would have Sark killed, maybe even before I got to see him. Or he'd make me watch, just like with—

Stop it. You need to keep it together or you'll never get to see him.

I took a deep breath, trying to calm myself. I missed Sark so badly that it hurt. I needed to see him, needed to hug him, and needed him to tell me that everything would be okay, even when I didn't see how it could be okay.

Who am I kidding? I was overselling to myself, trying to ignore the fact that Sark probably wouldn't want to see me at all.

Suddenly, I felt a hand on my arm. I half screamed and fell out of my chair. Lindsey was kneeling in front of me, a startled but sad expression on her face.

"Arie, are you okay?"

I froze. "How do you know my name?"

"Just calm down and sit—"

"How do you know my name?"

She took a deep breath, pulled herself up off the ground and sat in my chair. "Deron found your file. We have one on everyone we know of who has ever come in contact with Alexis. They're fairly outdated, but yours was there."

She waited for me to say something, but I just stared at her from my spot on the floor.

"This is what I do," she continued. "I help people involved in this kind of situation—we have a program specifically for supporting infecteds. I can protect you and give you whatever you need. I want to help you, if you'll let me."

No thanks. "If you want to help me then you'll let me see him."

"Why would you *want* to see him?" she asked in exasperation, breaking through her professionalism. "He's your handler—*the* Mr. Sark, no less. I can't even imagine the things that he's done to you, and instead of running away you want to walk right in and say hello?"

"Things changed," I responded, my voice trembling slightly. "It's not like that anymore."

"Then what *is* it like, Arie? Enlighten me." She gestured to me. "Because if he had anything to do with what you look like right now…" she trailed off in disgust, taking a minute to compose herself. "It's not human, how you've been treated. I understand that you need help, but Sark is not going to give it to you. I don't know what he managed to convince you of, but—"

"He didn't convince me of anything. He didn't lie to me, he didn't trick me, and he's not manipulating me." I choked slightly before adding, "He's the only family I've got left."

Lindsey rested her head in her hand. I waited for her to come up with more questions, not sure how many more I could take, but instead she sighed.

"Okay." She stood slowly out of the chair and walked toward the door. "The boys won't like it, but I'll see what I can do."

3

I waited forever, curled up in a ball on the floor in the corner. There was no clock in the barren room, but I could hear ticking as if there were a huge one right next to me. Each tick seemed to echo noisily in my skull.

Tick. *This is taking too long.* Tock. *She doesn't believe me.* Tick. *She's probably trying to decide what to do with me.* Tock. *Maybe she's called her superiors.* Tick. *Dalton works in this agency.* Tock. *Maybe Lindsey called him.*

She wouldn't know she was doing anything wrong; she would just be doing her job. Calling someone in charge would make sense. She would call him, explain that a random girl showed up and asked to see Sark, and wait for an answer. Dalton would know that it was me and warn that I'm a dangerous criminal. He would instruct Lindsey to keep me secured until he got here. It would be that easy.

My hands started shaking at the thought. I wrapped my arms tight around my legs and rested my head on my knees. I had to get out of here. I couldn't wait any longer for Lindsey to make a decision and she probably wasn't going to give me what I wanted anyway. And even if I could somehow get to Sark, what happens if he hated me and said he never wanted to see me again? I'd be back at square one. Maybe I should just leave while I still could. But I hated not knowing for certain what he would do. I hated admitting that I didn't know him well enough anymore to guess his reaction.

I can't take that chance. I couldn't walk out of here without knowing for sure.

But that shaky conclusion wasn't enough—if Dalton did show up then all would be lost. He would be so mad at me. Furious. I didn't remember the last time I had looked him in the eye, much less defied everything he ever said and broke out. And, as far as I knew, he was on his way here.

The door finally opened but I couldn't look. I shrunk away, not able to force my head up.

Go away please.

Eventually light footsteps sounded, getting louder until they stopped right in front of me. I heard their joints crack faintly as they kneeled down. I wanted to disappear, to melt into the wall, to run far away. This had been such a stupid idea.

"Arie?" The voice almost choked on my name.

Every muscle in my body tightened, and my heart skipped a beat. It wasn't Lindsey, or Dalton, or either of the other agents—it was *his* voice, the one that I had replayed in my memories over and over but hadn't heard out loud for months.

Instantly my head snapped up. There he was, right in front of me, his blue eyes full of so many emotions: shock, fear, confusion, relief, despair. Anger. Pain. He winced slightly when I met his gaze and it paralyzed me.

Time seemed to be frozen in that moment. We just stared at each other for a bit. I didn't know how long, but it felt like an eternity. I tried to read the indecipherable expression in his eyes. I couldn't tell what he was thinking.

I really shouldn't have come. I didn't think I could miss him more than I already did but seeing him amplified it by thousands. I wanted so badly to hear him talk, to hear him laugh, to see him smile. Anything. Anything was better than sitting right across from him, apologies stuck in my throat, and feeling a million miles away.

Finally, Sark smiled in stunned amazement, his small half smile that I missed so much, and I knew that I had done the right thing. Even if he was mad at me, he was glad I came. He had missed me too.

That freed me from my frozen state. I lurched forward and threw my arms around him, burying my face in his shoulder. He hugged me so tightly that I couldn't breathe, crushing me against him. It wasn't until I felt his shirt dampen under my cheek that I realized I was crying.

Sark is here, I thought in euphoric disbelief. *He's here, with me, right now.*

All too soon, Sark let go of me and pushed me softly away from him so he could look at me. His mouth was open, as if he were about to say something, but suddenly he stiffened. He wasn't looking at me in the eyes anymore; he was looking at my face as a whole for the first time. I hadn't seen my reflection in months, but I was sure I wasn't a pretty sight.

Sark looked different too. Gone was the sophisticated Sark who pretended to be much older than he was—the guy in front of me definitely put off the twenty-something single male vibe. I couldn't remember a time when he just wore jeans and a t-shirt, but he was now donning both along with a black leather jacket. His hair was slightly longer and messier compared to his usual pristine look, and he was paler than when I had last seen him. But underneath all of that, I could sense the emptiness, the impossibly oppressing grief. He had been suffering a lot since I'd been gone.

He lifted his hand and touched my temple lightly. Despite his gentleness, I flinched at the shooting pain the touch brought—I likely had a bruise there. His hands balled into tight fists, his jaw clenched, and a strange noise went through his teeth.

He figured it out, I realized, not sure what to feel. *He knows where I've been.*

Sark didn't say a word. He closed his eyes and took several deep breaths. When he opened them again, I saw something else in them: resolve.

Without explaining anything, Sark stood up off of the ground and reached down to pull me up. I momentarily lost my balance, but Sark kept me standing. My legs still weren't used to holding me up. He turned around and I saw that Lindsey was standing in the doorway watching us, her expression unreadable. Sark nodded once at her, and she pressed her lips into a thin line.

"You can't leave anything out," she told him, not hiding her distrust. "I hope you realize that."

Sark nodded again and Lindsey sighed.

"This should be interesting," she muttered before addressing me in a much kinder tone. "Arie, you're going to have to go with Brody for a while, okay?"

I took a step back and grabbed Sark's arm, hiding behind him as I peeked over his shoulder. There was no way I was going anywhere without him in this place.

"I have to go answer their questions," Sark told me quietly. Even with the low volume, I could tell that only a hint of his once prominent accent had survived. "Explain some things."

"But you just got here," I protested, my voice cracking, as I tightened my grip on his arm. "You can't leave again."

"I'll be back," he responded, his voice rough, as he fought to keep himself together. "I promise. I'm not going to leave you here."

Lindsey walked forward and took my arm. Gently she started pulling me toward the door. Fear ripped through me, and I dug my heels into the ground.

"No!" I yelled and yanked my arm out of her hand, retreating backwards until I ran into Sark. He grabbed me by my shoulders to keep me from falling over.

"Just let me take her there," he said to Lindsey, "wherever she's going. She's not going to let you take her by yourself." He tightened his grip on my shoulders slightly, which gave me a bit of comfort.

She looked back and forth between me and Sark a few times before answering.

"Fine." She gestured for us to follow her before walking out the door.

Sark didn't meet my eyes as he grabbed my hand and started leading me down the hallway. I would've stopped to protest, but the younger agent I assumed was Brody followed close behind us. All I could do was hang on to Sark and try to stay calm.

Lindsey led us deeper into the building before stopping at a heavily locked door.

"You can just stay in here," she told me as she used a key to unlock it. She stood and held open the door as Sark took me around her and into the room.

It was more of a cell than a room. A small metal bed took up the left side with a single white pillow and sheet on top of a thin mattress. A square metal table and a chair were in the middle; to the right a door led into what I guessed was a bathroom. The stiff carpet was an ugly navy blue that didn't go well with the off-white walls. One bare light bulb attached to the ceiling gave the only light the room had to offer.

Sark had to drag me inside. He tried to get me to sit down on the bed, but I wouldn't budge.

"I'm coming back," he reassured me before I could ask him not to go. "Just give me a few hours and I'll be back. I'm not leaving you here."

Tears stung my eyes. I opened my mouth but no words came out. The thought of him walking out—and the fear that he might not come back—was too much to handle. I clung to his jacket, but he pried my fingers off and disappeared out the door. I stepped forward to try and follow but Brody came inside, blocking my exit. In my haste to retreat away from him, I tripped over my foot and fell backwards onto the floor.

"You okay kid?" he asked, though he sounded like

he didn't really care. I just stared at him.

When I didn't answer, he went on. "Are you hungry? Carter said to get you whatever you wanted."

I watched him, waiting for some form of hostility in his demeanor, but I could only find annoyance. Finally, I shook my head.

He raised an eyebrow in surprise. "You don't want any food? You've got to be starving."

I shook my head again. Food was the very last thing on my mind. He eyed me doubtfully but let it go.

"All right then." Brody pointed to a small red button on the wall next to the door. "If you need anything, press that. Don't try to leave. It'll only create problems for both you and Sark. Got it?"

I nodded. He huffed in irritation, gave a last glance around the room, then shut the door behind him. I heard a click from the other side as he locked it.

The second I was alone, I started to lose my nerve, if I'd even had it in the first place. My cell at Dalton's place had been a lot smaller, darker, and dirtier than this but they both had a locked door. My throat felt like sandpaper, my hands shook violently, and I started hyperventilating. Pulling myself across the floor, I huddled into the small corner between the bed and the wall, distancing myself from the door. I grabbed the pillow off of the bed and hugged it to my chest, burying my face in it so I wouldn't have to look at the ugly room.

They could take him, I thought in terror. *They could take him anywhere and I wouldn't know. They could tell Dalton, and he would make sure I never saw Sark again. Just like...*

Even after all these months, it was still nearly incapacitating to think of Erika. The scene of her death would always be on replay over and over in my mind. I would never be able to forget it. But now I had another death scene to add to my grisly inner movie: Micah, the only friend I'd had in the last eight months.

Hasn't Dalton done plenty? Why can't he just leave Sark alone?

As if killing Micah wasn't enough—no, not just killing him: brutally murdering him as I watched, helpless—Dalton would definitely kill Sark if he had the chance, especially considering the whole 'successful breakout thing' I had going on.

I can't give him that chance.

Even though it hurt, I tried to imagine what Micah would be telling me if I was still locked up with him at Dalton's prison. He would reassure me that everything would be fine, that Sark would come back. He would help me to calm down while talking about the bright future we might have someday if we ever got out.

"Sunshine and roses, Arie," he'd say. "That's where we're headed." And I would almost smile in spite of myself.

But Micah wasn't here right now. Micah was dead. Sark wasn't here either and, if I wasn't careful, he could end up dead too.

The walls seemed to cave in around me as I clutched my head tighter and pressed my face into the musty pillow, counting my breaths and waiting for whatever would come. Like everything else, it seemed to take forever.

4

Lindsey came back a few hours later—at least I assumed it was a few hours. It felt like days. She appraised me in my 'curled in the corner' state before coming and sitting on the very edge of the bed. She rubbed her temples and let out a long breath.

"Where is he?" I squeaked out.

"He's still here." She turned her head to look at me. "He told me a lot of...absurd things. Hard to believe."

"Whatever he told you is true," I said. "One hundred percent."

She raised an eyebrow. "You stand by everything he said without even hearing it?"

I nodded. Sark knew what he was doing.

"You had a brother," she stated, watching my reaction. "A brother you loved very much. And when he passed away, you needed a new one."

I tried not to give a reaction, not sure where she was going.

"And Sark, being your handler at the time, followed you after you ran away. A while later he found out about your brother and the real effect his death had on you. Am I correct so far?"

I nodded again.

"Strangely enough, you two became friends through this—family even. Sark became your new brother." She smoothed out a wrinkle in the black skirt she was wearing. "Following this change, things started to go wrong. I realize that you're an infected and things often go wrong, but more than usual. Did it ever occur to you why that was?"

I just glared at her, beginning to see where she was headed.

"Did it ever occur to you that Sark may not be as sincere as he claimed? That maybe he saw his opportunity and took it?"

"You're a little late," I said, my voice icy. "We've already been through this."

"So there *was* a time when you questioned Sark?"

"Of course there was but it's way over now."

"You believe what he says?"

"Do you?"

She sighed. "Honestly Arie, I don't know." She clasped her hands together, her tone as if she were debriefing herself. "Factually, it doesn't really add up, but he seems sincere. Not just sincere...but really torn up. After all these years of hearing about the ruthless

Mr. Sark being Alexis' new prodigy, then meeting that man…they aren't the same. I was expecting a man who had lost his humanity, but instead he's a man burning in his own hell. He's been dormant since we caught him and then you show up and suddenly he's willing to tell us anything as long as we don't hurt you. That doesn't add up. Unless…"

"Unless he's telling the truth," I finished, "which he is."

Lindsey started tapping her fingers against her leg. "I'm assuming you know this, but Dalton works in this agency." I froze at the name, and she shook her head reassuringly. "Not in our location, but in this agency. I've worked with him before. I know he can be quite implausible at times and he's prone to letting power go to his head. He may be my superior but that doesn't mean he has to get away with what he did. We could turn him in. The issue is, we only have Sark's theory that Dalton was the one that kidnapped you. We would need your testimony if anything were to progress."

I dropped my gaze to study the frayed fabric of the pillow, unable to meet her eyes.

"I know it may seem frightening, but he deserves it, Arie. Not just because what he did to you. Erika was his assistant." I snapped my head up at the name to see condolences in Lindsey's eyes. "I worked with her. I knew her. She didn't deserve the end Dalton gave her. We both know that."

I didn't know how to respond. I knew she was right, but I couldn't turn Dalton in, for my sake. For Sark's. As much as I wanted Dalton behind bars, I just couldn't do it. He'd embedded that much in me.

"Just think about it," Lindsey added. "It would do more good than you're willing to consider."

She waited for me to respond but I just rested my head on the pillow again. I heard her sigh, stand up and walk out of the room.

As exhausted as I was, I tried to keep myself from falling asleep. Sleep had not been kind to me as of late and the last thing I needed was to trigger a full-on screaming fest. That was difficult to do, though, when I hadn't had any real sleep in weeks. I found myself lightly dozing, then pulled my head up from the pillow to keep myself from settling any deeper. That was when I saw Sark sitting on the ground in front of me, watching me with a worried expression.

A minute or so passed in silence before I spoke.

"Hi," I said quietly.

The corners of his mouth barely pulled up. "Hi."

I just sat there. Sark watched me for another few minutes before closing his eyes and letting out a long breath.

"Lindsey will be back anytime. Before she gets here, can I ask you something?"

I waited until he opened his eyes to nod.

"Please don't lie to me." He cleared his throat, but his voice was still rough as he struggled with the words. "When did he take you? Was it that day in Florida?"

Be careful, I told myself.

"That girl—the burnt one—that wasn't you?"

I shook my head.

"So, you were behind the mirror. The whole time. And you saw...everything."

Everything? I dropped my eyes to study the pillow again. The image of Erika's limp body was forever seared into my memory. *Yeah I saw everything.*

"So, you...you know then, right?" He had to clear his throat again. "About her?"

I jerked my head up and down once and felt part of his aura relax in contradicting relief.

"It was then, wasn't it? That's when Dalton took you?"

I didn't answer, but he knew it was a yes. He took another deep breath, trying to stay calm.

"Eight months," he whispered harshly under his breath.

I hesitated before scooting over so I could rest my head against his shoulder. He wrapped his arm around me tightly. It was the safest feeling in the world.

The door clicked and Lindsey came in. She didn't seem to be surprised that we were both on the floor. She just went and sat on the bed again, setting a water bottle on the ground in front of me. Her body still held a professional posture, but the look in her eyes told me she was tired. Tired, stressed, and very conflicted.

"Brody said you didn't want any food," she told me. "Were you too afraid of him to ask? I'll get you whatever you want."

I shook my head slowly.

Lindsey raised an eyebrow. "No? You've got to be starving; you're skin and bone. When was the last time you ate?"

I shrugged.

"And you don't want food?"

I shook my head.

"If I brought you something, would you eat it?"

I shook my head again.

"Would you at least drink the water?" she asked, adding a bit more authority to her tone.

Sark grabbed the bottle and put it in my hand, curling my fingers around it for me. They both waited expectantly. I sighed and unscrewed the lid. I had only planned on taking a sip, but the second the water hit my throat something exploded inside of me. I gulped the whole thing down in a matter of seconds, choking some of it up.

"Careful," Lindsey said as I used the back of my hand to wipe the water off my mouth. "Take it slow."

"Thanks," I mumbled. I screwed the cap back on the bottle and set it on the floor.

"So," she started, "I'm assuming that you won't see a doctor."

I shook my head fast, making me a bit dizzy.

"Not even the one we have here?"

"No."

"Then I'm going to ask you some questions and you've got to actually answer me and be honest." Lindsey looked at me the way the lawyers did when they expected the criminal to lie. "If I think you're downplaying anything in the slightest, I'm sedating you and handing you over to the doctor anyway."

I shuddered and Sark's arm tightened slightly around me. "I'll tell you anything if I can stay awake."

She nodded. "Fair enough. You don't remember the last time you ate, correct?"

"No."

"But you don't want to eat?"

"No."

"Why?"

"I don't know...I'm not really hungry anymore."

"Well, okay then." I could see her making a mental note to fix that later. "How have you been sleeping?"

"I don't. I have nightmares."

"We have narcotics that are safe to—"

"No," I interrupted. "No drugs."

She nodded again, making another mental note.

"Have you been sick recently?"

"I don't get sick anymore."

"Anymore?"

"Since infection."

Lindsey started tapping her foot against the ground. "What about your skin? Any irritation anywhere?"

"Um...it stings when I'm outside and the sun is up. Lots of light hurts my eyes too."

"And why is that?"

"I, um...haven't been outside...much." *Or at all.*

"Where did the bruises come from?" Lindsey asked. She attempted to make it sound like just another thing on her list, but I could sense a slight shift in the words.

I dropped my gaze to the floor. I had to be careful now.

"Bruises?" My voice was too high, giving away my feigned innocence.

"The purple blood clots on your face?" Some anger slipped through her controlled voice. "Where did they come from?"

"I, um, don't remember."

"Of course you don't." She looked up at the ceiling as if the answers to all her problems would be written up there, then took a breath and looked back at me. I thought she was going to press the point, but she let it go. "Do you have any other open wounds? Anything that might get infected?"

I opened my mouth to say no, but my ankles whined in protest. I *had* said that I'd be honest...

I uncurled myself out of Sark's grip and rolled my dirty pant legs up a few inches. Around each ankle was a thick band of exposed flesh, stained with dirt, grime and blood. Lindsey gasped and something that almost sounded like a growl came from Sark. I, for one, was pleased at what I saw.

"Never mind," I said as I rolled my pants back down.

"What do you mean 'never mind'?" Lindsey asked incredulously.

"They look better than they did earlier. They'll be fine."

She closed her eyes and took another deep breath before responding.

"Let me guess: you don't remember how that happened either?

"No."

"Look Arie," she said, "I understand what you're doing here, but you've got to stop. Admit that it was Dalton. Tell me what he did so I can punish him for it. I'll protect you—and Sark if you want—and it will all be over."

"I...I can't," I said, shrinking back into the wall.

"Yes, you can."

"But he...he would be...mad." I hid my face in my arms, my body starting to shake. "It would be bad. He would..."

"Kill you?" Lindsey asked.

"I don't think so. But he would kill other people...like..."

"Like me?" Sark finished almost inaudibly.

I nodded miserably and I felt myself unhinge. I looked up at Lindsey as tears began to stream down my face and everything began to spill out.

"Don't make me go back!" I cried. "Please, I'll do anything! I'll just sit here and be out of the way. You won't even notice me, I swear. I just can't go back, and he can never find out where I am. I...I left and he would be so mad and...and he...he would hurt Sark but I just got him back and I can't lose him again and…I can't…please…I can't go…and he…" I choked off and started sobbing.

"You're not going back, Arie," Lindsey told me, her voice firm. "I'm keeping you and Sark right here. There is nothing for you to be afraid of. He won't get to either of you."

She looked around the room like she suddenly remembered something. "This probably isn't the best environment for you, huh? I'm going to go talk to Brody and see what I can work out. It's going to be fine." And with that, she got up and strode out the door.

The second she was gone, Sark pulled me into him, cradling me against his chest as if I were five years old. I clung to him, trying to remind myself that he was really there. That I wasn't alone anymore. Slowly, my sobbing quieted and my breathing was almost as slow as Sark's. I felt a few drops on my head. I looked up and saw a single line of tears going down his face.

"I'm so sorry," he whispered in my ear. "So sorry."

He composed himself much more quickly than I did and took several deep breaths. He started stroking my hair softly, just like he used to. The feeling was so familiar, so natural and comforting, that I calmed down almost immediately. My eyelids became heavier until I couldn't hold them open. I tried to fight the drowsiness that had enveloped me, but it was a halfhearted effort.

"Go to sleep," Sark told me.

I shook my head violently. "You could be gone," I said, my words tangled together to the point of unintelligible. "I have to stay awake so they can't take you away."

"No, Arie. I'll be here when you wake up."

I wanted to protest, but I didn't have it in me.

"Promise?" I mumbled.

"Yeah. I promise."

That was the last thing I heard before unconsciousness pulled me under, still aware of Sark's protective arms around me.

5

It was the headache that woke me up. The imaginary construction crew that seemed to have set up shop in my head chipped away at my brain, striking so hard I was afraid by the time they were done I'd only have a pile of rubble left in my cranium. I curled into a tighter ball, wrapping my arms around myself. Through the clamor, I eventually became aware of hushed voices talking not far from me.

"It's not the most convenient idea," Lindsey was saying, "but it's all I can offer right now."

"It's great," Sark responded, his voice sincere. "Thank you." There was a slight pause. "For her."

"This isn't just for her. I'll admit I'm not your biggest fan, but I think I'm almost ready to start believing you."

"I don't expect you to."

"That's why I do. Nobody else seems to agree with me, which is why this is so complicated. My authority only extends so far."

"I appreciate it." There was a slight false note in his voice, like he almost turned the statement into a question. It was still so strange for me to hear it without the accent he had kept up for years, though, somehow, it was still distinctly his voice.

Lindsey caught the dip in his tone. "But?"

Another pause. "I guess…I'm just wondering why."

"Why I want to believe you?"

"Yes."

"I *want* to believe you for Arie. Right now, you're her whole world."

"That isn't all of it, though, is it? I doubt you would give this generosity to someone like me solely based on a girl."

"You're right. You have a part in it." Lindsey hesitated. "You...nobody can fake that kind of…pain. That look you get every time you see her…so severely injured…you can't fabricate that. I don't care who you are."

A few moments of silence.

"Well…" Sark cleared his throat. "Thank you for being honest."

"You've been honest with me, now I'll be honest with you. That's how trust works."

I was more alert now, but still not quite fully awake. It was like my headache was a barrier between me and reality.

"Do you think she'll be able to move on?" Lindsey asked, her voice losing its professional edge.

"I don't know," Sark answered. "If she's the same, then maybe."

"She seems like she was a fighter."

"The stubbornest girl I've ever met," he agreed. "But I don't know how far the damage extends."

"Would she tell you?"

"Probably not."

"Really? It seems like she trusts you completely."

Sark's voice took on a bitter tone. "My track record isn't looking too good right now, and she's not the type to open up to strangers."

My splitting headache must've been written all over my face, because I heard someone get up and walk over to me.

"Arie?" Sark asked, putting a hand on my shoulder. "Are you okay?"

My eyelids fluttered but I couldn't keep them open. I felt like someone was running a chainsaw through my brain.

"Yeah," I managed to get out. "I'm fine."

"What's wrong?"

"Nothing." I rubbed my temples. "My head just hurts."

"Does that happen a lot?"

I slowly opened my eyes and waited until everything came into focus. I was on the bed now; Sark was kneeling next to me and Lindsey was sitting at the table.

"I don't know. Sometimes, I guess."

I grabbed his arm and pulled myself to sitting. Sark moved to sit next to me so I could lean up against him. He reached down and picked up a new water bottle from the floor, then handed it to me.

"How long was I asleep?" I asked as I unscrewed the lid.

"Only a few hours," Sark answered.

Lindsey stood up and dragged her chair over to us. Sitting on it so she was facing me, she waited expectantly for me to drink. Like the first time, I gulped it down too fast and choked. Sark took the water bottle from me as I coughed. I composed myself quickly, then pulled my legs up and wrapped my arms around them, resting my chin on my knees. Finally I looked at Lindsey and waited for whatever she had to say.

"Feeling any better?" she asked.

I shrugged. "The headache is getting better. It will take a little bit to go away."

She nodded. "Well, the good news is you don't have to stay here anymore."

"Where am I going?" I asked nervously.

"I've made arrangements for you and Sark to go to one of our residences. It's just a small house, nothing elaborate by any means."

"And we just get to live there?" It sounded too good to be true.

"It gets a little complicated," Lindsey admitted, "but I think it will work."

"What's complicated?"

"Legally Sark is still a criminal and I can't just let him go, but I *can* change his prison quarters—as long as it's somewhere still under my jurisdiction. That's all I can do until I can work through the legalities of his situation." She gave a quick glance to Sark.

"Can't you get in trouble for doing all of this?"

Lindsey laughed once, a cynical sound. "No one cares what I do anymore."

"Why?"

"If you haven't noticed, our division is going downhill. It's just me, Brody and Deron that are left, and we're one of the only divisions still somewhat functioning. They put me in charge hoping I would finish running it into the ground so they can shut it down for good. The agency as a whole is crumbling into dust. They're too focused on their own problems to give us a second glance."

"But Brody and Deron…"

She jerked her chin up slightly, her eyes turning indignant. "They don't see it my way. But that's why I'm in charge."

Sark handed me the water again. This time I drank slower and had no problems.

"Are there any concerns you have?" Lindsey asked me. "Anything that you don't feel comfortable with or want to be taken into consideration?"

I thought for a minute before shaking my head.

"Not as long as it works, I guess."

"It will work. I'm sure it will." She smoothed her skirt out. "Are you ready?"

"Already?" I had been expecting to wait awhile to get everything set up.

"I got everything finalized while you were asleep. I don't want you to stay here any longer than you have to."

"Thank you," I said fervently. "You didn't have to do this."

She smiled softly. "You're welcome. I was getting bored listening to Brody and Deron argue all day—it's nice to have something new to do." She stood up and gestured to the door. "Shall we?"

Sark stood and grabbed my hand to pull me up. The

room started spinning for a second, but I was able to keep myself from falling. He followed Lindsey out the door, leading me along. We went down the hallway, past the conference room, and took a right. Lindsey opened another door and light from the afternoon sun flooded the dim hallway. The sunshine seemed to cut into my eyes, escalating my once diminishing headache. I stumbled backwards a few steps, still holding onto Sark's arm.

"I'm fine," I said before he could ask. I just squinted and tried to ignore the pain until my eyes adjusted.

We went outside into a small parking lot where a few cars were parked. Lindsey was already in the driver's seat of a small black one; Sark and I stepped into the backseat. She drove out of the parking lot with Brody and Deron in another car following close behind.

Lindsey noticed me watching them out the back window.

"They insisted on coming," she explained, scoffing. "As if my capabilities aren't up to par with theirs."

"They don't like me," I stated, turning back to face the front.

"It's more that they don't trust you, but yes." Lindsey glanced at me apologetically in the rearview mirror. "Sorry."

The feeling is mutual. "It's okay. Lots of people don't like me."

Speaking of people that don't like me…

"What happened to Alexis?" I asked, hoping the question would distract Lindsey as I looked to Sark. He understood what I meant.

I glanced pointedly at Lindsey. *Did you tell her? Does she know I'm the key to the formula?*

Sark shook his head slightly and I breathed a sigh of

relief.

"Something must've happened," Lindsey answered slowly, her eyes going from the road, to me, to Sark, to the road. She caught on that we'd exchanged something that she missed. "Alexis has been messy lately."

"Messy?"

"He's extremely secretive, of course, but he's been slipping up. It's hard to tell exactly why but it seems like his whole cult organization is in a mass panic. It started…actually it probably started about the time you disappeared." She glanced at me in the mirror, almost annoyed but not quite. "Do you want to tell me anything about that?"

I shook my head. "I got nothing."

She pursed her lips. "Of course not."

Sark gave a quick nod to me and I knew he would answer my questions about his old boss later.

We drove for about fifteen minutes. I watched the beautiful scenery of Colorado pass by in fascination. The barren trees stood with grave elegance; the frozen streets sparkled in the sun; the mountains rose majestically from the earth. Was the snow always so perfectly white? Had the clouds always looked so soft and feathery?

The world couldn't have just gotten prettier while I was gone, I decided. *It had to have always been this gorgeous.* How could I not have noticed?

Lindsey pulled into an old neighborhood, stopping at a simple white house on a corner. It was a small, one-story building with a narrow driveway but no garage. Some black shingles were missing from the roof and the paint was peeling to reveal yellowed walls.

"It's not much," Lindsey said, "but it's quiet around here. Everyone on this side of the street has a separate house for the winter somewhere sunny. It gets pretty cold here in the Rockies." She opened her car door. "Let's go in."

Sark and I got out of the car and followed Lindsey up the two concrete steps to the front door. Brody and Deron pulled up along the curb, studying me through the window. I avoided their gazes and trailed Lindsey into the house.

The front door opened into a small kitchen and living area. There was a worn brown leather couch, a flat screen TV, and a small fireplace in the living room. A square table took up the space between the couch and the kitchen counter. To the left of the table was a narrow hallway.

Lindsey set a key on the counter. "That's to the front door." She gestured to different parts of the room. "The TV has cable; the remote is on the mantle. Just flip the switch to turn on the fireplace. Last time I checked, all of the kitchen appliances worked." She pointed to the hallway. "There are two bedrooms down there. One has an old desk and computer if you need it. Each room has its own bathroom and the water works. Any questions?"

I looked around the kitchen in wonder. *When was the last time I was in a house?*

"Uh no," I muttered, distracted. "I don't think so."

Lindsey thought for a moment before walking over and opening a skinny door next to the fridge, showing a pantry full of basic food. She out pulled a package of crackers and came up to me.

"Eat," she ordered sternly, pressing the plastic sleeve into my hand. I ripped it open and took one out, beginning to nibble on the end of it. The salty flavor was shocking to my lethargic taste buds. My stomach rumbled at its new contents, not quite sure what to do with them.

Satisfied that I was attempting to eat, Lindsey turned her attention to Sark. She handed him a thin black rubber wristband and he took it obediently.

"Put this on," she instructed. "Once I activate it, you can't take it off. The machine back at our place registers everything, so we'll know if you decide to try anything."

Sark slid the band over his hand and waited for her to go on. Lindsey walked over to a white panel covered in buttons on the wall in the kitchen. Sark followed.

"Scan the silver side in here and press this button," she said, watching to make sure he did it right. "You have to do that every time you come in. Do the same when you leave but press this button instead. This will make sure you're here when you need to be and track you when you're not. I can give you three hours a day outside of the house—use it how you want."

Lindsey turned so she could look at both of us. "I can't stress this enough: if you are caught doing anything—I mean *anything*—that could be considered even potentially suspicious, it's over. Arie, you might get pardoned because of your circumstances, but Sark would be gone before you could blink, and I wouldn't be able to do anything. So please be careful. No stupid mistakes."

Both Sark and I nodded. We were familiar with stupid mistakes.

"Okay, one more thing." She pulled a mini remote out of her pocket and handed it to me. I put the crackers on the table so I could study it. It was thin, black, and smooth with one red button at the top. "I'm giving this to you because I get the feeling you're more prone to problems. Sark said you don't like cell phones, so I got you this. Press the button and it will call me automatically. I'll be able to track the frequency and find you, wherever you are. Although I want you to stay around Sark, strangely enough."

Lindsey let out a long sigh, then glanced over her shoulder toward the front door.

"Brody would kill me if he knew I was showing you this," she said, lowering the volume of her voice, "but you might need it."

She motioned for us to follow her into the hallway. Bending down, she moved a plank of wood to reveal a silver pistol.

"There's one under each bed too," she whispered. "I'm not giving permission, but if for some reason I can't get to you in time…"

Sark nodded once, a grim expression on his face. Lindsey slid the wood back in place and straightened up.

"I think that's it." She walked back to the front door and we followed.

"You," she pointed to me, "eat. Don't overdo it but *do* something. Try to get some sleep. If anything changes or gets worse regarding your health, you tell me. Call me for anything." She wrinkled her nose. "And a shower would help. There are supplies and extra clothes in the hall bathroom closet."

Then she turned to Sark. "You *make* Arie eat and sleep. If you notice her condition worsening in any way, call me. Make sure you check in at the right times or Brody will break down the door. I'll come by tomorrow night and see how she's doing."

She adjusted her jacket before giving me a small nod. "You take care of yourself."

"Thank you," I told her, nodding back. Then she

left.

I stared at the front door for a second before turning around to see Sark sitting at the table, studying his wristband. He looked up at me once I turned. There was a beat of silence.

"You look tired," he told me, his voice neutral.

"So do you."

"Will you be honest with me?"

I hesitated, wrapping my arms tightly around myself. "Maybe."

"When was the last time you slept more than just three hours?"

I shrugged.

"And you haven't eaten either?"

I shook my head.

His eyebrows furrowed. "How are you still standing?"

I decided to take the mostly honest approach, purposely leaving out some details. "It took a few days. To find you and to get here. I saved up…an energy supply, I guess."

"And how's that supply doing?"

"It's almost gone," I admitted. "But I think I have enough for a shower."

That broke Sark's stone face: he smiled. "Well thank goodness for that."

I grinned slightly, and the motion felt weird. *When was the last time I smiled?*

"Now will you be honest with me?" I asked, the volume of my voice dropping. "It will sound stupid but…"

He turned serious again. "Of course."

I closed my eyes and took a deep breath. "If I go look in a mirror…what…is it going to freak me out?" I opened my eyes to see his forlorn expression.

"It's pretty bad," he answered quietly.

"If I go look now…would you come with me?"

If he was surprised or annoyed by my request, I couldn't tell. He just nodded and stood up, letting me take his arm before we went slowly down the hall and into the bathroom. It was too dark to see anything besides outlines of our shapes.

"Ready?" he asked.

"Yeah," I answered, my voice small. Sark waited a half a second, then flipped the light switch.

In the reflection Sark stood, the grief amplified in his eyes, with something hanging onto his arm. A mix of a gasp and a shriek escaped my lips when I realized that the creature was me. My filmy skin was grossly ashen, stretched tight across my face. Lindsey had been right: I was skin and bone. My cheekbones stuck out, giving me a gaunt appearance, and my lips were so pale you could barely even see them. It looked like an animal had died on top of my head—my hair was matted, greasy and impossibly entangled, with thin grey streaks going through it. My face was covered with three giant purple wounds. The blood had congealed, creating a dark red layer on top of the mutilated flesh.

There was no way that thing was me. But it shrieked when I did, it moved when I did, and it let a few tears escape when I did. Even worse: it had my eyes. My blue eyes that were so empty and ghastly but easily recognizable. That thing was me.

"It's disgusting," I mumbled to myself, raising a bony hand to my bruised cheek. "He was right."

I could hear Dalton's voice in my head. *You're such an ugly little rat—look at you, you're hideous! Does that come with being an infected, Arie? Looking like an accident?* I had always liked to hope that he'd been lying to me, but now I saw that he wasn't exaggerating in the slightest.

"Who was right?" Sark asked.

"I, uh…nothing. Never mind." I couldn't rip my eyes away from the mutant in the mirror. *What* happened *to me?*

Sark shifted on his feet, trying to decide what to do.

"It will fade," he said, attempting to reassure me. "Give yourself a few weeks and you'll get back to normal."

But I'm not normal, I thought automatically. *No amount of time will ever change that.* I nodded anyway, flinching when the thing in the mirror nodded too.

Sark took that as his cue. He opened his mouth to say something but decided against it and left. I shut the door, leaning against it, trying to keep myself in check.

Finally tearing my gaze away from the mirror, I searched through every drawer until I found a brush. It occurred to me that I didn't have any sort of belongings. Not a thing. It seemed as though Lindsey had already stocked up on everything I might need, but it still felt weird to know that nothing in this house was mine. Nothing on this planet was, really.

I yanked the brush through my hair. It made it about a centimeter before coming to a halt.

This is a disaster. I'm *a disaster.*

I spent ten minutes on my hair before deciding it wasn't worth it. Half of it had come out in my hand anyway, and I was worried that if I went on for much longer, I would end up bald. I couldn't decide if that would be an improvement to my look or not.

Turning on the water, I sat on the edge of the bathtub and ran my hand under the stream. The liquid felt like satin against my skin, and I marveled at the sensation. How many thousands of times had water run over my hand? Did it always feel this way? I couldn't remember.

I had been telling the truth about my energy level—it was running out. With a sigh, I got undressed and stepped into the shower. I had to keep my face from getting wet: the water felt wonderful on the rest of my body but the wounds on my face didn't agree. That was a challenge because of the unpredictable water pressure, the ancient showerhead spurting out water in random patterns, but I managed. I scrubbed my head with shampoo, hoping to relieve my hair from its grime. A ton more came out in my hand, and I had to keep myself from crying again.

How could I have gotten to this point?

Eventually I gave up on the scrubbing. I was having a hard time keeping myself standing. I turned off the water and stepped out of the bathtub, almost tripping over the side. Opening up the small closet to my right, I hunted through musty fabrics until I found some old giant grey sweats and a t-shirt. I pulled the clothes on quickly and tried to brush through my hair again. The feeling of wet mops against my back was uncomfortable, so I twisted my hair into a bun on my head.

Maybe if it's up then it won't keep falling out.

Once my hair was out of the way, I looked in the mirror again, hoping I'd made progress. The creature didn't look any better, just a soggy version of its previous self.

I was really dragging my feet now. My thin body seemed to weigh thousands. I was about to give up and leave when something caught my eye.

A toothbrush! I snatched it off the cabinet and searched for toothpaste, not caring how tired I was. When I found a small tube, I squeezed the minty goo onto the brush and began cleaning my teeth. The bristles in my mouth created an odd but welcome sensation. Just by brushing my teeth, I felt slightly more human.

I trudged out of the bathroom and into the living room. Sark was sitting on the couch, staring at the floor, still as a statue. The only movement he made was his thumb on his left hand rubbing his finger. It took me a moment to realize that he used to wear a ring there.

The spell broke when I came in. He turned to look at me, his eyes expressionless.

"Do I look bald to you?" I asked, glancing around the room. I was starting to feel lightheaded.

He stifled a laugh, trying to tell if I was serious or not. "Um, no. Why would you think that?"

"All my…" I forgot what I was going to say for a moment. I closed my eyes to try and focus. "All my hair was falling out...in the water."

"Your hair looks fine," Sark said when I didn't continue, concern coloring his tone.

"Oh…okay…" I swayed on my feet, falling into the wall behind me.

"Arie?" Sark asked. I felt his hand on my arm, but his voice sounded far away.

I must've blacked out for a second, because suddenly I was sitting on what felt like the couch.

"Arie?" Sark was calling. "Please talk to me."

"No, I'm...I'm fine…" My words were slurred and quiet. They sounded funny.

Sark said something but I couldn't concentrate enough to make it out. He sounded really worried though. I had to make him not worried.

"Is that...is it...I'm going to sleep now," I said, deciding to ignore the feeling that I didn't like sleeping. "Is that...is that okay?"

"Yes," he answered, out of breath, like he'd just ran down the street after me. "Of course it is. Just..." He trailed off, seeming unsure what he was going to say.

I couldn't tell if I formed the words 'thank you' before I was out.

6

I slept for a long time, in sporadic intervals. The first time I woke up, I only stayed coherent long enough to take a drink of water. I was still on the couch—Sark never left my side, and I didn't complain. I wanted to tell him he didn't have to stay with me, but I fell back asleep before I got the chance. That happened several other times before the nightmare started.

I was in a house, one that I recognized. Something stirred in my chest when I realized where: it was Sark's house in Chicago, a long time ago. I wandered down the hallway into my bedroom. It looked exactly the same as I remembered it: unmade bed, books stacked on the shelf, clothes shoved in the corner. I ran my fingers over the top of my comforter, feeling increasingly unsettled. Something wasn't right.

Someone called my name, and my heart flinched. It was Erika. I didn't remember why, but I felt like I'd missed her. I didn't know where she'd been, but I wanted to see her. I walked back into the hallway and saw her standing a few feet away from me. Her curly black hair was pulled into a perfect ponytail and her skin was slightly darker than it was when we first met. She smiled her dazzling smile when she saw me, and I couldn't help but smile back.

Suddenly I heard Micah's voice echoing in the distance.

"Get out of here, Arie! He's coming!"

I didn't know what Micah was talking about, but it scared me. Erika started walking toward the commotion, away from me, and an urgency built inside of me. She shouldn't go down there. I followed her, hoping to stop her. The farther we went the more alarmed I became. She remained out of my reach, and I couldn't call out to her.

An earsplitting scream sounded, and I stopped dead in my tracks. I'd heard that scream before. It was Micah. Micah was dying. Again.

Erika broke into a run, wanting to help him. But I remembered now—Dalton killed Micah and he killed Erika too. She was running right to him.

"No, Erika!" I yelled. "Don't go!"

She didn't hear me, and I ran after her. Slowly the stretched-out hallway melted into our house in Florida.

No, no, no.

When I finally got to the end of the hallway, I burst into the living room. A crumpled, disfigured body was on the floor—Micah. I was too late for him. Erika was standing in the middle of the room, facing me, a worried and perplexed expression on her face. Dalton was behind her. She didn't know he was there; she was just watching me.

I rushed forward to push her out of the way, but I crashed into something hard. Glass. A giant glass wall. Dalton smirked at me.

"No!" I screamed, pounding on the glass. "Erika, get out!"

No matter how much I screamed or how hard I beat against the glass, it was no use. Dalton lifted his gun and pulled the trigger. Erika fell limp to the floor.

"Erika! Erika!"

Something was fighting against me now, overpowering me in my torn apart state of mind. My body was pinned by an invisible force, making me finally give up. I knew there was no use fighting. I knew that Dalton always won and took me away in the end.

My eyes snapped open. I wasn't in Florida; I was in Colorado. There was no invisible force. Sark was restraining me from behind, securing my head to his shoulder. The second I realized it was him I knew what happened. The nightmares were why I dreaded sleeping in the first place.

Horror rushed through me, and I yanked myself away from Sark. He must've decided I was awake because he let me go. I turned myself around and gasped, seeing a fresh scratch on his face, his eyes full of shock and anguish. My knuckles were bleeding, and I thought my face was too, but I didn't care.

"I'm sorry!" I hid my head in my arms, not able to confront his expression and the pain that I had inflicted. Why did I let myself go to sleep? "I'm so sorry! I didn't...I didn't mean to..."

He doesn't care if you meant to. He cares that it happened. So far, he had been welcoming, but I had a feeling the welcome wagon was rolling out of town. *How could you do that to him? Idiot!*

I peeked up at him briefly. He was still frozen, staring at me, a tiny drop of blood staining his face.

"I'm so sorry," I said again before jumping up and dashing down the hallway. I was so dizzy that I crashed into the wall, but I made it into the bedroom that I had just deemed as my own. Slamming the door shut, I leaned against it and sunk to the floor.

You're so stupid! He doesn't need this and he doesn't need you. Take your moronic problems somewhere else.

A moment later, Sark tried to come in. I pushed my back up against the door to keep it from opening.

"Arie, please let me in." He was calm but his voice still had remnants of the pain he couldn't hide.

I didn't answer.

"It's okay. I'm not… mad or anything like that. We used to deal with these nightmares all the time, remember?"

Erika wasn't dead then.

He tried the door again but had no luck. I just couldn't face him trying to say he was okay when I knew he wasn't. I knew he was angry—angry at me— and I wished he would just say it. Waiting around for it was draining.

Finally, he stopped pushing on the door. I didn't know what to do, so I just stayed on the floor with my head in my hands, trying very hard not to think.

Sark came back eventually. I knew he would, but part of me expected him to just take off. This time when he tried the door, I was too tired to fight. He opened it as far as it would go with me in the way and slid inside the room. I peeked through my fingers and watched his feet. He kneeled down in front of me.

"Would you do me a favor?" he asked, his voice soft.

I hesitated before looking up. Once I saw the package of crackers and water bottle he was carrying, I realized what he had in mind.

"Just start with two," he said before I could say anything. "If you eat two and drink half of this then I won't make you have anything else for the rest of the day."

I decided not to argue. I needed to make *up* for what I'd done to him, not make everything *worse*. Arguing about food wasn't going to help. I took the package and bottle from him and started working on a cracker.

Sark sighed and ran a hand through his hair.

"Look, Arie," he said, and I braced myself. I wasn't ready for any real discussion on any subject. "I know that…that this is strange and…and hard for you. And I would be lying if I said that it wasn't strange and hard for me too. It's going to be…difficult to get things back to…" He trailed off and started over. "I know that things will never really be normal again, and I'm sorry for that. Really, I am. But I don't want you to think that I can't help you. I don't want you to worry about me. Right now, you need to focus on yourself."

I was still staring at the cracker that I wasn't really eating. Listening to him lie this thoroughly was almost painful, however noble his intentions were. I didn't want to hear him say another word like that, so I just nodded without looking up and said, "I know."

If he had been planning on saying more, he didn't.

He just waited for me to eat. Finally, I gave up and shoved the whole cracker in my mouth, taking a drink of water to go with it. My stomach grumbled but didn't freak out. That was a good sign.

Sark glanced around the room, as if trying to be nonchalant, before looking at me again. "Would you be okay here by yourself for a bit?" he asked. "I wouldn't be gone long, but if you're not okay then it's fine."

That caught my attention. "Where are you going?"

He looked at the ground now. "I just have something I have to do and I'm not sure you should leave the house yet. You still look pretty fragile."

Where in the world would he be going? It's not like he has friends around here or anything. It occurred to me that I actually didn't know that. I'd been gone for eight months, and Lindsey had caught Sark in this general area. Was this where he'd been while I was gone?

"You have to go today?" I asked.

He shuffled his position slightly. "Yeah, I can't wait any longer."

"Why?"

"I just need to go check on something." By the sound of his voice, he knew that wasn't enough to convince me. He was right.

"If you're going somewhere, I'm coming." He probably wanted some time away from me—he probably wanted to get as far away from me as possible—and me being clingy wasn't going to help fix our relationship. But I wasn't going to stay here by myself, and I wasn't going to let him get away with vague answers.

Sark furrowed his eyebrows. "I'm not sure that's such a good idea."

"Well, where are you going?"

He debated for a minute, and I ate another cracker. Maybe if I was willing to eat, he would let me go.

Sark rubbed his jaw, then sighed. "Fine. But you have to do *exactly* what I say. No spur of the moment ideas."

Is it that bad? Where would he be going that was so dangerous?

"When are we leaving?" I asked, now a little nervous.

"Are you sure?"

"When are we leaving?"

He sighed and stood up. "Now." Reaching down, he pulled me to my feet. "Find a jacket and some shoes and let's go," he said as he left the room.

For a second I stood, contemplating, wondering if I should just stay. Sark obviously wanted to go by himself, and I didn't want to make him more upset than he already was. But the secrecy really bothered me. What wasn't he telling me?

I hurried and got ready to go, afraid that he would just leave without me. When I came into the kitchen, he was scanning the wristband in the tracker machine.

"We're walking," he said without looking at me. "It's not far, but are you sure you can make it?"

"I'll be fine." Actually, I wasn't sure, but it was not the time to wonder.

He nodded and walked over to the front door, opening it and gesturing for me to go. I didn't hesitate as I went out the door into the blinding, unfamiliar world.

7

Walking is hard.

That was the conclusion I came to after we went the first block. By the third I was slowing down. Sark noticed and tried to tell me to go back, but I waved him off and tried to be faster. There was no way I was going back. Sark let me hang onto his arm and he kind of pulled me along. He went slowly enough that I could keep up, but fast enough that I didn't feel like he was going easy on me. I couldn't tell if my presence annoyed him or not, so I tried to stay out of his way as I continued to trip over my own feet.

The trip was farther than Sark thought. I could tell

he was getting slightly frustrated, but he was also anxious. He kept glancing over at me, making sure not to meet my eyes, but he never said anything, so I didn't either. I had pulled the hood from my jacket over my head in an effort to hide my gross face from the world, not able to keep myself from stiffening every time somebody passed us.

Sark led me through the neighborhood and into a city. I watched the snowy sidewalk, trusting he was going in the right direction, as each step got harder. I was already exhausted, silently hoping Sark would point to the nearest place and say we'd arrived. That never happened. I was wondering how in the world I was going to make it back when Sark finally stopped. He had gone around the back of a building and was looking at a door on the side in the alley. He took a deep breath, then turned to me.

"You stay right here," he said, taking my shoulders and positioning me against the wall next to the door. "Right here. I'm serious. Don't move. I'll be right back."

What? He was going to leave me outside? What the heck was he doing?

Before I could ask, Sark went inside and the door shut behind him.

I pulled the hood off my head and felt the crisp breeze against my face. It felt amazing, but I couldn't really enjoy it. What was Sark doing? Why couldn't I go inside?

Why can't *I go inside?* I reasoned with myself. *What's he going to do? Yell at me? Tell me to get out? Tell me to get lost?* I had been anticipating that all three of those would happen in the near future so I figured I didn't have much to lose. And my curiosity was burning. I was gone—I had missed so much. Maybe he caught up with old friends, if he actually had those. Worse, maybe he made new ones. Better ones. Maybe it was like a TV show where he had a whole other family and was trying to lessen the blow as different worlds collided.

That's stupid. Why do you care so much anyway? After all, I was gone and I didn't come back. I had lost all dibs on being Sark's best and only friend. It would make sense that he moved on. He deserved to. He was entitled to that. And here I was, messing all of that up.

But I have to know. I just have to. That way I can do whatever's best for both of us.

Without taking much more time to justify myself, I slowly turned the handle on the door. It wasn't locked. Gently I pushed it open and stepped inside.

It was dark. Following the sound of voices, I hesitantly made my way to the far wall and peeked around a corner into a bright room. Sark was standing a few feet in front of me with his back to me, talking to someone. There were a few more people scattered around the big area, but I didn't recognize any of them. None of them noticed me.

Sark must've adopted an extra sense that has to do with me, because a second after I came in, he stiffened and turned around. I expected irritation or anger. He only looked stressed and worried. When he turned, he exposed me to the girl he was talking to.

Her black eyes widened when she saw me, the emotion escalating from surprise to disbelief. A small shriek escaped her lips. Immediately, everyone in the room looked to see what happened.

I shrunk back, hating the fact that everyone was staring at me and more people were coming into the room, but I couldn't make myself leave. Because this was Alaina and she was my best friend. At least, she *had* been.

The scene was frozen. Moments passed before Alaina walked up to me slowly, as if approaching a rabid animal, her hand halfway outstretched, before stopping right in front of me.

"Arie?" she whispered, her voice almost reverent.

I nodded. A faint gasp went through her teeth, and I waited in nervous anticipation, unsure of what to do. There was no easing into coming back from the dead—the shock value must've been pretty intense.

Alaina gave a small disbelieving grin, then threw her arms around me and I hugged her back tightly in relief. I hadn't realized how much I had missed her until now.

I felt her tense up before she pulled away from me, her black eyes heating up as she took in my face. I was distracted by the people coming into the room—people that I knew.

Liam, Alaina's older brother, was the first to catch up to us. The second he saw me, he froze right in his tracks. It was so sudden that his siblings who'd been following—Mark and Mara—crashed into him. Two others came right behind them: Brennan and Lucy. They were infecteds, two of my best friends that I hadn't seen in forever. They joined the line of people who were staring at me in astonishment.

I stepped back automatically and tripped on my own foot. Thankfully I caught myself before I fell. Sark stepped toward me, but didn't say anything. He was watching my reaction to their reaction.

"You're alive," Liam muttered under his breath.

"Arie," Alaina started, very slowly, "where have

you been?"

I opened my mouth, but I couldn't make any words come out.

What am I supposed to say? Are there guidelines for what you should say when your friends find out you're not really dead?

My concentration kept flicking to the teenagers that flowed into the room. Their eyes were confused, but there was a subtle layer underneath that I recognized. They were distrustful, scared but strong. They were infecteds. All of them.

"Who are they?" I asked, barely able to make my voice audible.

"They're infecteds," Sark answered, stepping closer and matching my volume. "They aren't going to hurt you."

Based on the death glares I was receiving, I sincerely doubted that. One of the kids, a beefy guy with sandy blond hair, stepped forward, breaking up the line of my friendly spectators.

"*This* is her?" he asked. "Are you serious?"

"Peter," Sark said, glaring, as a warning. A warning this Peter guy didn't take seriously.

"You're supposed to be Alexis' little pet? *You*? The key?" He was in my face now, and I cringed away. Sark stepped in between us.

"Back off. Now."

"What, we're supposed to be all nice just 'cause she looks like roadkill? If it weren't for her maybe there would be more of us left."

I peeked around Sark, interrupting whatever he was going to say.

"Left?" I still couldn't make my voice very loud. "What do you mean?"

By this point Brennan had composed himself. He pushed Peter away from me before answering my question.

"After you...left...Alexis kind of panicked."

"We all thought you were dead," Peter cut in.

"He started infecting new waves of people to try and recreate you," Brennan continued, trying to keep his voice even, as he fingered one of the many thread bracelets that lined both of his wrists. "He ordered the immediate extermination of the rest of us."

More of us left? My heart started beating faster as I looked around the room. *These are all of us left?* That couldn't be right. There were maybe thirty or forty people here—at last count there had been at least a couple hundred infecteds.

Yeah, but when was that last count? There weren't enough infecteds, yet there were too many. Too many people in one room, all focused on me.

"You mean...everyone else is...dead?" I asked, scanning the crowd. Too many, but not nearly enough. I felt dizzy as I tried to grasp this idea.

I thought of what Peter had said. *Maybe if it weren't for her, there would be more of us left.*

My knees buckled, but Sark caught me by the arm. Suddenly everything came back to me—everything from what seemed like my past life. I was still the key to the formula. Alexis knew that and still wanted me and the power I could have. Except I had escaped. I had died. And he had to figure something out.

They're all dead. They're all dead because of me.

"Arie?" Sark whispered in my ear.

I didn't answer. This was wrong.

Without an explanation, Sark pulled me deeper inside the building. I let him drag me, my mind at a loss and not willing to work. We went through a new door and into what looked like a kitchen. He brought me to a chair that was next to the wall and I collapsed into it, my legs grateful for a break, staring in a daze at nothing in particular.

I heard the soft buzz of voices. Sark left for a moment, then came back, bending down in front of me so he could look at me head on.

"Arie?" he asked again, waving a hand in front of my face. "Come on, look at me."

Finally, I blinked. "What?" I glanced around, really looking at the room for the first time. Cabinets lined the walls all the way around the room and a giant rectangle counter took up the middle of the space. I noticed two fridges, two ovens, and a microwave. Liam and his twin siblings were huddled by the door to my right. Across the room, Brennan, Lucy, and a several others I didn't know were leaning against the counter. Alaina stood a few feet behind Sark. Everyone was watching me.

Sark cleared his throat and I redirected my attention back to him. He gave me a glass of water, curling both of his hands around mine to make sure I didn't drop it.

"You need to drink this," he said, trying to hide the concern in his voice. "All of it. Okay?"

"I don't think I like water," I mumbled, distracted.

"Yes, you do."

"Okay." I brought the cup to my lip without really thinking and wasn't prepared for the liquid. I choked on it and coughed a few times. Handing the glass back to Sark, I pulled my legs to my chest and rested my chin on my knees, closing my eyes.

"Does your head hurt?" Sark asked. I nodded. As soon as I acknowledged it, the headache seemed to get worse.

I heard Sark stand up and take a few steps.

"What the heck is going on?" Alaina asked. She lowered her voice, but I could still hear. "You disappear for weeks without telling anyone, then show up with Arie? How did you find her?"

"I didn't find her," Sark answered. "She found me." He went on to explain that a few weeks ago he was caught by Lindsey and kept in her building. Then I showed up, demanded to see him, and convinced Lindsey to let him stay somewhere else.

"Does that lady know you're here?" Alaina asked. Sark must've nodded because she went on in frustration. "Are you serious? How are we—"

"I told her only what she needed to know. Plus, infecteds are part of her job description. She won't be a problem."

"You're sure?"

"I wouldn't have said anything if I wasn't."

Silence. A minute passed. I couldn't help but think it was weird to hear Sark and Alaina talk like this—like I wasn't the thing that kept them civil to each other.

"So where was she?" It was Brennan's voice now. "It couldn't...I mean…"

"She won't actually admit it, but it was Dalton." The murderous hatred Sark gave the name seemed to heat up the room. "He faked her death so we wouldn't try to find her."

A solemn heaviness enveloped the room. All was silent for several minutes. I couldn't tell if my headache was getting better or worse. Maybe it was just staying the same.

Alaina was the first to say anything. "You mean…this whole time?"

"She won't say exactly what happened," Sark went

on, seething. "But her face alone is enough to guess."

"Why didn't she tell that Lindsey chick?" Alaina asked. "Let's get the psycho locked up."

"Dalton works in the same agency as Lindsey. Arie's too afraid of him to do anything, even admit it to me."

I shifted on the chair. It was uncomfortable and my body just wanted to go to sleep. My mind was extremely opposed to that idea and the battle that ensued between them increased my headache.

"She's exhausted. She'll be fine for a while and then she just drops—can't even hold a coherent conversation—and her nightmares came back. She won't sleep; she won't eat. I can tell she's in pain all the time, even when she doesn't say so, and she talks to herself without even realizing it. Everything scares her. She won't talk to me…" Sark sighed in such complete defeat that I thought he might crumble to bits right there on the floor. "I don't know what to do."

Suddenly, he stopped talking and I heard footsteps.

"Arie?" he asked, his voice low and right next to me. "Arie, can you hear me?"

I tried to lift my head to respond, but it was too heavy. Someone held my head up for me so I wouldn't fall off the chair.

"You need to go to sleep," Sark said. "Can you do that?"

I shook my head awkwardly. "I don't…I don't sleep."

"You need to now, okay?"

"But I…" I tried to think of an excuse. "But we have to get home on time."

"We will."

"No…we got…in minutes…"

Sark picked me up and started carrying me somewhere. I couldn't open my eyes to see where.

"Go to sleep," he told me. "It'll be okay."

I wanted to believe him—and refute him—but before I could do either, the world seemed to slip from me. No matter how hard I fought it, I was gone.

8

The dream this time wasn't as bad as the first, and, thankfully, not as long. I wandered in complete darkness for a lingering length of time. Just hours of me trying to figure out where to go. Suddenly, I sensed a presence. I was no longer alone. I didn't get to see who it was before I woke up.

I momentarily panicked when I didn't recognize my surroundings. I was curled on a couch in a small room, the door ajar. The pounding in my head had reduced to only an ache, and I felt much more alert. Concentrating, I tried to figure out what to do, when I heard Sark's voice coming from outside. I picked myself up off the couch and, with wobbly and unsteady steps, hesitantly walked through the door.

Sark was sitting in a chair at the head of a loose circle. Alaina, Liam, Mark, Brennan, Lucy and a few others I didn't recognize were sitting around him, all with the same worried look on their face. Whatever they were talking about, it wasn't good.

They all stopped when I came in. Sark had his back to me, so he didn't see me until I put a hand out to lean on his chair. He went into panic mode for a second, then realized I was mentally there.

"Are you okay?" he asked. "You weren't asleep for very long."

I nodded, glancing self-consciously at the group of people. I could tell they were waiting for me to make the first move.

"Hi," I said, my hands fidgeting.

They all stared at me. The awkwardness was thick enough to choke on.

"Hi," Brennan finally responded. His signature spiky black hair and giant white smile helped calm me, strangely enough.

Duh, he's your friend.

"I'm sorry about earlier," I apologized. "I don't know what I said or…didn't say. I just don't make sense sometimes."

"Nah, it's fine." He stood up, came over to me and gave me a hug. His skinny arms made me feel right at home. "I'm...*insanely* glad to see you, Arie. Welcome back."

I gave a small grin. That was the first time anyone had said that to me. "Thanks."

Brennan kept an arm around me and pointed to the group. "I believe introductions are in order."

The two boys I didn't know looked at Brennan with questioning eyes but went along with it.

"I'm Tristan Foster," one of them said. He had chocolate eyes and was wearing a shark tooth necklace.

"He's one of our emergency guys," Brennan supplied. "If something goes wrong, he'll get it figured out." He pointed to the other kid. "And this is our tech guy. He can hack into nearly anything, and he's a beast at those claw machines."

"I'm Carlton Kenton," the hacker said, flipping his shaggy hair out of his face and giving me a small grin. "But just call me Carl."

"I'm Arie," I responded lamely before realizing that they already knew that. Everyone shifted uncomfortably in their seats, and I felt increasingly out of place.

"So…" Brennan started. "Things have been pretty crazy, huh?"

"Yeah." I brushed my hair behind my ear. "Yeah, you could say that."

"How long have you been back?"

"Um…I'm not sure. A few days maybe?"

"How's the weather treating you?" He grinned. "It's pretty cold out here."

I couldn't help but chuckle slightly. Brennan always made everything so relaxed, even if danger was staring us right in the face.

"It's definitely weird—it was hot when I left and now it's freezing. It's hard to wrap my head around. How long have you been here?"

"The longest of anyone besides Alaina. That makes us honorary veterans." He saluted me jokingly. "First in line for lunch and everything."

"Well congratulations, soldier. I'd imagine you…"

I trailed off, something catching my eye. Slowly, I walked around the circle of people to the wall across the room. It was covered with thin rectangular papers, each having its own name and date, and colored cut out hearts glued on. My eyes scanned them quickly, but all I really cared about was the bigger paper at the top.

Arie Nolan: November 1, 1995 - May 6, 2013

I stared, reading it over and over again, not really sure what to feel. That was for me—my memorial. I realized that the rest of the papers must be memorials too. I read them now with renewed interest. Some had only names, some only dates, and some were just blank. The sickening part was how many there were: the display took up the whole wall. So much to look at, but my eyes kept jumping back up to that top paper.

"We can take it down if you want," Brennan said quietly. He had walked up behind me.

It took me a moment to respond. "So, these…they're all gone?"

He stepped forward to stand next to me, studying the wall with reverence.

"We didn't know all of them. Everybody here knows someone that didn't make it, and others we just heard about. Some of them will be nameless forever." He turned to look at me. "Your name doesn't need to be up there, if you don't want it to be. You didn't really die." He sounded like he was telling himself more than he was telling me.

"It feels like it sometimes," I whispered, wrapping my arms around myself.

"I bet."

I took a shaky breath in preparation. "So, what

happened?"

"Sark was in Chicago with Alaina when he first heard," Brennan answered slowly, his tone like a voiceover on a war video. "Alexis shut him out of every system he could, but Sark can still access some low-level databases when he wants to. That's how he knew about the extermination order. Alaina and her family relocated here to keep from being found out while they tried to let infecteds know what was going on."

Brennan shook his head sadly. "Most of us died in the first month, just 'cause none of us knew. Instead of handlers kidnapping us for usual experiments, they would try to shoot us on sight. Eventually word started traveling that something was up. Alaina contacted me and told me what was happening, and I passed it on." He glanced sideways at me. "You always stayed away from the infected networking, but we've become pretty connected. It wasn't long before Alexis lost the element of surprise."

"And you came here?"

"Yep. Lucy and I came here, and several infecteds followed. Eventually we decided to set up our community here: we take in everyone who finds us, go outside as little as possible, and try not to get discovered by Alexis." He shrugged. "If we do it right, we stay alive."

"Wow," I breathed, looking over the names again.

"Yeah. It's hard, but it works." He forced a joking grin. "You missed all the action."

I missed everything.

I turned to Brennan, a pit in my stomach, thinking of the glares I had received earlier.

"That's why they looked at me like that when I came in, huh? I killed all their friends."

Brennan dropped his gaze to the floor and shifted on his feet. "Arie—"

"Oh good," a voice boomed from behind. I jumped and whipped around to see Peter. "She's awake. That's just fantastic."

I took an automatic step back when he sauntered right up to me. Brennan stepped in between us, but his skinny frame looked impossibly small next to Peter's broad shoulders. I couldn't even imagine what I looked like next to him.

Peter gestured to the wall without looking at it. "You checking out the memorial?" he asked mockingly. "It's only fitting that your name is up there, considering you pretty much killed the rest of them."

Sark appeared next to me out of nowhere, and I could feel the fury rolling off of him. "Get out."

"Aw come on," Peter replied, gesturing to me. "I'm just trying to welcome our new addition. Nobody else is glad to see her. I tried to tell them she's one of us, but I didn't have much luck. She doesn't look much like an infected, or even a person. Are you sure you didn't find her in the garbage?"

I grabbed Sark's arm when I realized he was going to hit him. Peter was a jerk, but he was right about a lot of things—including people not being happy to see me.

"I'm leaving now," I told Peter, "so you don't have to worry about it." I felt Sark clench his fists, but, thankfully, he didn't use them. "We have to go back anyway."

I turned to the group that was still seated in the circle. Liam, Mark and Alaina had all stood up, as if they were about to intervene. The rest were still staring.

What the crap are they looking at? I'm not that interesting.

"I'm sorry," I told them. "I didn't mean to be a problem. I'm going now."

"You'll come back though, right?" It was Alaina who spoke this time, with an anxious expression on her face. "You're not just going to…disappear again, right?"

"Oh yes," Peter said sarcastically. "Please come back soon."

"Um…I don't know." *Nobody really wants me here.*

Suddenly, fast footsteps pounded sharply against the stairs. A little boy appeared in the doorway. He was about eight years old, and his unkempt hair had grown to almost cover his big blue eyes. To my shock, I realized it was Hadley.

"Arie!" he shouted in joy. He ran forward and jumped onto me, knocking me into the wall. "Arie, Arie, Arie!"

I had to bend awkwardly to make myself kneel on the floor. He threw his arms around my neck.

"I knew it! I knew you didn't die! I knew it!"

"Hadley…how…what are you doing here?" I was so happy to see him—he was like a little brother to me—but the fact that he was here probably meant something bad.

"All the infecteds come here," he said, pulling away from me, as if it were obvious. "And now you're here too! Isn't that great?"

"We didn't know where he came from," Brennan explained. "He said that he knew you, but we never knew for sure."

"I *told* you," Hadley huffed in irritation. "Mom and Dad needed to protect me from The Mr. and Arie saved me. We got to play for a whole week! It was the best ever!"

'The Mr.' is what Hadley called his handler. As far as we knew, Hadley was the youngest infected alive. His parents did everything to protect him, and I ran into their family when I was trying to make my own escape from Sark over a year ago. We had saved each other.

"Perfect," Peter muttered, "the rat and the roadkill together. There's a dream team for you."

"When I got here they said you were dead," Hadley told me, his lip quivering for a moment. "But I didn't think you were. I knew you would come back. And you did!"

I couldn't help but smile. "Yes I did. Just for you." I glanced around the room hopefully. "Where are your parents? Are they here too?"

Hadley's face fell, all happiness draining right out of him. His eyes filled with tears as he looked at the ground.

"Well…they had to get me here, you know, to be safe but…we were being chased and it was scary. They…died." He pointed to a piece of paper covered in a ton of red hearts on the memorial.

Frank and Alicia Lewis — June 10, 2013

"I put lots of hearts on theirs," Hadley said, "because I missed them. I put some on yours too because I missed you too. But then I decided that everyone should have hearts on them because there has to be someone that misses them."

"Hadley…I'm so sorry." I didn't know what to say. What do you say when it's your fault?

He wiped his tears with the back of his hand. "It's okay. They're happy now. I know they are. And they brought you back to me. So it's okay. I still miss them a lot sometimes." He shook his head, like that would make it all go away. "I'm glad I got to see you. Everyone upstairs said that I couldn't, but I snuck down anyway. I used my sneaking skills, just like you taught me."

"Yeah, um, good job." I was staring at the wall again.

There are too many papers. Way too many names.

Sark reached down and grabbed my arm, gently pulling me to my feet. Hadley caught on immediately.

"Are you leaving?" He jumped up from the ground. "You just got here! You can't—"

"She'll be back," Sark said. "We'll come back later." Without waiting for anyone to say anything else, he started leading me toward the door. I couldn't tear my eyes away from the wall—from my name—until it was out of sight.

There were a ton of people waiting as I walked through with Sark. They all stopped talking when we passed by, and I had to stare at the ground and pretend like they weren't looking at me.

These are my people. This is the only place I could fit in, and I'm still the outcast. I knew I deserved to be, but it still made me sad.

Before Sark could get me out, Alaina caught up to us. She gave me another quick hug, then looked me in the eye.

"Come back, okay? Please? I can't…I missed you."

"I missed you too." Really, I did. I just wasn't sure if she did.

"We'll be back," Sark said again. "Sometime."

Alaina nodded and he pulled me out the door.

We walked back in silence. A thousand questions

were ringing in my head, but I couldn't bring myself to voice any of them. I felt like I didn't deserve to know, like all of the tragedies and secrets and relationships I'd missed out on weren't mine to ask about. Sark didn't so much as look at me the whole way back and I started to feel sick. It was coming. He couldn't hide his anger at me forever. I guess I would just hang onto him as long as I could.

The trip back was just as exhausting as the trip there. We went into the house and I immediately collapsed onto the couch. All I could think of was the wall covered in names and Peter's voice.

If it weren't for her maybe there would be more of us left. It's only fitting that your name is up there, considering you pretty much killed the rest of them.

He was right. I had killed them. And Micah. And Erika.

I'm a monster.

9

I couldn't fight the sleep again. I was wandering through the darkness, just like I had earlier. The smell of blood stained the air. I didn't know whose it was, but it didn't really matter. Somebody was dead and that was reason enough to mourn.

Strangely, I knew where to go. I didn't know how I knew, or where I was going—my feet just carried me through the darkness. I went for hours. Nothing seemed to change.

Suddenly I felt a presence, the slight sound of someone breathing echoing through the black. I wasn't alone anymore.

Turning around, I tried to squint and make out a shape in the dark. Quiet tapping sounded and I couldn't decide whether to follow it or get away from it. The stench of blood grew stronger; I could taste it in my mouth.

A gunshot sounded, much closer to me than I would've liked. I backed up, away from the sound, and crashed into something, falling to the floor. The lights came on and I screamed at the sight. Erika's lifeless body was lying next to me on the ground, accompanied by hundreds of bodies all around me. They were all teenagers except for two adults that I recognized as Hadley's parents.

Somebody stood above the massacre, almost suspended in the air. His face was disfigured, changing from Alexis to Dalton every time I blinked. He smiled coldly at me, but he was looking at my hands. I followed his gaze to see my hands dripping in blood—blood that wasn't mine. A gun was in my lap…the gun that…

I screamed until my eyes finally opened and I was freed from the nightmare. I found myself on the floor of my bedroom, blankets tangled in my limbs, and two people leaning over me. Sark sighed in relief when he saw me awake, but Lindsey's mouth was still hanging open in horror. I sat up and put my head between my knees, trying to make my breaths even.

I'm a murderer. I have to do something, help them somehow. I've got to…what can I do?

"And this happens often?" Lindsey asked, trying to downplay her alarm.

"All the time," Sark muttered. "Arie? You're awake now. Everything is fine."

I shook my head. Everything was not fine. Everyone was dead.

"Arie, it's over," Sark tried again. "It's all—"

"No it's not!" I snapped my head up to glare at him. "Nothing is just *over*."

Lindsey looked back and forth between the two of us. Sark was watching me, keeping his face smooth. I wanted to yell at him. How could he be so calm about this? I wanted him to be upset, be angry, be disgusted with me. I wanted him to *do* something.

I grabbed onto the side of the bed and pulled myself up. The sun was streaming brightly behind the curtains over the window, so I guessed it was afternoon again. I'd slept for a long time. I went out to the kitchen and searched through the cabinets until I found a cup. Filling it up in the sink, I drank the water slowly to keep from choking.

Lindsey came into the kitchen first. She leaned up against the counter in front of me, crossed her arms, and waited until I finished drinking. Sark went and sat on the couch without looking at either of us. The TV flipped on, the volume turned almost all the way down. I didn't care enough to look and see what he was watching.

"How are you doing?" Lindsey asked, her voice conversational but concerned.

I stared at the cup in my hand. "I'm fine. I'm getting better."

She cleared her throat so I would look up at her. "I want a real answer. How are you?"

I took a deep breath. Genuine concern from someone really ate at me. I didn't really know what to say, so I just shook my head.

She tipped her head in Sark's general direction, a silent question. I shook my head again.

No, things are not going well between us.

Everything seems to be falling apart.

As much as I appreciated Lindsey, I wanted Erika. I wanted Erika to hug me, to reassure me, to tell me everything was okay even when she knew I wouldn't believe it. I wanted her here with me. And I knew Sark wanted her too.

"I've got to get back," Lindsey said quietly, "but I'll come check on you. Maybe I'll bring you dinner tomorrow." She tapped her fingers against her arm, as if counting something in her head. "Call me if you need anything." She gave me a small encouraging grin before turning and walking out the door.

I stood there in the kitchen for a minute, not really sure what to do. Sark was still sitting on the couch. I doubted he wanted to see or talk to me. There wasn't really anything for me to do. I didn't have the stamina or the strength to go anywhere—and where would I go? Alaina and Hadley had wanted me to come back but…did they really? I couldn't imagine why they would. And there was no way I would go without Sark.

So…what now?

I set my cup down on the counter and went back into my room. Opening the small closet, I searched through the odd array of old clothes until I found a thick white coat. It was a little too big, but it was warm. I put on two pairs of socks and some boots before walking back into the living room. I didn't look at Sark as I went past him and out the front door.

The driveway was covered in thick snow, ridden with two deep lines of tire tracks. I started with those. Combining the efforts of my hands and boots, I pushed the snow away, creating a free spot on the pavement. I sat down on the cement, pleased that it was close enough to the house that I could lean up against the wall.

The sun was out, but it did little to warm the frigid air. I closed my eyes and let it wash over my face. It had never occurred to me before that even sunshine had a feeling. It was soft yet almost prickly, like a blanket that's a tiny bit scratchy in a good way. I stayed like that for a while, just sitting there, enjoying the sun with a slight wind blowing through my hair.

I was outside for a long time. I wasn't in any hurry for anything else and it just felt nice. Lindsey had been right—it was really quiet. I never saw one person in the tiny neighborhood, and only one car drove by. The stillness was calming and peaceful. It also was a great place to think, something that I did not want to do. I just let my brain be empty and focused on the magnificent world around me.

My hands were icy and I liked it. I drew shapes in the snow—circles, squares, triangles, stars, flowers. I wrote my name with my finger in block letters, cursive, and even tried it backwards. The snow was fluffy and flaky, like frozen bits of sparkly cotton. It was beautiful. I'd always loved summer much more than winter, but the snow was unusually comforting.

After a little bit, I realized that I had drawn people, little stick figures in the snow. I pretended to not know what I meant by them, but it was obvious, and I continued despite the morbid feeling. Once I had about thirty of them I stopped. Saying a silent prayer in my head, I put them to rest.

I'm sorry, I told them. *I'm sorry for what happened to you.*

I owed it to them to do something; I just needed to figure out what. I knew I could never make up for those who had been lost—that was a given—but I had to make up for my eight-month absence. The infecteds deserved some sort of effort from me.

Note to self: start putting together a plan of action. I was weak now, but that could change. It would take time, smarts, and energy to come up with something worthwhile, but I would do it. I'd ask Sark about it, and maybe even Alaina. After all, as long as I was back from the dead, I might as well be useful somehow.

I racked my brain for ideas, but I felt so uninformed, and my efforts began to wane. Eventually, it started to snow. Nothing heavy, just tiny dots of crystal. I caught them in the palm of my hand, watching as their intricate patterns faded when they melted into water. I repeated this several times before he came out.

Sark stopped suddenly in surprise when he saw me. He must've thought that I actually left. He took in my arrangement without giving any emotion away—if he could tell that I had drawn dead people in the snow, he didn't show it.

Finally, he asked, "What are you doing?"

I stared at the snow. "Nothing."

"Aren't you cold?"

"Yeah."

"Doesn't that bother you?"

"It feels good." Actually, my numb hands and face were starting to think otherwise, but I didn't want to tell him that.

He nodded and looked up at the sky. "Do you miss it? Being outside?"

"More than I ever thought I would."

He dug the heel of his shoe into the snow, making a crunching sound. "Lindsey brought some food over. Do you think you could eat?"

My stomach wasn't completely opposed to the idea,

and I did want to go back inside. Shakily, I got to my feet, gave one last glance to the dead people in the snow, and walked past Sark and into the house.

I took off my coat and went straight to the pantry. Nothing looked particularly good, but for the first time in forever I was actually hungry. I took a loaf of French bread out, tore off a piece, and started eating it. Sark came inside as I was looking through the fridge. He just stood there, watching me. I ignored him. Strangely, a cucumber sounded good, so I took one out of the fridge.

"Are you hungry?" I asked Sark as I found a cutting board and knife.

He missed a beat before responding. "No. I ate while you were asleep."

For some reason, I didn't believe him. "Are you sure?"

"Yeah."

I washed the cucumber and put it on the cutting board. Grabbing the knife, I tried to cut it, 'tried' being the operative word. No matter how hard I pushed I couldn't cut the stupid cucumber. The knife finally slipped jaggedly into the vegetable and sliced my finger open.

"Seriously?" I muttered, sucking on the bleeding wound.

Sark came over and took the knife from me. "I'll do it." Again, he kept all emotion out of his voice, but I sensed annoyance.

He should be annoyed. How stupid do you have to be to not be able to cut a freaking cucumber?

Feeling useless, I sat on a chair. Sark focused on the cucumber, cutting it into a bunch of little pieces, then scooted the board over to me. I put one in my mouth, taking a moment to appreciate the delicious flavor. Had cucumbers always been this good?

"Thanks," I said.

He nodded but wouldn't meet my eyes, turning to put the knife in the sink and wash his hands. Finally, I couldn't take it anymore. This had gone on long enough.

"When were you going to tell me?"

He hesitated before answering. "About what?"

"About Alaina?" I asked, slightly irritated. What did he think I was talking about? "About Hadley? About all of them? About Alexis?"

Sark dried his hands on a towel, then turned to face me. He still had a stone face going. "I don't know. I didn't know if you could handle it yet."

"So…what? You were just going to wait until I figured it out?"

"No."

"Then what?"

"I was going to wait. See how you did. But I had to go make sure they were still okay, and you insisted on coming. I figured you would probably follow me inside but…" He sighed. "I don't know."

"Didn't you think it was important for me to know?"

"Well yeah, of course I did."

"Then why wouldn't you tell me?"

"You would barely take a drink of water, Arie," Sark said, rather harshly. "I felt the need to prioritize. I'm sorry if it didn't turn out the way you wanted."

His tone made me drop my gaze. I watched my fingers play with the cucumbers, my voice losing its conviction. "I just…would've appreciated a little warning."

"I told you to wait outside."

"Not…you know what I mean. I had no idea what

to do."

"And you think *I* know what to do?" His sudden anger startled me, and I glanced up to see him boiling, about to explode. "You think *I* know how to handle myself when you come back from the dead? Because I don't."

"I never expected you to. I never expected anyone to. *I* don't even know." It was coming now. I could feel it. The negative emotion he had been trying so hard to hide was all about to blow.

"I know you don't." Sark took a deep breath, bringing him back into Zen mode. "And I don't expect you to either."

I slammed my hand down on the counter, making both of us jump.

"Will you just say it?" I asked exasperatedly. "I really can't take it anymore."

"Say what?"

"You know. Don't play stupid."

He just stared at me, his forehead creasing in confusion.

"I *murdered* every single one of those infecteds. And you're not the least bit repulsed?"

He gave me a half glare. "That had nothing to do with you."

"That had *everything* to do with me."

"Arie, you can't blame yourself for—"

"Stop it! Stop saying stuff like that! I don't want you to try and make me feel better. Cut the crap and just be honest with me."

"What? I *have* been honest with you."

"No you haven't. You've been lying through your teeth ever since I got here, and I'm sick of it. You don't have to be the saint, Sark."

"What are you talking about?"

I squashed a piece of cucumber with my hand in frustration. "You know what I'm talking about. You think you can hide it, but I know it's there. You had everything worked out for you, then I had to come track you down and force myself back into your life. You can't pretend to be happy to see me forever. Everything would've been fine if I—"

"You were dead, Arie!" Sark's hands clenched into fists, his face contorted with furious anguish. "Dead! Can you imagine that for just a moment? You were *both* dead." He choked slightly on the words. "She was my wife. My *wife*. And you were like…I don't know…my sister? My daughter? You were my life. You both were. And you were both gone."

I leaned forward, opening my mouth to say something—to stop him—but he beat me to it.

"There was no life for you to ruin or interrupt because *you* were it. And I had to explain over and over and over again what happened to you, because so many other people cared about you too." His voice got louder as he spoke. "And I had to watch as they screamed and they cried and they all wondered why. Why were you the one to die, instead of me? I had no answer for them. And I was there when they put your name up on the wall, when they honored your death, some of them not understanding who you were. And even though it killed me every single day, I stayed with those infecteds. I helped them because I knew it's what you would've wanted me to do."

He was yelling now, hands clenched so tight on the edge of the table I thought it would snap. "Have you ever noticed how much Lucy looks like you? Or that Alaina rolls her eyes just like you? Or that Hadley talks

82

about you non-stop? I had to tell the poor kid to shut up because I couldn't take it anymore!"

"Stop it!" I screamed, standing up out of my chair, unable to keep myself from crying. "Stop lying to me!"

Sark's eyes widened in disbelief. "You think I'm *lying* to you? You think I'm making all this up?"

"It kills me to hear that! It kills me that you feel like you have to lie to me! So stop! Just tell me to get lost and move on!" Anything, even his hatred of me, would be better than this.

"What are you—"

"I know you hate me! I know you blame me! So just say it! Pretending like you don't just kills me more." I felt the floodgates open, the gates I'd been trying so hard to keep shut. "I'm sorry about Erika! I'm sorry I didn't get away from both of you before you got hurt. I'm sorry I was selfish and put you in danger. I'm sorry, okay? I'm sorry I hung on forever and was too stupid to figure it out."

"Figure *what* out, Arie? You had eight months to figure things out! Eight months to stare at the wall and wait for a rescue that *never came*! How stupid do you have to be to not figure it out?"

I recoiled like he slapped me. "Thanks for the heads up. It's not like I hadn't almost died a million times before. I should've gotten used to—"

"To what? You being murdered?"

"You should've just told me!" I yelled at him, pulling on my ponytail in frustration. "Sitting there for months, watching myself go crazy, only to realize how freaking stupid I was." The torturing words escaped me before I could stop them. "*Of course* nobody was coming for me! Nobody was coming because everyone found out what I was, everyone knew I killed her, and everyone *wanted* me to be dead!"

I snapped my mouth shut and bit my tongue. I had made myself swear that I would never say that out loud. Even if I found Sark and he said it to me, I was never going to tell him that myself.

Sark froze, as if I had just pressed the pause button on *The Arie Nolan Show*. The only thing that changed was his eyes. They went from disbelief, to realization, then thrown into a blazing furnace with the door locked behind him. He deflated like a popped balloon as the fury left his system.

He closed his eyes and let out a long breath that I thought would never end. When he spoke, his voice was so quiet, I had to strain to hear.

"Did he tell you that?" The anguish and animosity were bubbling under the surface of his overly calm tone. "Did Dalton tell you that?"

"It doesn't matter who told me," I said, keeping my voice low to try to hide the cracking. "Because it's true. Isn't it?"

Sark opened his mouth, but no words came out. A sound came from his throat, like he was choking on something. "You...you didn't...you didn't really believe that. Did you?"

"You know what?" I cleared my throat. "I don't even know why we're having this conversation."

Without waiting for him to answer, praying that he wouldn't stop me, I turned and stalked out the door, grabbing my coat on the way. I didn't look back as I ran away from the house that I temporarily called home.

10

I couldn't run very well. After maybe sixty seconds I had to slow down to a walk. It bothered me. I was used to only two options when dealing with my problems: either I ran from them, or I was chained up and literally forced to face them. This slow walking stuff was stupid and unsettling.

It was only a matter of minutes before I was lost. When we had gone to the infecteds' place, I hadn't been paying attention to where we were going. Now I had no idea where I was or which direction to go. Not that I had a destination in mind, but it was scary and saddening. The beautiful world mocked me, laughing that I no longer fit in it. I was lost in every sense of the word.

I walked until my legs wouldn't carry me anymore. I found an icy bench under a barren tree and sat on it, wrapping my arms around myself. It was freezing, but I didn't really care. The stinging that came from the frigid weather was almost welcoming.

Once I sat down, I realized that I was still crying. I had known this was coming, but it came so much differently than I thought it would. The anger, the yelling, the frustration…I had expected that. But him lying like that, so thoroughly, so convincingly, saying exactly what I had been blindly and vainly hoping for—that was cruel. He could've just told me the truth. Twisting it like that just made it worse for both of us.

But the pain in his voice was so *real*. Was he really that good of a liar?

Suddenly, the conversation I had with Lindsey popped into my head.

That doesn't add up, she had said. *Unless…*

Unless he's telling the truth, which he is.

I had known that for sure. Sark only would've lied to Lindsey if he felt that it was right.

An idea was forming in my head, one that might have been there the whole time and I didn't see it, but it seemed so obvious that I couldn't believe I didn't consider it until now.

I didn't want to chase it. The injured girl—the most prominent side of me right now—wasn't having anything to do with that idea.

Dalton was right, she seemed to say. *It's your fault. Everybody hates you for it.*

After months of her saying that over and over, it was hard for me to not believe her.

I decided to give up on that topic. I stared at the

snow, watched as it changed with each new ray of sunlight. After a while, there was less sunlight to go around. The sun was setting and I still had no idea what to do.

Before I could begin to panic, he found me. I didn't know how, but he did. He came and sat next to me, leaning his elbows on his knees, and just stared ahead. I kept my eyes on the snow, wishing that I had used my time alone to come up with something to say.

"Did you know about her?" It took me a moment to realize that I had said the words out loud. Sark stiffened slightly, then let out a long breath and relaxed.

Way to go, idiot.

"I, um, never mind." I tried to backpedal, but it was too late. "Sorry, I didn't mean to—"

"Yeah, I knew." He sounded tired but prepared. He was ready for this conversation. I decided that I had already buried myself this far, so I might as well just take the chance.

"How long did you know?"

"Not the whole time. Her assignment was to me, and she didn't give that up for a while."

"What made her tell you?"

"She loved you, Arie. Because of her job, she'd known who you were for a long time before she met you and had always respected you. From the first day she met you, she felt a special connection and she wanted to help. Then after spending so much time together…she couldn't separate herself from your situation."

He took a deep breath. I waited patiently, and he spilled it all out.

"The day we met her—the night I tried to drown you—she called Dalton in a panic." His voice was reminiscent and kind of sad, but his mouth still twisted around Dalton's name. "He had something against her and made her come back to us. She was absolutely terrified. She was convinced I was going to kill her, which was why she felt like you should be her best friend. Of course, it freaked you out, but she didn't care. She felt connected to you by your mutual fear of me."

He started rubbing his thumb against his left ring finger again. Whether he noticed or not, he didn't show it.

"Is that why she talked so much?" I couldn't help asking.

Sark actually laughed. "Yeah, she didn't know how to handle her stress. So she would just talk, going on forever about every topic under the sun. She kept the TV on to give her ideas."

"And you didn't think that was weird?"

"Of course I did, but I…there was a lot going on. You were staying in my house and I had to keep myself from tearing you apart. That's where most of my focus went. I had no idea why she was there but…I liked her there. And I wanted her to stay."

"And she did."

"She did." He nodded. "For you. She would chastise me about my behavior toward you. It was in a very subtle way—she didn't want to get me angry—but she was determined to protect you. She felt guilty about forcing you to stay in my house, so she tried to make up for it, taking it upon herself to be responsible for whatever happened."

"Why did she make me stay?"

"Dalton told her to. She thought the idea was to apprehend me eventually, but things started to not add up: he shifted his focus from me to you. Everyone knew he was crazy—as she found out more about you, she realized what he really wanted. And she decided she wasn't going to just give you up."

I grinned. That was such an Erika thing to do. "When did she decide that?"

"Do you remember…well I'm sure you do. The day Felix almost killed you."

I winced in spite of myself. "Yeah."

Sark glanced at me for a second. "That…freaked her out. Once I finally found you and brought you back to the house, you were covered in blood. You looked like you could be dead. She lost it. Yelling, screaming, crying, trying to get you away from me."

He had to clear his throat and I realized how difficult that must be for him to think about now. "Eventually, she just broke down and told me everything: about her, about Dalton, about you. She kept ranging from calm to hysterical—she was certain that I was going to kill her. Of course, I was having my own…issues at the time." He smiled sadly. "You managed to completely derail both of us."

"So what happened?" I asked, leaning forward slightly, hanging onto his every word.

"Eventually she realized that I wasn't really…there. And even…even when she was scared for her own life…despite everything, she wanted to help me. It didn't take much of her probing before my resolve broke too. And I…Arie, I told her everything. *Everything.* From the day my mom got sick until that day you almost died."

He leaned back against the bench, still looking ahead. "It didn't come all at once, of course. I had buried all of that for so long…so we just sat on the floor for hours, hoping you'd wake up, as we told each other all about our miserable lives. And instead of hating me more than she already should, she tried to understand me." He grinned almost sadly. "If you had asked her, she would've said she saw it coming all along. She would've said that she already knew she was going to fall in love with me and she was just waiting for me to catch up."

I caught myself smiling. "And this all happened when I was asleep?"

"Yep."

"Wow. You get knocked out for twenty-four hours and you miss everything."

Sark laughed. "With you, yeah, that seems to be the case. It was pretty effortless after that—as if we really had been together that whole time rather than separately conspiring against you. We never really looked back. We just had to convince you."

"Actually…that makes a lot of sense." When I thought about it, that day really had been the turning point. Obviously it was for Sark, considering our enlightening conversation later that night, but it was Erika's too. She acted slightly differently after I woke up that morning.

"It was funny sometimes, watching you two together. She was *so* convinced that you would act like…" He chuckled. "No offense, but like a normal person. We'd have bets about how you would react to something, and I'd win almost every time. Your paranoia was a thorn in her side."

"Yeah," I said, remembering how upset we'd both get over something so small. "It was."

It was getting dark now. The sun had almost completely disappeared behind the mountains. We both shifted our positions on the bench, knowing where this had to end up. Their cute messed up love story was going to be over soon and neither of us liked the finale.

"You…you can tell me to shut up if you want," I said, trying to choose my words carefully. "Really, I won't care if you—"

"I want you to ask me anything," he interrupted, turning his head to look at me. "I know you've been wondering…for a long time now. And it's not fair for me to not tell you something that you deserve to know. She was like a second mom to you."

"But…I mean, it can't be easy to…to talk about her."

"Ah, no." He cleared his throat. "No it's not easy. But I knew this was coming. I'm sorry I wasn't prepared for it earlier. And I figure it's probably got to be pretty hard for you to talk about her too. It's just…it's just what's got to happen, you know?"

"Yeah."

Sark turned his whole body now, so he was angled toward me, and I did the same. Then he took a deep breath and gestured to me.

"Go ahead. What were you going to say?"

"I'm pretty sure you know."

"I'm pretty sure I do too."

He didn't look like he was going to go on, so I went.

"Why didn't you tell me she worked for him? I mean, I know I'm not the most…I don't know. I was just wondering if there was a reason or not."

He nodded to himself. "Honestly, there wasn't a real *reason*, I guess. We just both agreed that you had enough to deal with and we didn't know how you would respond. She didn't know if you viewed Dalton as an ally or not—she was terrified you would feel betrayed by her and get angry. So we just left it alone. We knew we would have to tell you eventually.”

“That’s why she was so panicked,” I realized, thinking back, “the day Alexis caught us and Dalton’s men were chasing me.”

“Yeah. If we hadn’t gotten mixed up with Alexis, she might’ve told you then.” A darker edge hardened his voice. “Of course, we didn’t realize what a psychotic government agent Dalton was at the time, but…” he trailed off.

He stopped for a minute, just looking at me expectantly. I didn’t know what he was waiting for.

“You’re missing something,” he finally said. “There’s a question you left out—though I’d imagine it’s harder for you than the rest of them.”

“What?”

“Was her death your fault and do I blame you for it?”

I dropped my gaze, watching my hands as I fumbled my fingers around each other.

“I had no idea that’s what you’d be thinking,” Sark went on when I didn’t. “I knew you were sad—not to mention scarred—and you probably missed her quite a bit, but…I mean, I had no idea. I’ve had eight months to think too, you know, to replay it all. I thought you blamed me.”

I looked up at him now. His expression was sorrowful but enlightened. That idea that I had thought of, the one I didn’t know if I could believe, was starting to slip back into my head. It was such a Sark thing to do. He was the king of putting the blame on himself.

“I understood that you’ve had a…horrible few months but recognized that you weren’t really talking to me. You were trying to stay out of my way as you glued yourself to me. I thought you were upset at me, that you couldn't trust me anymore after I couldn't protect either of you. Worse, I didn't even come look for you." His words took on a darker tone. "I figured you didn't know what else to do but come find me. You were scared, alone, and badly injured, and I was your only option."

"Are you serious?" I asked, anger rising in me. "My only option? That's the stupidest thing I've ever heard."

"No, it's not." Sark clenched his hands into fists. "The idea that I would…that I would *want* you dead, that I would *hope* you were dead…" He cleared his throat. "*That's* the stupidest thing I've ever heard. And if I didn't know you so well, I wouldn't believe it."

I shook my head. "Why? Why is it so hard to believe that you might want me dead? Or at least out of the way. With the whole key thing, then after…she died…"

"Arie, you have no idea what went on after you were gone. It took me a few weeks before I could drag myself up to go back to Chicago. Telling Alaina was the first thing I did. And the first thing she asked was if it was possible—no disgust, no fear, no judgment. Just concern for you. If you were the key, was it really that easy for you to die?"

"You thought of that?" I asked, my voice small. I didn't want to let him know how much that stung. Not that I held it against him or anything, but if he had just *acted* on that…

"Thought of that?" He rubbed the side of his head. "It ate us up for months. Both Brennan and Lucy had the same reaction. We weren't convinced you were gone. There were several times I even bought plane tickets so we could start to look for you." I could hear the torture creeping into his quieting voice. "Eventually we decided that we needed to let it go. That it was just wishful thinking and we needed to try and move on. And that is the *worst* mistake I have ever or will ever make."

Sark drummed his fingers against the back of the bench. "We were so happy to see you, Arie, and that will never change. But we all—Alaina and I especially—died a little when you came back. Because we all *knew* this whole time that you were alive. We didn't realize it, but we knew. And if we would've just—"

"Don't," I said, an aching in my chest. "Don't do that to yourself. Please? That's just—"

"The truth?" he asked bitterly. His revulsion at himself, rather than me, was disarming.

Hesitantly, I scooted down the bench and rested my head against his shoulder.

"I'm sorry," I whispered. "About everything."

He sighed in defeat. "I am too. But Arie?"

I hid my face in my hands, not sure if I could face what was coming. I hadn't prepared for this.

Sark leaned away from me, putting his hand on my shoulder.

"Arie?" He eyes were so sad, so broken, as they pleaded along with him. "If you only take one thing from this, if you only remember one part of this entire conversation, you need to know that I could never want you away from me, okay? None of this mess was your fault and I will never hold it against you. Erika loved you so much and she wouldn't blame you either. She would do it all over again just to spend that time with you. She would want you here. And I want you here too."

I shook my head fiercely, trying but failing to keep my tears inside.

"I know it's hard for you to understand now," he went on, a new kind of urgency in his voice. "I can't undo months of irrational lies Dalton fed you in just a thirty-minute conversation. I know that. But please just try."

I buried my face in his shoulder, the emotions running through me confusing. Of course, I was happy that he would take me back, but...I couldn't really believe it. My heart was trying to reject any positivity in an effort to protect itself, and I couldn't tell if it was working or not.

"It will take some time," Sark said, resting his head on top of mine and wrapping his arms around me. "But soon you're going to be happy to be back."

"I am happy to see you," I told him. "I missed you a lot."

He laughed once, making my head shake. "I missed you too Arie. More than you will ever know."

I wasn't sure if I believed that, but it was still nice to hear.

Sark reached into his jacket pocket and pulled out a bundle of papers tied together with a black string. He twirled it in his hand once before offering it to me. I took it and glanced over some of the papers sticking out, a faint gasp going through my lips when I saw they were covered in Erika's handwriting.

"They were meant for you," Sark said, his voice quiet. "She wrote you letters almost every day, like a journal for her. I thought you might want to have them."

"Are you sure?" I handled the package reverently, now realizing what it was.

"Absolutely. I've read them enough anyway."

"Wow. Thank you."

"Of course."

There wasn't enough light for me to make actual words out, but the perfectly swirled shape of her handwriting was enough. I almost felt like she was here, watching us with a smile on her face.

"We should probably get going," Sark said after a minute. "It's going to be completely dark soon."

Even though I had been sitting for a while, I felt way too tired to stand up from the bench. The idea of walking all the way back—when I didn't even know the way—made me want to just pass out on the spot.

I was trying to work up the energy to move when Sark scooped me up and started carrying me down the sidewalk.

"What are you doing?" I asked, looking up at the blackening night sky.

He smiled faintly. "I'm carrying you. I'm assuming that's okay. You don't look like you're really excited about walking."

"You can't carry me all the way home."

He scoffed. "Of course I can."

"But we're so far away."

"It's not hard. You weigh next to nothing. Maybe if you ate more than a cracker, I wouldn't be able to."

I hesitated, my eyebrows furrowing. "I'm not sure if that's a compliment or not."

He just laughed and it was the happiest sound I'd heard him make since I found him. Somewhat satisfied, I rested my head against his shoulder and relaxed, holding the bundle of letters tight to my chest. I couldn't help but feel warm despite the cold around me, deciding that life might be worth the effort after all.

11

My dream that night was the kind you shouldn't tell people about because they think you're either crazy or on serious drugs. I couldn't remember all of it, but it had something to do with snowmen that looked like people coming to life and trying to suffocate me with blue snow. It was terrifying. Thankfully, Sark woke me up before the snowmen actually killed me.

Despite the sleep disruption, I had quite a productive morning. First, I decided to take a shower. My reflection hadn't really improved and my hair still fell out, but it was nice to be clean. It seemed like such a luxury now even though it wiped me of any existing energy. I had enough to make it to the couch, but that was about it. Sark managed to convince me to eat something, so I had a piece of bread and a cup of apple juice.

Once I was settled, Sark decided to go take his own shower while I relaxed on the couch. I decided to take the opportunity to look at Erika's letters more closely. For some reason, I felt like I needed to be alone to read them.

Hesitantly, I untied the little string and began to leaf through the papers. It seemed like they had been put in chronological order, so I took out the first one, cuddled up in a musty blanket, and started reading.

Dear Arie,

Wow. What a day.

You would probably feel strange if you knew I was writing you like this. Honestly, I feel strange about it too. But at the same time, it feels right. You will probably never read this and that's okay. Maybe someday I'll let you know how therapeutic this is, writing to you.

Arie, I have no idea what to do. None. At all. The whole universe as we know it is coming to an end.

I've been keeping up on you for a while, but I finally met you in person yesterday. Only yesterday. Isn't that crazy? The past twenty-four hours have been so insane that it feels like it's been twenty million.

You almost died last night. Do you realize that? Died. As in, not alive anymore forever. Sark tried to drown you. And I could tell that you were scared, but he tried to kill you Arie. Kill you! How could you be that calm about it? How could you keep your cool the way you did? I've heard the stories, but Sark is worse than anything I could've imagined. He's much scarier in person, the way his blue eyes seem to delve into the darkest parts of your soul and you're sure he's going to use your worst nightmares against you. I mean, drowning a teenage girl? That's insane! I hope we can get you out of this as soon as possible. A person like you shouldn't have to deal with a person like Sark. And, really, I shouldn't either.

Dalton said I had to go back. He said I can't lose you or Sark. What can I do? I can only follow orders. If it weren't for Dalton, I could be in jail right now and he's not one to give second chances. I have to do everything he says, even if it means walking back to a murderer. That's insane. And I was thinking all morning about how I would begin tracking you both down and guess who walks in? Sark came to <u>my job</u>. Isn't that what professional killers do? Is he a professional killer, like a hit man? I don't know, but I wouldn't be surprised.

What else was I supposed to do? I don't know how to act! I guess I took classes and stuff in high school, but now I'm acting for my life! So I just went for it, totally being a complete idiot, and now…

I have a date. Tonight. With Sark.

I'm sorry I dragged you into it, but I didn't know what else to do. Dalton specifically said not to lose sight of you either. I figured I'd get you both in the same place again and hope he doesn't kill either of us.

This was a stupid idea. What was I thinking? A date? Really? That's the stupidest thing I could've done! But I'm stuck with it. After all, it's not like I can cancel or anything.

I have your bracelet and I'm sorry, but you might be the only way I can survive. Because if Sark miraculously doesn't kill me tonight then I might die of stress. I pretend like I'm here for you, to protect you, like I'm a professional, like I know what I'm doing, but the truth is I need you to keep me sane. You know more and are more capable in this situation than I could ever hope to be, even though I will probably never tell you so.

This is insane. I'm going to die. I am going to die. Even if I manage to survive the stupid date, Dalton will make me come back. And then what? It's just a matter of time. Sark will figure it all out eventually and I'll be in for it. But I don't have a choice. I'm so scared.

I had to read the last bit a few times because my hands were shaking. It was confusing, trying to work through the emotions. The shock. My version of that day was so different…and I thought hers had been much different too. At the same time, it made sense. Erika *had* been a normal person the whole time. I just didn't know.

Footsteps sounded from the other room. I folded the letter back up and stuffed the bundle in the crevice of the couch. A second later, Sark came in wearing jeans and a thermal shirt. He plopped down next to me, purposely squishing me against the couch and flicking his wet hair in my face. I tried to be annoyed, but I ended up laughing as I attempted to push him off. I wasn't strong enough and he finally just moved over.

"You're a dork," I said, not able to wipe the smile off of my face. It still surprised me to see him in such casual clothes when I was used to him exclusively wearing button ups and fancy shoes.

"Well it's good to know that some things don't change."

I rolled my eyes, but his grin looked like it would

leave stretch marks on his face, and I couldn't help but laugh.

"So," I started once he had settled, "what are you doing today?"

"I believe you mean *we*," he corrected. "What are *we* doing today?"

"I don't know. That's why I was asking you."

"Well I regret to inform you that I will not be leaving your side for the next…long time, so you better get used to me tagging along on your adventures."

"Now they're my adventures?"

"Yep. You're the exciting one around here."

"What happened?" I asked, confused. "You are in such a good mood."

He shrugged. "I don't know. I guess you just make me happy."

"You don't have to say that."

"No I don't, but it *is* my civic duty to be honest."

I raised an eyebrow. "Have you been drinking?"

He laughed. "Nope. Not a drop."

I couldn't help but smile again at his antics—I'd missed them. "Your voice sounds different." I commented. "I mean, it's still the same, but…"

Sark grinned. "Well, it's still mine. Minus the fake accent, of course. I decided I probably didn't need it anymore."

"You don't. This is better, I think."

With a grateful tip of his head, Sark cleared his throat. "Okay, so back to business. Is there anything you want to do today?"

I thought for a moment. "Not really. What about you?"

He hesitated for a second, his expression turning a bit more serious. "At some point I do need to go check on Alaina.”

Dropping my gaze, I watched my fidgeting hands, not really sure how to respond.

“What do you want to do?” Sark asked. “I know Alaina would probably be mad if I came without you, but I don’t know if I really want you there either.”

The thought made me uncomfortable. “*Nobody* wants me there.”

“Alaina does. Brennan does. Liam, Mark, Mara, Lucy—”

“They don’t count.”

“Why not?”

“Because they knew me before. They have the obligation to pretend to like me.”

Sark rolled his eyes. “You’re impossible.”

“You saw everyone’s face when I walked inside. And they have every right to think badly of me.”

“It’s nothing personal, Arie,” he told me. “Most of them have watched friends and family be slaughtered by Alexis over the past eight months. They were angry and hurt and wanted someone to blame—blaming the dead key was an easy way to go. Once they get to know you, that will change.”

“That’s exactly my point: none of them *want* to get to know me.”

He sighed. “Hadley would never forgive me if I showed up without you.”

“I think everybody would be just fine if you showed up alone.”

“Actually, a lot of them don’t like me.”

That caught my attention. I thought of the way he sat at the head of their circle, every eye on him and hanging on every word. “Yeah right.”

“I’m serious. They don’t trust me. I make them

nervous.”

“Why?”

“I used to work for Alexis. I’m the definition of their worst nightmare. If it weren’t for Alaina and the fact that I pay for their food, they would try to run from me or kick me out.”

“Huh.” I thought for a second. “But some of them like you.”

“Some of them, I guess. That took some time though.”

I remembered when I had the impossible task of convincing Alaina that Sark wasn’t a danger anymore—since I’d been gone she must’ve had to do that over and over again. “Who was the hardest to convince?”

“Alaina wasn’t sold at first, but she got over it pretty fast. Lucy still is a little wary from time to time. Hadley was convinced I was literally the devil for a while.” He shrugged. “We make it work.”

“That’s…amazing of you. Why are you doing so much for them?”

“Because.” Sark cleared his throat, managing to keep a light tone. “I knew if you would’ve been there, you wouldn’t have hesitated to do everything you could. I made for a lousy replacement.”

“You’ve done more than I could have.”

He shook his head. “It was the least I could do.”

“I’m serious.” I hugged his arm. “Thank you.”

“Of course.”

What would I have done if I had been here? How could I have helped them? It wasn’t like I could assist with any sort of funding issues, but I wondered if I could’ve saved any of the ones who were lost.

But I guess if I hadn’t left eight months ago, Alexis

wouldn't have started killing them off in the first place.

The whole idea was driving me insane. I felt a devout sense to help, but didn't know how.

"Oh no," Sark said. "What's that face for?"

He brought me out of my deep thought. "What face? It's just my face."

"That's the face you make when you're thinking hard, putting a plan together."

"Really?" I tried to imagine what my face looked like for future reference.

He nodded. "You mind filling me in?"

"No, it's nothing." I started fingering my hair. "I'm just…like, what are we—or they, I guess—doing about Alexis? They aren't just going to live in hiding forever, are they?"

"Isn't that what you guys were doing in the beginning anyway?"

"You know what I mean."

Sark hesitated, as if he was choosing his words carefully. "Everyone has their own idea about what we should and shouldn't do, but the point is that not much can be done. We are smaller, weaker, and in the dark in comparison to Alexis. Right now, we are focusing on surviving and will move from there when the opportunity presents itself."

"So basically nothing."

He shook his head. "I didn't say that. Different plans are always being made. We are just at the point where nothing can be carried out. Everyone has worked too hard to get here to just throw it all away." He used his tone to try and close the subject.

Everyone but me. I haven't done anything but get people in trouble.

I looked at Sark with imploring eyes. "So what can

I do?"

Sark's face fell. I now knew for sure he had been trying to avoid this. "Arie—"

"You said so yourself, if I had been here I would've done everything I could. And so far I've done nothing. I want to help, Sark. Alexis has probably relocated, but maybe—"

"Whoa, Arie, slow down," Sark interrupted, his voice almost nervous. "You need to steer clear of anything involving Alexis. Taking risks is not going to benefit anyone."

"But, Sark, I want to help."

"And you can, but you just got back. Give it some time. You have enough to work through right now."

I huffed in irritation. "Okay."

"No, Arie, I want you to promise me." Sark leaned forward, his eyes stern but agitated. "Promise me you won't do anything about anything unless you talk to me about it first."

"Anything about anything, huh?" I muttered. "That's an awfully big range."

"Arie."

I rolled my eyes. "Fine." Slyly hiding my hand underneath my blanket, I crossed my fingers. "I promise I won't do 'anything about anything' without your consent."

Unless a really good chance comes up. Then I'm totally taking it.

Sark relaxed back into the couch. "Thank you."

"Yeah, don't mention it." I was annoyed, but part of me couldn't help but appreciate the fact that Sark was so concerned. I'd missed him *so* much.

We sat for a minute in silence, just hanging out. It was nice. For the first time, I felt like I was home.

Sark picked up the remote and pointed it at the TV, then stopped. Hesitating a moment, he lowered the remote and broke the silence. "Can I ask you something? You don't have to answer if you don't want to."

I shrugged, slightly nervous. "Sure."

"Who is Micah?"

I stiffened, recoiling a little at hearing the name out loud. "How do you know Micah?"

"You talk to yourself a lot," he answered, his voice cautious. "Most of it doesn't make sense, but you still do. Micah is a frequent topic. Sometimes when you're having a nightmare you scream his name. I was just curious."

When I didn't respond he continued. I could tell by his voice he regretted bringing it up.

"I just wanted to know if he was a good guy or a bad guy. That's it."

"He was a good guy," I finally answered, staring at the blank wall.

"He was with you? With Dalton?"

I bit my lip and looked at the ground.

You can't admit it. Dalton threatened.

"Okay, how about this?" Sark asked. "Hypothetically, if you ever happened to be in a prison-like establishment over the last eight months, would Micah have been with you?"

"I never actually saw him." I could barely hear my own voice. "We talked through the air vents."

"Arie, if he is still there or needs any help, you know I would do anything, right? Whatever it takes, we'd get him out."

I rested my head on my knee, willing the tears not to come. I had been crying way too much lately.

"Micah isn't there anymore. He…he didn't…make it."

Sark didn't respond, and for some reason I felt like I needed to get something out.

"They killed him. No, not just killed him. They tore him apart."

"Why?"

I didn't know why I was telling him this. It hurt but it was almost a relieving kind of hurt.

"We would take off the air vent covers and talk. It was too dark to actually see each other, but we could make out shapes. It was enough, you know, just to have each other there. Dal—" I cut myself off, recognizing what I almost did.

"It's okay." I saw Sark nod in encouragement out of the corner of my eye. "Dalton…?"

My throat dried up like the Sahara. "He gets angry. He's reckless. Doesn't think. It wasn't so bad, being there, until he got mad. One day…he came in furious. I don't know why, but it was scary. I'm lucky, I guess, that I survived that episode. Micah didn't. I saw the whole thing, the shadows in the air vent. The sounds were worse, I think."

Finally, I realized what I was doing, and slammed on the brakes of the memory replay. I lifted my head to see Sark's painfully shocked expression.

"I'm sorry," I said, feeling stupid now. "I didn't…just forget about it. I'm sorry, I didn't mean to just…unload like that."

Sark shook his head. "You don't need to be sorry. I want you to tell me. It's good for you to talk about it."

"No, it was stupid of me. But thanks…I just…miss Micah. A lot." My voice cracked on the last words. "And I missed you. So much. It all hurts."

Sark just put his arm around me, staying silent. I appreciated it. Sometimes hurt people needed to talk to get it out rather than get a reply. And Sark had been hurt before.

What a broken pair we were. Being broken is a bit easier, though, when someone is broken with you—not because it's easier to deal with, but because you know you're not alone.

12

I dozed on and off for a bit. Sark had the TV on, flipping between the news and a reality dance show. The dance show was definitely more entertaining, at least for me, and he kept it on when he knew I was awake. The host was a teenage girl, and everyone had to copy the moves that she did. A middle-aged man and a little girl were the contestants, and though I had my money on the girl, I didn't get to see who won.

After a few hours of just hanging out, Sark decided he needed to go see the infected, and I hesitantly decided to go with him. I wasn't really sure why. Sark seemed more relieved than anxious, which made me feel a bit better. The thought of being away from him—and staying by myself—was a scary idea to both of us.

We had to walk again, something that wasn't my favorite, but I managed to make it. I must've been getting stronger because it wasn't as bad as the first time. Sark said he'd work on getting Lindsey to approve a car for us, but I wasn't super hopeful. For now, walking was fine.

Sark went right into the club, and I hung back, allowing him to pull me after him. People were milling around, some looking rather bored, until we walked in. It was like someone put a spotlight on me and announced, *Hey, look everyone: the girl who you all hate is here! Please make sure she feels your wrath.*

I could feel the heated glares I received burning a hole through my face, but Sark didn't pay them any attention. He pulled me across the room and down the stairs. I kept my eyes down, trying to tune out the faint mutterings of the people we passed by until we were in the basement.

Alaina was sprawled out on a couch, flipping through the channels of a static TV with little interest. Mark, Brennan and Lucy were sitting on the floor in front of her, playing some sort of card game with Hadley. Mara was on a stool next to the couch reading a book, and Liam was snoring on a leather chair on the other side. Four kids were sitting at a table in the far corner, heavily absorbed in stacks of books and loose papers.

Sark walked in without hesitating and sat on an empty chair next to Mara, but I automatically stopped in the doorway, not really feeling like I was allowed to enter. Alaina straightened up when she saw us, a deer-in-the-headlights expression on her face. Mara smiled warmly at both of us, and Lucy gave a little wave. Mark and Brennan both shouted, "It's Arie!" at the same time, causing the four kids to look up, Hadley to turn around, and Liam to bolt upright. Both Mark and Brennan started laughing at Liam's hair sticking up everywhere, and his face turned red as he quickly tried to fix it.

Well, at least I knew how to make an entrance.

Hadley jumped up and ran over to me, throwing his arms around my waist.

"You came back!" he yelled. "I knew you would!"

"Yeah," I said, keeping my voice quiet and hoping he would catch on.

Everyone besides Sark was staring at me, making my choice to come seem less and less like a good idea. I brushed my hair out of my face, even though it wasn't really *in* my face, and wrung my hands. I felt like this was getting a bit ridiculous.

"Hi," I told the floor. *You'd think this would get easier.*

"Hey, what's up?" Brennan asked as he expertly shuffled a deck of cards.

"Nothing much."

Hadley pulled on my shirt. "Wait right here, I have to go get something to show you." I barely caught the end of his sentence before he was bolting up the stairs. Not sure what to do with myself, I sat cross-legged on the floor next to Sark's chair as he started talking.

"How's it been going?"

"About the same," Alaina answered, her voice a bit dazed. "Food is getting low, but that's about it. Neil gets back any day."

That caught my attention. Neil was the guy that took care of Alaina and her siblings since her mom had died and her dad wasn't around. I didn't even think to wonder where he was.

"Where did he go?" I asked.

Alaina did a faint double take when I spoke, but she still met my eyes.

"He, uh, goes on business sometimes. That's how we got this building in the first place. He moved the club in Chicago to here, but it doesn't always work…he's been gone the last few weeks. He should be back any day."

"Huh." I guess that made sense. This building couldn't have just appeared. "Where are Andrew and Chelsea?" They were two members of Alaina's family that I hadn't seen around.

She blew her hair out of her face, her black eyes heated with resentment. "They wanted to have a 'normal' life, so they're going to school a couple hours away from here, since we aren't so good at being normal. I'd say we see them from time to time, but we don't."

"Oh." I stopped talking then, feeling like I'd said too much.

Footsteps sounded on the stairs, then Hadley appeared carrying his pillow with a big grin on his face. He set it on the floor in front of me and sat down.

"It seems like everything has been quiet," Sark went on.

"Yeah, Peter has kept himself from starting anything," Alaina said, a new kind of guard in her voice. "Everyone has been…talking a lot. Most agree." She rolled her eyes in anger. "Arguing hasn't been as much of a problem."

Sark pressed his mouth into a thin line and nodded.

Talking about what? It seemed like things were usually pretty dormant around here. What could cause such a rift?

It took me a minute to realize that Hadley was talking to me. When I hadn't responded, Brennan snapped his fingers in front of my face.

"Arie? Hello?"

I glanced up, then dropped my eyes sheepishly.

"Sorry." I brushed my hair behind my ear. "Concentrating isn't a strong point anymore."

"Nah, it's cool." Brennan waved it off as if it were no big deal. Mark tried to give me an encouraging grin, but it was too forced. I gave a small smile, feeling super awkward, which just made me sad. Mark and I used to be buddies.

Hadley bounced up and down in his seat. "Arie, are you ready? Can I show you?"

"Yeah. Go ahead."

"Okay." He picked his pillow up and dumped out his pillowcase. A crumpled paper airplane, a piece of twine, a teddy bear, and four rocks tumbled to the floor.

Hadley grabbed the four rocks one by one and handed them to me. "This is Jeffrey. This is Charles. This is Sheldon. And this is Brock."

I gave a small grin. "Brock the rock?"

"Yeah, isn't it great? They're like my pet rocks, but they don't need food or anything like that. Alaina said those are the kind of pets I can have here."

"That's awesome. I bet they really like it here."

He nodded. "They do. They like it a lot. I do too." He took the rocks back from me and started playing a game where they all try to blow up the others' spaceships.

Sometimes it was weird to watch Hadley for an extended period of time, just because his behavior never added up—that was a big side effect he suffered from infection. He was given the formula when he was six, which must've been too much for his brain to handle because it completely flipped. His body still grows and functions normally, so he looks like an almost-nine-year-old, but his brain is all over the place. One day he's eight, the next he's five, and the next he's ten…the pattern was never consistent. You could have an intelligent discussion on life with him and five minutes later you'd find him having a tantrum because evil alien robots ruined his new turbo car. It really just depended on the moment, but his curiosity and energy for life never changed.

Nobody could figure out why Hadley reacted to the formula the way he did, but, then again, nobody as young as Hadley had ever survived the infection process. I guess that's just what happened. To me though, he was always just Hadley, the younger brother I never had.

Sark continued to talk to Alaina as I played with Hadley and his pet rocks for a while. Eventually Hadley bolted up the stairs again, in search of more paper so he could make more airplanes—his favorite pastime.

A buzzing of voices from upstairs got louder, as if someone was arguing, and all of our heads turned toward the door.

"So Arie," Brennan started, obviously attempting to distract me. "What have you been up to? Do anything exciting?"

"I took a nap," I said, not really thinking. I was focused on the voices. Alaina had said that the infecteds hadn't been arguing as much because they were agreeing on something. Something that Sark wasn't too crazy about.

"Naps are good," Brennan said. "I'm glad you came

back for a visit."

That sentence put it all together for me. I looked to the door and back to Brennan, then sighed and rested my head in my hand.

"You don't have to say that Brennan."

"Arie—"

"No, I get it. Really. You don't have to pretend."

"We're not pretending, Arie." This time it was Alaina. I turned to see her almost angry expression. "We love you and, news flash, we want you here whether you like it or not. So, get over it."

I opened my mouth to argue, but I couldn't think of anything. I could only give a small grin.

"I think that's the nicest thing you've ever said to me."

Now she suppressed a smile. "Don't mention it."

And with just that small exchange, I already felt like I was closer to getting my best friend back. Wherever she had gone.

It's not where she *went, idiot. It's where* you *went.*

"Arie!" I heard Hadley holler from up the stairs. "Arie, Arie, Arie!"

What does he want? I really really didn't want to go upstairs. Downstairs was much safer.

Hadley's voice sounded urgent though, so with a sigh, I gave a quick glance to Sark before pulling myself off the ground and walking up the stairs. When I got into the main room, I found it was crowded with people coming to see what the commotion was. I was about to retreat to the basement when I heard Hadley again.

"Arie! Arie!"

Going against my screaming nerves, I started fighting through the group. I got many grunts of annoyance, but a few people let me through once they saw me. I finally got to the center and discovered what the problem was.

Everyone was crowded around Peter—a few infecteds were holding the crowd back. Peter had Hadley by the hair as a drop of blood fell from Hadley's lip.

"What are you *doing*?" I shouted, half afraid of the volume of my own voice. The other half was driven to overtaking anger. I rushed over, jerked Hadley out of Peter's grasp, and hid him behind my body. Peter rolled his eyes at me.

"I told you!" Hadley declared, giving Peter a smug smile from behind me.

"Roadkill to the rescue," Peter said, rolling his eyes. When I glared pointedly, he realized that I was looking for an explanation. "The kid's freaking annoying. He makes a good punching bag sometimes."

My mouth fell open in shocked disgust. "Are you serious? He's eight!"

Peter's expression darkened. He grabbed my jaw, his grip crushingly tight, and dragged my face close to his.

"If you're sticking around here, you need to understand the order of things." He clenched his hand, and I couldn't help but whimper at the pressure. "Trash like you belong underneath the rest—"

I brought my knee up and slammed it into his stomach, forcing him to release me, and I stumbled backwards into Hadley. Peter raised his fist angrily and I instantly remembered my place. Gritting my teeth, I cowered back, expecting the worst.

For some reason, my reaction made Peter freeze. It was only for a second, then Sark appeared and barreled right into him. Peter caught himself before he fell to the floor, and I grabbed Sark's arm before he could do anything else.

"Everyone shut up!" Alaina yelled as she placed herself in between Sark and Peter. The room went silent. I didn't realize how much power she had until now.

"I thought you could figure this out on your own," she went on, "but apparently you all are too stupid and need some help." She gestured to me. "This is Arie. Yes, the Arie that we thought was dead. She is not. Obviously."

Peter scoffed, but Alaina gave him a class-A Alaina glare and he stayed quiet.

She sighed. "And yes, Arie is the key to the infecting formula."

I couldn't help but wince. I was still used to my secret being a secret. Now it felt like the whole world knew. Well, I guess *my* whole world did know.

"However," Alaina's voice took on an edge of steel, "that does not mean that she is different from any one of you pathetic people. She is still an infected and she is still one of us. Anyone who acts differently will be tried for mutiny. Any questions?"

A rumble went through the crowd. Alaina answered before anyone could ask.

"No, she is not a spy, she does not work for Alexis, and she is not a monster. I've known her for two years now and she doesn't even come close to any of those myths that detail what the key is like. She is just like us and has the most to lose if we get caught. If it weren't for her—"

"We wouldn't be here," Peter finished, now glaring at me. "And we would *all* be alive."

"You're right," Alaina said, folding her arms across

her chest. "We wouldn't be here. If Arie hadn't kept her secret for as long as she did, then Alexis would've killed us off a long time ago and we wouldn't have had Sark to keep us above water."

Another grumble went through the crowd, but it wasn't as hostile.

"You all know I'm right," Alaina said. "So shut up and get over yourselves." She turned to look at me. "Did I miss anything?"

I was too startled to respond, and Alaina took that as a yes. She waved to the crowd, a dismissal. I didn't think that would do anything, but slowly people started to disperse.

Amidst all of it, someone came through the crowd. A balding middle-aged man walked up to us—a man I recognized as Neil. His eyes widened in shock when he saw me.

"Yeah, Arie's alive," Alaina said, flipping her hair. "You missed it all."

Neil stared at me a moment before shaking his head.

"Well, I guess I shouldn't be surprised," he said, taking off his jacket. "You weren't really one to just give up."

Neil and I had never been best buds, but the sight of him relaxed me. I gave him a small smile before releasing my hold on Sark's arm and bending down to Hadley.

"Are you okay?" I asked, brushing his hair out of his eyes.

He just grinned and threw his arms around me. "I knew you would come! I told Peter you were better than him and he didn't believe me, but I knew it. I knew you would show him." He looked at me seriously. "You're a hero."

I glanced around to the infecteds standing around, watching me. Some looks were angry, some were confused, some were pitiful.

"Okay, that's very nice Hadley, but let's not tell people that anymore."

His eyebrows furrowed. "Why not? It's just the truth."

"Because…" I trailed off, not quite sure how to answer.

Because I'm not the person you remember Hadley.

"Just because, okay?" I stood up and patted his head.

He started to protest at my vague answer, but Mara came to my rescue, asking for my help kneading massive amounts of dough at the counter. I was grateful for the distraction, the work giving me something to concentrate on. Mara was kneading her own bread dough next to me; Alaina and Lucy were sitting to our left watching us and eating pretzels.

Sark needed to go bring Neil up to speed on what had happened during both of their absences, and it took a minute to convince him that I could stand without him right next to me. He finally left, but—I assumed upon his instruction—Alaina, Mara and Lucy were with me, and Mark, Brennan and Liam were sitting just a few yards away. It was irritating and comforting at the same time. I didn't need babying, but it was nice to know that they cared so much.

Suddenly Alaina snickered. Mara and I looked up to see her amused expression and Lucy's smile. Alaina leaned a little bit closer to us so she could whisper.

"You've been missing this Arie. It's hilarious." She pointed a discreet finger at the scene across the room. Sark was literally backed into a corner, a blankly annoyed expression on his face. A shorter girl twirling her wavy black hair was standing in front of him, her back to me. The way she was holding her body told me she was trying to make an impression.

"That's Sasha," Alaina went on to explain, stifling giggles along with Lucy and Mara. "She has the hugest crush on Sark. And he can't stand her."

Sark must've felt us looking at him because he met our gaze. He gave me the 'please save me' glare and all four of us burst into laughter.

"How long has that been going on?" I asked, trying to keep my giggling from being too loud.

"Since the day she got here," Alaina said. "She's thicker than a brick wall—won't take any hints. Watching her talk to Sark is better than anything on TV."

We all continued to watch as Sasha continued to talk. Once Sark realized that I wasn't going to get him out of his situation, he rolled his eyes. He said something quick to her, then stepped around her and started heading toward me. Sasha whipped around to see where he was going. Her face was framed by her flawless dark curls, her expression disbelieving. Her face clouded over when she saw Sark was headed for me. Popping the gum she had in her mouth, she turned and stalked away.

Sasha's exit had caused another round of chuckles from us. Sark sighed in irritation when he got to us, leaning on the counter in front of me.

"Thanks," he said, annoyed. "You were a big help."

I nodded to my hands stuck in the dough, not able to hide my smile. "I was busy."

"You could've thrown some at her."

The seriousness of his tone reignited our laughter.

Sark rolled his eyes again but cracked a smile. He pushed me, teasing but still gentle, as he passed me and went into the kitchen.

"I'll be expecting help next time," he called as the door shut behind him. Alaina, Mara, and Lucy all watched him with a renewed interest.

"You know," Lucy said softly, turning back to me, "I don't remember the last time he smiled like that."

Alaina grabbed a pretzel and popped it in her mouth. "He died when you left Arie." I noticed that everyone said *left* now to describe my situation, rather than *died*. "You should've seen him, just moping around all day. Not that I blamed him but…it was pretty bad. Especially for Sark."

I concentrated on the dough again, not really sure how to respond to that. Alaina waved her hand in my face until I looked back up at her.

"My point was that he missed you," she clarified. "And we can tell how excited he is to have you back. I just wanted to make sure you knew that."

The corners of my mouth pulled up, but someone interrupted our conversation before I could answer.

"I just heard a rumor and I'm dying to know if it's true."

I didn't have to turn to know it was Peter walking up behind me. He leaned on the counter in front of me, where Sark had been, then stole a pretzel from a furious Alaina.

"I heard you had a run in with Alexis—he had you for three weeks—and you still convinced him you weren't the key."

Alaina looked like she was going to go for him. Behind Peter I saw Liam, Mark, and Brennan looking in our direction, starting to stand up, but I just shook my head at them. I didn't mind talking to Peter as long as he didn't bash my face in or anything.

"Yep. That was almost a year ago," I answered, keeping my eyes on my working hands.

"So they knew who you were before they knew your secret?"

"Oh yeah. They weren't big fans to begin with."

"She's the one that broke Jefferson's leg," Alaina said, her voice telling him to take a hike.

Peter raised an eyebrow. "What?"

A small group of infecteds close to us turned their heads toward me.

"That was you?" a girl asked, her voice taking on a reverent tone.

I just nodded.

A lanky boy with glasses falling off his nose pushed through the group.

"Are you serious?" he asked, a smile growing on his face. "That was legendary! I never thought I'd get to meet the person who did it."

"No, no, no," Peter said. "There is no way that was you. You're too…"

"Just because she looks like a train wreck doesn't mean she can't kick some serious butt," Alaina said before looking at me. "No offense."

"None taken." I had seen myself in the mirror.

Sark appeared next to me, and I nodded once so he knew I was okay.

"Were you there?" Peter asked him, still disbelieving.

"For what?" Sark asked flatly.

"She really broke Jefferson's leg?"

Sark chuckled, the sound generated double takes from several infecteds. "I know it's hard to believe now, but you don't want to mess with Arie. Give her some time to get better and she'll dance circles around you."

Before I could tell Peter to disregard that, the boy with the glasses spoke up again.

"But how did you do it?"

"I kicked him…?" I didn't really get the point of the question. There are only so many ways to break someone's leg.

"No, I mean *how* did you do it?" He pushed his glasses farther up his nose. "Weren't you terrified?"

The attention and praise made me uncomfortable, my body tensing up at all of the pairs of eyes trained on me in anticipation. Sark tipped his head to the side slightly, telling me to take the opportunity.

Let them get to know you, I could almost hear him saying. The trouble was, I wasn't Arie the brave crusader anymore. We were talking about a girl who no longer existed.

"Yes and no," I finally answered, trying to be honest. "Of course I was scared, but…I don't like people spitting in my face. Or whacking me with a crowbar. I don't do well with either of those."

Peter let out a whistle between his teeth. "Well, no kidding," he muttered.

"Alaina can tell you the story some time," I said, trying but failing to keep from smiling. "She's an excellent storyteller."

The kid with the glasses and the group he was with all nodded in appreciation before walking away.

"What was that all about?" I asked Alaina quietly.

"I told you, Arie," she said, popping another pretzel in her mouth. "That *was* legendary. That was a huge deal for the rest of us. We've all had stuff thrown in our faces, but few of us are brave enough to actually do anything about it."

Mara started cleaning up her hands and I realized that my bread dough was pretty much done. I started peeling it off of me, some of it up to my elbow.

"Speaking of faces," Peter said, stealing another pretzel from Alaina. She smacked the back of his head, but he just smirked at her before looking back at me. "What happened to yours?"

I didn't answer. Somehow, though, I knew he wasn't going to let it go.

"So that government guy—Dalton, right?—kidnapped you for no apparent reason," Peter continued when I didn't, "kept you forever, not knowing your secret, and he's still looking for you."

I sighed. *Word gets around fast, doesn't it?*

"And Alexis thinks you're dead. If he or Jefferson knew you were alive they would try to find you, which, I've gathered, would be bad news. Not to mention the fact that you managed to turn one of their best agents against them," Peter nodded at Sark, "which is a whole other story."

"Yep."

"So just by being infected, you're pretty valuable." He stared into space for a moment, lost in thought. Then he snapped back into it, giving me a mean little grin. "I guess I'm really just wondering if you're actually worth all of that."

Sark let a warning sound through his teeth; everyone else glared at Peter.

I gave him a wry smile, wiping my hands off on a towel. "That's the million-dollar question, isn't it?"

Sark didn't want to stay long after that. We had to be back to the house anyway. I said my small number of goodbyes and promised to return.

"So how was it?" Sark asked once we were on our way.

"Um…better, I think. Not as bad as the first time."

"They'll warm up to you," he said. "Just give it some time."

"At this rate, I'll be eighty by the time that happens."

Sark rolled his eyes. "Lighten up, will you? Open your mind to the idea that you might actually be an interesting person to know."

"I'll get working on that," I responded sarcastically. "Right after I end world hunger."

"Excuse me for infringing on your busy schedule. Just remember it probably wouldn't kill you to be a tad more positive."

He had been mostly joking—I thought—but I chewed over the comment for the rest of the way home, trying to gauge how much I was still me and how much I'd changed. I couldn't decide if I was okay with the results.

13

After we got home, I practically died on the couch. I tried to rest rather than sleep—the nightmares made me more exhausted than I already was—leaving me in a weird in-between state: I wasn't actually asleep, but I wasn't coherent either. It was nice. A long time went by before new sounds echoed through the quiet house. I didn't have time to make sense of what they were; I felt Sark pick me up and carry me to my bed. Way too tired to open my eyes and tell him I wasn't actually asleep, I just went along with the free ride.

Eventually, my mind focused enough to make out hushed voices from the other room. Lindsey was here.

I'd forgotten she'd said that she would bring us dinner. Sluggishly, I dragged myself out of bed, knowing I should at least make an effort to say hi.

I stepped out into the hallway, attempting to mat down my messed-up hair as the bickering voices became clearer.

"She has to stay as far away from that as possible," Sark was arguing quietly. I stopped once I realized he was talking about me. "I'm not taking any risks."

"She doesn't really have a choice," Lindsey said, her voice firm. "She's the central point of this. You take her out of the equation, and you don't stand a chance. They will do whatever it takes to get you out of the way."

"I can accept that."

"And maybe you can, but *she* can't. Talk about taking risks, what happens to her when you get carted off?" It was silent for a few moments. "In that room is a terrified, exposed little girl who is trying to recover from severe physical, mental, and emotional abuse. She needs someone and she's deemed that someone as you."

"I'm not letting her get dragged into the middle of this."

"Look around, Sark. She *is* in the middle of this and there is nothing you can do to change that. Do whatever you have to for yourself, but don't push her away from the situation and expect it to work out."

I could imagine Sark's impatience, how he would be running his hand through his hair in frustration.

"You realize what you're arguing for here?"

"Yes, I do, and yes it's a strange world, but I care about Arie and won't let your obligations destroy what little stability she's created for herself."

"And what if I'm not the stability she needs?"

"You aren't. But to her you are and that's all that really matters right now."

Footsteps sounded, clinking of something against the counter, then more footsteps.

"I wouldn't be here if I didn't think you had a chance," Lindsey said, a bit calmer. "I know it's slim, but you've got a reason to try now. You owe her at least that much."

Silence. My legs started shaking from standing still so long, but there was no way I was moving now. The old floor was unreliable.

"What do they want?" Sark finally asked, his tone resigned.

"Everything," Lindsey answered. "You know that. The little bit you gave proved to be worthwhile. We were able to catch up with Demarko and Rollins—it's not huge, but it's something. You'd be surprised at what they'd be willing to give you for just some intel. They've heard the stories—they can respect it."

Demarko and Rollins? The names didn't sound familiar. *What are they talking about?*

"How much?" Sark asked.

"It got you here, didn't it?"

Finally, I couldn't take it anymore. My legs were dying. I shifted my weight slightly, hoping to ease the pressure, but a loud creak in the old floor sounded. I froze up like a burglar caught with the jewels in hand.

I heard Sark sigh. "Arie, come out here."

I debated for a second, then decided hiding wasn't worth it. Sark knew me too well.

Stepping down the hallway, I stopped at the corner, hugging the wall as I turned into the living room. Sark and Lindsey were standing across from each other, obviously engaged in some sort of argument. A file of papers was strewn on the couch, and the smell of fresh Chinese takeout wafted from the kitchen.

I looked at Sark guardedly, wrapping my arms around myself. "You're leaving, aren't you?"

Lindsey gave a knowing glance to Sark, as if I had just proven her point. He ignored her, taking a step toward me and running a hand through his hair.

"No, Arie. I would never leave you."

"Then what were you talking about?"

Lindsey gestured to the couch. "Sit down and we can talk about it. You're a part of this too."

I just kept my eyes on Sark, waiting for an answer.

He let out a long breath. "Something has come up."

"I can see that."

"I have to go to…a thing."

I raised my eyebrow. "Well, that explains everything."

His explanation was slow and careful. "There's a…trial within their agency that they want me to go to."

I guess that made sense. I kept forgetting the fact that Sark was technically arrested. "When is it?"

"In three days."

I looked at Lindsey now. "Okay, so what do I need to do?"

Sark clamped his teeth shut and I glanced back at him.

"Oh, you better believe I'm coming."

"No." Sark glared at me. "Absolut—"

Lindsey took a step forward, interrupting him. "If you don't show up, they'll assume you were going to say something that would incriminate Sark so he wouldn't allow you to come. They would lock him up without listening to a single word."

Sark muttered something under his breath—

something indecent I had no doubt.

"You know, I'd feel better if I saw you eat something," Lindsey said. "Why don't you dish up some dinner and I'll tell you everything you want to know."

I thought for a minute before walking stiffly into the kitchen. Going fast, I dished up a small spoonful of rice and chicken, then made my way back to the couch. Lindsey sat down two cushions away from me, but Sark stayed standing.

"So, what's going on?" I asked.

Sark gave Lindsey a specific look—obviously trying to communicate something—and she sighed.

I let out an impatient breath. "Look, I think we've proven that keeping things from me never works out," I said, "so can you just treat me like an adult and tell me what's happening?"

"It's not complicated, Arie," Lindsey told me. "Like Sark said, he has to go to this...*trial.* It's just a matter of what happens afterward."

I started picking at my food, eating a bit here and there. "Do you think we have a chance?"

"Yes, I really do." Lindsey crossed her legs. "That's why this is important. It's not every day an infected fights to keep her handler from going to prison. It's a big deal for our agency."

Sark let a harsh breath through his teeth, folding his arms across his chest.

It's going to take a lot for him to let me come. I made a mental note to start thinking of ways I could change his mind.

"Really, what matters now is what Sark decides to do," Lindsey went on, a challenge in her tone.

Sark glared at her. "I never said that I wouldn't

talk—"

Lindsey shrugged her shoulders. "Then I don't see the problem."

I didn't understand the reason for the double meanings behind everything—they were ticked off at each other and weren't trying to hide it.

"Talk about what?" I asked. "Like, give them our story?"

"Yes, that's definitely part of it," Lindsey answered. "The board is mostly interested in our earlier agreement with Sark that was made when he was caught a month ago. The small bit of information Sark traded to get you both here went far, so they're willing to do a lot for you both if he keeps it up, and your involvement could keep him from going to prison at all."

He traded information for this? "Wait, what kind of information?" I took another bite, hoping my compliance would help.

Lindsey's eyebrows furrowed. "About Alexis' organization." She glanced at Sark. "Did you not tell her this?"

I choked on my rice, coughing as several grains went flying, before my mouth fell open in shock.

"You did *what*?"

Sark sighed, rubbing his temple with his hand. "It's not a big deal, Arie."

"Not a big deal? Are you serious?" I started tripping over my words, urgently trying to fix what had already happened. "Do you…he could…and with—"

"Arie—"

"Do you realize how stupid that is? How he could…I mean, he already hates you. And you're just going to—"

"Arie, it's fine. I'm being careful about it."

"How do you 'be careful' about it? It's just going to give him more motivation to find you and—"

"That's how this works, Arie," Lindsey interrupted. "Either Sark is charged as a criminal or he gives others up to limit his punishments. If he didn't know so much then it wouldn't matter."

I looked at Sark again. He nodded.

Sark knows what he's doing. At least he should.

Something vibrated, and Lindsey pulled her phone out of her pocket, giving it a quick scan.

"Look, I've got to go," she said, gathering up her papers. "Do you guys have any questions?"

Sark just took a step away from us, turning so his back was now to us. I took that as a 'no.'

"So, I just show up and talk?" I asked. "Answer questions?"

"Yes, that's it. Just be honest and they'll have no reason to do anything to you."

"Um, okay. We'll be there. Anything else?"

She looked at me with a raised eyebrow. "Uh, no. Just be ready and take this seriously. Both of you."

I pointed to the kitchen. "Thanks for dinner."

"I'd believe it if you actually ate it."

She was right. My small pile of food had hardly been touched.

"Thanks anyway."

She gave a small grin as she stood up. "Okay then. Call me if you need me." And she left.

Sark hadn't moved. I waited for him to say something, knowing he would want to. After a minute, he sighed.

"You really think you're coming?" he asked the wall.

"You really think I'd just stay home?"

He sighed. "I'm just worried that—"

"No, you don't get to give that speech. *I'm* just worried that you're going to get yourself killed spilling information. But that's no big deal, is it?" I stood up and walked into the kitchen, setting my full plate on the counter.

The more I thought about it, the more it freaked me out. I had been so preoccupied with the idea of Dalton getting to Sark that I'd completely forgotten about Alexis. Dalton was too afraid of Sark to do anything besides kill him. Alexis was an entirely different story. He would be furious, and he would be doing everything possible to track Sark down. And Alexis wouldn't just kill him—he would make him pay for betraying and humiliating him, especially after Sark had worked for him for all those years. For keeping me, the one thing Alexis wanted more than anything, out of his reach. It would be bloody.

I had to grab the side of the counter to keep from falling over.

"Do you realize what he would do to you?" I demanded. "He's already got to be looking for you. You can't just…set up a trail for yourself like that. What if he found out and tracked you here?"

"It's okay—" he started, walking up to me.

"No, it's not just *okay*. I can't even…" I shuddered. "I can't even imagine what he would do to you. And you think it's *okay* to—"

"Arie." Sark grabbed my shoulders, forcing me to look in his stern eyes. "It's okay." He said each word distinctly, as if he were talking to a little kid. "Calm down. Yes, I gave Lindsey the information she wanted. Yes, it's a bit risky, but it's not a problem. I wouldn't do it if I really thought it would end badly."

"But Lindsey—"

"Lindsey gets excited. They don't get anywhere in her agency, especially her division. Combine that with the fact that I'm the only living person who has ever defected from Alexis and they're hanging onto every word I say. It fueled their fire when what I said actually worked. Honestly, I'm surprised any of it was up to date." He let go of me. "Like I said: no big deal. You don't need to be worried."

I lurched forward and hugged him tightly, afraid he was going to disappear. "You can't scare me like that," I whispered. "It freaks me out. You're…you're too important to me."

He hesitated, still as a statue, before wrapping his arms around me. "I'm sorry. I'll tell you from now on."

"You better."

We spent the rest of the night watching crime TV shows, which seemed to slowly thaw out Sark's icy mood. He took it upon himself to make me finish my dinner. I ended up eating almost half of my plate, which I thought was pretty good, but Sark pointed out that there wasn't that much on it in the first place. Leave it to him to kill my victory.

I turned in around nine, barely able to keep my eyes open, and passed out once my head hit the pillow. It only felt like a few hours later when I woke up. Disoriented, I couldn't believe it was morning already. I stumbled out of bed, yawning, and went into the living room. It was empty.

Sark was usually up before me. Confused, I walked down the hallway and into his bedroom, his door ajar. It was empty too.

Where did he go?

"Sark?" I called, walking back to the living room.

"Hello?"

He wouldn't just leave. He would make sure to tell me.

I had started to turn back into the hallway when somebody grabbed me from behind and dragged me backwards into my room. I shrieked, kicking my legs and flailing my arms everywhere. My captor threw me onto the ground by my bed. Sark was next to me, crumpled and tied up. His face was beaten, and he was breathing heavy—I couldn't tell if he was conscious or not.

The man who grabbed me had a hood over his head, hiding his identity, and stood guard over us. I turned to Sark and shook his shoulder.

"Sark?" I whispered, panic building in me as I watched my captor standing as a statue in front of us. "Sark, wake up."

He groaned, wincing, trying to open his eyes. "Get out of here, Arie," he whispered back, his voice rough with pain and urgency. "Get out now."

Even if I was going to obey, I didn't have time. A man strode into the room: Alexis. His presence brought a coldness that sent a chill up my spine, the resentment and animosity emanating from him making me scramble back to the wall.

He found us.

We stared at each other for a minute, his dark wavy hair framing his merciless eyes. I was frozen in terror; he seemed to be deciding what to do. We both glanced at Sark at the same time.

"No!" I lurched forward as he did, getting to Sark first, but someone seized me by the hair and threw me across the room. I crashed into the wall and fell to the floor on the other side of the bed. When I looked up, my attacker was gone.

Alexis had pulled Sark to his knees and was holding a knife to his throat. The bed was in between us, but even if I was closer, I didn't know what I could do. Alexis' eyes held me captive as he moved the knife up to Sark's temple, cutting down his face, and Sark clamped his teeth together.

Watch, Alexis' eyes seemed to say. *Watch as I cut him to pieces.*

"Don't," I choked out, my desperation nearly killing me. "Please don't hurt him. I'll do anything."

You had your chance, his eyes told me. *You lost. Did you really think you deserved him anyway?*

The knife was getting dangerously close to Sark's neck. Then it disappeared. I didn't know where it went, but Alexis moved his arm a certain way and Sark howled in pain.

"Stop it!" I screamed, watching as blood started dripping from the corners of Sark's mouth. "Stop it now!"

A crashing sound echoed near me, and I was distracted for a moment, trying to find the source. The sound only escalated Alexis' plan. He reached into his jacket, and I knew what would be coming out: a gun.

A gun! I dove under the bed, my hands frantically searching. Lindsey had said there was a gun under here. My hand finally wrapped around the smooth weapon, and I yanked it out. My arm was still under the bed when I heard a gunshot, and I screamed.

"Arie!" someone shouted. I opened my eyes at his voice, bewildered at what I saw.

All the lights had been turned off. It was still dark outside the window. I was sitting in the corner, clenching the gun that I was aiming straight in front of me. Kneeling on the other side of the barrel was Sark. Besides his terrified expression, he seemed fine, his arms loosely raised as if in surrender. In other words, he wasn't dead.

"Arie," he said slowly, eyeing the weapon I was aiming at him in my shaking hands, "give me the gun. Right now."

My heart was still pounding, my head dizzy. Sark was dead. He had…Alexis had…I saw him bleeding. I had heard the gun. I had been too late.

A spot behind Sark's head caught my attention. A small hole in the wall.

Did I do that?

Sark took advantage of my brief distraction. He pitched forward and snatched the gun out of my hand, pulling out the magazine before sliding both across the room. Breathing hard, he rested his head against his knee and put his hands over the back of his neck.

I almost shot him. The thought echoed uselessly in the back of my traumatized brain. *I could've killed him.*

After a minute, he looked up and examined me in my frozen state. My arms were still extended as if I were holding the gun. He took several more deep breaths before he could talk.

"You scared me," he said almost inaudibly.

"You…you were…you almost…" My voice trembled and tears started to roll down my face.

"I know." He pulled me into a hug right as I burst into sobs. "We're safe. It wasn't real. You're safe." Carefully, he picked me up off of the ground and put me back in my bed, wrapping my blankets around me, then sat down on the floor next to my bed, keeping a comforting hand on my arm. I clutched his wrist tightly in my other hand, burying my face in my pillow.

Eventually I ran out of tears. Violent dry sobs shook my body, which drained me of the energy I had left, causing me to drift in and out of hazy consciousness for hours. When I finally came to myself, I turned to see that the clock read six in the morning.

Sark cleared his throat, and I looked to see him in the same spot as earlier, my hand still gripping his wrist.

"You okay?" he asked me softly.

"I'm sorry," I whispered, my voice thick and cracked. I knew the apology could never be enough. "I'm so sorry."

Sark took a breath, as if to respond, but I interrupted. I couldn't hear his 'it's okay' speech right now.

"How close was it?"

"Not close enough." He was determined to play it off cool, though I could sense he was still a little shaken.

"How close?"

"You've developed the insanely creepy talent of sleeping with your eyes halfway open. I didn't realize you were asleep until after you pulled out the gun."

I thought how he was kneeling right in front of me, the bullet hole in the wall level with his head. It was so close.

I cringed. "I'm so sorry. Next time…don't come in. Just let me live it until it's over."

He shook his head. "Not a chance. You could hurt yourself so easily."

I couldn't really argue with that. One time, I had a dream that someone was smothering me, and it felt so real that I actually stopped breathing. If Sark and Erika hadn't been right next to me…

"I'm sorry," I said again, thinking of how horrible this must be for him.

Sark just shrugged. "You've had a…stressful year.

I think a good breakdown every once in a while is entitled. Honestly, you've been holding it together quite well, all things considered."

"You shouldn't have to suffer through it too."

"It's not that bad." His voice faltered, emphasizing the lie in his eyes.

"Yeah right."

"It's my job." His tone was teasing, but he couldn't keep it up. "And I've…I've got a lot of making up to do."

We were silent and I felt increasingly calm. It reminded me of those days after we got to Florida—Sark and I had been so beat up that we couldn't get up. So we'd sit in my bed or on the couch and watch movies all day. The memory was so jarring, felt so real in the moment, that I half expected Erika to walk in with a plate of her new edible creation that wasn't always so edible. My heart ached when I remembered that would never happen again.

My eyelids were heavy and when I closed them for a moment, I fell back asleep. When I woke up almost an hour later, I was completely alert, finding Sark asleep on my floor.

He must be exhausted. He couldn't have had that much more sleep than me. I grabbed one of the blankets off of my bed and spread it out over him.

Afraid of letting my mind wander, I reached under the pillow next to me and pulled out Erika's letters. I had read a few of them over the past few days. They either made me feel peaceful or made me want to cry. Sometimes they did both.

Arie—

If there is anything I can tell you, anything that I

would want you to know, it's that people have layers. And people can change.

You almost died again yesterday. I guess that probably isn't a huge surprise to you, huh? Maybe I can be as brave as you someday. Because when I ran downstairs and saw you underneath all of those shelves, Felix heading for you...I froze. I panicked. And you were so calm and determined. You fought back. I hope someday I can tell you how amazing I think you are.

I understand why you ran away—I mean, who wouldn't?—but when Sark went off on his own to find you, I was wishing you had stayed. I was certain he wanted us to split up so I wouldn't be around for whatever he was going to do to you. And when he came back with you, you were so bloody and beaten. It was just awful. Like I said, I wish I could've been as brave as you, but I wasn't. I lost it, big time. I realized in that moment how much I've grown to love you, Arie, and the thought that you might not wake up because I had dragged you back here in the first place was just too much to deal with.

Things didn't turn out any way I could've predicted. I blubbered like a complete idiot, but Sark didn't kill me. Actually, he and I ended up talking for a long time. And wow.

I wish he would tell you, Arie. So badly. It wouldn't mean nearly as much coming from me, and you probably wouldn't believe me anyway. He needs to tell you so you can understand, so you can see for yourself. He's not who you think he is, Arie. He's not who anybody thought he was. He's done some bad things, for sure, but he's amazing. Strong and brave, but gentle too, and highly misunderstood. Don't kill me for saying this but I think he's a lot like you.

I glanced at Sark passed out on the floor, thinking about my story, just awestruck at how it had woven into an intricate piece of old European art: it was interesting to look at and impossible to explain, but you couldn't help but feel that there was some sort of purpose to it. At least I hoped.

14

We spent the next three days just hanging out. I finally convinced Sark that I was going to the trial, which meant that I had to get ready too. I didn't want to look like roadkill for something as important as this. The purple wounds on my face had started flaking—the skin that fell off was nasty but underneath it was brand new, better looking skin. I figured that with some help most of it would be pretty much gone by the day of the trial.

The only thing that I needed was something to wear. I didn't realize that until Alaina brought it up. It was the day before the trial, and we were at the infecteds' place.

It had been easier to be there since my last visit: news of my involvement in Jefferson's leg breaking had spread like wildfire, and the heated glares were getting more and more infrequent.

I was sitting at the counter with Sark, Alaina, and Lucy, watching Mara work her magic with food. Several groups of infecteds hovered behind us—it seemed someone was always following me now. I tried to distract myself by explaining the trial to Alaina, but after a few minutes I realized that I didn't actually know much about it.

"So, what are you going to wear?" Alaina asked.

"Actually…I have no idea," I admitted. "I don't think the hand-me-down giant sweatshirt will make a good impression."

"You need to go all out," Mara told me. "You've got to look sophisticated so they take you seriously."

"I don't have anything close to that." *I actually don't have anything period. Nothing in that house is mine.*

"All right." Alaina stood up and gestured to me. "You know that I wouldn't offer this unless it was an absolute emergency. Brace yourself: we're going shopping."

I raised an eyebrow. "Shopping?"

"I know, I know. Stores are often 'public places', which means that there will be actual," she made a face, "*human beings*. But, because of my knowledge and skill, I can show you places that are never crowded. We'll be back in no time." She snapped her fingers. "Piece of cake."

"I'm not sure that's a good idea," Sark piped up, glancing from me to Alaina.

"Do you want to come *shopping* with us?" Alaina

eyed him doubtfully.

He grinned. "Absolutely not. That's sure to be a disaster." His smile faded. "Which is why—"

"I can take care of Arie." Alaina folded her arms in indignation.

"I don't need anyone taking care of me," I said, annoyed.

"You say that now," Sark said, "but you'll get there and something will get you to lock up. Before you know it, they'll be calling the police because of a girl screaming in their store."

I glared darkly at him. "I'm not going to start screaming in the store."

He lifted his hands up in surrender. "I'm just saying it could very easily happen. You know that. And I wouldn't—"

"We'll be fine," I said, now determined to prove him wrong. "Come on Alaina. Let's go." I stood up and started walking.

Alaina smirked and followed me. "That's my girl."

I stopped once we got outside. Alaina gave me a confused look, but I just sighed, frustrated. "Hold on."

I turned around and went back inside. Sark was waiting for me, still sitting in his chair, a small smile on his face. I stopped right in front of him.

"You don't have any money, do you?" he asked, not doing a thing to hide his amusement.

I gritted my teeth. "No."

He had already gotten a wad of cash ready. He offered it to me but retracted his hand when I reached for it.

"If you're going then you have to take a phone," he told me, nodding to a small cell phone that was already on the counter. "No exceptions on that one."

"Fine." I put the phone in my pocket, then reached for the money again.

"Be careful," Sark told me, keeping the money away from me. "Please. This really scares me."

"I know."

"No, you don't. I would make you stay here, but I know it's a lost cause, so please just be safe."

"I will."

Sark appraised me for a minute, then hesitantly gave me the money.

"After two hours, I'll start looking for you. After two and a half, I'll call Lindsey."

"Two hours," I repeated, so he knew I got it. Then I turned around and went back to Alaina, who was leaning against the doorframe. She gave me a triumphant smile as we walked out the door again.

It wasn't snowing, but the thick layer on the ground seemed pretty fresh. I stuffed my hands in my jacket pockets and trudged after Alaina. We walked in silence that was slightly uncomfortable, but not really. It made me long for the easygoing relationship we used to have.

"You know, Arie," she started, slowing her pace a little so I was next to her. "I'm getting pretty sick of this."

"Of what?"

"You. Me. Acting like we met each other a week ago rather than two years ago."

"Oh. Yeah…me too."

She pursed her lips, something she did when she was fighting emotional display.

"I mean, Sark and all of them gave me the whole speech: the Arie you lost won't be the Arie that came back and all that crap—and I get that—but…I miss you, Arie. A lot."

"I miss you too." Suddenly I was overcome with anger. Scowling at the snow, I clenched my hands into fists.

Alaina noticed. "What?"

"I hate this." I kicked some snow up as I walked. "I hate that everything was taken. Everything was screwed up. For everyone." I glanced over at her hopefully. "Can I just have five seconds? I swear it will be quick."

She smiled. "I was afraid you were never going to ask."

"Everything is different now. *Everything.* I mean, you know that because it is for you too. It's weird to talk to each other, it's weird to be together. It's weird for anyone to be in the same room as me. Sark and I just started talking like normal a few days ago and he's…I don't know. Erika is gone, my secret isn't a secret, and I'm…I'm different. And I hate it. This isn't…this isn't my life. My life is gone." I took a deep breath to keep my voice from cracking. "I always talked about how much it sucked, but I really want it back."

Alaina looked straight ahead and kept her face smooth, but her eyes gave her away.

"I'm sorry," I said, feeling a little self-conscious.

"Don't be sorry." She tried to smile. "That's what I'm here for. It sounds like you don't get that out much."

I shook my head. "I don't feel like I can tell Sark everything, especially about…well…"

"Erika?"

I nodded. "It kills him too much. I already hurt him enough on a daily basis."

"He loves you, Arie," she said, a new edge to her voice. "We all do."

Alaina stopped then, pointing at the building next to us. Judging from the window display, it seemed to be a small clothing store—the sign was so worn that I couldn't even make out the name.

"Ready?" Alaina asked.

I took a deep breath and nodded. "I guess."

We went inside and I instantly tensed up. There were only four people in the place, including the worker, but the store was so small that I felt like it was hopelessly crowded. Alaina grabbed my arm and started pulling me toward the back.

"Are you sure you can handle this?" she whispered.

I wanted to say no and get out of there, but I remembered Sark. I could feel the stubbornness he always teased me about bubbling up inside of me.

"Yeah. Just…just stay by me, okay?" I felt really stupid and childish, but Alaina nodded, and I knew she was taking me seriously. She wasn't my best friend for nothing.

"So, I'm thinking black," Alaina said, slipping into authority mode, "because black dresses are sophisticated, right?"

I couldn't help but grin. "Right."

We went through all six racks of dresses. I was busy checking over my shoulder and watching other people; Alaina took charge of actually finding stuff. Within fifteen minutes, her arms were full.

"Wow," I said in disbelief. "I thought you hated shopping."

"Just because I hate it doesn't mean I'm not good at it. When I was eight, I could spot the perfect pink dress from ten miles away." We laughed, imagining a mini flame-haired punk in a pink dress. "My mom was heartbroken when I turned fourteen and decided the only thing I wanted was black skinny jeans."

We found the fitting rooms and shut ourselves in the

biggest one. I felt a little more relaxed when we were alone.

Alaina hung up the dresses on a hook, trying to look absentminded. "When was the last time you ate?"

I rolled my eyes, seeing right through her. "That has Sark written all over it."

"Fine, you got me. I just want to make sure you're eating."

"I'm eating fine," I muttered, slightly annoyed. *I can take care of myself.*

"Considering the incredibly tiny diameter of your arm, I'm thinking probably not."

"Since when are you Miss Responsibility?" I asked.

She turned to face me, expression deadpan. "Since my best friend died and I had to take in forty infecteds while trying not to be murdered."

My mouth fell open in shock. Leave it to Alaina to tell the truth.

She shrugged. "You asked."

I took a deep breath, shaking my head as if to clear it. "Right."

"Look," she said as she took a dress off its hanger, "I know you hate babysitters—I would hate it if everyone was all over me—but you can't blame us for being worried."

I sighed. "I guess I'd rather you be worried than not caring. I just…I don't know."

"I know. It's got to be annoying."

"It is. Especially when I know I need it."

Alaina helped me into the first couple dresses, all of which didn't work. When we got to the fifth one I realized how terrible of an idea this was.

"This is a waste of time." I stared at the reflection in the floor length mirror. The dress only emphasized what was wrong with me: my bones sticking out, yellowish skin, dark circles under my eyes, lifeless hair. If anything, it made me look less like a person and more like a…thing, I guess.

"Why? This one is totally perfect." Alaina started playing with my ponytail from behind. "I think you'll have to put your hair up. It fits the look better."

"No. Alaina…I look horrible. Sick. You can tell something is seriously wrong with me. A dress isn't going to hide that." I sat down on the wooden bench, suddenly exhausted. "Can we just go back?"

Alaina sighed, then sat cross-legged on the bubblegum ridden floor in front of me, which was pretty nasty, but she didn't seem to care.

"Can I ask you something?" Her voice was quiet as she rubbed the top of her boot with her thumb.

I shrugged. "Sure."

"Sark said…he told me a little bit about the shouting match you guys had. He said that you said that this whole time…while you were gone you thought we weren't coming for you…because we wanted you dead." She took a couple of deep breaths, then looked up to meet my gaze. Her black eyes were torn up, but still angry. "How could you even *consider* that? How could you…I mean, we're like your family, Arie. And you—"

I shook my head. "Alaina—"

"I just can't believe that! I know we were stupid, Arie, I know that. I know we messed up on bailing you out and you must hate us for that. But how could you think we wouldn't care? How could…I mean, we found out you were dead and Mark—*Mark*, the jokester that never stops—wouldn't leave his room for a month."

"Alaina! Please stop."

"I'm sorry. I just don't get it."

I took a deep breath in an effort to prepare myself. I knew she was going to be mad at me for bringing this up—I didn't even know if *I* was going to be able to finish—but it was the only way I could think to explain.

Do I even want to explain?

"Remember that one time when Lennon caught us, one of the times when Sark wasn't there, and he locked us in the basement for a few days and we almost got heat stroke? He was really mad about you flooding his house and he was punishing us—mostly you—for it?"

Her eyes widened when she saw where I was going. "No. We're not talking about this."

"We were basically dying but that wasn't the worst part—it was what he would say to us. To you."

"Shut up now."

"What did he say?" I asked softly.

At first I thought she'd keep fighting me on it, but she gave up and answered, her voice trembling. "He said I was an accident. I was a mistake. I was so worthless that my dad wouldn't stick around for me, and I was such a screw up that I killed my own mom. The car crash that killed her was my fault, that I knew it was. He said how much my dad must…what he would think if he knew…and how disappointed my mom would be if she could see me now…" Her voice got progressively quieter until she was just mouthing words. Words I knew she'd repeated to herself countless times over the years.

I cleared my thick throat. "And a few days later— when we escaped—you said something to me. I remember it, even after all this time. Do you remember?"

She let out a long breath that seemed to last forever.

Then she pursed her lips and rubbed her temples.

"I said that if I had to live like that one day longer…if I had to listen to that one more time…and get a beating right after to reinforce it…I would learn to believe it. I would learn to live it. And—"

"It would destroy me," we both finished in unison.

There was a beat of silence. I wrapped my arms around myself, wishing I could shrink to the size of an ant.

"You were right," I finally whispered. "That's exactly how it works."

Alaina stood and sat next to me on the bench, putting her arm around me. I buried my face in her shoulder.

I didn't know how long we sat there, just thinking and mourning, knowing we could do nothing to fix anything. It was therapeutic somehow. We talked about so many things without even talking at all, and just being in my best friend's presence made me feel like things might get better.

Eventually Alaina grabbed my hand and stood us both up. She looked me in the eye, smiling a little.

"First off, don't apologize," she ordered, "because I know that's what you're thinking. I needed it about as much as you did 'cause I've missed your guts so freaking much. Second, that's the dress you're getting. We're going to need to grab some shoes and jewelry on our way out. And third, you are still my best friend. I don't care about what Dalton says or any other psycho idiot out there. You are my sister and nobody is *ever* going to take that away from me." She cleared her throat before adding, "Never again. And fourth—"

"This is a long list," I interrupted teasingly.

She grinned. "Yeah, it's a good one. Fourth, I am so

incredibly ecstatic to have you back. I really am. I know that I was really…surprised when you showed up and it took me awhile to start acting somewhat normal. And I realize now how you must have interpreted that. So, I want you to know that I love you, I'm fighting for you, I'm here to help you, and that will never change." She let out a long breath. "Okay, I'm done."

I gave her a hug. "Thank you."

She took another shaky breath. "And if you…if you can ever forgive me—"

I squeezed her tighter. "Don't go there. It's okay."

"I'm just sorry. So sorry."

"I know. I am too."

I got dressed and we went back into the store. There were still a couple people around, but they were all wrapped up in their own shopping endeavors. I followed Alaina around as she picked up some lethal black heels.

"There's no way I'll be able to walk in those," I protested.

"These are perfect! You'll be sitting down the whole time anyway. You just have to make it in and out. Sark won't let you fall."

"That's literally the worst idea I've ever heard."

She was already gone before I finished. A second later she reappeared with a box of makeup.

"I'm guessing you need some of this. And I grabbed an extra thing of cover up—your face isn't quite there yet."

I grinned. "You're the best."

She bowed gracefully. "I know, I know. Tips are appreciated but not required."

I almost died of anxiety when we were checking out. Thankfully Alaina did most of the work, which I was grateful for. I knew this kind of thing scared her too, and we both breathed a sigh of relief when we stepped outside and started walking back.

Neither of us spoke for a minute. I could tell she was trying to figure something out, so I just waited for her.

Finally, she broke the silence. "Can I ask you something else? Since we're still in the land of semi-forbidden topics and may be leaving soon."

I shrugged, somewhat nervous. "Sure."

"I don't want to overstep," she reassured me. "I've just been dying to know some things and I could never really ask Sark, so…" she trailed off, waiting for real permission.

"Yeah." I stuffed my hands in my pockets. "Go ahead."

She dove in, talking quickly as if we'd had this conversation a million times before. "I mean, I know you probably never wanted to talk about your, um, secret, which is why you never brought it up to me, ever, or any of us, ever, but I could've—"

"I didn't tell you to protect you," I interrupted, my voice getting a bit smaller. "And to protect myself. It's not that I didn't trust you, I just didn't know what to do, or how you would react, or—"

"No, I get it." She let a false note slip into her voice.

"I'm sorry," I said, not really sure what else to say. "I just made it a rule not to tell anybody. It seemed like the right way to go."

"Wait, you didn't tell anyone?"

I was surprised that she was surprised. "Um, no. That was kind of the point."

"Not even Sark?"

"No. My family were the only people that knew, then Kieran died, so it's just my parents that know—

knew. I guess everyone knows now.”

We rounded a corner, shuffling our feet in the snow as small gusts of wind went through our hair.

“How’d they find out?” Alaina asked after a moment of quiet. “Sark and Erika. ‘Cause when Sark showed up to tell me, he knew.”

I gritted my teeth. “I made a stupid, *stupid*, idiotic mistake.”

Alaina muttered something incoherent before saying, “Yeah? And what was that?”

“Uh, one day I was out by myself and realized Dalton’s men were following me, which didn’t make sense at the time, but…” I shivered and started over. “They were following me, and I was certain that they knew I was the key. I completely freaked out, breaking the one rule I had set for myself. I called Erika and admitted that I had codes that someone would want—”

“Codes?” Alaina interrupted, her eyebrows furrowing. “What codes?”

“I don’t know. I overheard my dad say one time that I could ‘provide codes’ but I have no idea what that means.”

She shook her head. “Huh. Okay.”

“Anyway, Erika was confused, but Sark knew exactly what I was talking about. I met them at a parking garage so we could get out of there.” I cleared my throat. “But Jefferson was in town. I guess he had seen me walking around and followed me to the garage. He was shocked when I ran *to* Sark instead of *away* from him.”

“So Sark had to make something up,” Alaina guessed.

I nodded. “He told Jefferson all about how he was getting nowhere with me, so he tried to go a different route and gained my trust. And I was a complete sucker, so it worked."

Alaina winced slightly. "Ouch. I'll bet that was fun."

"Yeah." My hands fidgeted in my pockets. "It was pretty brutal to hear. For Erika too."

"She didn't know?"

"Not at first. Sark had to make absolute sure Alexis bought his story, especially after Lennon had reported him. If Alexis had suspected anything at all, he would've killed Sark and Erika in two seconds flat. Sark had to be extremely careful and it cost us all a lot. I know he hates himself for it."

"So how'd you get out?" Alaina asked, flipping her hair out of her face. "I know Sark's a scary genius, but I don't really see how this could work."

I shifted the shopping bag on my shoulder, unable to decide if this visit to the past was bothering me or not.

"Well, uh, after an eternity they brought me into a big room with Alexis and asked me about the key. I didn't know what they were talking about, since I figured Sark had told them my secret on day one, but eventually I realized that they didn't know. So I lied, just like I had been doing for months before that."

"And they believed you?" There was a hint of awe in her voice.

I shrugged. "I guess. I passed out. When I woke up, we were in Sark's house. He told them he wanted to be the one to kill me and they didn't care. Everything would've been just fine if I hadn't spilled my guts over the phone."

"No," Alaina gasped, as if she were watching a TV show. "They found your conversation?"

"Yeah. Felix came to the house and almost killed Sark. We were able to get out in time and I convinced Sark to let me stop at your place to warn you. Then we took off for Florida."

I counted eleven steps in the snow before Alaina responded. "You were going to tell me then, weren't you?" she asked, her voice quieter. "You came to say Alexis found out about Sark, my psychotic handler Lennon was coming after me, and you were in serious danger 'cause you were the freaking key."

"I just left the last part out." My attempt at a joking tone fell flatter than a squished pancake. I sighed. "I couldn't do it. There was nothing you could've done anyway."

"I wouldn't have thought any less of you," she whispered under her breath. "If you had told me. That wouldn't have changed anything."

"I know," I lied.

Alaina's hands started twitching. She was slipping into her obsessive mode, using the tone that told me she wouldn't stop until she had worked through this. "Sometimes I just don't know how I didn't see it. I mean, it's not like I actually believed the key existed, but still. Every time I or any other infected brought the subject up, you would always lock up and try to get around it."

I rolled my eyes at my own ignorance. "How did that not give me away?"

"I don't know. You've always been such a…" She searched for the right word. "Compassionate soul, Arie. I've never really understood that. You always take in everyone's pain and make it your own. I figured you just couldn't handle that amount of pain."

We both snorted at the irony. "But that wasn't it,"

she continued. "I'll admit, running from psychos has always been hard for me—for everyone, really—and some days I just gave up. I would let Lennon find me, and not put up an ounce of fight, then throw a giant pity party. Every infected I met had those days, but with you that was never an option. There was no room for capture in your plan, and the second someone had grabbed you—literally the very second—you were already figuring out how to escape."

She laughed once. "Honestly, it was cool, but sometimes it drove me insane. Now I realize that you were doing it because—"

"I was really just a coward?" I supplied.

"No. It's just different than I thought. It makes sense. I'm just mad I didn't figure it out earlier."

"Well now you know." I hesitated before adding in a quieter voice, "I'm sorry."

"Stop saying that, Arie!" She hit me with her shopping bag. "How stupid do you think we are? We know none of this is your fault. Sark explained as much as he could—"

"Sark doesn't know everything," I interrupted. "He shouldn't have to deal with—"

She skidded to a stop, grabbing my shoulder to stop me too. "He's not *dealing* with anything and he's not dealing with you. He loved you so much that it literally killed him. I mean, he went to a lot of bars, but you should've seen some of the holes I had to drag him out of—"

I shook my head. "Please don't."

Alaina sighed. "Look, I could paint you a nasty picture, but I know you don't want it, so I won't. But you should know that when you died, he went to hell, and we were all sure he was never coming back."

I took a shaky breath, willing myself to not imagine anything.

Of course he had issues, I reasoned with myself. *He lost his wife.*

Alaina seemed to know what I was thinking, tightening her grip on my shoulder. "It wasn't just Erika, you know."

I nodded, not sure exactly what I was feeling, but Alaina let it go. She gave me a small grin before we started walking again.

"Thanks for coming," I said after a moment, watching my footprints in the snow as we approached the club. "I would've been lost without you. Actually, I wouldn't have come and then I would've had to show up looking awful tomorrow. So thank you."

"Thank *you.* I haven't been out of the club for a long time." She opened the front door. "I was going to go crazy if I didn't get a change of scenery."

The second we walked inside I realized that we must've been late. Sark was pacing up and down the length of the counter. Brennan, Lucy, Mark, Mara, and Liam were all sitting at the counter, semi worried expressions on their faces. It seemed that they had given up on telling Sark that everything was fine.

"It's a miracle!" Alaina exclaimed mockingly as we walked up to them. "We didn't die."

Sark jumped at Alaina's voice, spun around, and gave me a hug. Then he let me go and released a long breath.

"Two hours and twelve minutes," he said, eyeing me sternly. Alaina gave me an 'I told you so' look from behind his shoulder.

"Did you have a heart attack?" I muttered, still not over his comments from earlier.

"Almost. Did you have any problems?"

"Nope. Alaina's got a gift. It was slick." I pulled out the cash that we didn't spend. "Do you realize that you gave me five hundred dollars? What the heck did you think I was buying?"

Sark studied me for a moment before grinning. "I didn't know how much you wanted. I wasn't even sure five hundred was enough, knowing you two."

I couldn't tell if he was joking or not since Alaina and I were probably the last two people on this planet that would spend five hundred dollars on a dress. Rolling my eyes, I threw the cash at him.

"So what did you get?" Mara asked excitedly.

Lucy was almost bouncing in her seat. "You have to show us."

Alaina pulled the dress out of the bag she was carrying, holding it up like a game show model. It was pretty simple—a soft black fabric, knee length, with a slight v neckline and short sleeves—but it generated many oohs and ahs from our spectators. Lucy took it from Alaina so she and Mara could examine it more closely.

"So yeah," Alaina said, flipping her hair. "Arie is going to kill it tomorrow."

"You better come tell us about it," Brennan said, "because we'll be dying to hear how it went." Mark and Liam nodded.

"*If* we come back," I said automatically, then stiffened. I turned to Sark. "We *are* going to come back, right?"

Sark's face fell, instantly turning from joking to serious. His eyes went down the line of each of us before looking at the floor. "There is a chance it won't be smooth sailing. There are so many things…" He ran a hand through his hair, then looked at Alaina. "Arie will come back, with or without me. I'll make sure that happens. I can't promise that there won't be issues. We're just going to have to be careful."

I caught on to his warning, knowing it was something he was trying to hide from me. I started putting the pieces together, a pit forming in my stomach.

"Who's going to be there?" I asked.

"I don't know," Sark said, keeping his voice even. "A few of the higher officers in the agency, I would guess."

My hands started shaking softly. "Lindsey would never let—"

"No. Lindsey would never let Dalton come. She would make sure it was someone else."

"But they might work with him," I said, thinking out loud. "They might have talked with him. He might have told them about me."

"You're a victim, Arie," Sark said, his words harsh. "What could he possibly tell them?"

I knew this too well; Dalton had threatened so many times.

That I'm a criminal. That I'm dangerous. That I'm an unstable infected that he tried to neutralize but I broke out and now I'm running rampant. That they need to do everything in their power to get me back to him, for the sake of everyone else. Because I murdered an innocent girl in their agency in cold blood. Because I'm a deceptive killer.

And he wouldn't even be lying.

I sucked in a sharp breath. "A lot."

In a daze, I grabbed my bags of new pretty things, waved goodbye, and walked out the door.

I went a block and a half before Sark caught up to me. He reached out and took my bags from me.

"What are you doing?" I asked, not sure if I was annoyed or not.

He shrugged. "Attempting to be a gentleman. It looks like I'm failing."

"Oh. Sorry. Thanks."

"Of course."

We went another block. I had finally got the route between the infecteds' place and our house down, so I actually knew where we were going.

"Is that why you don't want me to come?" I couldn't help asking.

He looked up at the sky. "There are about a million reasons why I don't want you to come."

"Name a few. I can handle it, I promise."

He sighed but surprised me by answering. "It's going to be long, it's going to be exhausting, and it's going to require a lot of...reflecting. Reflecting on things that are probably hard to think about, let alone tell a group of strangers. We will be separated the whole time, so if you do have an episode then I won't be there to help. The agents will likely be harsh and cruel, with no patience toward you at all, which could just trigger an episode faster. There is a good chance that they're already biased against you—much of their agency only tolerate infecteds—and will be more so since you're arguing for me and not against me. And that's just a few."

"Wow," I breathed. "That's..."

"Mostly I'm afraid they're going to start grilling you so hard that you'll snap. Any mistakes you make will be used against you, even small ones. If you start freaking out, they'll probably brand you as mentally unstable and lock you up in a hospital facility. Or they'll decide that you're dangerous and try to apprehend you. And all of this will take place without me there to do anything." He cleared his throat, but his voice was a bit rougher. "They could take you within the first five minutes and you would be missing by the time I realized something had happened. You would be gone again."

"That's not going to happen," I said, not really sure if it was for me or for him.

"I know it's not. But it could. I'm just as worried about you as you are about me. At least if they took me, it would be for a good reason."

"There's no good reason to take either of us," I responded darkly.

"I wish that were true."

"It is."

"I'm a criminal, Arie." His hands clenched slightly. "I know you forget, you make allowances for me, but not everyone can or should. I let you make allowances for me because I love being with you. But I can't erase years of felonies by claiming to be a changed man. It doesn't work like that."

"That's why this is so important," I said. "We have to show them that you deserve to be granted your freedom."

"The only reason I don't lock myself up in prison is you. Despite everything I've ever done to you, you're still willing to keep me around."

It took me a few steps to swallow that. "It's more than that. You know that, right? I don't just tolerate you."

"I know. You rely on me. You need me. And I need you." He gave me a half smile. "So let's just keep our little family going, okay?"

"Okay," I said, only because I really didn't like this conversation.

We got home and I hung up my new dress in the closet. It stood out dramatically among the old, tattered clothes that were gathering dust. I admired it for a moment before shutting the closet door.

Sark was warming up something in the microwave, but I didn't really feel like eating. Instead I took a shower, shaved the jungle of hair off my legs, and brushed my teeth thoroughly before climbing into bed.

"Goodnight," I called, too lazy to get up.

Sark walked into my room and leaned up against the doorframe.

"Get some sleep," he said. "Tomorrow is going to be a long day."

"You too."

"It's going to be okay, Arie. You know that, right?"

"No," I admitted, "but it's a nice thought."

He opened his mouth to say something, then stopped himself. Finally he smiled, though it didn't reach his eyes. "Goodnight." He turned off the light and shut the door behind him.

I closed my eyes hesitantly, afraid of going to sleep. I had no idea what tonight's nightmares would bring.

But to my surprise, I had a nightmare-free night— the first I'd had in a long time.

15

I slept like a rock, so when Sark came to wake me up my neck was stiff.

"Come on, Sleeping Beauty," he said, shaking my shoulder. "Rise and shine."

I growled and threw my hand out, hitting what felt like his face.

"Ow!" He chuckled. "I'm sorry, I know you're tired and you're actually sleeping, but we got to go."

I put my pillow over my head. "Shut up."

"Don't make me throw water on you. Because I will."

"I'm coming." I didn't know if he could understand

me through the pillow, but I think he got the main idea.

"Lindsey left us a car, so we don't have to walk," Sark said as he stood up. "We're leaving in an hour." I heard him walk out of the room.

Five more minutes. I just need five more minutes. I was so tired that it hurt to open my eyes. I let myself relax as I tried to cultivate the courage to drag myself up, not willing to give up the warmth and comfort of my bed. At that moment, nothing was worth losing it.

A second later, I heard Sark's quick footsteps down the hallway.

"Arie, what are you doing?"

What is his problem?

"Five more minutes," I mumbled from under the pillow. He started pulling my blankets off of me, and I held onto them with an iron grip.

"You fell back asleep. We have to leave in twenty minutes. Come on! Get up."

It took a half a second for that to sink in, then I bolted upright, the room spinning. "What?"

"Twenty minutes, Arie." He grabbed my arms and dragged me out of bed, holding onto me until he was sure I wouldn't fall over, then he left.

"Twenty minutes," he called as he went down the hallway.

I stumbled into the bathroom, frantically trying to rub the sleep out of my eyes. I turned the cold water on and splashed some on my face in an effort to focus.

Twenty minutes. I looked hopelessly at the sleep-deprived zombie in the mirror. *I've got twenty minutes to resurrect that.* My chances didn't look good.

I grabbed my makeup and started going to work. Layers of cover up on my face hid almost all traces of purple spots, which I was grateful for. I looked slightly more human with a somewhat normal skin tone. That was the only success I had though. My frustration was building as I lost control of the eyeliner pen and drew all over my face.

You would think a teenage girl could remember how to put on makeup.

After poking myself in the eye three times with the mascara brush, I gave up. I slammed the makeup box shut, grabbed the supplies I needed, and stalked into my room.

I changed into my dress, having to bend my arm awkwardly to zip it up all the way. It was a bit too big, but manageable. Really, I just wanted my sweats back. Dresses were so uncomfortable.

Oh well. I can survive for a day.

All that was left was the disaster that was my hair. I went to the floor-length mirror hanging next to my bedroom door. My hair was already in a ponytail, so I started twisting it around into different shapes.

Hair. Hair…how do I do hair? How could I forget how to do my own hair?

At the expense of many elastics and bobby pins, I was finally able to secure my hair into a simple bun—nothing fancy since I had no time or patience for anything else. There were sections of hair above my ear that had broken and were too short, so I just let them hang there and frame my face. Grabbing a can of hairspray, I went over my head a few times hoping that it all would stay put.

I grabbed the lipstick that Alaina had picked and smeared it on my lips. She had gotten the color just right—it was red enough to stand out but wasn't crazy bright. I owed her big time.

Sitting on the edge of my bed, I slipped on the heels

of death that were sure to cause me trouble, then stood up and took a wobbly step to the mirror, taking in the whole look for the first time.

It was crushingly disappointing that I had expended so much energy to make myself pretty and this was all I could produce. That was a common problem I faced since infection. I thought it came from the months of looking and feeling like a creature that had crawled out from a graveyard, which made something like shopping extremely difficult, but that usually wasn't important. Being an infected is all about blending in, not making a statement. I wasn't used to this.

Oh well. We can't have everything.

"Wow." I jumped at Sark's voice and turned to see he was leaning up against the doorframe, wearing a crisp black suit. "You clean up nice for only having twenty minutes."

"You get what you pay for," I muttered, moving to walk around him.

He grabbed my arm to stop me. "I'm serious. You look great. I can't even tell your face used to be purple."

That was nice of him to say, but I felt like he was just acting out of obligation. I mean, what else was he supposed to say? 'Nice try but you still look awful'?

"You too," I told him. "Without the leather jacket you look like less of a punk."

He laughed, which made me crack a small smile.

"Ready?" he asked.

I shrugged. "I guess."

He gestured for me to go first, so I went down the hallway and out the front door. Sark started to ask if I wanted a jacket, but I waved him off. I was already sweating with anxiety and the cold helped calm me.

It was still dark outside, as it was barely after six in

the morning. I walked carefully down the driveway, stumbling in the heels from time to time. A small black car was parked in front of the house. Sark opened the door and helped me into the passenger seat. Then he got inside, started the car, and pulled away.

I smoothed my skirt out about a billion times even though there were no wrinkles. After a minute, Sark reached out and took one of my barely shaking hands. I looked over to see him staring straight ahead, jaw clenched, with his other hand holding onto the wheel a little too tightly. He was nervous. No, he was more than nervous—he was scared. His stress increased my own.

"Two things," he said, his voice too calm. Too even. He was trying very hard to hide his anxiety. "Be a hundred percent honest, but…keep your secret to yourself. They know that you're infected, they know that Alexis wants the key, but they don't need to know that you are the key. I don't trust them with that."

I nodded. There was no telling how they would react.

"And second, don't tell them about Dalton. Keep them in the dark, just like you did with Lindsey. Give them the idea that you were taken, but not who it was. I will make the judgment call on that one."

"Why?" Not that I wanted to give details about my imprisonment, but I had thought that Sark was an advocate of getting Dalton in trouble.

"Because you could be right—I don't know if they've had contact with him or not. If I'm sure that it would give us a good edge, then I'll tell them what I think, but…just leave it out. You'll have plenty to discuss besides that anyway. Okay?"

"Okay."

He squeezed my hand. "If something happens—if

something goes wrong—you fight. Scream, make as much noise as possible, and get out. Do whatever it takes. Run as far as you can, meet up with Alaina. She'll help you. But just go, okay?"

My voice was barely above a whisper. "What about you?"

He sighed. "If I hear you then I'll come get you, but…I can't make promises. And you can't stick around. You need to run, with or without me. Can you promise me that?"

"I'm not walking out of there without you," I said, jerking my chin up.

His jaw and hands clamped at the same time. "Oh yes you are. You do whatever it takes to get out. Do not come back for me. Understand?"

"No."

Sark slammed on the brakes at a stoplight, even though he could've easily made it through the yellow. He turned to look at me, controlled anger threatening to explode.

"I will turn around, go back home, lock you in a closet, and come back myself. Once they see that you're not with me, I'm done. Is that what you want?"

I gritted my teeth. "That's not fair."

"Life's not fair."

I could tell by his tone he was serious—he really would lock me in a closet. I would have no chance to help him in that scenario.

"Fine." Both of us knew it wasn't much of a promise. He let out a long breath through his teeth. The light turned green, and we started down the road again.

It was the longest, yet the shortest car ride I've ever had. I played with Sark's hand, folding up each finger then straightening them back out. The simple activity did little to take my mind off of the butterflies in my stomach morphing into rabid bears clawing at each other.

Sark parked in the small parking lot of Lindsey's building, which was now full of several cars. My heart skipped a beat when I saw them.

This is really happening.

Sark got out and opened my door for me, offering his hand so I didn't trip stepping out of the car. I took his arm as we walked up the pavement stairs to the door, almost falling at least seven times.

"The shoes?" Sark asked, smiling a little to himself.

"Alaina's idea. A pretty terrible one."

"They look great. Walking isn't all that important anyway."

"She seemed to think so too."

We got to the door, where Lindsey was waiting for us. She did a faint double take when she saw us, raising her eyebrows as she opened the door and ushered us inside. I looked around the drab building, my hands starting to shake. I hated this place.

It took a few moments for me to realize Lindsey had been talking. She looked at me expectantly, waiting for me to respond.

I gave a small grin. "Yeah, okay."

Her eyes narrowed slightly. "You didn't hear a thing I just said, did you?"

"Uh…"

"I'll take that as a no."

"No. Sorry."

Her eyes softened. "It's going to be okay."

I just nodded, not trusting my voice to be even. I could tell she wasn't convinced, but she turned and started walking. Taking Sark's arm to reassure me, I hesitantly followed.

We went down a hallway, then turned down another. Lindsey stopped at the end where it forked into opposite directions. A group of four men in official-looking suits, along with Brody and Deron, were waiting for us there, every angry and cautious eye on Sark. I tensed up when we stopped right next to them.

"All right," Lindsey said, turning to look at me. "This is it." Two of the men gestured for me to follow them, down the hallway to the right.

My heart was pounding so hard that I was surprised nobody could hear it. I glanced at Sark, who looked like he was desperately fighting the urge to grab me and make a run for it. I honestly couldn't tell if he was winning or not, increasing my fear, making me realize that this wasn't going to be what I had prepared for. This was going to be worse than Sark had ever let on.

"It's going to be fine," I told him quietly, able to keep my voice from shaking. "I'll see you in a little bit."

Sark nodded in a jerky motion. Using every last ounce of my willpower, I let go of his arm and started walking with the two men. Everything in my body was fighting it, screaming at me to go back. But I forced myself to keep going.

I looked back and saw Sark going the opposite direction, the other two men flanking him guns at the ready. I kept forgetting they saw him as a dangerous person. Although, I guess he *was* if you were on his bad side.

He turned and looked at me too, right before we both disappeared around a corner. I could see in his eyes that we were thinking that same thing.

That could've been the last time we ever see each other.

16

The two men walked behind me, so I had no idea where to go. I just focused on putting one foot in front of the other and not throwing up. When we got to an open door with a man waiting outside of it, I assumed it was time to stop. All three men herded me inside.

It was a medium-sized room, the walls gray and slick, formal and detached. A long rectangular metal table stood in front of a small square metal one. Three men were sitting at the wood table: two thirty something guys, one pale and one dark, on either side of an older guy. I was led to the metal table and sat on a metal chair that was bolted to the floor. It was cold. The whole room was cold. I shivered slightly, focusing my attention on the men that were seated. I caught a nod that the oldest one gave to one of the guys that had brought me here, which was when I noticed that he had handcuffs.

"With all due respect, sir," I said, my voice louder and clearer than I was expecting. "I don't need to be restrained. I'm here as a willing participant."

The older man raised an eyebrow. "Is that so?" His voice was deep and gruff, like a commanding officer.

I nodded, hoping that I looked like I knew what I was doing. The handcuffs would push me over the edge, exposing me as the weak link I was. I couldn't afford to have them.

The sound of the door shutting and locking echoed in the room, making the hair on the back of my neck stand up. I was trapped in here. Even if I could somehow break through the door, I didn't think I'd be able to fight off all three guards that I could sense were standing behind me.

This could get ugly.

"Let's get started then." He opened up a notebook on the table and started scanning through it. "I'm Agent Locke, these are Agents Odell and Rodriguez. They are here to assist me in your interrogation. You will speak only when spoken to, and you will answer every question honestly and to the best of your knowledge. If there is any suspicion of you lying or leaving information out, you will be dismissed and all previous answers given will be void. Do you understand?"

I had a pretty good idea of what 'dismissed' meant, and I wasn't going to find out if I was right.

"Yes sir."

"Well, Ms. Nolan—"

"Arie," I clarified. Locke looked up at me with a

question in his eyes. "It's Arie."

"Arie, then. We are here to discuss the history as well as present circumstances of Mr. Sark, and to decide his future. Now that you are safely secured and protected from Mr. Sark, do you wish to change your stance on his innocence?"

I narrowed my eyes slightly. "No."

"You realize that no harm would come to you at this point if you were to say yes?" His tone was a bit harder, and I knew what he was trying to do.

"I know."

All three of the men stared me down, as if their glares could force me to do what they wanted.

"You are completely at liberty to—" Locke started.

"I'm sorry sir, but I was under the impression that I was here to discuss my side of Sark's story and come to a conclusion about where he stands, not to have my beliefs challenged." I met Locke's stare evenly, ignoring my nerves that were telling me it was a bad idea.

Locke let out a long breath, like he was changing his tactics to match mine.

"Very well then. Let's begin."

I soon realized that Locke was definitely the one in charge. He was the only one that spoke while the other two just took notes. Their expressions were smooth, but their eyes were harder. Angrier. They didn't like why I was here.

I sat straight up, hands clasped in my lap, looking ahead. I tried to keep my answers short and to the point, not giving too much away. The questions started off easy but got progressively harder.

"How long have you known Mr. Sark?"

"About two years. Maybe two and a half."

"Did you know that Mr. Sark is actually an alias?"

"Yes."

"Do you know his real identity?"

"Yes."

"And what is it?"

"Aiden. Aiden McCoy."

"Yet you still refer to him as Sark. Why?"

"I don't know…I've always known him as Sark. I don't think he would want to be called Aiden anyway."

"Why not?"

"Um…because of his mom. It's a difficult thing for him to talk about."

The topic of Sark's past went on for a while, and I gave the best answers that I could. It was weird to talk about Sark's personal stuff to strangers, especially when he wasn't even there.

"Mr. Sark has mentioned that he was married for a short time. Were you aware of this?"

A lump formed in my throat. "Yes."

"To the late Ms. Erika Malone?"

"Yes."

"Did you know Ms. Malone?"

I could only nod.

"Based on your observations, was Ms. Malone ever forced into or harmed by her relationship with Mr. Sark?"

I clamped my teeth. "No."

"What makes you say that?"

"They loved each other. He died when she did."

"Which is something else we need to discuss." Locke flipped a page in his notebook. "You said you met Mr. Sark two years ago?"

I nodded. "Close to that."

"And at the time, Mr. Sark was affiliated with and

an active participant in Mr. Alexis' organization?"

"Yes."

"He was your handler, correct?"

"Yes."

"Describe what that means."

I did a double take. "What?"

"In your words, your experience, what is Mr. Sark's job as a handler?"

"Uh, his job *was* to follow me. To track me and to…" I searched for the right word. "Test me."

"And what does that entail?"

"Um…pushing my limits. To see how far I could go as an infected."

"You say that as if it's a training exercise." Locke gave me a stern look. "It's essentially torture, is it not? Unrestrained experiments?"

I took a shaky breath. "Yeah."

"Give some examples."

"What?"

"Give some examples of said instances."

"Uh, I…" My hands fidgeted. "I don't think…it's just painful. And damaging."

"And, as your handler, Mr. Sark benefits greatly by this torture."

"He *did*." This was frustrating me. "But not anymore."

Locke looked frustrated too. "You're talking as if Mr. Sark is no longer employed by Alexis."

"He's not."

"And what makes you say that?"

"I would take an assassination attempt to be something like a pink slip, wouldn't you?"

Locke leaned back in his chair, studying me for a moment. I was afraid I had overstepped the respectful line that Locke seemed to have drawn, but he didn't get mad.

"Let's start with the story then. Describe in your own words the events that brought you to Mr. Sark and what led you to believe that he's a 'changed' man."

Without any warning, a man came in through a door behind the wooden table; he walked forward, handed Locke a packet of papers, then left again. Locke took several minutes studying the papers before gesturing for me to go on.

I took a deep breath and started from the very beginning: my dad infecting me, running away, Sark chasing me forever, meeting Erika and the craziness that followed. I described the difference in Sark's behavior, how he risked his life for me over and over—including saving me from Alexis, which marked him as a huge target. I slowed down when I got to Florida.

"We lived there for a few months, then things…fell apart."

"Are you referring to Ms. Malone's death?"

I nodded. The other two agents looked up at me with interest; this whole time they had just been writing.

"Mr. Sark failed to mention who her killer actually was. He said that the assailant hid his identity, killed Ms. Malone, then kidnapped you."

That's Sark's way of telling me not to say anything.

"Which would mean, Ms. Nolan, that you are aware of the identity of Ms. Malone's killer. Is that correct?"

For the first time, I dropped my eyes to my hands in my lap. I twisted my fingers, not really sure what to do.

"Ms. Nolan," Locke said again, rather sharply. "Who was the assailant?"

"I…I can't tell you," I answered quietly. My hands started to shake.

"Why not?"

"Because. He would kill him."

"Mr. Sark would kill who?"

"No." I twisted my finger again. "He…the assailant would kill Sark."

Papers shuffled. My answer surprised them. "And why would he do that?"

"To punish me."

"You realize Ms. Nolan that by you not giving a name, you're leaving opportunity for belief that Mr. Sark was the assailant."

My head snapped up. "What? That's…that's just sick. Sark would never…I mean…kill Erika? Do that to me? No. No, there is no way—"

"But you understand why that's an issue, right?"

I gritted my teeth. "No. I don't see the problem at all."

Locke let out a frustrated breath. "Would you describe your past or present relationship with Mr. Sark as harmful or abusive in any way?"

"It used to be, I guess. But we didn't really have a relationship then. We just hated each other. Now, though, not at all. Sark would never hurt me."

"But he did?"

I glared at him. "Yes. He did."

"In the years since you've known him, have you ever had, or do you currently have a romantic attraction or involvement with Mr. Sark?"

I couldn't help being appalled at the question. "Ew, no! Sark? He's cute, but he's like my brother."

Half of Locke's mouth pulled into a tiny smile, something I didn't know he was capable of. "That's funny. He said the exact same thing about you." The smile disappeared as quickly as it came. "So, you were held captive for eight months, then broke out. What took so long?"

I blinked in surprise. "Excuse me?"

"If conditions were so bad then why didn't you escape earlier?"

I raised an eyebrow. "Are you serious?"

"Yes, Ms. Nolan, I am."

Who does he think he is?

"Have you ever been in prison, Agent Locke? It's not exactly built for escape. Especially when everyone is bent on making you stay there."

Locke put down his pen and leaned back in his chair. "This is where I get confused, Ms. Nolan, so help me clear it up. If you're such an innocent little girl, then why would someone go to such great lengths to lock you up?"

The accusation in his tone infuriated me, but I knew I had to keep it under control. "If I knew the answer to that question, Agent Locke, I would sleep a little better at night."

"I'm going to be honest with you, Ms. Nolan." Locke leaned forward and rested his elbows on the desk. "I don't like you. I don't like your kind. Infecteds to me are tragic accidents that need to be permanently erased before they cause problems. I don't trust them, and I don't trust you. That being said, I understand your place in this world. You are often cast down, usually the victim, especially if Alexis knows about you. I know that if you were imprisoned, it would likely be for something that wasn't your fault." He said the words as if he was bestowing a great honor upon me.

"Thank you," I said curtly. "I'm glad my eight months of hell isn't a joke to you."

"My job is to protect people, Ms. Nolan. It's a job I

take very seriously."

"I think you should."

Locke then delved into the topic of Alexis' cult, something that I didn't know as much about. I explained my part in it as best as I could, but the overall organization of it was still a mystery to me. I mentioned Jefferson's leg injury incident in passing.

"You said you were present when Mr. Jefferson was injured," Locke said when I was done. "We kept tabs on this; we didn't really know the extent."

"Yeah, I was there." I brushed my hair out of my face sheepishly before adding, "I was the one who did it."

Of course that brought on a whole new wave of questions that were more specific about the incident, catching the interest of the other two agents.

"Everyone in that organization hates me," I finished. "You and I are on the same side in the sense that we need to bring them down. I'll never be safe as long as they are around. And neither will Sark."

Locke studied his notebook for a moment. "The idea has been circulating that we should test Sark's loyalty by sending him in as a double agent. If he had the intentions that you believe, there is a lot we could stand to gain by it."

"Wait..." My heart started beating faster as I wondered what had really been going on while I'd been locked in this room. "You mean send him to Alexis?"

Locke glanced up at me. "Yes. Mr. Sark is high up in the organization, is he not?"

"No!" I yelled in horror, jumping up from my chair. "Are you crazy? You can't do that! He would...you can't...that would..."

The two men standing behind me each grabbed one

of my arms. The three men sitting at the table all stared at me in shock.

"Please don't send him in," I said, fighting the men's hold. "He wouldn't last an hour. Alexis would…" I cringed, remembering my dream. "Please, you can't do that."

I yanked my right arm free, and the guy moved to grab me again. Instantly, I dropped my eyes and cowered away, a faint shriek almost escaping my lips.

I overstepped, I thought in a panic. *They're angry.*

I waited in terror, but nothing happened. I felt the man holding my left arm release me. It was a few seconds after that I dared to peek.

Locke had composed himself, but Odell and Rodriguez were still shaken. Locke nodded to the man next to me. The man slowly took my left wrist and pulled me backwards into my chair. He wasn't rough, but he was firm. Then he handcuffed my left wrist to the chair arm. I tried very hard to pretend like it wasn't there.

"So," Locke said, as if nothing had happened, "I take it you are opposed to the idea?"

"Yes," I answered, breathing hard. "Extremely."

"You said Mr. Sark wouldn't last an hour. What did you mean by that?"

I desperately tried to find the right words so he would understand. "Alexis is a very…proud person. And a very powerful one. He hates Sark about as much as he hates me, maybe even more. Sark betrayed him, humiliated him, and got away with it. Alexis would want to punish him, punish me, and remind everyone else who is in charge. Sark would be made as an example." I cringed again. "And it would be horrible."

"You believe that?"

"I know that."

Locke let out a long breath, then started gathering up his papers. "Well Ms. Nolan, that is enough for now."

He stood up, Odell and Rodriguez right after him, then they all walked out the door without further explanation. The three guards followed, and I was left handcuffed to the chair, alone.

17

Time ceased to mean much to me. I waited and waited. I strained to hear sounds from outside the room. I pulled on the handcuff until my wrist ached. I picked at my fingernails until they started bleeding. But mostly, I worried.

They could be taking him right now. I didn't do good enough. I know I didn't. I upset them and now they're going to take Sark away.

I wondered what they would do with me, since it was doubtful they would just let me go. They could charge me as an accomplice, or just lock me away too. I didn't know if they technically needed a legal reason for it either: this was much more serious than I ever would've thought. They did know my name though, which could be a problem. I wasn't an orphan—Sark wasn't my legal guardian anyway—so if they took him then they might send me back to my parents. I cringed at the thought. I hadn't even considered that.

I had started working through rough breakout plans in my head when the door opened. I breathed a sigh of relief when I saw it was Lindsey. She handed me a water bottle, which I immediately gulped down, then leaned against the table in front of me.

She rubbed her arms. "Sorry. It's cold in here."

"I don't care. It's fine." I pointed to the door. "What are they doing?"

"They were talking for a few hours, comparing notes with the men who questioned Sark. Now they're all in there with him."

I winced, imagining how that would be. "How's he doing?"

Lindsey clasped her hands together. "They're grilling him quite hard, but he's holding his own. He's losing his mind worrying about you. I finally had to come check on you, so he'd actually focus on answering the questions."

"I probably can't see him, huh?" I asked, defeat in my voice.

"No. Keaton would kill you."

"Who's Keaton?"

"The guy that started Sark's interrogation. He's really the one in charge." She nodded at me. "Locke did mention that you were quite firm in your responses and held it together until the end. I wasn't sure how well you were going to do under this kind of pressure."

Translation: you've been a wimp since I met you

and I didn't think you could handle this.

"I just get defensive when it comes to stuff about Sark," I told her. "Logic tends to go out the window."

I took another drink of water then set the bottle on the table, catching Lindsey's glance at my bloody fingernails. Her face remained passive, but her eyes held a sense of disapproval.

I blew out a long breath. "When Sark told me this was a trial, he made it sound like…I don't know…"

"A nice talk in a courtroom with an unbiased judge telling you everything would be fine?" Lindsey supplied, an edge to her voice.

"Yeah. Pretty much."

"Honestly, Arie, part of this is my fault. This interrogation should've happened a month ago when I first brought Sark to our office. I put it on hold because I wanted to take the credit, not realizing how hard it would be to get Sark to talk without motivation, which, for Sark, means you. You're the one that makes this work." She gritted her teeth. "Granted, that didn't mean he had to lie to you about what this really was. It looks like you could've used some preparation," she added, glancing at my bloody fingers again.

"I wish he would've told me," I decided. "It wouldn't have made a difference though. I suck at this kind of thing. I shouldn't be involved in something so important."

"You're doing great, Arie. I'm just sorry you had to get dragged into it."

I shrugged. "It doesn't matter. They're going to take him." I couldn't keep my voice from trembling. "We were doomed from the start. I don't know what I was expecting, but...he was scared and he knew I would be too, so he didn't tell me." I rested my head in my free hand.

"I wouldn't count yourself out just yet," Lindsey told me. "There are too many factors that go into this. Our agency detests Sark for what he's done over the past several years, but if they feel like he can make up for that then things will change. These men will always go for the bigger fish if they can." She gestured to me. "And your participation goes a long way. More than you know."

My eyebrows furrowed. "Why? I'm just a beat-up infected who looks homeless most of the time. I can't really offer anything."

She shook her head. "You have a story, Arie, and your story will always be the most valuable thing you have to offer. Remember that." She smoothed out her skirt and straightened up. "Before I go, there's something I need to ask you. Have you had any contact with our agency in the past? Professionally, I mean?"

I stared at my hand fidgeting in my lap, willing my voice to be even. "Yeah. I used to have a point of contact back before Sark turned it around. I'd hoped he would be able to put Sark away one day." I rolled my eyes at the irony.

"Really? Who was your case officer?"

Four beats of silence. "Dalton."

More silence. I watched my hand start to shake softly.

Lindsey let out a short breath. "You know, Arie, it's very brave of you to be here."

"I don't really want to be," I admitted.

"I don't blame you." She folded her arms across her chest. "But know that if this doesn't work out, I will get you the best conditions possible for you to continue your life. If Sark loses today, it doesn't have to be over for you."

I didn't answer. After all, Sark was the only reason I wasn't completely insane, or still locked up, or dead. If it was over for Sark, it was over for me.

Lindsey sighed, then turned and started walking to the door. I listened to the clacking of her heels against the floor for a moment before looking up.

"Lindsey?" I asked. "Why did you believe us?"

She stopped and turned around, a thoughtful expression on her face, tapping her fingers against her arm as she bit her lip.

"You are quite influential, Arie," she answered slowly. "More than you think you are. Don't take this the wrong way, but there are some aspects of you and your life that some may envy, despite the many challenges you have. I guess I really believed you because I wanted to and felt like I should. And both you and Sark have proven to me that it was the right decision."

"Huh." I couldn't tell how I was supposed to respond to that. "Well, thank you. I guess."

She gave me a small grin. "Good luck." Then she turned and walked out the door.

I was left to my silent ponderings for another block of time, mulling over Lindsey's answer and my situation. There was no way I would allow myself to get locked up again. I decided that for the most part I could trust Lindsey—at least, I could trust her to keep me alive and free. When it came to releasing Sark, or helping the infecteds, or figuring out what I should do as the key…I was on my own. And that was kind of a terrifying thought.

Without warning, the door opened again. I was expecting Lindsey, so it was surprising—and panic inducing—when a line of men started filing through.

Keep it together. This is important.

Locke, Odell and Rodriguez all took their seats again, and the two guards assumed their positions behind me. There were three new men I didn't know. Two of them sat down at the wooden table while the third walked toward me. Alarmed, I saw his round face and mostly bald head resembled Dalton, eyes callous and unforgiving. However, Dalton's eyes often boiled with uncontrolled rage, while this man's eyes were frosty and wary—eyes that had seen too much cruelty in the world.

He must be Keaton.

Keaton came right up to the metal table and put his hands on it, forcing me to lean as far away from him as I could, trying not to show how much he scared me. He pointed to my right hand, a disapproving and irritated look on his face. Before I could make sense of what that meant, one of the guards grabbed my right wrist and handcuffed it to the chair arm. I gritted my teeth and closed my eyes, trying to keep from freaking out.

It's fine, it's fine, it's fine. No big deal. No big deal at all.

After a few seconds I opened my eyes to see Keaton staring at me, a little more pleased. I could almost hear what he was thinking: *Does that bother you? Good.*

I already hated this guy.

"Ms. Nolan," he said with such authority that I automatically flinched. He was used to being large and in charge.

"It's Arie," I responded, my teeth still clamped shut.

He ignored me. "Your interrogation has been reviewed and we are close to reaching our decision. There are a few things we have to confirm first."

I nodded, not really sure what he was waiting for.

"This was a classified case that has since been discontinued," Keaton went on. "We used to have an agent assimilated in Alexis' organization: he was there for several years, slowly leaking low level information back to us. He was apprehended and killed a year ago this February."

"I'm sorry to hear that," I offered. He just glared at me when I spoke, so I waited.

"He sent one last transmission, one that was lost somewhere in between us and him. By the time it was recovered it didn't make much sense. Now, it seems to have some relevance. It was just five simple words."

Keaton pulled a folded piece of paper out of his jacket pocket and placed it on the table in front of me. When I didn't move, he gestured impatiently for me to read it.

"Sark defected. Girl gone. Chaos," I read quietly. My hands started to shake, but, thanks to the handcuffs, I couldn't hide them.

Keaton nodded, then started walking back and forth in front of me. "He was right. Alexis has always been one for pristine order and secrecy. We could not decipher much, but we knew that something was wrong. Something had changed. And what would be more chaotic than having an important and knowledgeable agent defect without being caught?"

I could tell that these words were rehearsed—this is what they had been discussing. I just kept my eyes down and didn't interrupt.

"Alexis tightened security tremendously, which is quite a feat considering how it already was. Our agent was easily found and killed immediately. Without his transmission, the security change would seem to come out of nowhere. It all lines up quite nicely, doesn't it?"

I started to feel a tiny spark of hope. If Keaton really believed what he was saying then he was on track to letting Sark go. But if I had learned anything in my life, it was that you could never trust hope—always expect the worst, anticipate all disasters, and work for the best.

Suddenly he stopped pacing. He turned and came up to the table again, leaning so far forward that I could feel his peppermint-scented breath on my face. He waited until I finally looked up to meet his cold green eyes.

"I'm going to be honest with you Ms. Nolan." His voice took on a dark edge. "We have the evidence needed to exonerate Sark. Between both of your confessions and our own findings, we have enough to clear him."

For some reason, I found no satisfaction. This is what I'd been begging for. Why did it feel so wrong?

"This agency is crumbling, Ms. Nolan. The FBI has stepped in, our funding has been cut, and we are the laughingstock of government officials. Almost nothing can save us at this point. However, we would gain huge advances, huge steps forward, if we were able to claim responsibility for putting someone like Sark in prison."

I froze when I realized where he was going with this.

Keaton smiled slightly, a sickening sight. "I personally would love to see Sark behind bars. And since that's what's going to save my job, that's what is going to happen. As of twenty minutes ago, Mr. Sark is officially sentenced to life in prison, and I am going to push for the death penalty."

He leaned back a bit, letting that sink in for a moment. I started hyperventilating, my hands shaking so hard that the handcuff chains rattled against the chair, filling the room with the eerie clinking sound.

He's gone. Sark is gone.

"No," I whispered, the panic threatening to take over. "You can't do that."

"I'm afraid I already did. There is nothing anyone can do at this point." His grin grew slightly. "Such a shame."

Keaton straightened up, watching my shocked, still form.

"This still leaves a few questions for you, Ms. Nolan. I don't claim to know everything, but I assume that you are the girl the transmission was referring to, which would mean you are much more involved in this than I first guessed."

Sark is gone. How could I have let this happen?

"You said that your father was the one who infected you, but I find that very hard to believe. How much would a father have to hate his daughter to do something as horrible as infection? The way I see it, you have to be lying. It's the only thing that makes sense."

Keaton walked behind me now, bending down to talk in my ear.

"Did Sark infect you?" he asked, his voice harsher than before.

"No." The words burned coming out of my mouth. "My dad did."

"Your dad did? Tell me, was your father the one who kept you imprisoned all these months? Could he not stand the sight of his daughter becoming such an inferior mess that attracts the company of someone like Sark?"

I gritted my teeth. "Sark made a lot of bad decisions. I know that better than anyone. He—"

"Sark is in our custody because he's a revolting criminal."

"Don't kid yourself," I scoffed. "Sark is only in your custody because he found a conscience."

"A conscience." He folded his arms across his chest. "You mean he found you?"

I just sat there, stunned into silence.

Keaton started pacing in front of me again. "I've been trying to profile you, Ms. Nolan, but I'm having a difficult time understanding, so please help me out. Agent Carter told me all about the dire condition you were in when you arrived at her office, yet you came here today all dressed up. You obviously need help, but you aren't playing the victim card at all, even as you're asking for impossible circumstances. You're important to Alexis so you stay away from him—that makes sense as an infected—but you risk everything to break out your handler." He stopped directly in front of my table. "The only plausible explanation is that you're working with them. Whether you're acting for your own interests or being forced into it, you're an accomplice."

"Accomplice?" I breathed, imagining the tiny cell accomplices must end up in. "I'm not—"

Keaton slammed his fist on the table, making me half shriek.

"Sark might have been the only person on this miserable planet who could actually tolerate you, but now he is gone." He got in my face again, his voice getting louder. "He's on his way to most vile prison on this earth to live out the next week before he dies. Why do you deserve anything less than that?"

My hands shook like my voice. "I didn't do anything wrong." My conviction faltered as my mind flashed to Erika, Micah, infecteds—people who had been done wrong because of me. "I didn't."

"You're defending Sark," Keaton said, as if that were a federal offence. "You're working with him."

"Shut up." Small tears were starting to form in my eyes. "You don't know anything."

"I know Sark deserves every bit of what's coming to him, and you shouldn't get off much easier."

"We are family!" I exclaimed, trying so hard to keep my tears in my eyes. I would not cry in front of this jerk. "Family! Why is that so hard to understand? Sark is here because he's trying to do the right thing, to listen to his conscience and turn it around so he can help our weird family. So he can give us our best chance. And if you take that away then you're no better than the scumbags who make our lives hell."

The tears were coming. I couldn't stop them. Not seeing any form of escape, I rested my head on the freezing metal table as water trickled down my face, waiting for the world to just start crumbling away.

All was silent. I held my breath to keep from sniffling. Keaton would *not* know I was crying. Even if he forced me into the tiniest, nastiest cell on earth, he would not get my tears. I could hang on to that much dignity.

More silence. Finally Keaton spoke, in a much quieter tone than before. "What is it you want, Ms. Nolan?"

"I want Sark," I answered, not caring what they thought. "I want Sark and I want to go home."

Silence rung again until I heard the sound of chairs scraping and footsteps tapping against the floor, then the door latching back in place. I was alone again.

My head got sore from the hard table, which added to the giant headache that was stirring. I was at a complete and total loss.

What do I do?

I didn't know how long they were going to keep me here. What would they even do with me? Lock me up so I could never tell what went on today? That would make the most sense. None of them wanted me around—that much I could tell.

But that was the least of my problems. If Keaton could really get the death penalty by the end of the week…

This can't be happening, I repeated to myself. *This can't be happening.*

It felt like hours, maybe days later when the door opened again.

This is it. I hadn't decided what kind of fight I was going to put up. I felt like just laying down and dying.

The second his hand touched my arm I knew that's probably what happened. I had gone so crazy that I just died. There were worse ways to go, I guess.

"Wake up," he said softly.

"Am I dead?" I blurted.

He chuckled. "Do you want to be?"

Oh no. "Am I dreaming? Is that what this is?"

"No, Arie, we can go home."

I turned my head to see for myself. Sark was kneeling next to my chair, his tie loosened around his neck, his hair a mess, his eyes exhausted. But it was him.

"Really?" I asked.

He grinned, his face worn. "Yeah. It's real."

"But…" I tried to work through my confusion as Sark unlocked my handcuffs. "But you're supposed to be gone. Keaton said—"

"Keaton was lying to you." His jaw clenched

slightly, his tone barely hiding his resentment. "He wanted to see if you would still hold your ground when you thought you'd lost—if you'd give me up in the end."

I jumped out my seat and pretty much fell into him, throwing my arms around his neck. I was too tired to cry, but I was still shaking. He hugged me tightly.

"I thought you were gone," I whispered.

"Nah. You can't get rid of me that easy." He stood and pulled me up with him. "Let's get out of here, okay?"

I nodded, swaying on my feet. Sark took off his jacket and wrapped it around my trembling body. I stuffed my arms in the too long sleeves while he leaned down and slid my shoes off.

"I think you might kill yourself in these right now."

I nodded again, my eyelids heavy. Holding my shoes in one hand and taking my arm in the other, he slowly dragged me out of the room and I stumbled, half blind down the hallway with him. Lindsey met us at the door.

"Just come back tomorrow morning," she told Sark. "You can finish it all then. You both deserve some sleep." She patted my arm once. "You did great, Arie."

"I'll see you tomorrow," I said, but it sounded kinda mushed.

Sark pulled me out the door and into the icy night. I didn't remember going down the stairs—suddenly we were in the car. I grabbed my legs and tucked them underneath me, snuggling into the seat.

"Don't fall asleep while you're driving," I mumbled to him somewhat urgently. He had to be at least as tired as me, and I was in no shape to drive. "After everything…it would be stupid for us to die in a car accident."

The last thing I heard was his laugh echoing through the warm car.

18

Two thoughts hit me once I became conscious. The first was that I had another night with no nightmare, my body stiff from sleeping so long with no interruption. The clock said it was almost four in the afternoon.

The second thought was Sark. I was in my bed, still wearing my dress and wrapped in his jacket. I remembered that he had brought me home last night, but I was terrified that he was gone. I had been sleeping forever. Anything could have happened.

I dragged myself out of bed and staggered down the hallway. The living room was empty, so I continued down to his room. I breathed a sigh of relief when I saw him still in bed. Last night he must've just died. He was still in his clothes from yesterday, but they were all wrinkled, and his shoes were even on. He was staring at the ceiling, just relaxing, but he looked a little off. He grinned faintly when he saw me appear in the doorway.

"Are you okay?" I asked as I sat down on the edge of his bed. "You look a little…I don't know. Not good."

"Yeah, I'm just tired." He put his hand on my forehead. "Are you feeling okay?"

I did a quick mental check. "Fine, why?"

"You had a fever last night. A really high one. I was too tired to do anything about it." He felt different sides of my head before dropping his hand. "It's gone now. Do you feel sick?"

"No." I thought for a moment. "I don't get sick anymore. I haven't had so much as a cough since infection."

His eyebrows furrowed. "Hmm. I don't know. I guess it's good that it's gone."

"So, what happened last night?" I asked, curiosity building. "How did you convince them?"

He let out a long breath, a tired sound. "I don't really know. They started by asking me basic questions, then questions about you—"

"Did you ever tell them about Dalton?" I interrupted hastily, leaning forward slightly.

"No." He hesitated, a hint of caution in his eyes. "Why, what did they say to you?"

"Just that you said the assailant kept his identity a secret, so you didn't know who it was."

"Did they ask you if you knew?"

"Well yeah."

"What did you say?"

"That I couldn't tell them."

"I'll bet they really went for that."

"Yeah, they didn't like me much."

"You and me both."

I gestured for him to keep going. "So, they asked you questions about me…"

"Yeah. They were…interested in you." His tone told me there was a problem with that. "After that—"

"What do you mean?" I asked. "Interested?"

He sighed, attempting to pretend like he wasn't mad. "You are a *person*, Arie, and it really…upsets me when someone views you otherwise. I don't care who they are."

"Oh." I had gotten that vibe too, but it was something I was used to. "Me too."

"Yeah, I wonder why," he said, rolling his eyes.

I ignored him. "So after that…"

"They asked me why I decided to defect, so I told that story. Then they left for several hours to talk it over before everyone came back. I had to lay out everything I knew about Alexis' organization. Everything. That alone took four hours. They talked about the transmission, said I was cleared on condition, then Keaton went to talk to you."

My eyebrows furrowed and I watched his face carefully. "What conditions?"

"Actually, nothing too bad, all things considered. I have to stay in Lindsey's area for the next twelve months, come in for regular checks, and be on call for any information or assistance they need." He shrugged. "It could have been a lot worse."

"I'm assuming that 'information' involves telling more about Alexis?" I asked, not liking where this was going.

"You worry too much," Sark said, clearly not

worried at all. "This is the best scenario we could've gotten." He glanced at the clock, taking a deep breath. "I've got to go back to finish it up. Do you want to come or stay here?"

"What do you have to do?"

He rubbed his forehead. "Uh…sign a few papers, get some…honestly, I wasn't really paying attention. Lindsey just said it wouldn't take long, and I could do it today if I wanted to. I said yes without thinking."

I still didn't feel good about leaving Sark, especially having him go to that office by himself. What if he didn't come back?

Am I just a clingy annoying worrier or what?

"I don't care," I said, trying to keep it cool. "What do you think? Is it worth coming?"

"If you really don't care…I'd rather you come. I know you must hate that place, but…" He grinned. "I'm just the insanely overprotective older brother. Deal with it."

I rolled my eyes. "Yeah, 'cause you're a real pain."

Sark's face took on a more serious expression, but it was a cautious one. He was treading carefully.

"You know," he started, attempting a conversational tone. "A few minutes ago…that was the closest thing I've heard you say concerning Dalton— the closest you've been to actually admitting it was him."

I turned my head and dropped my eyes, suddenly becoming very interested in the ugly maroon carpet.

"Arie, I think it's time you turned him in."

"No."

"You can't keep living with him hanging over your head, knowing that he's out there. Honestly, *I* can't keep living knowing he's out there. You've got to be able to move on."

"I can't," I said, adding a sharp edge to my tone with the hope of ending the conversation.

"What are you so afraid of? He kidnapped you, did who knows what to you for eight months—after committing murder, no less—all while posing as an honorable government officer." Sark shook his head. "There isn't anyone in the world who wouldn't take your side on this."

It's not that easy.

I stood up. "I've got to go fix my hair if I'm really coming with you."

He grabbed my arm before I could leave, waiting until I finally turned to meet his gaze. "Please just consider it. Really consider it. You deserve to move on."

I couldn't help but imagine for a moment, just a small moment, what it would be like if I did turn him in. If the fear, the confinement, the shackling despair was gone. If I *could* move on. Even in theory, the relief washed over me in overwhelming buckets.

Sark could tell I was thinking about it, so I pulled my arm away and walked out the room before he could convince me of anything.

"We're leaving in five," he called after me. "Fix your hair then let's go."

I went into the bathroom and looked in the mirror. My hair wasn't as big of a mess as I'd thought—that was always a bonus. I just wiped the smudged makeup off my face and grabbed some brown slipper boots from my closet on my way out, not caring that they didn't match my dress or Sark's jacket. It wasn't like I had anyone to impress.

When I got to the living room, I saw that Sark

seemed to be on the same page as me. He didn't bother to fix his appearance either.

"It's too early," he explained, making me laugh.

"I know this will sound really weird," I said as we got in the car, "but I was wondering if we could stop somewhere."

Sark glanced at me, pulling the car out of the driveway. "What did you have in mind? Are you hungry?"

"Actually, yes," I admitted, feeling kind of stupid.

"I'll get you whatever you want."

"I really want…some hot chocolate. And French fries. Is that weird?"

He laughed. "Yeah, it is, but that's okay."

Neither of us felt like going inside anywhere, so we took advantage of beautiful modern conveniences and went through the drive thru. As requested, I got a hot chocolate and some fries, while Sark loaded himself up with a giant burger. We ate in the car as we drove the rest of the way to Lindsey's office, and it was arguably the best meal I'd ever had.

Lindsey was waiting for us when we got there, everything ready to go. Sark sat and signed a bunch of important-looking papers, while I doodled on a sticky note and hummed random songs that came into my head. I noticed something on the inside of my right wrist—a small black scab, almost perfectly circular. For the life of me, I couldn't remember where it came from, though I was certain that it wasn't there yesterday. It itched like crazy, creating a burning sensation whenever I scratched it.

After about an hour, Sark finally finished. Lindsey handed him a metal tray filled with an array of things: a wallet, some keys, a phone, a few folded papers, spare change, and a pocketknife. I assumed it was everything that Sark had on him when he was caught.

"Lindsey?" I asked as Sark was grabbing his belongings. "Where's the bathroom? I've got ink all over my hands."

"Go out this door to the left, take the first right, and it's halfway down that hallway," she answered. "Do you want me to show you?"

"No, I'll find it. Thanks." I went out the door, following her directions until I found it. Turning on the water in the sink, I scrubbed most of the ink off my hands, then worked on the burn mark for a minute, accidentally ripping off the black skin. To my alarm, it didn't bleed. Instead, it revealed a new patch of skin the same circular shape. The problem was that it was blue. Light blue skin.

What the crap is this?

It felt just like normal skin, no scar or tear or anything. It was if I had drawn on myself with blue marker. I scrubbed water on that too, but nothing happened, so I finally just gave up.

I walked out of the bathroom and back into the hallway, studying the mark on my wrist. It took me a moment before I sensed that somebody was watching me. I turned around and froze, my heart skipping a beat before pounding like crazy. I couldn't even make myself breath. Standing several yards away from me with a shocked expression on his face was Dalton.

We both stared at each other, trying to understand what was happening. I saw as his eyes went from confused, to understanding, to furious. I knew he had figured it out. He knew why I was here.

An earsplitting scream shattered the silence as I turned and ran the other direction. I got back to the room and slammed the door shut, my shaking hands somehow turning the lock. Sark was behind me in an instant, grabbing me by my shoulders.

"Arie, what—"

I spun around and shoved him away from the door. He crashed backwards into the table, but I caught his arm to keep him from falling. Rattling sounded as someone tried the doorknob.

"You're making a mistake here, Arie," I heard Dalton say from the other side of the door, his tone telling me I was in gigantic amounts of trouble.

A scary sound came from Sark as he snatched me by my wrist and dragged me behind his body, shielding me and pressing me against the wall.

The door handle shook again. "Get out here now."

I automatically started to obey, but Sark kept his arms back, trapping me where I was.

"Did you hear me?" Dalton asked, his rage escalating. "Move before I come in there and beat your wretched face. You're looking too much like yourself; it makes me sick."

I dropped my head, as if in apology even though he couldn't see me. He was right.

Then I heard a sound that made my heart stop: keys jingling.

"I'll give you one more chance, Arie. I know you came here looking for Sark—I can find him much faster than you can and put a bullet in his head. Get out here and we'll leave without you killing anyone. Didn't you learn anything from Erika?"

Sark growled and lunged toward the door, but I held him back like my life depended on it.

He can't know Sark is in here, I thought in a panic. *He would kill him now.* But I couldn't just wait for him to come inside. *What do I do?*

"You're making the wrong choice," Dalton said. They keys sounded again as the door handle twisted.

I didn't know what my plan was, but I ducked under Sark's arm and dashed to the door, feeling Sark's fingers barely miss grabbing my arm. The door opened at the same time, and I crashed into Dalton, shocking us both, but neither of us fell. Dalton automatically wrapped one hand around my neck, forcing the back of my head against his shoulder, and aimed his gun at the other person in the room. I felt his surprise double when he registered it was Sark.

"Well, well," Dalton said, out of breath. "I should've known."

Sark glowered at him with murder in his eyes, the gun the only thing keeping his trembling body stationary. He opened his mouth, but he was so livid he couldn't speak.

Don't do anything Sark, please. He wants a reason to get you out of the way, to justify murder in his messed-up head.

Suddenly, I heard Lindsey's alarmed voice calling my name from down the hallway.

She heard me scream.

Dalton huffed in frustration. "Listen to me you little tramp," he seethed in my ear. "You got lucky today, but now I know where to look for you. Trust me when I say it's only a matter of time. And if you ever tell the people here about me," he tightened his grip around my neck, "then I'll make sure you never see Sark again, one way or another. The rules haven't changed."

He released me, then smashed his gun into the side of my head. My knees gave out, but Sark caught me before I fell. By the time I had turned around, Dalton had disappeared, and Lindsey was standing in the doorway.

"What happened?" she asked, an appalled expression on her face.

I didn't know why Dalton was afraid of Lindsey seeing him—especially if he was her superior—but I didn't care. I only knew that Dalton had been here, and he had threatened and he was serious. There was no way I was going to turn him in now, despite my thoughts earlier. I was as good as dead.

The rules haven't changed.

I had to protect Sark. And I had to make sure Sark didn't get himself in trouble.

I made the decision in less than a second. Before Sark could say a word, I grabbed his wrist and dragged him out the door. He protested and tried to pull away, but my grip was like a vise. I focused everything on putting one foot in front of the other and keeping Sark with me. He wasn't used to me being so strong: I won.

Lindsey followed us, firing off questions to understand what happened, but I didn't listen. Every time I felt like Sark was going to answer, I tightened my hand on his wrist. He sucked in a sharp breath, so I knew it hurt, and kept quiet.

We got to the parking lot. I went around to the driver's side of our car, opened the door, and all but threw Sark inside before slamming the door on him. Lindsey tried to stop me, but I shoved her away and got in the car.

"Drive," I ordered coldly.

Sark took a few deep breaths. "Arie, I—"

"Now!" I screamed, making him jump. He started the car and drove away without another word. I pulled my legs up and rested my head on my knees as my breathing got faster and more ragged.

That was close. He was here. He almost…Almost. Almost. Just almost. It was just almost.

I didn't look up until Sark stopped the car. When I did, I saw we were at the infecteds' place rather than home. Before I could ask what he was doing, he turned off the car and got out. He opened my door, grabbed me by my wrist, and yanked me out of the car. I was about to get mad, but then I saw his face. I knew it was time to stay quiet.

Sark stalked inside, dragging me through the club and down the stairs. Alaina, Brennan, Liam, and Lucy were down there, along with several others I only recognized. Sark paid them no attention. He went across the room and stopped in front of a small door—the storage closet. Jerking it open, he forced me inside and I fell to the floor, not able to get out before he slammed the door and trapped me in total darkness. I reached up for the handle, but he had locked it somehow.

"Sark?" I asked hesitantly, his behavior scaring me.

Alaina wasn't really okay with his actions. "What are you doing?" I heard her demand from outside.

"Do not let her out," he ordered, his voice so furious that even I flinched away from the door. "Not until I get back. Not for anything."

"Sark?" I asked again, my panic building. "Sark, what are you doing?"

He ignored me. "Dalton is here. In Denver. Right now."

"What?" Alaina asked. "How do you know?"

"We just ran into him." I heard someone walking around. "Almost got Arie again."

I froze when I heard the sound of a gun cocking.

"No! You don't understand!" I shouted, pounding

my fists on the door. "Sark, he's going to kill you!"

Again, he paid me no mind. "I'll be back later." Footsteps sounded toward the stairs.

"No!" I desperately tried the handle again. No luck. "Sark! Sark come back! Please come back!"

I heard footsteps stomp up the stairs. He was leaving. He was going to die.

"Sark!" I screamed as loud as I could, killing my throat. "Sark, please, you can't!"

"Arie," Alaina said softly from right behind the door.

"Alaina, you have to stop him," I begged. "Please, you have to. He's going to get himself killed."

"Arie, I can't."

"You have to!" I shrieked back fiercely, slapping my hand on the door. "You can't just let him die!"

"I'm sorry."

I pounded my fists again. "Sark!"

"He needs to do this, Arie." It was Brennan now. "Sark can handle himself—you know that. He'll be okay."

Faster, lighter footsteps came down the stairs.

"Arie?" Hadley's voice was an octave higher with fear. "Arie, where are you?"

"Hadley! Hadley let me out!" I hit the door. "Hadley, please!"

I heard the sounds of people moving, of Brennan and Lucy talking in hushed voices.

"What are you doing to her?" Hadley demanded in horror. "Arie! Arie!"

"Hadley! Hadley, let me out!"

His voice got quieter and quieter until it was gone. He was the last hope I had.

I screamed until my voice died. I pounded my fists

until they ached so badly that I had to stop. I grabbed a couple of cans from one of the shelves and threw them at the door. Finally, I just curled into a ball on the floor and stared at the tiny line of light that came from under the door.

After what seemed like forever, I heard Alaina's soft voice again.

"Arie, are you okay?"

I took a few rough breaths, then swallowed. It burned my throat.

"How long?" I asked, my voice hoarse and lifeless.

"It's been two hours," she answered. "Almost three."

"Please just let me out."

She sighed. "I wish I could."

"Do you always do what he tells you?"

"I have to. I owe him. But you shouldn't be so worried. Sark is Sark—he's always been the best. Why are you so sold Dalton can kill him?"

"Because. Dalton said he would. He keeps those promises."

After that, I tuned her out. I stared at the light and tried to keep my imagination at bay. The image of Micah dying kept coming to me, except his screams were now Sark's.

"How long?" I would ask after each eternity. Alaina would answer—it usually had only been an hour or two—then I would go back to ignoring. The more I asked, the more panicked I got. Because there was the chance that every time I asked, he was already dead.

After seven hours I started dozing off and on. It was the hazy kind of sleep, the kind that trapped you between dreams and reality, both of which were nightmares.

It was a long time when I asked again. I wasn't sure if Alaina would be awake, but she was.

"How long?"

"It's six in the morning," she answered after a moment, somewhat groggy. "It's been a long time."

I was about to ask her if she would let me out now, when slow heavy footsteps made their way down the stairs. They stopped in the middle of the room. Silence.

"Did you find him?" Alaina finally asked, her tone cautious.

Sark let out a long breath. "No. Not a trace." His voice sounded as dead as I felt. "Is she asleep?"

"No."

"How long did she…"

"A long time." She sounded slightly disapproving, but didn't press it.

Another long breath. A few footsteps. The handle twisting. The door opening. I stared straight ahead at his dirty shoes. I waited for him to talk, to pull me up, to do something. He did nothing. I wasn't sure if I would've been angrier if he did try to help me than I was when he did nothing.

Finally, I summed up some energy and hauled myself up off the ground. I refused to look at him, but I saw that Alaina was on the ground next to the closet. She had slept there, making me feel a tiny bit bad about what I said to her. I decided I would apologize later.

After a moment I met his gaze, which just reminded me of a ghost town: exhausted, sad, and empty.

Do you have any idea what you put me through?

I took a step toward him and hit him as hard as I could across the face. Without waiting to see the damage, I went around him and to the stairs.

"Next time you decide to take your insanity out on

her," I heard Alaina say as I went up the stairs, "don't ask me to help."

The club was dark and vacant, as everyone was sleeping in the other room. I walked out into the freezing night unnoticed.

It was snowing lightly, the crystal dots twinkling like stars under the streetlights. It was beautiful. I couldn't tell if that made me feel better or worse, but it was relaxing either way.

I got lost at least four times. Eventually I noticed his car—he was following me. This infuriated me, but I didn't do anything about it. I just ignored him and kept going, even though I knew it probably wasn't in the right direction.

It took me much longer than it should have to get home. I walked inside without hesitation, hearing the car door open and shut behind me. I hurried into my room and slammed the door before he could catch up to me, hoping that he got the message. If he came in here, I would lose it. I would probably try to kill him myself.

I kicked off my wet shoes and slid out of Sark's jacket, throwing it in the corner. Taking the stupid dress off, I pulled on sweats and a sweatshirt. Being outside for so long had frozen me to the core. Then I climbed into bed, pulled my blankets tight around me, and stared at the ceiling, knowing sleep was a lost cause. I made shapes in the rough parts of the ceiling and tried hard not to think. I'd found a fox, wolf, mermaid, alien chicken, and George Washington when I heard it.

It was a thumping crashing kind of sound. Really loud. Scared me to death. And it was coming from the direction of Sark's room.

At that point things were a little confusing. My instincts told me to get away from the scary noise. They also told me to protect Sark. With a mix of a gasp and a sigh, I got up out of bed, silently opened the door, and crept down the hallway.

His door was shut. I put my ear up against it to see if I could hear anything else. All was quiet. I decided that if someone were really trying to kill him, I would hear it. That meant it was safe to go on, but I didn't know if I wanted to. Annoyed at myself, Sark, and the world, I slowly turned the handle and pushed open the door.

All the lights were off. The pillows and blankets from his bed were strewn all over the floor, and the square nightstand next to it was tipped over. The lamp that used to be on it was across the room in a ton of pieces. I scanned my eyes over the space until I found Sark. He had changed into his own sweats and t-shirt, but that's as far as he had gotten on the sane train. He was huddled in the corner holding a glass bottle half full of clear liquid. An empty one was on the floor next to him, along with two full ones, emitting the smell that was making its way into my nose. They weren't full of water.

"Oh no," I muttered, feeling a hundred times heavier. Sark had dropped drinking when he met Erika: she had thrown that practice right out the window. In the past eight months though…anything could have happened.

I walked up to his spot in the corner, not meeting his eyes. Leaning down, I picked up all of the bottles and took them in the kitchen, knowing I would have to deal with them later. Sark had been alone—with alcohol— all night. There was no telling how drunk he was or what damage had been done.

Hesitantly, I went back into his room; he hadn't

moved. I kneeled down so I was eye level with him and finally met his stare. Whatever anger I had been feeling toward him quickly dissolved. He was looking at me with such a sad, heartbreaking expression, at a complete and total loss.

"Sark," I said softly, putting a hand on the bottle he was holding. "You don't need this." Slowly, I pulled it out of his grip. He held on tight but was no match for me. I reached over and stood the table back up before setting the bottle on top of it. He stared at it, his eyes empty.

"Sark?" I asked, getting worried. "Sark, it's me. It's Arie."

He flinched at the sound of my voice but gave no response.

"Sark?" I asked again. "Can you hear me?"

His face clouded over as his eyes focused, and he scowled darkly at me. "Who are you?"

"I'm Arie. It's me, remember?"

He shook his head. "You aren't Arie. You're a fake."

"A fake?" I brushed my hair behind my ear. "What are you talk—"

Sark lunged forward and wrapped his hands tightly around my neck, choking me off.

"Who are you?" he shouted. "Where is she?"

"It's me," I managed to squeak out, carefully fighting his grip. I didn't want to hurt him. "I'm right here."

He shook me hard, murder in his eyes. "What did you do to her?"

"Nothing," I tried to say. "I'm Arie."

His hold just tightened as he glowered at me, and I clawed in desperation at his hands.

He's ready to kill me, I realized, my vision starting to darken around the edges. *Who does he think I am?*

I did my best to look him in the eyes. "Sark…please. It's me."

For a second I thought I'd lost him, but Sark mercifully released his hold. I slumped over, holding my neck, coughing and gasping for air.

"Arie?" he asked, the violent tone to his voice gone.

I nodded. It took me a moment to get myself together and straighten up. I was surprised to see Sark staring at me with distant eyes—as if he hadn't just tried to strangle me.

"What's wrong?" I asked, keeping my voice soft in an effort to keep him calm. He didn't look too thrilled by that question, so I gave a nod of encouragement and added, "It's okay, you can tell me."

Sark contemplated for a minute, desperation starting to creep into his expression as he ran his hands through his hair over and over.

"I can't do this, Arie," he told me. "I can't do this. I can't…I can't handle this. I'm sorry."

I shook my head. "You don't need to be sorry. It's okay."

"No, it's not." He held his head in his hands. "I can't protect you. I couldn't protect Erika. You both deserve better. A lot better."

"No…no, don't talk like that," I said, my heart aching. "You are the best we could've asked for. You are. I'm not just saying that."

"I should've died. It should have been me. Not her." His voice was so tortured that it was killing me. "I have nothing else to offer. She was perfect and beautiful and light. She made the world better. I make it darker."

"Sark, you can't—"

He snapped his head up. "Yes, I can. I ruined her. I should have let her go. I should have let *you* go. Now you're both gone."

"I'm right here." I put my hand on his arm. "I haven't gone anywhere."

"You aren't here," he said bitterly. "You aren't you. The Arie I know…she wouldn't have reacted that way. She wouldn't have let Dalton talk to her like that and be so…submissive, like…like an animal. It's sick, Arie. And it's not you."

A lump formed in my throat. I knew he was right.

Sark laughed, a semi crazy sound, making me jump. "You know that day, the day that you were gone?" His words were starting to slur together slightly. "And Dalton came to our house? Do you?"

"Yes," I said cautiously. "Of course I do."

"And you…they had knocked you around a little and you…you were scared. I could see it in your face. Then he backed you up in the corner, holding a gun to your head and you were even more scared. And you closed your eyes. And your hands were shaking. And you were scared. Weren't you?"

"Yeah." I shivered at the memory, wrapping my arms around myself.

He laughed again. "And he told you to tell him what he wanted to know. You opened up your eyes," he put his hand on my face, tapping his thumb right next to my eye, "and you stared him down. He had a gun to your head, and you were so scared, and you just stared at him, as if nothing could make you surrender. And even though I was scared too, I have never been prouder of you than I was in that moment."

I cleared my aching throat, hoping to keep my emotions in check.

He dropped his hand, his smile vanishing, despair filling him back up. "I would do anything in the world to get that girl back for you. I would do anything if you could be her again. Because I know you miss her too." His gaze left mine for a moment, straying to the bottle on the table. He went for it the same time I did, but I got to it first.

"You've had enough," I said, standing to hurry and put it in the kitchen. When I got back, he was still in the corner, resting his head against his knees. It was a pitiful sight.

I grabbed two blankets off the ground and kicked a pillow in Sark's direction. I wrapped one blanket around myself because I was still freezing, then went and sat next him, spreading the other blanket around him as best as I could. He grabbed my arm and clutched it to his chest, which was when I realized he was shaking.

I wondered how many of his nights over the past eight months had gone like this. How many hours had he spent in the dark, drunken in a corner by himself?

You should've been there for him. He needed you.

"Sark?" I asked quietly. "You should go to sleep."

He grumbled something in response that sounded like a 'no.'

"It's okay. You're going to be just fine. We both are." I carefully rested my head on his shoulder. "Just go to sleep. By the time you wake up tomo—later today, I guess, everything is going to be better. You'll see. That's a secret I've learned: everything seems worse at night. And sometimes you just have to cut your losses and go to bed, and when you wake up things don't seem so hopeless. It's a nice trick, really."

It took a while, but eventually he started to relax.

His breathing evened out as his rigid position slowly went slack. I grabbed the pillow from the floor and propped it against my leg so his head could rest against it and lay down. He didn't protest; he was asleep. It was relieving to know he was finally somewhere else, that he could escape for at least a little bit.

I untangled my now numb arm from his grip and fixed his blanket before settling into the corner. That was when I realized how shaken I was. I mean, I'd known Sark had issues—and they had only gotten worse over the years—but he'd always been almost…immortal in my mind. Unshakable. Indestructible. It was scary to see the strongest person I knew be brought to their knees.

I guess even the best of us fall sometimes. Isn't that kind of the point? I'd heard all the cheesy sayings before—it's not how many times you fall, it's how many times you get up—but I hadn't really understood them until I was infected. That was a misconception I felt like the world had: we always pair strength with invincibility and weakness with fear. But over the past few years, some of the strongest people I'd met were always afraid. I learned that fear doesn't make you weak, it makes you human. Endurance, survivability— that's what makes you strong. And sometimes endurance involves crying yourself to sleep in the corner. Everyone survives differently and you just have to do whatever it takes. Like it or not, that's just the way it works.

If more people understood that, the world would be a gentler place to live in.

19

I was burning. It was black, I was alone, and I was burning. My screams seemed to be trapped inside of me, everything confined within my body. It was excruciating, the worst pain I'd ever felt—and I had felt this burning before. This was how it felt to be infected. This was what it burned like when that horrid poison coursed through my veins for two weeks. It was the same. Except this time, I couldn't move. I couldn't make a sound.

My eyes jerked open, my breaths heavy and uneven. I had to bite my tongue to keep from crying—not because of the vivid dream, but because the pain hadn't left. It was coming from my arm.

I yanked my right sleeve of my sweatshirt up. To my horror, the blue spot of skin had grown, taking up the base of my wrist in a circular shape with different lines going through it, creating a symbol that seemed to attach to my veins. It had literally seared itself onto my skin.

And that wasn't even the worst part. The worst part was that I had seen this symbol before: it was the shape that had marked me while I was being infected, the shape that had marked me as the key to the formula. And it was back.

That can't be good.

Sark groaned softly. Neither of us had moved in our sleep. My body ached from sitting against the wall for so long, so I knew he couldn't have been comfortable on the floor either. I saw his eyes open and I hurried to move my sleeve back down. Now was not the time to bring up mysterious skin diseases.

He blinked a few times, then I felt him stiffen. He brought his hand up to his head, rubbing his temples for a minute, before taking a deep breath and turning to look at me. A small bruise had formed on his left cheek—I assumed from me—adding to his forlorn expression. He only looked at me for a second before putting his hand over his eyes.

"Do I even say sorry?" he asked, his voice hoarse. "Or am I past that point?"

I cleared my sore throat, but even then my voice was pretty much gone. "It's fine."

He sighed. "Arie, I—"

"No offense, but can we not do this now? I'm kinda too tired."

He nodded. "Yeah. Sure."

It was silent for a moment, and my wrist took the opportunity to remind me of my latest problem.

What does that mean? I wanted to ask Sark if he knew, but I was afraid he wasn't quite ready for something like that yet.

"What time is it?" he asked, his eyes still covered.

"I don't know." My voice was really high now, letting me know I was really losing it. "Based on the diminishing light outside, I'm thinking around six. You didn't fall asleep until almost seven this morning though, so I'm pretty sure it's justified."

Sark took his hand off of his eyes, noticing my hand. I panicked when I thought he had seen my blue mark, but then I realized he was looking at something else. He picked up my hand, his eyes saddening. It was bruised and bloody from me trying to break down the closet door last night.

I pulled my hand away and patted his shoulder. "Come on, get up. You need to drink some water."

He sat up slowly, wincing and putting his head between his knees. I stood up, my joints cracking loudly, and walked out into the kitchen. Grabbing a cup from the cupboard, I filled it up with water. When I turned to go back to his room, he was standing in the kitchen, looking like he had been hit by a truck. Both of our eyes went to the four bottles that I had left on the counter from last night.

I walked over to him and curled his hands around the cup of water before leading him firmly to a chair. Once he had sat down, I turned back and grabbed all of the bottles, emptied the toxic liquid in the sink, flipped the water on to wash it all down, then threw the bottles in the trash. When I glanced at Sark, he was staring at the wall and drinking his water, looking so hollow. A shell of a person.

What am I supposed to do with him? The silence wasn't quite uncomfortable, but pretty close. I refilled his water twice, tried to make him eat something, gave up, then sat on a chair next to him. Leaning my elbow on the table, I rested my head in my hand. Without anything to distract me, the burning on my arm got much worse. I gritted my teeth and winced.

"What?" Sark asked, concern coloring his lifeless tone.

"Nothing," I replied, not even looking up. I realized too late that my sleeve had moved slightly, barely exposing the tip of the blue.

Sark grabbed my wrist and pulled the sleeve up to my elbow, faster than I would've thought he was able. His mouth fell open in horror when he saw it. I was shocked too. At the bottom of the symbol, a line was forming, about a quarter inch thick. As if the thing was growing a stem. But the crazy thing was that I could literally see the mark slowly burning itself onto my skin. Like it was alive.

"Is that…is that the same one from infection?" Sark asked shakily.

"Yeah. Same one." I clenched my hand into a fist and yanked it out of his grip. Suddenly I felt like it was my secret—he didn't deserve to know.

"When did it show up?"

I shrugged in annoyance, so not in the mood for a lecture. "I don't know. A little bit ago."

"And you didn't tell me?" His anger just made me angry. "Don't you think this is something you should tell me about?"

"You weren't exactly around," I replied coldly. That shut him down pretty fast, which made me feel kind of bad.

Sark finished his water and stood up, looking around at nothing. He didn't seem quite stable and his face was much too pale.

"Sark?" I asked, standing up next to him. "Are you okay?"

He closed his eyes as if he was concentrating. "Yeah…I just…" He swayed on his feet, almost falling over, and I reached out to catch him.

"Hey, what's wrong?" His arm felt warm, so I put my hand on his forehead. "Holy crap, you're burning up! Are you…Sark, are you okay?"

He mumbled something incoherent in response, and I took that as a bad sign. I put his arm around my shoulder so I could support him as I dragged him back to his room. He collapsed into his bed, which was still a wreck from this morning. I collected everything from the floor and tried to remake it. Lifting his head up, I stuffed a pillow underneath it, then put the rest of them on the bed next to him. Spreading out his blankets over him, I surveyed his set up. He looked pretty dead.

I went into the bathroom and wet a cloth with cold water. When I came back, he hadn't moved a muscle. I checked to make sure he was breathing, just in case. Then I put the cloth on his forehead, relieved when he turned his head so it would stay on better.

"Feels nice," he said, barely audible, as he relaxed a bit.

I knew the best things for him were food and sleep, so I set out to make both of those happen. I went into the kitchen prepared to make something, then realized that I hadn't cooked in months. It felt strange to have no idea what to do.

Finally, I decided to take the safe route and heat up

canned soup. I searched the cupboards until I found the medicine I was looking for: some for his fever and some to knock him out cold. Filling his cup up with water, I took it all into Sark's room.

He opened his eyes when I came in, which I thought was a good sign. I set the cup and pills on the table, then handed him his bowl of soup.

"Eat up," I told him, taking the cloth off his face and going to wet it in fresh water. When I came back, he had sat up a tiny bit but was just staring at the bowl.

"What?" I asked somewhat jokingly, repositioning the cloth on him. "Food not good enough for you?"

The corners of his mouth pulled up, but he was still serious. "I'm not eating unless you eat."

"Funny." I rolled my eyes. "Come on. The sooner you eat, the sooner you can take this medicine. It's going to make you feel better."

He shook his head.

I sighed. "Really?"

"Yeah."

"Fine." I went into the kitchen and poured a small amount of the leftover soup into a bowl. Grabbing a spoon, I walked back to his room and sat on the other side of his bed. Once I put some in my mouth, he started eating too. He would stop from time to time to make sure I was keeping my end of the deal.

I showed him my empty bowl as proof once he finished his. "Happy now?"

He nodded, handing me empty dish. "Thank you."

"You're welcome." I gave him the pills and his cup. "Take these." Then I went and put the dishes in the kitchen sink, stopping in the living room as an idea came to me. Untangling as I went, I unplugged the TV and all its cords. Then I took the TV and satellite box into Sark's room, stole the nightstand from my room to put them on, and set it all up so he could watch from his bed.

Once the TV was on and he had the remote, he seemed a tiny bit better. I changed his cloth again, cleaned up the broken lamp pieces on the floor, then realized there was really nothing to do. I was about to leave when he broke our silence.

"Arie?" he asked hesitantly, almost fearful but not quite. "Would you…would you do me a favor?"

"Of course."

He let out a long breath. "Can you…can you stay here? I…I need to just…know you're here."

"Um, sure. Yeah." I sat next to him on the other side of his bed. "It's not like I have anything to do anyway."

It took a few minutes before he started to really relax. It wasn't long after that he was asleep, which was when I started to really relax. I didn't know what was wrong with him, but it was stressing me out.

I spent the night watching game shows and stupid comedy reruns—the only things the television had to offer, apparently. Didn't the cable companies account for girls who stayed up all night by themselves and needed something to watch? I guessed probably not. The commercials were more entertaining sometimes, though the same ones replayed over and over, which was annoying. There was one for some sort of election that played every single commercial break. It wasn't long before I had the *Believe in Anne Kutler!* campaign memorized.

Sark slept all night undisturbed, which I was grateful for. I didn't want to go to sleep, knowing that my nightmares would wake him up, so I just chilled by myself. He only woke up once, mumbling something about my name, but quickly fell back asleep when he knew I was still there.

The trial must've really freaked him out, I thought. *Reliving everything when he thought I was going to disappear…then having Dalton show up…* I shivered. It was enough to mess anybody up.

It was around nine the next morning when he woke up. He was upset that I didn't sleep, but I didn't give him the chance to press it. I made him eat—unfortunately he also made *me* eat—then I sat with him while he watched TV. He would go in and out of consciousness, talking to me from time to time. He didn't get worse, but he didn't really get better either.

I got sick of TV, and the only thing I could find in the house with potential was an abundance of yarn. I stole Sark's phone and looked up any sort of craft that only needed yarn: scarves, socks, and hats I'd never wear. Sark made fun of me, but it was halfhearted. He was just glad I had something to do that let me stay with him.

Four days went by the same way. I called Alaina to give her some of the details of the trial. She felt bad about not letting me out of the closet, but I told her it wasn't her fault and I wasn't mad.

"So how is Sark doing after that?" she asked, almost hesitantly. "Did he get his mind back yet?"

"Well…" I glanced down the hallway from my place in the kitchen. "He's sick. And essentially unresponsive. I don't know what to do for him."

"What do you mean? Did you call a doctor?"

"I tried, but he got so mad at me for even considering it that I just let it go."

"He's probably okay then," she reassured me. "He's gone through phases like this before. Just ride it out.

Yell at him a bit if he gets ridiculous. He'll come around; he always does. But call me if you need me to come over and kick his butt into gear or something."

I laughed faintly, part of her response bothering me though I didn't know why. "Okay. Thanks." I hung up the phone and stared at it for a minute, feeling pretty alone. Quickly, I shook the irrational thought out of my mind and went to work on dinner.

~~~

Shortly after dinner, Sark figured out I'd been giving him sleeping pills, which was funny since I thought he knew it the whole time. Apparently not—he was peeved. Thankfully, he made that connection *after* I'd given him tonight's dose, so I had one more night to regulate his sleeping habits. Now that he knew about the pills, Sark wouldn't take them anymore and would try to make me sleep instead. Tonight might be his last peaceful night.

Because of that, I decided to spend my evening elsewhere. I didn't want to fall asleep by accident and have a nightmare, waking him up. Walking quietly, I went into my room and grabbed the bundle of Erika's letters, but I didn't really want to stay in there. Instead, I grabbed a can of soda from the kitchen and went to sit on the floor in front of the fireplace in the living room. Watching the flames in the dark while feeling the warmth had always been one of my favorite things to do. It was mesmerizing, making me feel like I was resting without actually falling asleep.

Once, I settled in my place, I took out the letter I'd left off on. I honestly couldn't tell sometimes if I really loved reading them or if I wished Sark had never given
~~~

them to me. Of course, the heartbreaking and almost bitter feeling they brought never kept me from continuing.

Oh Arie.

Sark just got done explaining everything to me. I'm having a hard time processing it all, but I get the basics. You're different because you're infected, and you're infected because of the formula—I knew that—and you are the 'key' to that formula.

Oh Arie, you poor girl. How did someone like you get dealt something as awful as this?

The worst part is how you hold it all in. I think of how hard it must be for you, carrying around something so heavy and being entirely alone in it. Sark said that's why you were so terrified of him and Alexis. They were the ones who could make your nightmare come true.

Today was only the second time I've seen you have a nightmare, but I already hate them. It's just so sad. You were so scared, Arie, screaming 'it's my fault' over and over again, then woke up and wanted to know about reversing the formula. Of course, that's when Sark figured it all out, and he didn't take that well. You guys argued a little, but he left before he could lose it, making both of us really confused. I didn't know what was happening, but I knew it couldn't be anything good.

Then you started firing off questions—really good questions that you deserve answers to—and I had no idea what to do. I know I must seem crazy to you, which is completely justified. I couldn't decide if telling you about Dalton was the right thing to do, and I didn't have Sark there to back me up. So I totally chickened out.

Don't get me wrong, Arie—I didn't lie to you. I just

left some things out of my story. Like that internship my uncle got me? It was an internship with a government agency. I started out as the coffee girl, but eventually I moved up to a desk assistant for Dalton. At first it was the best thing that had ever happened to me—dream come true, you know?—but slowly I started seeing more of what Dalton was really like. He's kind of crazy— after all, he sent his untrained desk assistant to gain the trust of a known murderer—and everyone knows it too. He's obsessed (literally obsessed. It's scary) with proving that he deserves his job, which consists of catching Sark, and that will never happen. Dalton's not exactly the sharpest tool in the shed, and Sark can be a genius when he wants to.

Of course, now I'm starting to realize what's really going on. Dalton lied to me—this isn't about Sark. He wants to know more about you. He's never really been a big fan of yours (sorry) and he knows that there is something different about you, more than just infection—something that kept Sark so interested. Dalton would give anything to find out what.

He can never know you're the key. I'm sure you know this, but I feel like I need to drill it into your head. You need to stay away from him at all costs. Over time he'll just get more obsessed with figuring you out and I'm sure he would stop at nothing. He can't ever get to you. Ever.

Sark agrees with me. He's already fixed my cell phone so Dalton can't track me. I've cut off all of our communications. I will never speak to Dalton again. I quit. I can't be the person that leads him to you. I just can't. I love you too much, Arie.

I'm just so afraid of what he'll do when he figures out I betrayed him. You never want to see him when he's angry. If he ever finds either of us—I can't even imagine what would happen. Sark promises that he'll keep us safe and I find myself believing him. Who knew that I would fall for Sark so fast? Our relationship was born through fronts and deceit and yet I love him more than anything. I guess it's some sort of crazy Christmas miracle or something.

Oh, Merry Christmas! It's almost four in the morning, so I guess technically it's Christmas day. I'm so excited! I can't wait for you to open your presents! You are going to be so surprised and excited and it's going to be perfect! You definitely deserve a magical day. I think we could all use one. Poor Sark. He's sitting on the couch next to me, completely devastated. I've given up on telling him it'll be okay. He just cares about you so much and he kind of understands what this whole key thing could do to you. It's tearing him up.

You aren't alone in this, Arie. Just having you around has completely changed both of our lives, and we are going to fight to the end for you. You are worth infinitely more than your circumstances. I wish you could see that. I wish you could see yourself in our eyes.

Merry Christmas beautiful girl. Someday I hope you get the peace you deserve.

—E

There were so many things wrong with that, yet so many things right, that I didn't know what to feel first. After all the time I'd had to process it, I still had a hard time wrapping my head around Erika's side of the story. It seemed like her letters were rewriting history and predicting it all at the same time.

"But I'm so afraid of what he'll do when he figures

out I betrayed him. You never want to see him when he's angry. If he ever finds either of us—I can't even imagine what would happen."

I shuddered involuntarily. She would never know how right she was.

What are we going to do? About everything? About anything? Nobody could just sweep it all under the rug and get by forever. Eventually you had to face the problems and deal with them.

For the millionth time, I wished Erika were here. She could get through to Sark. She could pull him out of whatever pit he had dug himself into. We could go back to Florida and live in our beach house and be happy forever.

If only it were that easy.

A thud echoed from the hallway, close to my room, interrupting my thoughts.

Dang it. Sark had woken up. He was probably looking for me, hoping I was asleep, and wasn't going to be thrilled that I was using caffeine to keep me up.

Footsteps sounded, going down the hall and into the living room, stopping behind me. I took a deep breath and turned myself around. The defenses I had prepared came to a halt in my throat, my mouth hanging open without words. Because it wasn't Sark that was standing there. It was a stranger.

He was a few inches taller than me, with olive skin and cropped black hair. The kid was built, a giant brick wall, but he had to be close to my age. His dark eyes seemed to light up when he saw me, a perfect white smile flashing across his face. It was friendly, but the light from the fire showered him in odd shadows, creating a menacing feel.

I stood up in one quick motion, studying him. He

was infected, I could tell that. I didn't know how—infecteds looked like regular people—but I just knew.

Does that mean he's a threat?

"Who are you?" I asked, keeping my voice soft, but commanding. If he was going to be nice then I was too, but I wanted to make sure he knew that I was in charge.

"Wow, Arie," he said, his voice low to match mine, taking a step toward me. "I'm speechless."

"Um…do I know you?"

"Well, I've read so much about you that I feel like we're just so close."

I didn't like his voice. It was unnecessarily deep and gruff, like something was wrong with it. Like it was damaged.

"Are you here to join the infecteds?" I asked, still sorely confused. "Because you're at the wrong place."

He smiled wider, his eyes taking on an almost possessive expression. "No, I'm at the right place. I'm here for you."

Okay, this is creepy. "Is there something I can help you with?"

He laughed softly. "You're so polite, Arie. Being the key and all, you must have seen some bad stuff in your time, and yet you're still so polite. I think that's sweet."

"Why are you here?"

"You know, they lied to me." He slowly started walking toward me, and I matched each step with one backwards. "You are so much prettier than they said. It's an injustice to you, really. You're beautiful."

I willed my voice to be even. "Look, I don't know who you are, but you better start giving me some answers. I don't want—"

"I'm not here for trouble," he said, now right in

front of me. I was backed up to the wall. "I'll make it quick, I promise." His cheerfulness faltered, and he gave a regretful sigh. "It's just such a waste. You're just so beautiful. It's such a waste. Such a shame."

I raised an eyebrow. "Excuse me?"

In one insanely fast motion, he grabbed both of my arms in one hand and twisted them behind me, then pushed me against the wall so hard that I couldn't move them. He put his other hand over my mouth, securing duct tape over it, then pulled a knife out of nowhere and held it to my throat. I barely had time to blink.

"It's sad, really, that we were brought together like this," he went on, his tone so conversational that it was scary. "I think we could've been great friends. We're both infecteds—both *special* infecteds, even. I'm the most elite infected in the world right now, and you're the key to the whole thing. Pretty amazing, if you think about it."

I just stared at him.

"See, I'm so well trained that I get to do this for a living. Isn't that great? It usually is, except for jobs like this." He picked up some of my hair, handling it almost reverently. "It's hard when I get attached to the victim, and you're not making it any easier on me." He curled my hair around his finger. "You're just so beautiful. How am I going to kill you if you're so beautiful?"

My heart stuttered, nearly pounding out of my chest, and I tried to flinch away from him. *This guy is crazy. He is absolutely insane.*

He grinned at me, the kind of grin the wolf must've given to Red Riding Hood when he found her alone in the woods. "My employer is paying me so much for this, I guess I'll manage. That's the problem about being an assassin: you just have to pick your battles. In this case, the job comes before beauty. Sorry."

He let my hair fall back in place, using his thumb to smooth out the corner of the tape on my face, and I turned away from him. "Sorry about the tape, I'm sure it's annoying, but it's necessary." He nodded toward the hallway. "I can't have Sark come to your rescue when you start screaming. That would ruin the fun." He grabbed me by the throat. "Anyway, should we get started then?"

I kicked him in the shin as hard as I could, and he threw me to the ground. He stepped on my foot until my ankle cracked. I cried out, but, thanks to the tape, it was only a muffled sound. Then he reached down and grabbed me by my arm, twisting it behind me like I was a rag doll and we were playing a game.

He was stronger than me. Stronger and faster. Obviously, he wasn't kidding when he said that he was trained, but there was some other kind of power to him. Could he be more infected than me?

How is that possible?

"It must feel weird to you," he said in my ear, "to not have the upper hand on someone like me. Usually you're the best when it comes to infecteds." He yanked my arm, and I felt something detach in my shoulder, then he smashed his fist into the side of my head, and I crumpled to the ground. Dizzy, I managed to swing my legs out to knock him down too.

The psycho grabbed his knife and stabbed the middle of my left thigh. He took it out, then kept going, stabbing three times all the way down to my knee. Again, my cries were barely audible.

What do I do? I couldn't remember the last time I fought off someone.

I used my good leg and kicked him right in the jaw.

He fell over, and I tried to crawl away and pull the tape off. I had barely lifted the corner when he slammed into me, beating my face into the ground. Finally, I was able to push him off.

Sark! Sark, wake up! Of course I had to give him sleeping pills.

I tried to get up, but didn't make it too far. He came out of nowhere and picked me up by the neck, throwing me backwards. I fell into the standing lamp and it shattered underneath me. The shards buried themselves into my back.

The kid froze, looking toward the hallway. We both waited in anticipation, me with hope.

He had to have heard that. Come on, Sark.

Then I remembered: I clawed my way toward the hallway, aiming for the loose board with the gun underneath.

The intruder just laughed and yanked me up by my hair, then pulled me out the front door.

The icy night air flooded over my skin as he dragged me outside and down the street, still managing to keep up a fast pace. I fought his grip, but it was no use. The kid was a machine.

We stopped a few minutes later in an alley. My stomach dropped when I saw him heading for a dumpster.

I'm going to die in this alley, right now. He'll dump my body, and nobody will know.

In a last-ditch effort, I twisted myself around and took out one of his knees. He released me, but it was momentarily. Before I figured out which way was up, he had me by the neck again, a gun pressed to my chin.

"Just give it up, Arie," he whispered, a smile still on his face. "I knew you were a fighter, but this is a bit ridiculous. We're clocking in at twelve minutes. My standard is closer to three." Almost playfully, he tipped the gun down and shot me in the calf. I shrieked at the new burning.

"Well, it's been fun, Arie. Really it has. It was an honor to meet you, but I've got a schedule to keep." He shot me again in the shoulder before lifting the lid on the dumpster. "I left a message for Sark, so I imagine he'll be out looking for you now. Of course, you'll be dead by the time he finds you, but I thought you'd appreciate my courtesy."

Giving me another grin, he picked me up like a sack of garbage and threw me in the dumpster. "Goodnight Arie. Sweet dreams." Then the lid shut, and I was trapped in darkness.

I felt myself fading. My body weighed a million tons, fire emanating from where he had shot me. Every breath was another stab in my side, every blink a fight.

This isn't how it ends. You can't die. Come on.

Using insane amounts of effort, I was able to pull myself into a sitting position. Blindly, I searched through the garbage with my good hand, not allowing myself to consider what I might be touching. Eventually my fingers closed around a plastic rod that felt like a broom. I pitted it against the dumpster lid and pushed as hard as I could. After a minute of trying different angles, I was finally able to get the lid off.

Hurry, I thought, my mind sluggish. *You're running out of time.*

Next came the most difficult part: getting out. The garbage was high enough that I could probably roll myself out, but the fall would be brutal. I didn't really have a choice though. Counting to three, I used my good arm to hoist myself over the wall of the dumpster. There was a second of falling before I slammed onto the pavement. I screamed, but, thanks to the tape, it wasn't very loud.

I pulled the tape off of my face, then started dragging myself out of the alley. To my alarm, I couldn't move my right arm or my left leg—the ones that had been shot. My vision started to fade around the edges as I made it to the street. That was it. The pain overtook me, and I couldn't go any farther.

Keep going, I tried to urge myself, but to no avail. I didn't know where I would go anyway. I was going to die in the street. After everything I'd managed to survive, I was going to bleed out in a street, alone.

"Help!" I called even though the road was deserted. "Help, someone, please!"

Hoping to relieve my shoulder, I rolled onto my back, which was when I felt a lump in my back pocket. Figuring it was the last decision I'd get to make, I reached my free arm into my pocket and pulled out the remote tracker Lindsey had given me several weeks ago.

I couldn't remember putting it in my pocket, but right then I couldn't remember my own name. Using as much energy as I had left, I pressed the button over and over again until the remote slipped out of my bloody hand and rolled out of reach.

That's it. I'm bleeding out in a deserted street. I'm gone.

I blacked out several times, only aware of the changes between nothing and absolute fire beginning to spread throughout my body. Casting my eyes to the sky, sure they would be the last things I would ever see, I watched the innumerable stars, which made me feel slightly less alone. Then there was nothing again.

When I regained consciousness, I recognized Alaina's voice shouting commands that didn't make sense. I was able to crack my eyes open to a blinding light. Once my eyes adjusted, I saw I was back at the club with Sark, Alaina, Brennan, Lucy, and a girl and a boy I didn't know all standing around me. They were all busy doing something, everyone talking at the same time.

"We're out of everything else," Brennan was saying.

Lucy took something from him, coming closer to me. "Hey, Arie, you've got to take this, okay? It's just a little pill. No big deal." She put it in my mouth and put a cup of water to my lips. I choked but was able to swallow it down.

"That will take at least twenty minutes to get going," Brennan said.

"We don't have twenty minutes," Sark replied, his voice grim. He was filling up a tray with something. "The bullets are capsules on a time release—some sort of poison has been leaking into her for who knows how long. We have to get them out now."

"How many?" the girl asked.

"Two. One in her leg, one in her shoulder."

Alaina leaned over to me, putting something long and smooth in my mouth, then brushed my hair out of my face. "Bite down on this, okay? You're going to be fine."

Peter appeared next to her, standing behind my head. I felt someone grab my wrists and my uninjured ankle, holding me down, which probably wasn't a good thing. Peter put his hands on either side of my head and brought his face a little closer to mine so he could talk over everyone else.

"Eyes on me, roadkill," he said, wincing at something that I couldn't see. He was so nice that I almost didn't recognize his voice. "Keep your eyes on me."

Something wet touched me, bringing on a new kind of fire. Everything was hurting so badly that I couldn't tell where anything was coming from.

"Okay, Arie," I heard Sark say warily. "Take a deep breath and this will all be over."

If I thought I had been in pain before, it was nothing compared to what I felt now. I writhed and screamed, feeling everyone tighten their hold on me to keep me down. Peter held my head in place, forcing me to look at him.

"You're doing great," he kept saying, even when I was screaming so loudly that I couldn't hear him. "You're doing great. You're almost done."

The merciless seconds ticked by sluggishly. I tried to tell them to just let me die, but they must've not understood me because the pain didn't stop. For a harrowing few eternities it only got worse.

How can it get worse? Right when I thought the pain was literally going to kill me, it started to retreat. At first it was in such small increments that I didn't notice. But eventually I was able to start generating a thin layer of control.

Peter let go of me, putting his arm under my neck and supporting my head in the crook of his elbow. Then he pulled me into a halfway sitting position, keeping my body straight so I only bent at my waist.

I winced at the poking and tugging at my back, feeling the shards from the lamp being pulled out one by one. The medicine must've kicked in, because the pain started to be put down. It started to go to rest. The relief made me tired; I couldn't keep my eyes open anymore.

After a little bit, the tugging stopped. I felt Peter lay me back down and take the thing out of my mouth. Murmured voices continued to talk, but everything was quieter now. The only sounds I made were harsh breaths through my teeth.

Then a new hand was on my face, and I recognized the touch without looking: Sark. "It's over, Arie." His voice was strained but working on relief. "You're safe now. It's all over." He brushed the hair that was plastered to my sweaty face, wiped my face with a wet cloth, then just held it against my forehead. It felt amazing. "Arie? Can you hear me?"

I got out a mangled, "Yes" before adding, "He tried to kill me."

"Did you know who it was?"

"No…infected, but…never seen him." I furrowed my eyebrows. "Something was wrong…with him. His voice…was broken…he was crazy. Kept repeating himself."

"Did he say why he was there?"

"Um…hired to kill me…paid lots of money…really, really trained, but…he was infected…almost differently. Different than me."

The muscles in my hurt shoulder twitched, sending a spasm down my body. I couldn't trap the whimper behind my teeth. Taking deep breaths made it worse, so I could only gasp in short quick breaths, but my chest was moving up and down so fast that my shoulder was dying. I could find no middle ground.

"Sark?" My voice cracked. Add that with the gasping, and I didn't sound at all like myself.

"Yeah?"

"I'm…I'm scared."

"I know, Arie." He squeezed my hand gently. "I know you're scared, but it's going to be okay. You're safe now."

"Sark?" Another spasm. Another cry.

"Yeah?"

"I don't want to die." Tears started to fall down my face, though they might've already been there. "I know I said I did, but I really don't want to."

"Hey, it's okay." His voice started to crack too. "You're not going to die. You're going to be just fine."

My breathing caught, generating a mangled half scream.

"Arie, I know it's hard and you're scared, but you have to stay calm," he pleaded. "Can you do that for me?"

"I don't want to be here."

"Where do you want to be?"

A giant spasm went through me, almost jolting me off the table. I screamed, clenching my hands into fists, digging my fingernails into his skin.

"Arie, stay with me, okay?" Sark was trying to keep the alarm out of his voice. He started rubbing the cloth against my forehead, methodic and soothing. "Just a few more minutes and that medicine is going to knock you out. Just hold out for a little longer." He started running his fingers slowly through my hair, and I focused on the familiar sensation. "Tell me where you want to be."

"I want…in Florida."

"You want to be in Florida?" He couldn't hide the obvious pain in his voice. "With Erika?"

I tried to nod. "And you. And…Alaina comes sometimes. And Hadley. And other people. But then we're alone." I calmed a little at the idea. "Dalton…he isn't there. Not him or Alexis or Jefferson…or even Keaton. Nobody is chasing us. And guess what?"

"What?"

"I'm not the key anymore. I'm not even infected. I'm normal, just like you and Erika."

That fantasy was like a warm ball in my core, slowly spreading throughout my body. The pain seemed to numb a bit as it went, and I felt myself really calming down.

"I'm not scared anymore. You guys don't worry about me anymore. And I don't scream in the night anymore. You don't have to come wake me up. You can sleep all night. And now you don't get sick. I'm normal now, and you don't get sick." My voice got quieter, the words coming to me sluggishly. "I'm…I'm not…a freak anymore. I'm normal…and you're happier."

My breathing had finally evened out. The numbing warmth seeped into my brain, taking over, and my exhausted body willingly submitted. I stopped shaking and fidgeting, which made me feel even better. I could finally relax.

"Arie, you are perfect the way you are." Sark continued to rub the wet cloth along my face, talking quietly to me. "You're going to be just fine. We both are. Just calm down and go to sleep. By the time you wake up tomorrow, everything is going to be better. You know, someone once told me that everything seems worse at night. Sometimes you just have to cut your losses and go to sleep, and when you wake up things don't seem so bad. It's a nice trick, really."

His voice lulled me into unconsciousness again, where I stayed for a while, pain free. It was several hours later when I woke up on the couch downstairs. A pit of fire was in my stomach, burning through my insides, scalding me to the surface. Vaguely aware that my right arm was secured in a sling, I rolled myself off of the couch. A small shriek escaped me when I hit the ground, but I didn't care. Right now, the pain on the surface of my body didn't compare to what was festering in my core. Using my left hand, I dug my fingernails into the floor and started dragging myself across the room. My destination was so far away; I knew I wasn't going to make it in time.

"What are you doing?" someone asked from behind, making me jump. Peter kneeled down beside me, attempting to mask his alarm with amusement.

"Help," I said breathlessly, the agony in my body taking my voice. "I need help."

I assumed that he would spit some churlish remark and just leave, but he surprised me. Concern came into his eyes—concern he tried very hard to hide—as he looked from me to where I was trying to go. I knew he understood.

Effortlessly, he picked me up. I could tell he tried to be careful, but it still hurt like crazy. He carried me quickly into the bathroom, setting me gently on the floor.

"I'll get Sark," he said as he disappeared, shutting the door behind him.

Unfortunately, I needed help right then. It was coming. I struggled to lift my head but had no luck. Before I could do anything to brace myself, the bubbling pit in my stomach exploded and I threw up everywhere. My body shook violently, and I would've screamed if my throat wasn't otherwise occupied. The acid burned my throat and my mouth, but my insides felt a tiny molecule better. Whatever was in there was going to eat at me unless it came out.

When Sark opened the door, I was lying in a puddle of my own vomit. I was sure I wasn't a pretty sight, but he was still a sickly pale color. He dropped to his knees next to me, pulling me into a somewhat sitting position, and angled me so he was right behind me. I leaned back against him, grateful for the break from the floor.

Alaina and Lucy came in right after him, supplies in hand. Without a word, Lucy stepped around us and started cleaning the floor, while Alaina kneeled next to me.

"Sorry," I was able to get out. "You don't have to…it's really gross. Let me do it."

I reached for a wet cleaning cloth, but Alaina moved them away from me as she wiped off my arm with one. Sark took a cloth and started cleaning my face.

"What did you eat?" Alaina asked, her tone teasing, but still strained.

I wanted to come back with some sort of witty remark, but I didn't have the chance. My restless stomach exploded again, jerking my body forward. Thankfully, Alaina and Sark reacted insanely fast, and the toilet was right in front of me. Sark grabbed my head before I fell all the way forward, and held me there, while Alaina pulled the hair out of my face just in time. I retched again, everything except my stomach screaming in response.

When it was finally over, I collapsed back against Sark, gasping for air while tears streamed down my face. Everything just hurt so badly.

"What…is happening?" I asked in between torturous breaths. "This…this isn't normal."

"Your body is reacting," Sark explained quietly. He was tense as he continued to clean my face. "It's protecting itself. Those bullets weren't just bullets. They had some lethal substance in them. Your infected body is rejecting it before it can kill you like it would a normal person."

"So it's a good thing?"

"As much as it doesn't seem like it, yes."

I winced and gritted my teeth, trying to keep myself in check. I couldn't let the pain overtake me again. I had to stay in control.

Sark leaned my head forward a bit and started pulling gently on my hair. It took me a minute to realize that he was putting it into a loose ponytail. Then he rested my head back, and I felt him nod.

"Let me know if you need anything," Alaina said. She brushed my arm before I heard her and Lucy walk out.

"Sark?" I asked after a minute of silence. I couldn't make my voice very loud.

"Yeah?"

"Are you okay?"

He laughed once in disbelief, making my head shake a bit. "Are you serious?"

"Of course I am." I didn't understand the big deal. "You were…I mean, before…you weren't doing too well. And you don't look like you're feeling much better."

"I'm feeling just fine," he said, a little sarcastically. "Although you seem to give me recurring heart attacks, and I don't know if I'm going to survive many more."

"I'm—"

"Do not say you're sorry," he interrupted, his tone harsh, "or I really will lose my mind."

"Well, I am."

"Someone tried to kill you as I was snoring in the

other room. That hardly requires an apology."

"There was nothing you—"

"Don't. I swear, I will lose it."

I didn't have the energy to try to fight him on it. I just needed any form of distraction.

"Who would want to kill me?" I asked, my voice small.

Sark sighed. "Honestly, I don't know."

"Alexis?"

"Not a chance. He would never risk you like that, much less send someone to kill you."

"Dalton?"

"Maybe. It doesn't seem quite his style though. If anything, he would send someone to kill me."

"Yeah, you're right." No other ideas came to mind and that made me uneasy.

"We'll figure it out. And it won't happen again." He glanced at my heavily bandaged calf. "How did you get in here anyway?"

"Peter helped me." The second I said it, I realized how ridiculous that sentence sounded.

"Really?" Sark asked, surprise in his tone.

"Yeah. Why is he being so nice to me? Was that him helping stitch me up or did I just imagine it?"

"No, it was him." His tone told me he still wasn't a fan.

"Why?"

"He's always right there at the med station—he has been ever since he got here, despite the fact that he has next to no medical training. Besides Kayla and Daxton, none of us do, really, but we've all learned enough to try to save infecteds when they show up in bad shape. We haven't had any new ones in a while."

"Why does Peter hang around that? I wouldn't think

helping people would be top on his list."

"I'm assuming it's because of Leslie."

"Who's that?"

Sark dropped the volume of his voice slightly, as if afraid someone would hear. "She came here with Peter. They got mixed up with some handlers on their way. She got the worst of it, and when they arrived she was in really bad condition. We tried everything, but she didn't make it. Peter was desolate for weeks. He won't ever talk about her, so nobody knows who she actually was, but…it must've been a big deal. Ever since, he's been right at the med table, no matter who it is."

"Wow." That explained a lot. Peter hated me, but he couldn't help but see Leslie lying there instead of me. How sad.

"Don't let that fool you," Sark said, talking at normal volume again. "He's still an impulsive idiot."

"That's mean," I told him, my voice disapproving.

"Nice job, by the way," Sark said, changing the subject. "I don't leave your side for twelve hours straight, then run upstairs for two minutes, and *that's* when you decide to throw up. You could have planned that a bit better."

"Sorry." I rolled my eyes. "I'll keep that in mind for next time."

"Next time? You expect this will happen again?"

"With my luck, who knows?"

Sark laughed quietly. "You're right."

Shortly after, my break came to an end. I was sick again, but now I was noticing a decent change. The burning inside my body was starting to lessen. The outside was getting worse, but at least the searing acid inside of me was disappearing.

You've just got to pick your battles.

The next three hours continued with slow, tortuous progress. It was good though, because eventually all of the toxins were out of me. The second Sark was sure it was over, he gave me more drugs, allowing me to return to my nothingness and begin to really recover.

20

The next few days blurred together, the time going by in odd intervals. I slept on and off for a while, then decided to give it up. I couldn't tell if the sleep made me feel better or worse, and it scared me to be asleep. I didn't know when my nightmares were going to start up again and I wasn't eager for them to show. Plus, so much could happen while I was asleep. It wasn't worth it.

Sark made the executive decision to stay away from our house for the time being, which I thought was a great idea. Thankfully, Lindsey was nice enough to clear it for us, saying as long as he was in Denver his agreement wouldn't be void. That was a huge relief to me, but it seemed like Sark didn't really care much about it. He rarely left my side and was on guard for every disaster that could possibly happen to me. He never relaxed. If he absolutely had to go somewhere—which just consisted of the next room—he always made sure at least three other people were close to me. It was completely ridiculous, though I had to admit that it made me feel slightly better about my whole situation.

My mystery killer still scared me to death, but the whole encounter had become a hazy memory. A past nightmare. I did my best to pretend like it didn't happen, but that was hard to do when my right arm had been rendered useless. It was still secured safely in the sling, where it would most likely stay for a long time, especially considering I hadn't even been able to move my fingers yet.

I tried to pretend like my arm was fine by finding things to do that wouldn't require it to work. It turned out almost *everything* required two arms, or at least two hands. It frustrated me to no end.

Hadley tried to keep my frustrations at bay by finding things that I could do. He was the only one who acted the same around me. Everyone else looked at me like I was a ticking time bomb, and, honestly, I couldn't really blame them.

Today, Sark ran downstairs for something, leaving me in Hadley's charge. Liam, Mark, and Brennan were all within a few yards of me, but Hadley felt important when Sark specifically left him in charge. After making three paper airplanes for me, he proudly puffed up his chest and pulled out his favorite thing: Battleship. Not only was it the best game ever, he told me, but I could sit down the whole time and only needed one arm. I had to hand it to the kid, it was a good idea, but by the third game I was getting bored.

"How about A5?" I asked, resting my chin in my hand and scanning my red filled board. If I didn't get a hit soon, Hadley was going to win. Again.

"Miss," he answered smoothly. He prided himself on his flawless poker face. To me, he looked like a baby monkey that was constantly smelling something nasty.

"A miss?" I looked back over my losing board again. "Hadley, that can't be a miss."

"But it is."

"It can't be. There are no other places that could fit your big ship."

"But my big ship isn't there."

"Then where is it?"

His mouth dropped open. "I can't tell you! That's the whole point of the game."

I rolled my eyes, annoyed. "Fine. Your turn."

His monkey face came back as he studied his side carefully. His serious eyes met mine.

"G2." His tone suggested we were in a congressional debate rather than a game of Battleship.

I looked down at my board, knowing what I would find.

"Hit," I said. Unwillingly I added, "Sink."

Hadley's face lit up for a second before turning serious again. "One more ship and I win."

"What a surprise," I muttered. I fingered my right sleeve, tracing the bandage around my wrist. Sark had wrapped it when they were patching me up to hide my freaky glowing tattoo before anyone could see it, and I was grateful.

I grudgingly placed the red pin in my lost ship. Before I could take my turn, Sark came up the stairs. He crossed the room quickly and sat on a chair to my left, a calculating expression on his face.

"How many times has he beat you?" Sark asked, nodding toward Hadley.

"Two times," Hadley answered for me. "But it's going to be three. I have a plan."

"Yeah, it involves magically making all of his own ships disappear." I leaned back against the couch, having to adjust my position slightly to please my shoulder. "So, what's going on?"

Sark shrugged, pretending to be confused. "What do you mean?"

I glared at him. "Really? You're not fooling anyone; I hope you know that."

He let out a long breath, settling deeper into his chair. His thumb started brushing against his left ring finger again. It was something he did more and more, especially when he was stressed out.

"I was talking to Kayla downstairs about the capsules we dug out of you."

It took me a moment to remember who Kayla was— she was the blonde girl always at the desk downstairs and had helped me at the med table. "Why Kayla?"

He raised an eyebrow. "Have you ever talked to her?"

"Um, no. Not really."

"She's a genius. She was going to school to be a doctor before she had to run from her handler. If there is anyone to ask about this, it would be her."

"Huh." I didn't know why that surprised me so much. "Okay, so what did she say?"

Hadley huffed in impatience and slouched in his seat. I gestured for him to wait.

"She was examining the liquid inside of them—

pretty much the stuff you threw up—and it's…" Sark trailed off, wincing slightly. "Not good."

Oh great. "Not good how?"

He nodded toward my leg. "It's not nearly as severe in your leg, though you might have a slight limp forever, but your shoulder…" He shook his head and started over. "The poison in the capsules target your nerves, literally burning them up. Thankfully, your body rejected it before it could completely kill your nervous system, but your shoulder was fried. And there's a good chance…it will never come back."

I blinked in shock. "What?"

Sark winced again, his eyes mournful. "Your arm might be dead indefinitely." He went on quickly. "But we don't know that for sure. If we work with it, try to get it back…I mean, I don't know. It just depends on…a lot of things, I guess."

"So my…" I was having a hard time wrapping my head around it. "My right arm—like my *right arm*—is basically gone?"

"We don't know for sure yet. Up to this point you've been able to come back from every injury that's hit you, but…I'm not sure about this one."

I shook my head, as if that would clear it. I didn't want to try and process that at the moment.

"Okay…well, what else did she say?"

Sark seemed taken aback, as if he expected more of a reaction. When I didn't offer one, he hesitantly went on.

"Well, uh, we've pretty much proven that you can't be killed easily, but you know that. I'd imagine it would take advanced techniques—like those bullets—to put you out for good."

"So…?" I didn't really know where he was going

with this.

"So whoever that was really meant to kill you. And he knew how to do it too."

"Which means?"

Sark gave me a half glare. "You aren't really concerned about this, are you?"

I drummed my fingers against my leg. "Honestly, I'm still fed up with the Battleship game."

He gritted his teeth and looked away from me. I turned back to Hadley, who straightened right up, poker face on.

"Okay, um…" I scanned my board. "E6. That has to be a hit."

The corners of Hadley's mouth pulled up. "Miss."

I leaned forward. "That can't be a miss."

"But it is."

"But it can't be."

"But it is."

"Is this what you do all day? Magically win Battleship games?" I recalled Hadley's small attention span. "Don't you get bored?"

Hadley positioned something on his board as he answered.

"Sometimes people work up in the club, but everyone says I'm too little to do that. So I just play by myself or with my friends. Make up games and stuff. Sometimes we have Guitar Hero battles. Sometimes not. When we first got here, all the big kids were doing homework stuff, but they stopped a while ago except for Kayla and her friends." He shrugged. "We just have to make our own fun."

"What kind of homework?"

He wrinkled his nose. "Boring stuff. About the formula." He said the word like 'formlula.' "Sark brought all these papers of research or something."

That piqued my interest. *What were they researching?*

"Are the papers still here?"

"Yeah." He pointed to the stairs. "Downstairs in the boxes."

"Will you show me?"

"No," Sark answered, his voice hard. He was looking at Hadley. "Not now."

Hadley nodded obediently, then went back to studying his board.

"Why not?" I asked, annoyed. Sark just ignored me. "Fine. I'll go find them myself."

"You can't," Hadley said. "They're hiding." He pointed to the board. "Can we play now?"

I sighed. Everything was a thousand times more irritating than usual. Finally, I nodded. Hadley smiled.

Within four turns he had beat me again. I shut the game box with a little more force than was needed, thanked Hadley for the game, and started for the kitchen, aware of Sark following close behind.

Mara, Alaina, and Lucy were in there, getting ready to make dinner, which was what I was hoping for.

"Do you guys need any help?" I asked. "I'm dying for something to do."

"Are you serious?" Sark asked. I rolled my eyes in annoyance and ignored him.

Alaina suppressed a smile when she saw my expression. "Yeah, sure."

Before Sark could protest, Mara started rattling off things that I could do. "Kneading bread dough, washing and cutting vegetables, putting the soup together—"

"I already called dibs on the beverage," Alaina cut in, a mischievous look on her face. She pulled out a can of the powdered lemonade and a big pitcher.

"Why don't you work on the dishes?" Lucy suggested. "The dishwasher is huge, so it may take you awhile, but you could still empty it with one hand."

"Perfect," I answered. "Thanks." Sark began to protest, but I shut him down. He gave up and went to sit on a chair by the wall, pulling out his phone and muttering to himself.

I opened the dishwasher as Alaina stepped nonchalantly next to me.

"Long day?" she whispered, a smile in her voice.

"Yep."

"He driving you nuts?"

I sighed as I pulled out the first row of dishes. "No, I'm just in a really bad mood. I should apologize, but I don't feel like it."

"Nah, don't worry about it. It's funny to see Sark so annoyed at you."

I glanced at her. "Why?"

"Are you serious? In his eyes, you basically walk on water. It's good for him to realize you've got a nasty side too."

"Um…thank you?" I wasn't really sure if I should be offended or not. "I think."

Alaina just snickered and continued in her lemonade mixing. I focused on my task but couldn't get her comment out of my head.

The dishes took me forever. I didn't mind, but I just felt stupid, especially considering how tired it made me.

Arie, the key to the infecting formula, survived countless near-death experiences, but gets wiped out by the dishes. How stupid was that?

After nearly an hour, Alaina gave up on me. She grabbed the rest of the dishes out of the dishwasher in one huge stack.

"Hey," I protested. "I can do that."

"No offense, Arie," she said as she swiftly put them all away. "But we need dishes *today*, not next year."

I trailed after her, sneaking a few bowls when I could. Peter strode in, making his usual attempt to snag food before it was served. I ignored him and went to the sink before I realized that I only had one hand. Letting out a long breath, I tried to wash my left hand with itself. Peter came over, leaning against the counter next to me, a few stolen cucumbers in hand.

"Helping out in the kitchen, huh?" His arrogant aura grated on my nerves. I attempted to concentrate on my feeble hand washing endeavor, but Peter wasn't going to just let me go.

"Oh, I get it." He popped a cucumber in his mouth. "You miss your mom, right? Cooking in the kitchen and all that jazz."

I turned off the water, giving up on the washing my hand thing, and flipped my hand around on a towel like a dead fish, hoping to dry it. The tactic didn't work as well as I wanted. *Nothing* was working as well as I wanted.

What is with the world today?

"I bet your mom's not cooking anymore though, right?" Peter went on. "I don't envy the whole 'slave to Alexis' thing she's probably got going on."

I snapped my head toward him. "What?"

Genuine surprise crossed his face before Alaina slid between us, her back to me.

"Really, Peter?" she fumed. "Can you not be an idiot for more than five seconds?"

"You didn't tell her?" Peter was appalled. "Her own parents—"

"Shut up!" Alaina shoved him away.

I grabbed her arm and turned her around. "What's he talking about?"

She sighed, her eyes darting everywhere besides my face as she debated what to do. "Arie, just forget about it, okay?"

I glanced around the room, hoping to get some sort of idea. Mara and Lucy were still wrapped up in their jobs, trying to give us space. Sark was resting his head in his hand in defeat. Peter's wide eyes were going from me to Alaina, taking in the scene. None of them were going to give me anything. I squeezed Alaina's arm harder.

"Ow!" she protested, jerking her arm away from me.

"Tell me," I ordered darkly. "Tell me now."

She took a deep breath. "Look, Arie—"

"Skip the crap and tell me."

"I just don't know all the details so—"

"Just tell me!"

"Fine!" She threw her hands up in exasperation. "Right after you supposedly died, Alexis went and somehow 'convinced' your dad to come work with them to try and recreate you. Sark went to check, and it looks like they took your mom too. I don't know what they're doing, or what's happened to them, or if they're even alive. I'm sorry."

I felt the color drain out of my face as I stared at her in shock, trying to get a handle on what she was saying.

Alexis has Mom and Dad. Alexis has Mom and Dad. Why hadn't I ever considered that before? Why did I have such mixed emotions over it? Yeah, I hated my dad, but he was still my dad. He was crazy, but not Alexis kind of crazy. And Mom? The thought of her, strong in a fragile way, up against Alexis...I was mad at her, but I would never wish *that* on her. And that was if she was even alive.

Alaina snapped her fingers in front of my face. "Arie? Are you going to faint on me?" I managed to shake my head. She grabbed my damp left hand. "I'm really sorry. I really am. I don't—"

"I know." It took me a moment to realize that it was my voice. It sounded far away. I pulled my hand out of hers and stepped around her. Before I could walk out the door, Mara called to me.

"Arie, maybe you should eat something. It might help."

I turned to look at her, but I didn't really see her.

"No thank you. Not hungry."

"I didn't see you at breakfast this morning. When was the last time you ate?"

The room started to spin a tiny bit. "Um...I had...it was the...last night. I had those potato things you made."

Mara raised an eyebrow. "Arie, that was on Saturday."

"Yeah."

"Today is Wednesday."

"Oh." I closed my eyes, trying to concentrate.

"You're telling me you haven't eaten anything since Saturday?"

Pretty much. "I probably just forgot. I'm sure I had something…" I took a deep breath and opened my eyes. I could only zero in on Mara. "Look, thanks, but I'm not hungry. I just need a little bit of air and I'm sure I'll be fine." I made a quick decision, turning to Sark. "Is there a car around here I can use?"

He analyzed me for a half second before answering.

"Yeah. I'll show you." He stood up and I followed him through a door into a garage I'd never seen before. Four unassuming black cars that looked pretty much the same were parked in a line with a silver motorcycle at the end.

"Whose is that?" I asked, gesturing to the bike. I didn't think anyone around here had the money for that.

"Mine."

I couldn't help but laugh, surprising us both. "That's *yours*? Since when?"

He smiled. "You missed my rebellious phase. It probably wasn't my best idea, though I get the feeling you'd love it." He nodded toward me. "If you weren't so broken I'd take you on it now, but you'll have to wait until your arm gets better."

I noticed that he said *until* instead of *if* but didn't point it out. If he wanted to be overly optimistic then that was fine by me.

"I'll hold you to that. I just wouldn't show Sasha if I were you," I told him.

"Good thinking." His smile faded. "Arie, why do you need a car?"

I shrugged as best as I could. "I need some air," then added grudgingly, "I'm too tired to walk anywhere."

"Did you know there's a rule here about leaving?" he asked, only a little bit joking. I shook my head. "Infecteds have to clear it with me, Alaina, or Tristan if they want to leave. We have to know where they're going so we can make sure they make it back safely without any of Alexis' men following."

I gave him a 'really?' look. "So basically, you're saying I need permission?"

"Pretty much. And I say you can't leave unless I go with you."

"Why not?" I asked, trying not to sound too annoyed.

He rolled his eyes. "Oh, I don't know. Maybe it's the unknown assassin that almost killed you or the government agent seeking revenge. Maybe it's the fact that you're momentarily disabled. None of those are really important though, so I'm not sure why I'm so concerned."

"Okay, okay, I get it. Don't strain yourself." I thought for a moment, but I knew what would have to happen. "Fine. Will you come with me then?"

"Sure. Where are we going?"

"I don't care. I just miss the sky."

Sark grabbed a key off of a hook on the wall, then opened up the passenger door of the first car, gesturing for me to get inside. "I can do that."

I slid inside, kicked my shoes off, and pulled my legs up on the seat. Sark let me roll down my window, which was basically my favorite thing to do. Even though the air was icy, the wind against my face was the best feeling to me. Strangely enough, the wind was the thing I missed most about being outside.

"You know," I said as we sped down the road, "you're pretty much my favorite person in the whole world."

"Well, you're pretty much stuck with me," he said, "so you might as well get used to it." He was trying to suppress a grin though, so I thought I had said the right thing.

We drove for hours, sometimes talking, sometimes not. Eventually we were past the city and seemingly in the middle of nowhere. The farther we went, the more Sark relaxed, and I did too. Apparently, we both needed to get away.

Eventually my eyelids started to get heavy. I rolled up my window, my face numb, and settled back into my seat. Wincing, I turned and tried to get comfortable.

"How's your shoulder?" Sark asked. "Skip the 'fines' please."

"It's…" I winced again. "Present. And vocal. But not too bad."

"You should sleep."

"No thanks."

"I didn't say you *wanted* to; I said you *should*."

I didn't answer; I knew he was right. I hated when he was right, and I was wrong. Really, I just hated being wrong. That thought made something else come to mind.

"Sark?"

"Yeah?"

"Do I have a nasty side?"

Sark laughed once. "What?"

"You know, like a bad side. Like I'm in a bad mood a lot? Tell me honestly."

"I'll admit, you can get pretty scary, but that's the case with everyone. It's not like you're always in a bad mood."

I sensed something else to his tone. "But…?"

He sighed, tilting his head as he chose his words carefully. "No, you're really not. You just…I don't know. You're still the nice person you've always been, there's just something different. A spark is gone. You're not as happy as you used to be."

"Oh." That shouldn't have surprised me, but it made me kinda sad. "I'm sorry."

He shook his head. "Will you stop apologizing for everything?"

"Sorr—" I stopped myself in time.

Sark grinned. "See? There's still some Arie in there."

It was silent again for a minute. The darkness was getting more and more comfortable.

"Sark?"

"Yeah?"

"I'm sorry I haven't been very nice lately."

"Arie, it's not that bad. And, honestly, you have every right to be much worse."

"That's not an excuse. It's not fair to anyone. I'll be better."

I thought he would argue, but he just sighed. "You do that."

Another minute of silence.

"Sark?"

"Yeah?"

"Don't keep stuff away from me anymore. I think I'd rather just know."

He glanced sideways at me. "I…uh, look Arie, I didn't—"

"I don't really want to get into it now. Just promise me, okay?"

Another sigh. "Okay."

"Promise?"

"I promise."

I ran through my checklist in my head, then realized I forgot something.

"Sark?"

I heard him chuckle softly. "Yeah?"

"Thank you." I went on before he could refute me. "Don't say anything please. I'm just grateful for you."

The corners of Sark's mouth pulled up into a slight grin. "You know, I could say the same to you."

Satisfied, I closed my eyes and completely relaxed,

listening to the soft humming of the car. The next thing I knew, I was lost, standing on a road in the dark. I wandered through the blackness slowly, hands held out in front of me to keep from crashing into anything.

Hands? I raised my right arm. Normal. No pain or difficulty. I couldn't see what it looked like, but it felt as if it had never been hurt in the first place. With that new discovery, I hesitantly continued on my path.

Out of nowhere, I sensed a presence. A dangerous one. A murderous one. I started running blindly, feeling my pursuer on my tail. Then something pushed me from behind and I flew forward, crashing to the ground. The lights flashed on without any warning. I pulled myself up, prepared to face whatever was after me. Instead, I was shocked to find myself facing me.

Mirrors encircled me, reflecting my wide-eyed expression from a hundred different angles.

I blinked once, then screamed when the image changed. A monster was staring at me—a monster that *was* me. Huge spots of skin had been torn away, exposing large areas of mutilated flesh: electric blue flesh that almost glowed, like the mark on my arm. Her jaw was angled wrong, and her mouth seemed to be split in half. One side had a scarred lip that pulled it into a permanent scowl. The other side was normal, revealing a perfect white smile. Half of her hair had been ripped out; she was cut up and bleeding blue. My right eye stared back at me, while the left was a solid blue orb.

I backed away from the thing, colliding with the wall behind me. Whipping around, I screamed again when I saw the monster in the mirror. She was all around me.

She started moving. Each mirror showed her doing something different—rather, doing the same thing to different people. Erika, Alaina, Hadley, my parents, a shadow of Micah, Sark, and various infecteds, all being ripped to shreds. Literally. She was tearing them apart as they all shrieked and fought. But they had no chance. Hadley was completely gone within thirty seconds.

I yelled and pounded my fists, trying to break through any glass.

"Stop it! Stop, please, stop!" I begged. "Leave them alone!"

Simultaneously, all of the reflections froze and turned to face me, leaving their bloody victims on the ground. Her one eye bore into mine, a smirk on half her face.

"You can't run from me forever," she said in a perfect imitation of my voice. "I know you can feel me. I'm coming. There is nowhere that you can hide." She took a step closer, if that was even possible. I felt her breath on my face, reeking of blood. "I will win."

She stuck one ravaged arm out of the mirror, shoving me backwards. A pit of blackness swallowed me whole, suffocating me with fire as I fell into nothing.

My eyes opened to a starry night sky, which scared me even more.

Where is she? I glanced wildly around the open space, looking for some evidence that the monster had followed me here. Sark was the only one in sight. He was kneeling on the ground in front of me, trying to gently hold me down. My stomach dropped when I realized that if I couldn't see her, then I must *be* her.

"Don't touch me!" I shrieked, kicking Sark as hard as I could. He fell backwards, releasing his hold on me, and I started examining myself. My left arm was normal, my right still in the sling. I touched my face, my head, my hair, trying to find something that wasn't me. I was all there.

Sark got back up, a new fear in his eyes that he was attempting to hide. He reached for me again, but I kicked his hand.

"Get away from me!" I thought of him, and all those others, lying in an awful bloody heap after she was done with them. That visual was too much. I leaned over and threw up what little was left inside of me. Sark caught me before I fell onto my shoulder, sitting me back up against what I now realized was the car.

I hit his arm. "Don't touch me!"

"Okay." Sark held his hands in the air where I could see them. "Okay, look. I'm not touching you. It's just you and me. Nobody else."

"It's not me," I said, despair in my voice, as I continued to look around for her. I couldn't shake the feeling that she was still here. And it terrified me. "It's not me."

"It's not you," Sark said softly. "I know it's not you. You're okay now. It's just me."

I shook my head, whimpering and putting my hand on my hurt shoulder. My deep gasping was killing it.

"She's not here," I repeated to myself. "She's not here." I finally evened out my breathing, slumping back against the car, then surveyed the area. The car was pulled to the side of the road, the passenger door hanging open. Sark was watching me cautiously. He seemed tense, waiting for me to lose it again.

"I'm sorry." I could barely make my voice audible. "I don't know what's wrong with me."

Sark let out a long breath, relaxing a little bit. He turned and scooted back so he was sitting next to me, and I rested my head on his shoulder, suddenly exhausted. He gave me a few minutes to get it together before he started talking.

"That was pretty…brutal," he said quietly. "Worse than usual. What happened?"

I just shuddered, burying my face in my hand and hoping I would disappear. Then I noticed something on my left wrist. I felt Sark stiffen, and I knew he saw it too.

Pausing to make sure I wouldn't freak, Sark took my left hand and pulled my sleeve up. Sure enough, a blue circular symbol was glowing on the base of my wrist, the thin veins already starting to wrap up my arm.

"Oh no," I moaned, my hand beginning to shake.

Sark quickly pulled my sleeve back down, holding my hand in his. "Stay calm, okay? Panicking will only make it worse."

"Why is it coming back?" I asked, voice trembling.

"I don't know."

"Guess."

He sighed. "The only thing I can think of…is that maybe your power as the key only works at a certain time. Maybe there is a window and that's the only time it will manifest itself. And this…marks that."

"Oh." As much as it killed me, I knew he was right. It made sense.

I'm running out of time. I just didn't know the outcome. Would I turn into the monster? Is that what she meant when she said she was coming?

"But I don't know for sure," Sark said, hoping to keep me calm. "It could be anything. It could be nothing. I just…wish I knew."

Why am I such a freak?

We sat in silence for a few more minutes before Sark sighed again. "You know we have to go back now, right?"

I shook my head. "You go back. I'm staying here."

"I'm not—"

"It makes absolutely no sense for me to sit around in the same place and wait for someone to find me." I lifted up my left arm. "Especially with that thing. Especially if you're right. I've got to be far away from all of you when…whatever is going to happen happens."

"What makes you say that?" He tried to look at my face, but I kept my head down. "What aren't you telling me?"

"Nothing." A picture of the disgusting monster came into my head, and I cringed. "But I'm the key, Sark. We've known that for a long time now, and we've known that I would turn into something eventually. And it can't be anything good, right? I've got to make sure you all don't get hurt in the mix."

"That's not your job." He didn't sound convinced. "And unless you're hiding something from me, I don't think that's going to happen."

I rolled my eyes. "And you know everything, right?"

"Right."

"Look," I said, staring at the mountains ahead, "it's not that I want to leave. I don't. But I have to. Staying in one place is just begging for trouble, especially when Dalton and unknown crazy people know I'm around there. You should leave too."

"I can't—" Sark started.

"I know you can't." I kept my disappointment out of my voice. "You have to stay and help Alaina, and that's okay. But I have to go."

"And where would you go?" He started rubbing his thumb against his ring finger.

"I wouldn't go anywhere. That's the point."

"You hate living on the run like that."

"It beats the alternative." *I can't be the one that kills you all.*

"You really think you could do it?" The challenge in his voice wasn't like him. "You have one arm that works, you can barely walk, and you can't sleep for more than an hour without screaming. No offense, but you wouldn't last a day."

Before I could argue, he picked me up off the ground and slid me carefully back into the car. Slamming my door shut, he stalked around and got in himself.

"Sark," I said as he fumbled for the keys and started the car. "I really can't go back with you."

"Yes, you can." I could make out his shadow from the dashboard lights in the darkness: his jaw and hands were clenched tight. He was more upset than I thought.

"We both know I can't."

"Do we?" His voice was edgy as he sped down the street. "Because I'm thinking it's just you."

"You have to at least consider—"

"I have considered it. I've considered everything, and you're staying with me. End of discussion."

"But you have no idea what I could turn into," I protested.

"Oh, and you do?"

I refused to answer that. "Stop the car. I'm getting out."

He ignored me and pressed the gas pedal harder.

"Don't you get it?" I asked, my voice rising. "I don't *want* to go back. I don't *want* to sit around and wait for my worst nightmares to find me. I can't live with myself knowing that I could kill the rest of you just by existing." I tried to turn it on him the way he was turning it on me. "Is that what you want for me? Dragging me back there and forcing me to stay is just going to make me miserable. It's not going to fix anything."

"I'm not trying to fix anything," he said evenly. "And you'd be miserable no matter where you were. I'm just doing what I think is best."

"Best for who? I am going to kill you all." I didn't know how I could drive this into his head. "You know that better than all of us."

"I don't know anything."

"Yes, you do! Please, Sark, I can't do that to them. I can't do that to you. Do you think I want that hanging over my head?"

"We're not talking about this anymore."

"You can't do that."

"Arie, drop it."

"No. Why won't you at least try to look at this realistically?"

Sark shook his head. "I'm not doing this."

"Why are you—"

"Because I can't, Arie," he interrupted harshly, making me jump. "I know you should go, but I can't come with you, and I can't live like that again, wondering if you're okay, or if you've been caught, or if you're dead or alive." His hands tightened around the steering wheel. "I'm sorry, but I can't do it. So just accept the fact that you can't control everything and deal with it."

I sat in stunned silence, keeping my eyes on my hands. It was a few minutes before I felt like he was calm enough that I could speak.

"You know, Sark," I said quietly, "you can't control everything either. I know you try, but you can't."

He let out a breath that seemed to last forever. Then he said almost inaudibly, "I know."

We stopped talking after that. I knew he had to be tired, and I offered to drive, but of course he said no, so I settled into the silence, watching the road and trying my hardest to not fall asleep.

"So, are you going to tell me about it?" Sark asked after a while, when he'd cooled off a bit.

I decided to play stupid. "About what?"

"I've never seen you try so hard to stay awake. And you've never thrown up after a nightmare before. It must've been pretty bad."

It was. "And?"

"Are you going to tell me?"

"What's there to tell?"

"I'm taking that as a no."

I didn't answer; I wasn't getting into that now. Or ever.

Thankfully, Sark let it go. I went back to keeping myself awake, which was hard. The quiet darkness was calming. I yawned several times and had to wipe the water out of my eyes. Pulling the visor down, I looked in the mirror to try and get out what was left in my eye. But instead of my eyes staring back at me, I saw *hers*.

I screamed and threw the visor back up, instinctively kicking the dashboard in front of me, and Sark almost swerved off the road.

"What's wrong?" he demanded, trying to watch me and the road at the same time.

How could she be here? That was a dream! I glanced fearfully around the dark car, imagining what could be lurking beneath the shadows.

"Arie, behind us or in the mirror?" Sark asked, trying to decide if he should stop or floor it.

"Mirror," I answered breathlessly.

He slowed the car down, then reached over and pulled the visor down. I cringed, but only saw me. The terrified me, not the monster me.

"Sorry, I, uh…" I cleared my throat. "I thought I saw something. It's fine."

Sark let out a long breath through his teeth. "You can't scare me like that."

"Sorry."

I thought he was going to ask more about it, but he didn't. I had no idea what I would've said if he did. How could anyone explain that kind of insanity?

We drove the rest of the way in silence. Sark would glance at me from time to time, but never brought anything up. I knew he was thinking the same thing I was.

What is wrong with me?

21

The rest of February went on without much excitement. Mara took it upon herself to celebrate Valentine's Day. She drafted Hadley, Brennan, and Lucy to help her in her endeavors: Brennan and Lucy wanted to help change the monotonously dank atmosphere, while I was pretty sure Hadley just wanted an excuse to eat a bunch of sugar. The kitchen and main room were decorated with anything anyone could find that was red, Mara made every dessert under the sun, and valentine notes were written and passed out to everyone. A few infecteds got into the party, but most remained uninterested. Some people found it hard to celebrate when life sucked so much. Brennan said that the best time to celebrate was when life sucked the most.

Hadley presented me with my 'special' card made by him, Mark, and Lucy, that said I was a 'strong hero sent back from heaven' and was 'deeply missed' and that I 'made games funner.' It was probably one of the best things anyone has ever given me, and it helped me work into his celebratory spirit. Even Sark was part of it all. Hadley was hesitant at first, but eventually delivered Sark his own valentine covered in barely legible eight-year-old boy penmanship.

"You are a good at being a good guy even though you used to be scary. Thanks for bringing Arie back," was all it said. Sark thanked Hadley coolly, but I thought he appreciated it more than he let on. He hadn't taken it out of his wallet since.

I tried to stay out of everyone's way as best as I could, melting into the background and keeping myself busy. Since my last terrifying nightmare, I slept even less often. To my horror, that didn't keep the monstrous me away from me. She popped up *everywhere*: in the bathroom mirror, the ice, the black TV, and in my head every time I closed my eyes. Thankfully I had learned to expect her—I didn't visibly freak out anymore when I saw her. I was going to keep her mysterious existence a secret at all costs, even from Sark. He was keeping close watch over me, and I knew he was trying to figure out what was wrong. I just did my best to give him nothing to go on.

Hadley hung around me a lot too, which made the work I gave myself to do much more entertaining. He talked my ear off constantly and I listened absentmindedly. It was interesting to get to see the world from his eight-year-old perspective. Everything was so simple.

Today I was folding towels in the kitchen when he found me, towing a girl behind him. I'd seen her around before but had never talked to her—she was about twelve years old, fairly small, and really quiet. Her hazel eyes were locked on me in a way that made me uncomfortable.

"Arie!" Hadley called loudly, even though he was right next to me. "Arie, guess what?"

I used my one hand to fold the last towel. My hurt arm was out of the sling but hung uselessly at my side. "What?"

"I want to show you someone." He gestured to the girl. "This is my friend Jacklynn. We play sometimes. She's really nice. She's the one that helped me put hearts on the wall downstairs. It was even her idea! But I helped a lot too."

"Hi Jacklynn," I said, giving her a smile. "I'm Arie. It's nice to meet you."

She opened her mouth to talk, but Hadley beat her to it. "She hasn't met you yet because she was scared of you." Jacklynn's eyes went huge, but Hadley continued, oblivious. "She was scared to meet you, and I thought that was silly 'cause you're really nice. So, I said she should meet you. And now you did."

Jacklynn mumbled something incoherent, her eyes glued to her shuffling feet.

"Hey, it's okay," I told her. "I'm not really that scary. It's really nice to meet Hadley's friend. What are you guys going to do today?"

"We're going to play Battleship," Hadley informed me. "Then make paper airplanes but fly them downstairs so Alaina doesn't get mad this time."

"Good call. Have fun."

"Okay we will!" Hadley yelled, already out the door, dragging poor Jacklynn along with him.

I put the folded towels away, checked with Mara to see if I could do anything else, then decided to head downstairs to see what Hadley and Jacklynn were up to. Sark met me halfway there and came with me.

The basement only had a few stragglers—thankfully most people liked to hang out upstairs. Hadley and Jacklynn were sitting on the floor in the far corner, both heavily focused on their Battleship game. A small table covered in papers had been shoved into the other corner. Three kids sat around it—one I recognized as Kayla—completely absorbed in whatever it was they were reading. Carl and Liam were working on fixing the TV, while Alaina, Brennan, and Mark were watching from the couch.

I went over and watched the Battleship tournament between Hadley and Jacklynn for a bit. It couldn't hold my attention forever though, and eventually something caught my eye. I wandered hesitantly over to the table where Kayla and her friends were working.

Sure enough, I recognized the papers they were so engaged in: they were all of Sark's files he used to keep in his library, the ones about the formula. One of the folders even had a stain on it from when I had spilled my drink one day long ago. They seemed to be from another life.

Kayla noticed my interest, but didn't offer an explanation. I couldn't tell if she would be annoyed by me or not.

"What are you doing?" I finally asked as I tapped my foot against the ground. It was ridiculous that a simple interaction like this made me so nervous.

The two boys that were sitting with her looked up at

me—I realized that the dirty blond-haired one was the boy that dug a bullet out of me—then went right back to their reading.

Kayla adjusted her glasses and gestured to a thick file. "Stephen White was a genius."

"He was the formula guy, right?" I was working hard to remember information from so long ago. "He was the one who wanted to reverse it."

"Yeah."

"Well, did he…I mean, did he get close? Does it work?" I didn't know if I even dared to hope.

Kayla sighed, took her glasses off, and rubbed her temples. "Yeah, it does. That's the worst part."

"What?" The blow of her casual remark hit me harder than I was expecting. I collapsed into an empty chair next to her. "Are you serious?"

She cleaned her glasses as she spoke. "Stephen White dedicated his life to reversing the formula, which only seemed to interfere with Alexis' work rather than advance it," she explained. "Eventually, interests conflicted too much, and White took his work elsewhere. Alexis doesn't tolerate that. White's success only magnified the situation, and Alexis finally decided to demonstrate the consequences. Nobody has tried to leave since…until…" she trailed off uncertainly.

We both glanced at Sark at the same time, who had appeared next to us during our conversation. He didn't seem like he really approved of Kayla filling me in but did nothing to stop it. Alaina was there too, standing slightly behind him with a frustrated expression.

I turned back to Kayla. "But it worked? Why haven't we done anything?"

"No offense, Arie," Alaina said, "but you're a little late. We've been through this only a million times:

reversal is possible, but part of his work is missing. And even if we could figure it out—"

"Could we do it?"

"The logistics of it are quite extensive," Kayla said, "but infection is a pretty complex process itself. This research points to the idea that White actually had successful trials of reversal, but we can't confirm that. Alexis had prohibited that work, causing White to record it somewhere other than Alexis' database, which is all Sark has access to. Unless we find the organization who aided him, then we're stuck with what we have, and that doesn't seem likely to happen. Especially considering Phoenix was such a dead end—"

"What's in Phoenix?"

Kayla shuffled through some of her papers before picking up a file. "It took a bit of digging, but we discovered that White may have a link to a scientific research facility in Phoenix. Sark took some of us down there a few months ago to see what we could find."

"And there was nothing there," I supplied, disappointed.

"There *was* a facility, but it had been shut down. Nobody could tell us anything about it." She let the file drop to the table. "Dead end."

No, there's got to be something there we could use. Any kind of information that could point us in the right direction.

"But think about it, Arie," Alaina said, twisting her red hair around her finger. "Do we really want it to be reversed?"

What? Alaina was the very last person on this planet who would ever let that question leave her mouth, even in joking.

She went on before I could decide if she was

serious. "Even if we do manage to reverse it, Alexis is going to hunt us down and waste us all anyway. It doesn't matter if we're infected or not, we're on his hit list. And I'd rather be a stronger freak than a normal person if it came down to literally fighting him for my life."

The arguments I had planned to make never came out of my mouth. I sat for a moment, taking that foreign idea in, realizing that she was right. In a horrible way, she was absolutely right. We were in too far now.

But I can't afford to think like that.

"What about me?" I asked Kayla, the words spilling out faster than I wanted them to. I hated sounding so desperate. "Is there even a chance it would work?"

Kayla glanced at Sark again. I didn't have to turn to see his expression.

"Please just tell me," I said. "I'm already expecting the worst."

"I, uh…I can't…" She sighed. "Look, I can't make promises. This is all strictly speculation."

"That's all I'm asking for."

She bit her lip, contemplating for a moment. I figured Sark must've laid down the law pretty firmly about keeping me out but was hoping she'd see it my way. We were both infected. We had an unspoken connection that ran deeper than whatever scare tactics Sark could use, even if we didn't really know each other.

The dark-haired boy sitting across from us responded before she did. "And you want it reversed?" he asked curiously. "For yourself, I mean."

"Yeah, of course I do." I shook my head uncertainly. "Why wouldn't I?"

The boy shrugged. "If you wanted whatever power

you can have for yourself. I'm sure there's some way to give you all the superhuman abilities too, once the key fixes the formula."

That idea was so foreign to me that it took me a moment to understand what he was saying. "No. Absolutely not. I've never wanted any of it. I only care about getting rid of it so other people can't have it."

The boy raised an eyebrow. "Really?"

Why is he so surprised? "Yeah, really." I looked at Kayla, hoping that she would explain reversal to me now that my motives had been deemed pure.

"Each infected is a failure of the formula experiment," she said. "I'm assuming you're aware of this. There is nobody out there that is one hundred percent infected, and we are all varying degrees of infected ourselves." She gestured upstairs. "You know Dustin, the skinny boy with the Rubik's cubes?"

I nodded.

"I don't know for certain, but I would imagine he is less infected than Alaina: she's stronger, smarter, and faster—not just from the skill set she's developed but from infection itself. Let's say Dustin is twenty percent infected. That would put Alaina around forty-five percent infected. For reversal, you have a better chance of success the less infected you are, so reversal would most likely work on Dustin because of how little his infection extends, where it would be more of an uncertainty with Alaina."

I glanced at Alaina. She was glaring at the ground, her mouth pressed into a thin line. I wondered how many times she had had this conversation, either with Kayla or in her head. That couldn't be easy for her to hear.

If it won't work on Alaina, then there can't be much

hope for me.

"How much do you think I am infected?" I asked, leaning forward.

Instead of answering, Kayla looked to the blond kid sitting next to her. He detached himself from his reading to answer me.

"It's hard to give exact numbers, but I would easily peg you over sixty percent." His eyebrows furrowed, as if he were studying me. "You just don't seem…I guess I imagined you wouldn't be so…human. I thought the key would be more robotic, and dead inside, not really even a person anymore. But you're very much a person. It makes it more complicated this way."

"How so?"

The kid glanced at Sark again, which drove me insane, but at least he didn't stop talking.

"Your body is so intertwined with the formula—especially after several years of living with it—that reversal would be an extremely complex process, if it were even possible at all." He pointed his pen to a bunch of headache-inducing diagrams in front of him. "We would literally have to rip the formula from your biological makeup at the molecular level, which would completely decimate your anatomy." He slowed down his words, not meeting my eyes anymore. "It…it would probably reverse infection, but…what's left…"

The anticipation that had been building without permission suddenly exploded into actual hope. Why wasn't anyone more excited about this?

"So, it would work?" Just the thought of success was cause for celebration. I could stop the destruction. I could get rid of the monster. I could win.

I need to go to Phoenix. I've got to figure this out.

The boys and Kayla all stared at me with shocked

expressions.

Why are they so surprised? Of course I would be happy about this.

"Well yeah," Kayla said, eyeing me dubiously, "but you'd die."

My stomach fluttered. "Well, yeah, but that's it?"

"All right," Sark said, grabbing my hand and roughly pulling me out of the chair. "We're done here."

His cross objection seemed to be condemnation for everyone else. Kayla and the boys instantly went back to their work as if they'd never spoken to me in the first place. I knew they all obeyed Sark—most were probably still scared of him—but this was getting ridiculous. Even if I could talk to Kayla alone sometime, there was a good chance she wouldn't continue this conversation. Sark had a place here that I could never compete with.

Sark dragged me up the stairs before I could get another word out, Alaina following close behind. They backed me up into a corner, which was when I knew I had really stepped over some line.

How do they expect me to stay in line if they won't explain the boundaries?

"What has gotten into you, Arie?" Sark demanded, shaking his head in exasperation.

"What do you mean?" I loved Sark and all, but I needed space to breathe. "You should've told me that stuff a long time ago. Of course—"

"I'm not talking about that."

"Then *what*?"

"You're scared of your own reflection, you'll only do chores all day—which just tire you out—and Hadley is the only one you really talk to. You won't even try to work with your arm, or anything, really, and now you're sitting down to plot your own murder." He let out a long breath. "You're moving a little too fast downhill, don't you think?"

I opened my mouth to respond but couldn't really think of anything to say. Sark ran his hand through his hair, mumbled something under his breath, then finally turned and went back downstairs. I watched him go for a second before looking at Alaina.

She folded her arms across her chest. "Don't talk like that, Arie."

I threw my hand up in the air. "Like what?"

"Like you dying would be no big deal. It freaks him out." She cleared her throat. "And I'm not the biggest fan either."

I thought back on my conversation, realization dawning on me.

Reversal is the only thing I really want, but it would kill me, and I don't seem very concerned about that. Of course Sark would flip.

"Oh. I didn't mean it like that."

Alaina rolled her eyes. "Uh huh. Whatever." Then she left me in the corner.

A commotion erupted by the front door, and it took me a moment to figure out that a new infected had arrived. I couldn't get a glimpse of him but could hear as infecteds started rolling off a million questions. Walking slowly so not to draw attention to myself, I ducked behind the counter to listen, my intuition telling me something was wrong. Concentrating, I was able to make out the voices: babbling excitement that Alaina was trying to get ahold of, and a deep, gruff voice. It didn't sound right, like something was caught in his throat.

My body froze over. He wasn't a new infected—at

least not to me. The kid who tried to kill me was here, making conversation with the infecteds as if he were just an old friend.

"Was your handler following you?" Alaina was asking him. "Or anyone, really?"

"Nope," the kid answered coolly. "I've never had a handler. At least, not in the sense that you think."

"What? How does that work?"

"I don't know doll face, I guess I'm just special."

Hadley and Jacklynn came up the stairs, and he stopped when he saw me hiding behind the counter. I shook my head at him once.

Don't acknowledge me.

His face turned serious, and he ran back down the stairs, Jacklynn following.

Meanwhile, Alaina was about ready to rip my killer apart. "Look buddy, I don't care to know who you think you are, but if you're really going to stay here then you have to understand some rules. I don't know what kind of mommy issues you have, but I'm not here to—"

"Correct me if I'm wrong," he interrupted, "but I thought you were the one with the mommy issues, Alaina. And your dad isn't fond of you either, right?"

A shocked silence fell over the room, the kind of silence that had silence inside of it. You could hear a spider sneeze, the last sneeze a spider would ever sneeze because the world was about to end.

"How did you know that?" Alaina finally asked, her quiet voice shaking with fury. "How do you know my name?"

"I know everything about your messed up family." He continued to talk casually. "I know all about Hadley's parents, Peter's sister, Brennan's dark side, Lucy's uncle, Sasha's boyfriend, Tristan's guilt,

Kayla's brilliance. I know about the extermination order, about Neil and his 'club,' about your vain attempts to survive."

How does he know that? Who is this guy?

Hadley reappeared at the top of the stairs again, this time towing Sark behind him. Sark's eyes surveyed the room before resting on me. His head tipped toward the direction of the kid.

Is it him?

I nodded. Rage boiled in Sark's eyes, but his face remained smooth. He glanced up at the ceiling then back to me a few times before I understood what he meant.

The roof. He wants me to take the back stairs in the kitchen up to the roof. That way I could use the fire escape to get out of here without anyone noticing.

Sark nodded at me again, telling me he would take care of everyone else, then started typing on his phone. Bending down, he whispered something in Hadley's ear, causing Hadley to square his shoulders proudly, then they both went in separate directions: Hadley to the sleeping room and Sark outside.

The infecteds—well, mostly Alaina and Peter by the sound of it—were arguing with the kid, who seemed to know exactly how to get them riled up. A moment later, the kid shouted in surprised annoyance, and I heard something clunk against the ground.

Hadley's rocks. He was providing me with a distraction.

My reaction time was about as sprightly as a diseased turtle, but I hurried into the kitchen, praying the kid wouldn't notice. Scurrying past Mara and Lucy cleaning the stove, I jerked a heavy door open and started climbing the stairs as fast as my injured leg would let me. My calf exploded every time I went up a step, but I didn't allow myself to stop.

I had gone up one flight with two more to go when I heard the door open and shut, the sound echoing up the cavern.

"How's your leg holding up on these stairs?" the kid called, already halfway up the first flight. "Those bullets pack a wicked punch, don't they?"

Keep going, I pleaded with myself, though I knew it was no use. He was going to catch up to me. *Keep going.*

Mercifully, I reached the top of the stairs. I felt the wind as his hand barely missed grabbing my hair when I stumbled through the door and onto the roof. The bright sun beat down on me despite the frigid air, momentarily disorienting me. Registering that Sark was standing several yards away from me, I was somehow able to catch the gun that he threw. The second my fingers closed around the weapon, I skidded to a halt and spun around, stopping the kid in his tracks since the barrel of the gun was against his chest.

That was close, I thought, breathing hard. *That was way too close.*

"Hey beautiful," he greeted as if there wasn't a gun between us. "How ya been?"

"How have I…" I shook my head in disbelief. "Who are you? And why do you want me dead so badly?"

He chuckled. "Arie, there are a lot more people who want you dead than you realize. Of course, *I* don't really want you dead. I'm just doing my job. Remember?"

Sark stalked up next to me, his blazing eyes trained on the kid, aiming his own gun at him.

"Who sent you here?" I asked.

"Wouldn't you just love to know?"

I huffed in irritation. "Alexis? Dalton?"

The kid shook his head in amusement, beginning to pace slowly around the roof. Sark and I both stiffened, keeping our guns on him, but he didn't seem to notice. "I forget how naïve you all are. You think Alexis is the only one you should be afraid of? You think Dalton is the only one that's out to get you? There are more players in this game than you see. Alexis still doesn't know you're alive—which I would keep up as long as I could if I were you—but that really doesn't matter in the long run."

I shifted my weight; my leg was not handling the pressure well. "How would you know that? And all that about the infecteds…how do you know everything about them?"

"I told you: I know *everything*." His eyes narrowed like he was trying to see through me. "I know all about the demons you hide so well behind that pretty face of yours."

I blinked in surprise. *Could he really know about the monster in my head? The marks on my arms?*

"I know about your dad, your infection, and your life on the run; how you magically made Sark see the light; how Dalton killed Erika and kept you imprisoned for the last eight months."

I sucked in a sharp breath. *Who is this guy?*

"Come on, Arie, that's common knowledge by now. Plus, I've seen some of the security tapes." To my alarm, he looked to Sark. "You should've heard her, a few months in, screaming for you to come—"

I didn't know what happened. Some instinct took over, my finger pulled, and I shot the gun. The bullet went exactly where I had wanted it to go: whizzing right past the kid's face, so close that he probably felt the air as it went by. He froze, turning his attention back to my murderous expression.

"I missed on purpose," I told him, my voice cold.

For the first time, he seemed a bit shaken. "Yeah, I gathered that." Of course, his uneasiness only lasted for a second. He grinned playfully again. "Touchy subject, huh?"

"Shut up or I will shoot you."

"I'm just curious as to how much you actually remember," he went on. "With trauma like that, most people suppress—"

I pulled the trigger again, the bullet grazing his left shoulder. He flinched, pressing his palm against the bleeding wound, but it didn't really seem to bother him.

"All right, all right," he said. "I can take a hint."

"A bullet is a heck of a hint." I didn't know how I was keeping my voice even. This guy was going to crush me for that. Just because we had guns on him didn't mean anything.

"I get it. After all, we're all in the same hell, right? We're just playing with different devils."

"Whatever helps you sleep at night."

He clapped his hands together and glanced at his wrist, as if checking the time on a watch that wasn't there. "Well, Sark called your fun agent friends, so I imagine they'll be here in the next few minutes to take me to the slammer. I guess my work here is done."

My eyebrows furrowed. "Aren't you here to kill me?"

He laughed. "Arie, if I were here to kill you, you'd already be dead."

"Then why—"

"Things aren't always black and white," he said, a new seriousness to his tone. "You'd do well to remember that."

"But—"

"Hey," he interrupted, winking at me. "You've just got to pick your battles sometimes. Isn't that what you say?"

That brought me up short. "Um, yeah, I think so. How did you…I mean, do I know you?"

"Of course you do."

Sark let out a warning sound through his teeth and spared me the briefest glance. "Arie."

"Why don't I remember you?" I asked, ignoring Sark.

"Arie," Sark said again, stepping slightly in front of me.

"Honestly Arie, I'm a bit disappointed," the kid admitted, ignoring Sark too. "I know you've tried your hardest to forget, consciously or otherwise, but I thought you would've recognized me a long time ago. Granted, the light wasn't great, but…"

"What are you talking about?" Something was stirring in my head, trying to break through muddled memories of…what? I was sure I had never seen this guy before.

"Arie." Sark's fury was building. "He's lying."

"Although I have to admit that I have been curious about you," the kid continued, focusing on me. "I've been wondering what you've been up to since you broke out, if you did any of the things you said you would. Looks like life hasn't been too kind. No sunshine and roses for you, huh?"

It all clicked together then, the puzzle that I'd been unconsciously solving. The wall came down and I remembered. I could now see that the shape of my killer's face matched the memories of my shadowed best friend. My shadowed *dead* best friend.

I sucked in a sharp breath as my hands started shaking, and I lowered my gun. It was impossible.

"Micah?" I whispered reverently. Sark glanced back at me, but I paid him no attention.

Something shifted in the kid's eyes—something too subtle for me to figure out—as he cleared his throat. Then in a somewhat lighter voice, the voice that was forever etched into my memory, he said, "Hey Arie."

I felt like I'd been hit by a dump truck. "But I…I don't…how did…you were…this whole time?"

Micah's smile faltered slightly, but he tried to not show it. "Yep. I'm still kickin'. Pretty amazing, right?"

"You're infected?" I asked, my voice breaking on the words. In hindsight it made sense. There was no way any normal person would survive what Dalton had put Micah through. Was I really so focused on my own miseries that I never noticed? How could he not tell me something like that?

Micah's alive. Micah's alive. Why wasn't this more exciting? A reunion like this shouldn't be so angry and cold and confrontational. I should be…and Sark…Sark was mad because…

Micah almost murdered me.

No. No that wasn't right. Micah would never hurt me.

"Arie," Sark ordered sharply, "walk away right now."

"No," I said, not really thinking. The indignation, outrage, and bitterness swelling inside me took over. I pushed Sark out of the way and stalked up to Micah. "You tried to kill me?"

Micah actually winced, giving me a small amount of satisfaction, but managed to keep up his attitude. "It would seem that way."

Sark grabbed my arm and yanked me away. "Arie, you get—"

"No," I snapped, jerking myself out of his grip. "You stay out of this." Ignoring the heated glare I got, I turned back to Micah.

This makes no sense. "If we didn't know you were infected, then why were you locked up in that prison?"

"Easy." He shrugged. "So I could get to know you."

"What about Dalton?"

"We live in a paranoid world, Arie. It only takes one faked mistake to get yourself locked up, and the right people to make sure you're in the right place. Dalton was too focused on his vendetta against you to give me a real second thought."

"Until we became friends."

The corners of his mouth pulled up. "Right."

"And to think I used to feel guilty about that," I scoffed. "I can't believe how much I've beaten myself up over you and…" I trailed off, fury taking my words. "How could you do that to me? Do you realize what that…I almost…it almost killed me." I clenched my fists, fighting the urge to hit him. "And you just walked out. No, not just walked out. You *died.* You died in front of me, then walked out and left me to burn." I tossed my gun onto the ground in frustration.

Micah nodded toward the gun. "You don't want that?"

"No!" I shouted.

That seemed to surprise him. "Why not?"

"Because I have no desire to shoot my best friend, something that you don't seem to have a problem with."

"Arie, let's be honest." He was still so calm. How could he be so calm? "You wouldn't be here without me. You would still be sitting in that prison waiting to die. We both know you could've gotten out long before you did, but you'd given up and I knew I had to do something to get you out."

I laughed in disbelief, skirting around the accusations. "*You* didn't get me out. *You* left me there."

"I paved the way for you, Arie. I died so you would wake up and realize what you were allowing to happen to yourself. I left up the information on the computer so you would know where to find Sark. I took out the security system so you could make it through the front gates." He gestured to me. "I didn't get you out, but you wouldn't have gone anywhere without me."

I wrapped my good arm around myself, suddenly feeling sick. "You…you were…you staged it? You were manipulating me?"

Can't I make my own decisions anymore? Do I know anything?

He stepped toward me. "I wasn't trying to—"

"You tricked me." I slapped my hand against my forehead. "I'm such an idiot!"

"I tricked you into doing what you really wanted and needed to do," Micah said, his overly patient tone starting to slip. I was getting to him. "You just wouldn't get up and do it yourself. It's hard for me to believe you regret it."

I glanced at Sark, who stood frozen as a statue, his mouth hanging open in outraged shock, his eyes on me.

"Of course I don't regret it," I said quietly.

"For the record, I told you so." Micah nodded at Sark, only slightly teasing. "I told you they would want you back."

I took a shaky breath. "Why are you doing this to me?"

Micah sighed. "The thing is, Arie, there is so much going on that you don't know about. So much that you aren't ready to understand. This is bigger than you— you just haven't seen the whole picture yet. And once you do, you'll thank me." There was a bitterness to his tone that I couldn't figure out.

I huffed in irritation. "You're still not going to tell me who sent you?"

He couldn't hide it—I caught another wince underneath the bravado. "Nope."

"And that didn't...*bother* you at all?"

Micah looked at the wall again, his jaw set. "I take my job very seriously. I don't ask questions."

That stung, more than I was willing to admit. "Well I'm glad it works out for you," I said bitterly. "It seems like the perfect job for you."

His eyes glinted. "I wouldn't make assumptions," he muttered back.

"Maybe you should go talk to Dalton. I bet he could get you a great gig."

He sucked in a sharp breath, turning toward me furiously. "Don't you *ever* compare me to that—"

"It only makes sense," I spat back. "Is that why you were there? To get some training on how to make my life a living hell?"

"No! I would never—"

"Hurt me? News flash, you're a little late on that one."

"I couldn't...you were—"

"Let me guess." I rolled my eyes. "I was your little ray of sunshine. How sweet."

"You're not listening to me!"

"What's there to listen to? Filthy lies from a devil that loves to play both sides? Sorry, but I'm done listening to that."

"I'm not like them!" he yelled.

"You are *just* like them!" I screamed back. "And I hate you for it!"

Suddenly, the door to the stairs burst open, Brody, Deron, and Lindsey filing through. They were barely there for five minutes. Micah surrendered with a grin on his face, giving me one last wink before they took him away, which was when something dawned on me.

He put Lindsey's remote in my pocket, I realized, remembering the night he almost killed me. *He gave me a chance.*

The chaos in my head was overwhelming, and it took me a bit to remember where I was and that Sark was with me. I turned to him, locking up when I saw his face.

I was in trouble. Heaps of it.

Sark closed his eyes and took a deep breath, trying to keep himself in check. When he spoke, his words were slow and controlled. "Don't you ever, *ever*, go against me like that again. If I tell you to leave, you leave. Understand?"

I sighed. "Sark, I had to—"

His eyes snapped open. "Understand?"

"I had to talk to him," I said, my voice starting to shake. "I had to. It was important."

I needed him to accept this. I needed him to acknowledge the fact that I had just been hit with a blow that I might not recover from.

"I don't care how important it was," Sark snapped. "Do you realize what could've happened?"

"Of course I—"

"No, you don't. You obviously have no—"

"You don't understand this!" I yelled, taking a step

toward him. "You could *never* understand this."

"Fine then." His voice hardened as he gestured to me. "Explain it."

"He…he was my…more than my best friend."

"Apparently, since you chose to camp out with him instead."

"What's that supposed to mean?"

Sark gritted his teeth and shook his head. I could not believe he was acting like this.

"What is wrong with you?" I asked in exasperation. "Why are you being such a jerk?"

"*I'm* the jerk?" His voice got louder. "He was *paid* to murder you, and he almost got away with it."

"I know! I know what he did, but Micah saved me, Sark! He saved me in ways you don't even know."

"Yeah, you're right. He's a great friend, Arie," Sark said, his voice sardonic. "I'm really glad you've got him around, you know, when he's not out killing people."

"It beats having you," I countered impulsively. "At least Micah *tried* to keep me alive. You were only good for pity parties and drinking yourself to death."

As soon as I said the words, I begged the universe to let me take them back. Pain flashed in Sark's eyes, his mouth pressed into a thin line, as he nodded once.

I felt the color drain from my face, my veins scalding with regret. "No, Sark, I didn't…just let me…"

He turned and stalked away from me, heading down the fire escape.

"Sark, please wait. I'm sorry…I didn't mean that. You have to let me…I just…"

I tried to follow him, but it was no use. He was much faster than me, disappearing around the neighboring building before I could even figure out how to get on the stupid ladder. My leg finally gave out and I collapsed into the built-up snowbank on the roof.

This is insane.

A voice echoed in my head, making me freeze. It was my voice, but it wasn't me. It was *her*.

I told you, Arie. You can't win. I'm getting stronger, and you're getting weaker. It's only a matter of time.

"No." My hands started shaking. "No. I can fix this. I can…"

Do what? she sneered. *What can you possibly do?* She laughed when I didn't have an answer. *We both know that I'm right. You can keep denying it all you want, but the truth remains. I'm just happily watching as you run yourself and everyone around you into the ground. Sooner or later, I'll be the one in charge. You can't stop it.*

"Yes I can," I argued, an idea coming to me. "Watch me."

Hauling myself off of the ground, I went back inside. It took a few minutes to get the address I needed without getting caught, but soon I was in the garage, sliding into the first car. Starting the engine, I pressed the buttons on the screen next to the steering wheel, hoping I could figure out how to make it do what I wanted. Finally, I was able to set the navigation system to lead me to my destination: Phoenix, Arizona.

I'm going to get rid of you, I told her. *One way or another.*

Taking a deep breath, I turned on the heater and started driving down the street.

22

It was amazing what driving down the freeway at night while blasting music could do for someone. I felt like a different person.

According to the robot lady giving me directions from the car speakers, it would take almost thirteen hours to get to Phoenix, which wasn't ideal but whatever. If I accounted for the extremely quick stops I would have to make, I'd roll into town at about six in the morning. I'd go to the research facility Kayla was talking about, poke around a little bit, see what I could uncover, and go from there. Of course, there was a giant chance that this would be a complete waste of time. I didn't care. At least I was doing something somewhat useful. At least I was alone.

It was easier to be alone. It was easier to be hidden in a dark car by myself, knowing nobody was following me, with only the radio and the navigation lady to talk to. It was easier to pretend like nothing was wrong when I was the only one watching my performance.

The hardest part for me was keeping my excitement in check. Any kind of enthusiasm or expectation concerning this whole trip could lead to disastrous consequences, but I couldn't help myself. The 'what if this solves everything' was too much to pass up on, even if I only allowed a tiny bit of it in my head. Instead, I tried to think of other things, like guessing the songs on the radio, counting red cars, and looking at other states' license plates.

From time to time my thoughts would wander to Sark. I knew I should at least call him and let him know I was okay, but I felt like that would make everything worse. Granted, me running off to Phoenix without telling him was only going to make him angrier with me, which I couldn't bring myself to care about at the moment. I had just ruined everything already.

Better to ask forgiveness than permission.

The drive wasn't as bad as I thought it would be, time wise. I enjoyed the pressure-free time to myself, singing along with the radio at the top of my lungs, making friends with the nice navigator lady that I had named Barbara. It was when the gaslight went on the first time that I started to get uneasy. Heaven forbid I would have to get out of my safe car and venture into the world of a gas station.

I had known this whole idea would be risky—I wasn't stupid—so I had planned for this. Taking the next exit, I found a small convenience store and pulled into the parking lot.

The best part about commandeering one of Sark's cars was all the extra stuff he kept in it, including back up credit cards. I opened the glove box and took one out, flipping it around a few times in my hand before sliding it in my back pocket.

Okay, you can do this. In and out. No big deal.

I took a deep breath, then jerked the car door open and stepped outside, walking briskly through the automatic doors of the store and keeping my head down. Grabbing a basket, I went all the way to the back of the store before circling around to the aisle I needed. Being in such a bright space made me feel jumpy and exposed.

Hastily—but still trying to look normal—I grabbed an array of things off of the shelves: hair elastics, bobby pins, three blonde hair pieces, glasses with fake lenses, nail stickers, two different hoodies, a flashlight, a small notebook, a writing utensil, and a drawstring backpack. Then I went to the food section, making sure to get a six pack of soda, two water bottles, two bags of potato chips, two granola bars, a bag of chocolate covered pretzels, three travel sized boxes of cookie cereal, and a pack of spearmint gum. I knew I wouldn't be able to make myself go into many more stores—it was just too nerve-wracking for me—so I made sure I'd have enough supplies to last me through my long drive and the days spent in Phoenix.

That should be good, I thought. *Time to check out.*

I absolutely hated checking out. There should be a holiday to celebrate whoever invented self-checkout (Best. Idea. Ever.) and a law that says every store should have one. Including a small convenience store en route to Phoenix.

I hesitantly went up to the only lane available, pleased that there was no line. I'd be out of here in no time. The woman behind the counter gave me a sweet smile when I walked up, which told me she was one of those 'social' people and would talk to me. I added a bag of sour gummy worms to my stockpile for comfort.

"Did you find everything okay?" she asked politely.

Giving a small grin, I nodded, tapping my foot against the floor as I grabbed Sark's card from my pocket.

She surveyed my basket as she pulled things out, her huge smile unwavering. "This looks exciting. What's the occasion?"

"My friend's birthday," I mumbled in response.

"Oh fun! How old is she?"

I don't want to talk to you. "She's turning eighteen."

"That's such a great age. You have your whole life ahead of you, you know? There's just so many possibilities out there."

I bit my lip to hold back a snort. *Yeah, if only.*

The lady was young, but she worked at the pace of a senile great-grandmother. It felt like hours had passed when she finally bagged my last item and gestured for me to swipe my card, still beaming from ear to ear. I complied quickly, then panicked when the screen asked me for a PIN number.

What would Sark's PIN number be?

I knew if I hesitated that would come off suspicious, so I punched in the first thing that came into my head— my password for everything as a kid—and held my breath.

It worked and I couldn't help but smile a bit.

November first. My birthday.

"Thanks for coming in," the lady told me as she handed me a receipt. "Have a great night."

"You too." I took the receipt, grabbed my bags, and graciously fast walked back to my car.

Good job. I allowed myself two gummy worms for the victory. *That was slick.*

Yeah, good job, princess, the monster echoed in my head. I could almost see her rolling her freakish eyes. *Convenience stores are nasty places. I'm so proud.*

Shut up. I made a wish on some unknown star that Phoenix would hold something for me. I couldn't live with this chick in my head for much longer.

I spent about fifteen minutes applying my new supplies to myself, knowing it wasn't much, but at least it was something. People wouldn't look at me and think: *hey, isn't that the infected that's supposed to be dead?* At least, that was the idea.

After I secured the blonde pieces in my hair and put the stickers on my nails (what infected had the time to do their nails? Besides Sasha, of course), I slid the glasses onto my nose and took a quick look in the mirror. It would work.

It didn't take long for me to find a gas station and fill up the car. Before I knew it, I was speeding down the road, thinking how weird it was to be in this kind of groove again. Granted, living on the run was easier when you had a car and a credit card, but still. The 'disguise, blend, run, hide' patterns felt familiar and foreign all at the same time.

This used to be my life. I couldn't quite tell how I felt about that, so I decided to try to ignore it.

The rest of the drive wasn't bad, all things considered. I hit a slump between two and four—my consciousness was owed entirely to sugar—and had to stop for gas again, but that was it. No major catastrophes.

It was quarter after six when I passed the sign that welcomed me to Phoenix. Of course, there were a million people everywhere, rushing to get to work or school on time and begin their day. The traffic slowed me down; I drove around for several hours, making mental notes of where different things were located in relation to others. When traffic was at a standstill, I drew on a napkin, creating a rough map of the city. I was here on important business. Getting lost was not in the cards.

I felt like the car wasn't flexible enough, so I parked it at a grocery store four blocks away from the address I'd found in Kayla's files, packed my backpack full of supplies, and started walking.

I was halfway up the third block when I saw the sign, which made me pick up my pace. The sign was under construction, so it was partly covered by giant tarps, but I could see the word 'research.'

This has got to be it. Please still be here.

There were several big trucks parked at the site, construction workers milling around the vehicles and the property. I stopped in front of the spiffy establishment, looking at the front doors almost in longing, wondering what the crap I was supposed to do now.

One of the workers noticed me standing there gawking like an idiot. He strolled up to me, carrying a shovel, and I automatically assumed he was going to kill me.

"Can I do somethin' for you?" he asked, gruff but polite at the same time.

I bit my lip and started to shake my head, totally

prepared to walk really fast in the other direction.

Speak now or forever hold your peace.

"Actually, yes," I mumbled, then cleared my throat. "I was just wondering if you could give me some information. I'm looking for someone."

He propped his shovel against the ground to lean on, then gestured to me. "I'll do what I can."

"My, uh, uncle used to know a man who works here—or, at least, he did." I brushed my hair behind my ear. "His name was Stephen White. Do you know where I could find him?"

The man nodded to himself, his voice taking a distrustful tone. "And what business does your uncle have with White?"

"Well, he's sick, and he used to know Stephen White a long time ago. They were research partners or something like that." I shrugged. "I guess he's hoping to reconnect before…you know."

The man relaxed slightly. "Sorry to hear that. Wish I could help you out, but White hasn't shown his face around here in years."

Yeah, dead people usually don't do that. "Why not?"

"White used to be one of the top researchers here about…" He thought for a second. "Eight years ago, maybe. Really smart guy. He always had a million different projects goin' on at once. Worked here for years. Then one day, went to the boss askin' for money to fund a secret project. Wouldn't tell anyone about it, just said it was important. Of course, the boss said no, but that wasn't good enough. White looted 'em for all they were worth. He took off, this place went to ruin, and nobody has set eyes on him since. It's been almost five years and this place is finally ready to get back on its feet. It was a big deal, back in the day, you know. Front page news."

The man took a step closer to me, leaning in slightly. "Between you and me, I'd bet money he's dead as a doornail."

I raised an eyebrow. "Really? Why do you say that?"

"Word on the street was he was in somethin' deep. My guess is he owed some big shot a sack of Benjamins, and when the know-it-all didn't pay on time…" He dragged his thumb across his neck.

Why would White owe Alexis money? He was an employee. Alexis would've funded anything he needed, except…except reversal experiments.

"Do you have any idea what he might've been researching?" I asked. "What the secret project was?"

He shook his head. "No idea. White was high up in the biology and chemistry departments—probably somethin' to do with that, would be my guess anyway."

Reversal. That has to be what he was doing.

"So basically White was the one who got this place shut down?" I asked, just to make sure I had the story straight.

The man nodded, a glint of anger in his eyes. "My brother's in the presidency for the facility. I'm here with my construction crew to make a few renovations before it opens again next month."

"Construction, huh?" I muttered. "What happens to everything inside when you're doing construction?"

"It's all kept in a storage unit down on the east side. Safe keepin', you know? Wouldn't want any of that stuff damaged."

"No kidding." I folded my arms across my chest. "Well, thanks for your time."

He nodded. "Sorry about your uncle. Wish I could've been more help," he said as I turned to walk away.

You were a huge help, I thought, heading back to my car so I could check out my map and make a plan.

23

It took me the entire day to figure out the storage unit issue. I had to research storage places in the city and check out each one. Once I found the right place, I realized it should've been obvious: it was owned by a man with the last name Oscarson, which was the same name on the construction vehicles. Then I had to understand security measures and break in, all without getting caught. It was quite the ordeal, but I kinda liked it. I felt like a spy or something.

It was getting dark outside, and I was afraid to turn on any lights, so I had to use my flashlight. The unit was ginormous, full of so much science-y looking equipment that it made me a little sick. My high school chemistry class had not been kind to me, and it felt like science had thrown up over the whole building.

Going slowly, I stepped around machinery and models, not really sure what I was looking for. It was in the back corner that I saw the huge array of dozens of filing cabinets.

Bingo. This has got to be it. I grabbed my notebook, pencil, and a granola bar from my backpack, then went to work.

First, I wrote down a few notes on what the construction guy told me, just to make sure I didn't forget:

Research facility reopening next month after five (?) years of inactivity. White used to be high up (emphasis on biology and chemistry), wanted to fund secret project, stole the money and took off. Hasn't been back since. Assuming project had to do with reversal, considering money shouldn't have been a problem if Alexis approved.
Questions: how long ago was White killed? How much time lapsed between him stealing the money and his death? How long did he work on reversal and how far did he get?

Satisfied, I opened the nearest cabinet and started reading through the labels on the files, which ranged from animal breeds to the periodic table to rock formations, and everything in between. For hours, I was lost in a sea of science—it was awful.

This is impossible. I'm never going to find anything in here.

A headache was stirring as I opened the fourth cabinet marked 'chemistry department.' My eyes went down the row of manila folders until one caught my attention. Philo Castor.

Philo Castor! That's it! I ripped the folder from its place and opened to the first page. Castor was the man who first created the infecting formula a long time ago. If there was a file that would help me, it was this one.

The first few pages were complicated diagrams, full of weird shapes and symbols and numbers that meant absolutely nothing to me, except one that matched the mark on my arm.

Interesting.

I couldn't decipher what any of them were for, but I recognized them, and knew Kayla had copies of all of them back at the club. Whatever they were, they weren't new.

There was a small excerpt on Castor himself, but held nothing I didn't already know: he was a scientist in the Dark Ages with a utopian vision; his work was passed down through the years, often attracting cult-like organizations dedicated to bringing his vision forth, blah, blah, blah.

The next page was more what I was looking for, and I took brief notes as I read. It talked about the formula itself, about how it was designed to heighten the senses, strengthen the body, enhance the brain; how the subjects were to become fortified beings, almost super-human, their consciences erased and emotions void. But—like we already knew—it was incomplete. According to the file, the formula couldn't even produce a failed infected until after Castor's death. The formula killed on contact until the necessary changes were made, but even then it couldn't produce the perfect human it was created to make. Then it was discovered that someone could provide the missing components of the formula through their biological makeup.

The key. It's talking about me.

It was simple. If you could find the key, you add in their special biological makeup (whatever that means) and boom: you've got a working formula. As long as the key is in its peak phase, it will work.

Peak phase, huh? I glanced at my wrist even though my sleeve was covering it. *Is that what the tattoo means?*

However, if the key had been 'breached' then everything changed. I had never heard the term before, but it sounded like a big deal. If the key had been breached, extra steps had to be taken during the peak phase to ensure success. If even the slightest thing went wrong during those extra steps, it was all over—the key was void.

So Alexis would want me 'unbreached' or whatever that means. That would make it easier, which means I should work on getting myself breached. I wondered why I had never heard of that before. *Does Sark know about this? Does Alexis even know?*

I kept looking through the pages, but couldn't find anything else on breaches, infecteds, or keys. Nothing about glow in the dark tattoos, evil twins in your head, the time frame of when she might take over, or what 'take over' even meant.

Then I read: "Until the key finishes the formula, giving the formula to subjects will only result in unreliable products, each having varying degrees of the abilities that a finished formula promises. Speculation over reversing the effects of the formula by—"

I urgently turned the page to finish, almost ripping

it in my haste, only to see the back of the file.

"No!" I yelled, pounding my fist against the floor. I flipped through the file again, then glanced through the ones still in the cabinet. That was it. "No, no, no!"

Slamming the cabinet shut, I rested my head in my hands and groaned. I'd been so close. It had literally been right there. If only there was just one more page, if I could've just read the rest of that sentence, just a few more words…

And now I have nothing. Awesome.

I sat there stewing for another few minutes before collecting my belongings. I was tired and upset, and it was late. I'd go find a good place to sleep in the car, then figure out what to do in the morning. The thought of going back to Denver empty handed made me want to throw up.

Let's just deal with it later. That seemed to be my motto for everything lately.

Within five minutes I had repacked my backpack, put all the files back, closed the unit, and walked out into the night.

The parking lot I had left my car in was now empty. It must've been later than I'd guessed. Surveying the lot, I pulled the keys out of my jacket pocket, unlocked the car, and slipped inside, realizing too late that there was someone sitting in the passenger seat.

I screamed, but it was cut short when he slapped his hand over my mouth. Instinctively, I grabbed his wrist and twisted his arm the wrong way as hard as I could.

"Ow!" Sark exclaimed, yanking his hand away. "What was that for?"

It's just Sark. It's fine. I rested my head against the steering wheel and took a few deep breaths, calming myself down. "You can't do that to me."

"'You can't do that to me,'" he repeated derisively. "Right. But you can just run off to Phoenix without telling me. That makes perfect sense."

Here we go. "Sark—" I started.

"I don't want to hear it, Arie. Do you realize what you did? What if someone recognized you? What if someone knew—"

"No." Taking off the stupid glasses, I shook my head and reached for the car door handle. "I'm not doing this." Getting out of the car, I slammed the door shut and stalked the opposite direction, hearing his door open and shut too.

"Where do you think you're going?" he called after me.

I didn't answer. I kept going until he grabbed my arm and turned me around. "You're coming back with me. Now."

"No, Sark, I can't leave yet. I have to—"

"You have to *what*, Arie?" he yelled, and I flinched in spite of myself. "What could you possibly have to do?"

"I found the research place Kayla was talking about," I said, calmly trying to get through the wall of fury he'd built around himself. "I found it. I—"

"We already told you there was *nothing there*!" he cut me off. "What possessed you to think you could change that?"

"I talked to a man there," I continued anyway. "He told me everything was kept in a storage unit, so I went there and—"

"Let me guess: you couldn't find anything."

"There were files there, it's just…the reversal ones were…gone."

"What about you?" he asked, a hint of slow caution

drifting amid his barely contained eruption. "Did you find anything about the key?"

"Yeah, I did actually." I yanked the blonde pieces out of my hair. "I'm screwed! I'm so freaking screwed, but thanks so much for asking!"

I held my head in my hands, digging my fingernails into my skin, willing myself to keep it together.

This is tearing me apart.

"I'm sorry I left without telling you," I said slowly. "But I need to figure out how to not be the key. That's important and I need you to let me do that and not step in every five seconds. I mean, you're holding me on a leash here, Sark."

"A leash?" he repeated, half in awe, half mocking, and a hundred percent mad.

I lifted my head to see him looking up at the sky, muttering under his breath, trying to keep himself from getting more upset than he already was. This wasn't a good combination. We were both bombs wired to explode.

Just go home, I told myself, feeling the exhaustion starting to set in. *Just do what he says.*

"Fine," I muttered. "Let's go home." I stepped around him and stalked back to the car, getting in the passenger seat 'cause I knew he'd be even more peeved if I tried to drive.

He joined me about a minute later. Sliding into the driver's seat, he picked up the keys from where I had dropped them in the cup holder and put them in the ignition. But he didn't start the car. He just stared at the steering wheel.

"I'm sorry you feel that way," he started suddenly. He was mostly calm, but the underlying anger was still very present. "But you can't expect me to be clearheaded about reckless behavior. Not after…after…" he trailed off.

I hesitated. "After what?"

"After you…" He sighed. "After you died."

I waited, watching him watch the steering wheel, hoping he would continue and hoping he wouldn't.

"You know, that was the worst part…at times," he went on quietly, working to keep his voice even. "Seeing how you went in that glass room with a few scratches and came out charred to the bone. At least with…with Erika, I knew it was quick and relatively painless, but you…" He shook his head. "I've spent so much time obsessing over that little detail, those five minutes you were in the glass room, imagining what your last moments must've been like, wondering what might have happened if I had done something different—if I could've saved you. Every time I closed my eyes the last eight months, I saw you."

He cleared his throat, and his tone hardened up again. "So, forgive me if I seem to hold you on a leash, but I'd rather you be safe and angry at me than lose you again."

I wasn't sure what to say to that, but I was saved by a distraction. Sark's phone must've buzzed, because he took it out of his pocket. He only glanced at it for a second, but his eyes blazed as they read the message, then he muttered something under his breath.

Oh no. "What's wrong?"

"It's Lindsey," he told me curtly. "He got away." I didn't have to ask to know he was talking about Micah.

He stayed just to talk to me, to let me know who he was. That was it. I couldn't tell if his new freedom scared me or made me happy. *How am I supposed to react to this?*

"What if it happened to you?" I asked, keeping my eyes on my hands. "What if you had to watch Dalton murder me, then learn to live without me? And when I miraculously came back, instead of running up to you, crying, and saying how much I missed you…" I had to take a deep breath. "I tried to put a bullet in your head. Because I was getting paid for it. Because I thought it was fun. Would you have been okay with that?"

He didn't give me an answer.

"Would you?" I asked again.

"No," he eventually responded. "No, I wouldn't have." There was a beat of silence before he added, "I'm sorry your friend is a psychopathic murderer."

It wasn't supposed to be funny, but I couldn't help laughing darkly. "Yeah, me too."

And with that, Sark finally started the car and began our long journey home.

"So, we're going back to Denver?" I asked, somewhat hesitant. I didn't know if the whole 'Arie's killer is free now' situation would change his mind.

Sark just sighed. "For now."

What's that supposed to mean? I glanced at the clock, which told me it was just after one in the morning.

"How did you get here?"

"I tracked the GPS in this car and your credit card purchases, took the first flight once I figured out where you were, then ditched the rental car when I found this one abandoned in the parking lot."

"So…you haven't slept at all. Are you sure you're okay to drive? 'Cause I—"

"I'm fine, Arie." His tone completely shut me down.

Okay then. Taking my backpack off my back, I pulled out the bag of gummy worms, then kicked off my shoes and put my feet up against the dashboard.

Might as well be comfortable.

I used my teeth to viciously tear apart three gummy worms, hoping that carnivorous action would help appease my crushing frustration at nearly everything. It didn't.

Sark started talking out of nowhere. "So you found information on the key?"

I hesitated. "Yeah. I guess."

"Do you want to tell me about it?"

I killed another worm. "Does it look like I want to tell you about it?"

He raised an eyebrow, letting out a breath through his teeth. "Okay then."

Great. Sark hadn't calmed down much, but he was still trying to be somewhat nice. Snapping at him made me feel bad. Especially after what I'd put him through.

I held out my bag of gummy worms to him as a peace offering. A small, disbelieving grin came to his face as he glanced at it, then glanced at me before taking two out of the bag.

"You make no sense sometimes."

I smirked. "It's a talent."

We drove for hours in almost silence. Sark kept the radio on and I would hum along. I was worried he was going to fall asleep, so I waited for the moment when he would need me to step in—not that he would say anything of course—but the moment never came.

I pondered over my small number of findings in Phoenix, realizing more and more what a waste the whole trip had been. Yeah, I found out that the key could be 'breached' but that didn't get me far. And it didn't help the forty infecteds back home either.

It was stupid of me to have expectations, to get

excited, to think that I might actually have been able to solve something. The heavy disappointment I felt wasn't surprising, but it still wasn't fun.

I happened to glance into the side view mirror, which didn't show *my* reflection. The monster was back.

Nice try, princess, she said, smirking at me as she highlighted today's failures in my head. *Better luck next time.*

24

Someone once told me that nobody has ever choked to death from swallowing their pride. I'd always thought that was true, but ever since I got back from Phoenix, it seemed like there was something perpetually caught in my throat.

Everyone must've been somewhat involved in helping Sark figure out where I was, because everyone knew where I'd been when I got back. I was asked the same questions over and over again as if they were scripted:

You really just left by yourself to Phoenix? Yes.

What were you hoping to find? Information about

Stephen White or reversal.

Really? Yeah.

Well did you find anything? No.

Oh. So it wasn't really worth going? Yeah, probably.

Apparently, just leaving like I did broke about a million different rules they had, so everyone was upset, curious, and jealous all at the same time.

The first thing I did when I got back was track down Kayla. She was downstairs at the table again, the blond-haired boy by her side, still going over the same papers as when I had left.

I explained to them how I'd found the research center, how White had put them out of business, describing what I saw in the filing cabinets. They both listened with captivated interest—Sark and Alaina had followed me and were listening too—as I detailed my failed adventure.

"I found a file for Castor, which had a lot of information in it," I explained, "but someone took out everything about reversal. The last page didn't even finish the sentence."

"And there wasn't any clue as to where one might have taken it?" Kayla asked.

"I didn't get much time to really investigate," I answered, trying to keep the annoyance out of my voice since Sark was right behind me. "But I would say no. My guess is White took it with him when he ran off."

She sighed. "So, we're essentially back to square one."

"Yeah." I dropped my gaze to the floor. "Sorry."

"At least you tried something. That's more than any of us can say."

"Yeah, well I didn't find anything on reversal," I

said, looking to the blond boy now, "but I was hoping you could—what's your name?"

"Daxton," he answered.

"Okay, Daxton, I was hoping you might be able to explain something to me." I pulled out the small bit of notes I had taken and handed it to him. "There was a short section on the key, but…I'm not sure what it means."

Daxton positioned the paper on the table so he and Kayla could both look at it. "Okay, go."

I brushed my hair behind my ear. "It talked about a peak phase for the key, which I guess makes a lot of sense."

"That's what I would've guessed," Daxton supplied, nodding.

"But you have no way to tell when that would be?"

"Well…" He blew out a long breath. "I have no idea, but I would think you'd be able to tell. The formula would have some way of letting you know it's ready. Have you noticed anything odd lately?"

Besides a tattoo with a mind of its own? "Um, no. Not really."

"But without the peak whatever, it doesn't work?" Alaina interrupted. "Like, if Alexis had found out Arie was the key a year ago, or whenever he had Arie and Sark, whatever the power is wouldn't have worked 'cause it wasn't peaked?"

Daxton nodded. "Yeah. At least, that's the idea. This peak phase could be anywhere from ten minutes to ten years. We just don't know."

I pointed to the paper. "It also mentioned something about breaching the key. It said that if the key had been breached by the time the peak phase came around, extra steps would have to be taken to ensure success, but everything was void if something went wrong."

"But it didn't say what breached meant?" Kayla asked.

"No."

"You know, I've heard that word before," Daxton said, getting up to retrieve a folder from the other side of the table and handing it to me.

"There are stories people have written over the years," he explained, "regarding infection and such. Some even date back to Castor's time, right after he created the formula."

"The trouble is, we can't verify them," Kayla added. "We have to just take them for what they are, which is most likely fiction."

"There's some wicked stuff in there," Daxton went on. "The mutations are especially nasty. But there is a mention of someone being breached. It doesn't say exactly *what* it is, it just describes how…painful this subject thought it was."

Fantastic.

I opened the file and froze when I saw the images: grotesque bodies hunched on all fours like an animal, veins popping out, manic eyes, chunks of exposed electric blue flesh.

The sight of them took the breath out of me. "What the heck are those?" I asked, my voice small.

"Mutations," Daxton answered. "Like I said: nasty business."

The images aligned near perfection with the monster.

Is that what she is? A mutation?

That caught her attention. She scoffed. *You think they're talking about me?*

You're the only one around here with blue skin, so I'd say yes.

Oh really? She brought up a mental image of my arms. *Don't pretend like you're any better than me, princess.*

"What causes a mutation?" I asked, finally tearing my eyes away from the pictures.

Kayla tapped her pencil against her glasses. "It depends on the person, but usually it's age—whether the body is still in developing stages or not."

"Ever notice that the only living infecteds are all teenagers?" Daxton asked. "Or, at least, were that age at the time of their infection?"

I'd never really thought of that but now it made sense. "What happens to adults?"

"If the body—mostly the brain—is fully developed or almost, the formula takes extreme measures. It needs something to work with, a little bit to grow with. If there's too much to directly change among brain functions and anatomy, the subject dies or turns into one of those." He gestured to the pictures.

"There are always exceptions to the rule," Kayla added, "but that's usually how it goes. Daxton was twenty-one and he's one of the oldest non-mutated infecteds. At least that Alexis has record of."

"Huh. Wow." I thought for a second. "So if someone infected Sark—" I turned to look at Sark who didn't seem like he was enjoying the conversation. "You're twenty…?"

"Four."

Daxton shook his head. "I wouldn't expect anything pretty."

I gave one last glance to the pictures, making me shiver, before turning to what I was supposed to be looking at: breaching the key.

I scanned through the words quickly—very conscious of Sark reading over my shoulder—but soon found it was nothing I wanted to know. Just a page and a half full of moaning about how much breaching hurt.

Awesome.

"Like Kayla said," Daxton told me, "it's probably fiction. After all, this is strictly for the key, right? A one-time deal?"

"Right." I closed the folder and set it on the table. "I just have to figure out what it is, so I can do it to myself or get someone to do it to me."

Kayla and Daxton exchanged glances, and I heard Sark exhale sharply in disapproval.

I shook my head. "If there's a chance I can screw this whole key thing up, I've got to take it, no question. I don't care what it is." I stood up from my chair. "Let me know if you find anything, okay?"

Fingering my sleeve, I wondered for a half a second if I should show them my arms, just to see if they could pinpoint anything.

No, bad idea. Something that freaky needed to be kept to myself.

In the weeks that followed, Sark became my shadow. If I thought he had been keeping a close eye on me before, it was nothing compared to now. I couldn't take a breath without being aware of his calculating gaze, which partly annoyed me and partly scared me, driving me to lie every second of every day.

I'm fine. I'm fine. Nope, nothing is wrong. I'm fine, but thanks for asking.

My life became a game of convincing everyone I

had adjusted to being back when that wasn't even close to being true, trying my best to be as small of a burden as possible and gradually nursing my arm back to health. Of course, the freak monster in my head *loved* this game, constantly reminding me of what I did wrong and where I fell short. The less emotion I allowed myself, the less power she had, which was a hollow victory.

I knew my plan was working at least a little bit though, because Sark slowly started to back off as the weeks went by. Whether he actually believed my act or he was just giving up on me, I couldn't tell.

Needless to say, March wasn't that great. Not that I was really expecting it to be the best month of my life, but it was still numbingly disappointing.

I spent most of my time with Kayla and Daxton, obsessively reading file after file, case after case, looking for any form of clue that could point me in the right direction. It shouldn't have been surprising that I could never find anything—they'd been obsessing over the information a lot longer than I had, and, to be honest, were a lot smarter than me. If they couldn't find anything then I had no chance, but that didn't stop me from trying. It wasn't like I had anything else to do anyway.

Eventually I found the file entitled "The Key—Myths" which piqued a burning interest and sent me in a frenzied panic at the same time. Up until that point I'd shied away from these stories, partly to keep my faith alive and partly because I was too scared. When I was initially infected I always had a small vain hope that I could tell someone someday, like Alaina or maybe Brennan. I didn't want to know what the infected world already assumed about the key; I didn't want to dash the dream that kept me going.

I really didn't want to know. But, then again, I really really did.

I glanced around the table. Daxton was taking a fifteen-minute "power nap" in his chair. Kayla was heavily engrossed in whatever she was writing, attacking the paper with her pencil, the headphones in her ears a version of a "do not disturb" sign. Neither would notice me.

Hesitantly, I opened the file and started skimming. There were over twenty different accounts, some partially realistic and several that were just ridiculous—everything from blood drinking to Satanist practices, human sacrifices to cannibalism, Sirens to sociopaths. One even mentioned a werewolf, while another claimed the key had power over the elements. They all varied from each other, but I winced at the one word that was used over and over again in every single version: monster.

It was easy to understand why people hated me before they actually knew me. If these were the rumors going around, I wouldn't be too fond of the key either.

Daxton broke the silence out of nowhere, making me jump. "That's not you, is it?" he asked, his tone mostly joking.

I didn't find it all that funny. "Not yet."

That sobered him up pretty fast. I let out a long breath, closed the file and gave it back to him, my hand shaking ever so slightly.

That was a mistake.

The monster smirked. *Ignorance doesn't change facts, princess.*

Daxton looked at the file for a moment before taking it from me. "People would disregard these if they met you. You'd change their minds."

I dropped my gaze to my hands in my lap, planning on some sarcastic remark or just nothing in response, but I couldn't stop myself.

"Really?"

He shrugged. "You changed mine."

"Mine too," Kayla chimed in suddenly. She didn't miss a beat, though she was still hunched over the table, hand ferociously writing, with her headphones still in her ears.

I gave a small smile. "Thanks."

Daxton settled back into his chair, picking up yet another file he started flipping through.

"You could be worse," he said to himself.

I rolled my eyes. "You know, you're right: I could be a werewolf."

He laughed. "Yeah, that's too bad. I've always wanted to be friends with a werewolf."

"You missed your only chance."

"If you ever figure that one out—"

I grinned as I stood up. "You'll be the first to know." Then I went up the stairs, checking to make sure the sleeping room was empty before going up to the bookshelf in the back of the room. I'd had enough of hopeless formula garbage for one day; I needed to ground myself again. I reached behind the top shelf and pulled out my bundle of Erika's letters. Settling next to my pillow, I wrapped a blanket around me and started reading.

Arie,
Okay I know circumstances are scary, but I do love

Florida. It's warm and quiet and peaceful, and just gorgeous. Arie this is the place for us. I know we're hiding from a bunch of insane murderous men, but besides that it really couldn't get better. At least for me.

Arie, will you please stop beating yourself up? Please? It's painful to watch, really. We all knew Alexis would find out you were the key eventually. It wasn't your fault—never has been and never will be. Can you please accept this? It's killing me, and Sark too, to see you like this. It's okay. Breathe. The world hasn't ended yet.

I just worry about you. Your nightmares haven't stopped since we got here, and my heart just aches for you. Please don't think badly of me for never helping you with those. I have to put Sark in charge of that. Every night when I wake up to your screaming, it just brings back awful memories of that place, sitting in that cell next to you, just listening to you, not being able to do anything. I'm so sorry, but I can't do it. I know it can't be easy on Sark either, or you. I just can't handle it when you're in so much pain.

But I'm not writing to tell you about our problems— you're fully aware. Our lives may be hard, but there are so many beautiful things around us. Oh, I have to tell you the cutest thing that happened today! You were asleep, so you totally missed it, but it was adorable.

You haven't quite been able to walk right since we got here—and that's okay. It'll come back eventually— so you usually just hang out in bed. Sometimes you sleep, sometimes I can convince you to watch a movie, but you usually just sit. It's really sad.

Anyway, Sark hasn't quite healed up since those men nearly killed him, and he can't do much either. But, of course, it's no big deal. You know Sark: he always has to be the tough guy. Nothing ever bothers him. I can tell when he's hurting, but he would never say a word, so he likes using you as an excuse. He loves hanging out with you anyway, but by doing so he can relax without having to admit he needs it. Oh, Sark. What are we going to do with him?

Today he was feeling it worse than usual (he got no sleep last night, but don't feel bad) and convinced you to watch a movie with him. I went to clean the kitchen (it looked like a horribly boring movie. I felt bad for you) while you guys watched it and came back in about an hour later.

The movie must've been boring because it put you both to sleep. You sleep for most of the day anyway, so I don't know if you really notice, but Sark never falls asleep during the day. He's got to be exhausted, but he won't do it. Maybe it's some man ego thing. I don't know.

Anyway, it was the cutest thing I have ever seen. You're so tall, Arie, but you had somehow managed to curl yourself into this tiny ball, wrapped up in blankets on the bed. Sark was sitting next to you with his arm around you, and I could tell he fell asleep accidentally because his head was leaning at a funny angle against the wall. You both looked so content and peaceful. It was beautiful. I don't think you realize how special you are to Sark and how much you mean to him. I wish you could've seen the two of you—you would've understood. You have an exclusive place in his heart that will never be filled by anyone else.

I had to just sit and watch you for a bit. I couldn't help but think how lucky I am to have both of you in my life. You two are the best things that have ever happened to me. And I think of Sark and who he used to be...it's just a miracle. Out of the millions of things that have gone wrong in all of our lives, there are many things that have gone right.

Of course, it wasn't long before Sark woke up. He felt so bad about it, but I assured him it was no big deal. For me, it was a perfect moment—a gorgeous silver lining within the many clouds.

Make sure you always look for those, Arie. Great moments like that often get overlooked in the storm.

—E

I didn't remember that specific day, but I remembered that time. I remembered that feeling of being so scared, of complete and total failure, and yet feeling so content at the same time. Florida was the only place I felt like I belonged. And the worst part was that at that time, I'd had no idea what I had. I was too overwhelmed to really appreciate how I was living.

I guess they're right: you never truly know what you have until it's gone.

25

I didn't know why I remembered this, but in my English class once we were studying Robert Frost. "In three words," he said, "I can sum up everything I've learned about life: it goes on."

He was right. Even when it seemed like the world couldn't possibly keep turning, it did.

I realized today that I was eighteen years old—only seven short months away from nineteen. *Nineteen.* Where had the years gone? I guess when I was infected things got so crazy I just assumed the world would stop and let me catch up. Apparently it didn't get that memo because I would be nineteen in November.

Nineteen. I thought of my eight-year-old self, or

even twelve-year-old self, and all of the plans they had for the future, how they thought their life was going to turn out. How could they have guessed that a single injection would alter their life the way it did? I could say for sure that none of them—including me—had ever imagined that things would end up the way they did. I guess I just felt like I was wasting time or something.

Time. That seemed to be consuming everything lately.

A new infected showed up at the club (a real one, not a psychotic ex-best friend) but that was the only news anyone really had to offer. His name was Bowen: an awkward little thing, probably around fourteen, though I got the feeling he was a lot smarter than he let on. The excitement around him in the beginning was overwhelming, but it didn't last long. I felt bad for him. I knew how lonely it was to be the new face in a community like this.

Looking for Mara to give me a job to do, I was heading for the kitchen when I almost crashed into Alaina coming through the door. She rolled her eyes when she realized it was me. I assumed my increasing 'silence except during artificial conversations' thing I had going on severely annoyed her, though I was kind of afraid to ask.

I opened my mouth to apologize, but never really got the chance. Out of the corner of my eye, I saw Peter come into the room from upstairs, his body tense as he shut the door softly behind him. There were at least twelve other people in the room, and he motioned for all of them to be quiet. His eyes were on Alaina and me.

"What are you—" Alaina started.

"Shut up!" His low voice was harsh with fear. He

began to say something else, but loud footsteps sounded down the stairs, along with voices, which was weird. Nobody ever went up to the second floor; Neil's office was up there. The voices got more defined, and I recognized both of them. Neil was talking to someone.

My throat closed up; my blood went ice cold. Alaina slapped her hand over her mouth to muffle her gasp. Because it wasn't just *someone* coming down the stairs with Neil. His charismatic voice echoed behind the closed door, bringing back a million memories.

It was Lennon. Alaina's handler and member of the 'I hate Arie' club. An employee of Alexis, having the capacity to have us all killed in the blink of an eye. We were less than ten seconds away from being exposed.

Peter pushed us away from the door, but we couldn't really go anywhere. We barely had time to hide behind the bar when the door swung open and Neil walked in, Lennon following. He still stood tall, dignified, and arrogant—just like I remembered him— but there was a sickly and worn look to his face. The past year had not been good to Lennon either.

We're dead, we're dead, we are so dead. Alaina grabbed my hand tightly, her face white, her eyes locked on a spot on the bar. Honestly, I couldn't tell if she would throw up before me or not.

I risked a peek around the other side of the bar. Peter and everyone else pretended to be normal, but I didn't know what effect they were going for. We just had to hope that Lennon wouldn't recognize any of them. I saw Kayla slip downstairs, probably to warn those who were down there.

Sark. Sark is down there. If Lennon found Sark, then Sark was dead. No, he was worse than dead—he was caught.

Please stay downstairs. I huddled closer to Alaina, both of our bodies shaking. *Please listen to Kayla.*

"All right, listen up," Neil shouted to catch everyone's attention. It didn't really matter though—he already had everyone's attention. "This is Mr. Brown from…" He looked to Lennon. "Where did you say you were from?"

"The inspection agency downtown," Lennon answered smoothly. Alaina and I both shivered. "We're running a protocol check through all the businesses around here."

"Yeah. What he said." If Neil knew that 'Mr. Brown' could end our world, he didn't show it, which was good. "Just make sure to stay out of his way and show him around if needed."

Okay, we just have to somehow stay hidden, keep Lennon occupied and completely oblivious, and give him no reason to come back. I looked to Alaina, who I knew was thinking the same thing.

We have no chance.

"Well, feel free to get started," I heard Neil say. "Let me know if I can help you with anything."

"Thank you," Lennon answered. "I'll make it quick."

What do we do? I mouthed to Alaina. It was only a matter of time until Lennon saw us behind here, and I was sure his stupid 'protocol check' involved going downstairs. I didn't know if he'd remember Brennan and Lucy, but Sark was an obvious giveaway. Heck, everyone could be. Lennon could have files on all living infecteds and had already recognized everybody.

What do we do?

Alaina couldn't even answer, and I knew what she must be thinking. This was her worst nightmare:

Lennon finding her brother. They had a close call once before, which was the reason she ran away in the first place. Alaina lived her life so Lennon would never find Liam, and that was all about to crash down.

Many different footsteps were wandering around the floor, so I couldn't tell where Lennon was.

"Interesting arrangements," I heard Lennon call. I realized he must've seen the beds all over the floor in the other room. "Do you all sleep here?"

Neil must've gone upstairs, because it was Peter who answered.

"Yeah, sometimes. We all work really hard to try and get this place back up and running. It can be brutal hours, so Neil created accommodations. It works out for all of us."

"I see."

I bit my tongue. Lennon didn't sound convinced at all.

How could he be? What group of teenagers sleep in a club that's out of business?

"How's the weather out there?" Peter asked, somehow keeping a conversational tone. "It's lookin' like somethin's coming our way."

"Uh, yes." Lennon sounded distracted. "I heard there's quite the storm rolling in."

Mara came out from the kitchen, stopping just in my line of sight.

"Peter, there's a huge leak in the—" She stopped when she saw Lennon, her eyes widening. "Oh, um, never mind."

"I need to take a look at all problems in this building," Lennon said, his voice coming closer.

"Oh, no, it's not really a big deal," Mara said quickly. "Continue with everything. I'll just grab Peter later." She gave an anxious glance to Peter, which was just enough to pique Lennon's interest.

They're good. They're really good. I shuddered to think what must've happened here for them to gain the precise acting skills.

Just as we were hoping, Lennon took the bait. He strode into the kitchen, Peter and Mara following, making me and Alaina flinch when he went past the bar. He disappeared behind the door.

Okay, where do we go? Downstairs was a trap, and hiding in a closet was a bad idea. We could just run out the door, but…I didn't know if I could do it. Leave everyone here, leave Sark, and just hope that they didn't get caught? That wasn't going to happen, and I knew Alaina wouldn't be able to do it either.

Not really sure what to do, I grabbed Alaina's hand and pulled her up with me. The room was empty. I could make out shadows in the sleeping room—kids were probably trying to make it look more normal.

Going as fast as we could while staying silent, we walked around the bar and into the middle of the room, heading for Neil's closet.

We should've known he was smarter than that. We should've known he wouldn't fall so easily for a trick by some kids. And we'd forgotten how quiet he was.

"Oh Alaina," he said, his horrid voice alarmingly close behind us. "I was so hoping you'd be here."

I felt Alaina freeze behind me, and I did too, my terror paralyzing me. Then I heard Lennon gasp and knew it was all over.

He grabbed my shoulder and turned me around slowly, as if he thought I would disappear. I hesitantly met his astonished expression.

"Arie?" he asked under his breath.

"But…that's…that's impossible." He shook his head, trying to smooth over his shock. "I must admit, this is a story that I'm dying to hear."

I just stared at him, hands shaking, imagining the drones of guards Lennon probably had around the building right now. Several infecteds trickled into the room to see what was going on. Gasps. Muffled cries. Frantic whispering. The amount of sheer terror in the room was crushing.

It was over. Everything we'd worked for was void.

Finally, I was able to get out, "Yeah. It's a good one."

Lennon looked around at all the kids, a small smile on his face. He was realizing what he found. I wondered how much Alexis would reward him for this victory: over thirty outlawed infecteds and the resurrected key.

"Well, this is just fantastic," he said, his smile growing bigger. "I should've known you two would organize something like this. Of course, Arie…" He shook his head again. "Wow."

Suddenly, his bright eyes hardened slightly. "So, does this mean you know where one would find Sark?"

The lie came so naturally that I almost forgot I was lying.

"Sark?" My shaky voice had the perfect amount of incredulity. "Why would I know where Sark is?"

Lennon narrowed his eyes. "He got you out, didn't he? You couldn't have pulled something like this yourselves."

I tried my best to look confused. "No, he, uh, he got me out, I gave him what he wanted, and he left. I haven't seen him since."

He almost seemed disappointed but tried not to show it. I breathed a silent sigh of relief. Sark would be okay. We were all going to die, but Sark would escape his fate.

Get out of here Sark. You still have a chance.

I quite literally felt when he came into the room. Apparently, Sark didn't get the whole 'Sark's not here' part of my plan. He stepped right in front of Lennon's face, his fierce animosity bringing a silence to the already hushed room. I dropped my eyes to the ground in hopeless defeat, feeling Lennon's questioning gaze on me, as I held my breath. Sark's hateful presence immobilized us all.

"Well, well," Lennon said, the contempt in his voice clear. "You've been busy."

I saw a shadow move and heard a sickening crunching sound. Lennon's knees buckled, but he somehow managed to keep himself up. I didn't dare take my eyes off my shoes.

Sark delivered another painful blow, and I almost caught myself feeling bad for Lennon. You never wanted to be on Sark's bad side. Ever.

It wasn't until I heard a gun cock that I looked up. Sark's back was to me, his shoulders tense, gun aimed at Lennon. I was barely able to stop him in time.

"No," I said, lurching forward to grab Sark's arm. "You can't just shoot him."

Sark turned on me and my heart leapt in my throat. I took an automatic step back, feeling Alaina seize my arm, as my hands started shaking harder. He wasn't Sark. I could see it in his eyes—he was the scary Sark, the Sark that hunted me, the Sark that I hadn't seen since Erika had turned our lives upside down.

He deflated as soon as he saw my expression. Closing his eyes, he took a deep breath and relaxed slightly.

"Arie," he said through his teeth. "We can't leave him alive."

My mouth was so dry that I could barely form words. "Sark—"

His eyes snapped open. "Do you *want* Alexis to find you?"

I shuddered involuntarily. "No. But you can't—"

"I will do what I have to."

"You're not going to kill someone," I said, gaining my voice. "You don't do that."

Alaina let go of my arm and nodded. As much as we hated Lennon, we were better than standing back to watch Sark shoot him.

Peter took a step forward from across the room. "He's going to get us all murdered. You have to think of the majority here."

I glared at him. "Sark isn't going to murder him. If you want to go through with it, then be my guest."

Peter glared back at me, but knew he was beat. Peter wasn't *that* hard hearted.

"We'll do what it takes to survive," I told him, "but we aren't killers. That's them, not us."

Alaina nodded again, though her face was still white. Various infecteds glanced at each other, most in agreement, at least I hoped. After my long streak of silence and solitude, it felt bizarre to be back in the spotlight again.

Sark looked around at all of us before resting his gaze on me. The relief hit me hard when I saw the rest of the cruelty leave his eyes. He was still Sark. He never had to be the murderer again.

He sighed and turned back to Lennon, who was completely bewildered. I could see he was fearing for his life, but Sark's behavior—probably all of our behavior—was foreign to him. The idea that Sark would listen to me or that I would want him to be the good guy would never make sense in Lennon's head.

"Who have you contacted?" Sark demanded, still keeping the gun loosely aimed. The message was clear: he wouldn't shoot Lennon now, but Sark wouldn't hesitate at the slightest provocation. He would *look* for a reason to pull the trigger.

Lennon was trying hard to cover up his panic, not that I really blamed him—Sark was terrifying, and I knew Lennon had always been afraid of him. As much as he didn't want to admit it, Sark had always been better than him.

"Luckily for you, no one yet," Lennon said, a steely warning in his voice. "Of course, they'll be all over this area when I don't come back."

I didn't believe that, anticipating a full-on ambush any second, but Sark did. I guess after years of working together they had gained a handle on each other.

"What kind of response?" Sark was still in command mode.

"Security protocols have been scrapped, thanks to you. Any and all suspicion gets met with the White execution."

Sark pressed his mouth into a thin line, wincing slightly. That made the corners of Lennon's mouth pull up.

"You know it's all a matter of time, right? As much as I dread my situation, it pales astoundingly in comparison to yours. I imagine no one will be talking of Stephen White once Alexis gets through with you."

That made both Alaina and I cringe, causing Lennon's gaze to flick to us again. Sark waved his gun threateningly, as if by doing so he was saying *look at them the wrong way and you're dead.*

"Tristan, go get Neil," Sark ordered, his penetrating eyes still locked on Lennon. "Liam, Brennan, Peter, Daxton—start packing up. We are out of here in less than two hours."

Brennan spoke up from the back corner, Lucy hanging onto his arm.

"I don't think that's going to happen," he said.

As if on cue, a deafening clap of thunder sounded, followed by the immediate downpour of heavy rain against the roof.

"They've put out flood warnings and closed down some major roads downtown," Brennan added. "It's supposed to be nasty. I'd be surprised if we made it anywhere."

Sark gritted his teeth, thinking for a second. "Do it anyway and prep the place for flooding. If it doesn't get worse in the next thirty minutes, we're going."

That was the sendoff. Everyone scrambled away to do whatever emergency job they had been assigned when they were preparing for a disaster like this. Sark started dragging Lennon toward the basement, motioning for Peter and a few others to follow. Lennon shot me one more incredulous glance and the cord holding me in check officially snapped.

My secret was out: I was alive. I had failed yet again.

Backup plans started running through my head. It had been over a year now since my secret was uncovered and I had been able to keep Alexis away since then. He never found out about me because I stayed hidden, because I was away from the world, because…because I had been taken.

I wrapped my arms around myself once that

realization hit me, hating where this was going. The only way I was going to stay away from Alexis was if I went back to Dalton. In a sick and twisted way, Dalton saved me from Alexis.

Sark came back up the stairs, angry determination on his face—he was going to do everything he could to save these kids.

He strode quickly to where I was rooted in the middle of the room. It took me until then to realize that Alaina was still frozen next to me. Sark looked to her first, but she interrupted whatever he was going to say. To my surprise, she stepped forward and threw her arms around him, her eyes watering with the tears she was fighting. He hugged her back tightly.

"It's okay," he said, his tone a little too edgy. "He's not going to touch you. We'll get him out of here and you won't have to worry about it anymore."

Alaina nodded weakly then took a deep breath, pulling herself together. She let go of Sark and walked stiffly away.

Sark took one look at me. "You need to calm down. Look, nothing is going to happen. The idiot came here alone. We've got time. We're going to be okay."

"No, I…" How was I going to explain this? "I have to—"

"I know, you have to stay hidden. We'll keep you sa—"

"I have to go back," I said quietly.

Sark took a step closer to me. "What? Go back where?"

"Go back…to where they can't find me." I took a deep breath. "To Dalton."

Sark's eyes widened when he realized what I was getting at. I went on quickly before he could get too upset.

"I was there for eight months, and nobody ever figured it out. Not even the people who worked there. I could go back and just disappear again and they would never find—"

"Whoa, whoa, whoa." Sark grabbed me by the shoulders. "Do you hear yourself? I know you're panicking, but you can't honestly be considering—"

"Sark, I have to. I have to do whatever it takes to keep the key away from Alexis. No matter what."

Some of the color drained out of his face as he was deciding which approach to take. Finally, he set his jaw, harsh with determination.

"And how far do you think I would let you get?"

I cleared my throat to keep my weakening voice from cracking. "I never told you where it was."

Sark opened his mouth then shut it, the panic starting to show through in his eyes. "Arie, think about this for a minute, okay? Just think. That is the worst idea you've ever had. You're really scared right now, I understand, but you can't make stupid decisions based on that."

I started to argue, but was interrupted by Neil, Tristan, and Liam wanting to talk to Sark. Sark gave me the 'do not move' glare before turning to them. I waited until he was sufficiently distracted to slip away.

Across the room, I saw Alaina heading for the door, so I grabbed my jacket from off of its hook and followed her outside. Giant dark clouds loomed overhead, rain pelting against my body, a bitter wind adding to the insanity.

"Where are you going?" I asked once I'd caught up to her.

She was startled by my sudden appearance, but

annoyance soon took its place.

"Oh, so you're talking to me now?" She rolled her eyes. "I'm honored."

I ignored the comments. "Where are you going?"

"We have a small storage place a few blocks over," she answered grudgingly. "It's my job to make sure it doesn't blow up or anything."

I obviously missed the assigning of jobs, but I needed something to keep my mind distracted. I didn't know what to do.

"Can I come with you?"

Alaina just shrugged. I decided to take it as a yes. We walked down the sidewalk in silence, huge drops of rain flying in our faces and soaking through our clothes.

"Are you okay?" I couldn't help asking. "With Lennon here, I mean?"

She fought hard to keep her voice even. "I'm fine, Arie. I actually know how to keep myself together with stuff like this."

I sensed a few implications in her tone but chose to ignore them.

A ringing sounded from under the sounds of the storm. Alaina pulled out a cell phone, dragging me into the nearest alley, and answered it. I was pretty sure I knew who it was.

"Yeah?" she nearly shouted into the phone, putting one hand over her other ear so she could hear over the wind.

Her gaze flicked to me. "Yeah, she's with me. Why?"

She listened for a minute, shock slowly taking over her expression. Then she scowled.

"I'm not an idiot." Another second of listening. "Yeah, fine. Whatever." She hung up, sliding the phone back into her pocket before glaring at me.

"Dalton?" she demanded. "Really? You're just a special kind of stupid, aren't you?"

She stepped around me and started walking down the sidewalk again. I considered becoming a hobo and staying in the alley for the rest of my life but sighed and followed her.

"I'm just scared," I said under my breath.

I didn't think she would hear me over the wind, but she responded quietly.

"Me too."

We went the rest of the way in silence. I felt the urge to tell her everything, to explain myself, though I didn't know what to say.

We passed several mishaps on our way: car accidents, injured people, fallen trees. The storm was getting serious, and it seemed like it was just getting started. There was no way we'd be able to make it out tonight.

The storage building was closer than I thought, which was convenient. I followed Alaina's lead, obeying her instructions and helping her when she needed it. We covered a few leaks in the roof, fortified the one window, checked to make sure everything was still there, and locked it all back up again. In less than thirty minutes we were on our way back.

Ideas were flowing through my head—ideas involving taking off—but ultimately I decided against them. I was too cowardly.

Just one more night, I told myself. *Just one more sane night with everyone I love. I'll leave in the morning.*

At that, the monster scoffed at me and rolled her eyes. *Yeah, I'm sure they'll just be heartbroken.*

With a start I realized what she meant: nobody would notice if I never came back. They would just go on with their lives, like before I found them in the first place, but likely safer. Sark would notice, obviously, but he'd probably get over it. He did it before, right?

That uncomfortable idea kept me thinking until we got back to the club. Brennan, Mark, and Liam were outside, wrapping up some anti-flooding work on the basement windows.

"How's it looking?" Brennan asked Alaina, wiping some rain from his drenched face.

"The place should be fine. How about here? You think it'll hold?"

"That's all we can do now," he said. "We've just got to survive through the night and deal with it in the morning." He paused, grinning. "That would be a great book title, don't you think?" He waved his hand in the air dramatically. "Surviving through the night: teenagers endure pounding rain while evading their own demise. It's got a nice ring to it. We should write it."

Alaina rolled her eyes. "Nobody wants to read a book about us, Brennan."

"You never know," he said, winking at me, as we all stepped inside.

Everyone had been working to get this place as flood proof as possible—the reports coming in must've been worse than I'd thought. They had moved everything from the sleeping room to the main one, I assumed to minimalize damage if the building did flood. Mattresses, blankets, sleeping bags, and pillows were scattered all over the floor, like a glorified sleepover. The power must've gone out: small candles, lanterns, and flashlights were being used to light up the darkness. People were milling around and setting things up. Most were getting ready to retire to their temporary bed.

Alaina gave her report to Tristan and Neil, who passed it on to everyone else that needed to know. I caught Sark's eye from across the room, seeing him breathe a sigh of relief. Then Alaina and I went to find some dry clothes, seeing as we were soaked to the bone. We changed quickly, wringing out our hair and drying our faces with towels. I threw my hair up in a bun to keep it out of my face and put on two pairs of socks. Grabbing an extra blanket from the stockpile, we went back into the main room.

A large space heater had been added to the center of the room, everyone angling their makeshift beds toward it. Even with all of us in there, it was freezing. Alaina went and sat by Liam, while I made my way to Sark. He was sitting against the far wall, distanced from everyone else, with the gun back in hand. Lennon was bound with tight cords in the corner, his eyes covered with a blindfold. I tried very hard to ignore him as I went and sat on the other side of Sark.

"You okay?" Sark asked quietly. I knew he was referring to a million different things.

"Yeah," I answered, wrapping the blanket around my trembling body and resting my head on his shoulder. "Just cold."

Earsplitting thunder boomed overhead, making me and many others jump. The storm frightened all of us. It was a bad omen, and the uneasiness enveloped the room with extra pressure.

"Sark?" I asked, noticing that a few infecteds were already asleep. "Don't let me fall asleep, okay?" I didn't think my insane nightmares would go over well with anyone.

"I won't." Out of the corner of my eye, I saw him fingering his gun in his other hand and knew he wouldn't be sleeping tonight either.

I was surprised that anyone could fall asleep in the first place—it wasn't very quiet. The rain pounded against the building like angry fists, the space heater hummed loudly, and restless whispers echoed through the room. I glanced around, seeing who had been able to tune out the storm.

Alaina was already dozing against a tired Liam. Lucy was curled into an impossibly tiny ball in Brennan's lap as he stroked her hair. Mara was holding onto Mark's arm while they both stared into space. Dustin had snuck a Rubik's cube underneath his blankets, which he was absentmindedly twisting, and a few beds down from him was Peter, sharpening the giant blade of a knife. Sasha was filing her nails next to an alert Tristan. Carl was shooting his rubber wristband at the wall over and over; Jacklynn watched him from under her blanket with fearful eyes. Everyone was eerily on edge, just waiting for another disaster to strike.

Time passed slowly and unevenly. A few more people dropped off, but most couldn't sleep. I drifted a few times myself, but Sark would gently tap my shoulder before I could settle very deep. I just stared at the wall and let my mind be blank as I gradually warmed up.

After a while a new sound was added to the mix. It was quiet at first but got louder and more defined. I strained to hear until I realized it was someone crying. Eventually the crying broke into deep sobs as a small figure popped up from the ground a few yards in front of me.

I sat up straight. "Hadley?" I whispered, though it didn't really matter. His cries had already woken almost everyone up.

I saw his head turn a few times, then he ran toward me as fast as he could. He fell into me, slamming me against the wall, sobbing hysterically. I wrapped my arms around him, covering him with my blanket.

"Hey, what's wrong?" I asked, feeling his tears already soaking through my shirt.

I couldn't make out much of what he said, but I caught 'Mom and Dad' and knew what happened. A pang of hurt went through my heart.

"Shh, it's okay." I stroked his disheveled hair. "You're awake now."

Hadley peeked up at me, his lip trembling, as fat tears rolled down his face. "I want my mom and dad."

I had to take a deep breath to keep myself from crying—it was just so heartbreaking. What are you supposed to say to that?

"Do you dream about them a lot?" I asked.

He just nodded. "Most times it's a happy dream that makes me sad. But sometimes it's a scary dream and they…they…they bleed a lot…and…they…" His voice broke and he hid under the blanket again.

"Just calm down, okay?" I tried to sound as soothing as I could. "Calming down helps. When you see people die, especially when you love them a lot, you can't get them out of your head. And sometimes you dream about them, and you dream about them dying…over and over…and it's hard."

Hadley leaned back so he could look at me. "Do you dream about that girl a lot?"

"Erika?" I let out a shaky breath. "Yeah, I see her a lot."

Hadley nodded thoughtfully. "Where were you when she died?"

"Um…" I didn't really want to go into that, but I didn't want to let him down either. "I…I was trapped somewhere. Behind a mirror. She couldn't see me, but… I could see her." *I could see everything.*

"Was it scary?"

"It was one of the scariest times in my life."

"And then that guy kidnapped you, right?"

I sighed. "Yep."

"And were you scared 'cause we thought you were dead?"

"Yeah, I was."

"But you weren't dead, right? 'Cause you came back."

The corner of my mouth pulled up. "Right."

He chewed on that for a minute, leaning his head against my chest. Oddly, it seemed to calm him down. His tears slowly dried and he was quiet again for a long time.

He's so young. He shouldn't have to deal with monsters like this. Nobody should.

Finally, Hadley yawned, stretching his arms out wide. "I'm scared to go back to sleep."

"You can sleep by me if you want to."

"But you get those dreams too," he pointed out. "You can't make them go away."

"You're right, I can't. But do you know who's really good at that?"

"Who?"

I nodded my head to the right. "Sark. He's got a magic power for keeping scary dreams away. Every time I have one and he's there when I wake up, I don't have another one when I go back to sleep. He protects me. He can protect you too."

Hadley's eyes got a little bigger. "Really?"

"Yep."

He looked at Sark. "You can really do that?"

Sark grinned faintly. "Works every time."

"Okay." He jumped up from my lap to drag his pillow, blanket, and teddy bear back to me. Wrapping his blanket around himself, he plopped his pillow in my lap. He tried very hard to pretend like he wasn't scared anymore, but it wasn't really working. Clutching his bear, he laid his head down on his pillow, and I felt him trembling slightly under the blanket. After a few minutes of me fingering his hair, he popped his head up again.

"Arie?" His eyes were huge. "Would you sing me a song?"

I glanced quickly around the room. "No, Hadley, we have to be quiet. People are trying to sleep."

"No they aren't," he insisted, talking at normal volume and looking around. The annoyed looks we were getting didn't seem to faze him. "Nobody is sleeping. Everyone is too scared. I bet a song would help them too."

Before I could tell him absolutely not, he ducked into the next room.

"A song, huh?" Sark asked.

I shook my head. "It's not happening."

"It's been a long time since I heard you sing. I miss it."

Hadley reappeared dragging one of Liam's acoustic guitars behind him. He placed it carefully on the ground in front of me, then, folding his arms across his chest, he sat down and prepared to wait.

"I'm not playing a song now," I protested, still

trying to be quiet. "It's, like, one in the morning. People are trying to sleep."

"No they aren't," he insisted. "They're awake 'cause they're scared."

"No, they're awake because you're stomping around and being super loud."

"Please, Arie," he said, his lip starting to tremble slightly.

"What are you guys doing?" a soft voice asked from underneath a blanket. I peeked around Hadley to see Jacklynn. She was slowly crawling across the floor until she was sitting next to Hadley. I could make out her huddled form, her eyes terrified, as she was trying very hard not to cry.

Another huge clap of thunder sounded. I jumped, Hadley whimpered, and Jacklynn half shrieked before smacking her hand over her mouth. I put a hand on her shoulder, and she collapsed into me, throwing her arms around me as her whole body shook.

"Hey, it's okay. It's just some rain," I said. "We're going to be just fine."

"Is this a party or something?" I heard Brennan ask. I looked up to see that he and Lucy had scooted over to us too. Brennan glanced from the guitar to me with a raised eyebrow.

"Everyone is trying to sleep," I said again, but it fell flat. I had the feeling I was going to lose this battle.

"Honestly, I don't think you could make it much worse," he said. "If anything, people need to relax. There are too many stressed out kids in one room."

"Then you sing a freaking song. You have no problem doing that."

He grinned. "Nope. But everyone here is sick of me, and I think this might be good for you."

"Good for me, huh?" I scoffed. "We're to that now?"

"Please Arie," Hadley said again. He was clenching his bear to his chest, tears rolling down his face, as he hung on to Lucy's arm. Jacklynn was holding her other hand. They all looked at me in anticipation.

Knowing I would get no support from Sark, I picked up the guitar and strummed through the strings. It was a bit awkward—my right hand had a slow reaction time—but eventually I plucked out a few chords. Without looking up to see who might be listening, I hesitantly started singing a song. I kept my voice hushed, hoping nobody else could hear. My eyes went from my fingers to Hadley. The song wasn't anything good, but it seemed to be what he wanted. I just pretended that I was talking to him, saying that tonight might be scary but tomorrow would be better.

As soon as Hadley and Jacklynn had relaxed a bit, I stopped. I'd realized that many more had tuned in to our little show, which I wasn't really okay with. Hastily, I placed the guitar back on the ground.

"Hey, you know what this kinda reminds me of?" Brennan asked, glancing between all of us as if in secrecy.

"What?" Hadley and Jacklynn asked in unison.

"You remember who Jefferson is, right? He's like Alexis' vice president or something."

They both nodded, eyes wide, and Jacklynn shuddered.

"Have you ever heard the story of when Arie broke his leg?"

I rolled my eyes. "And how does tonight remind you of that?"

Brennan grinned. "Remember afterward? We made

friends with those hobos standing around the fire, and they were so drunk they didn't give us a second glance."

"Oh yeah." My eyebrows furrowed. "Why is that so fuzzy for me?"

"Well, you'd just gotten several crowbars to the skull," he answered. "You weren't all the way there that night."

I half smiled. "Didn't Alaina pretend to be drunk, or did I make that up?"

Brennan nodded and Lucy giggled softly.

"What did I do?" Alaina asked. She and Liam were sliding their way over, with Mark and Mara close behind.

"Pretended to be drunk to fit in with a few hobos?" I supplied.

Alaina laughed. "Oh yeah. That was funny."

"Wait, what happened?" Hadley asked, leaning forward in interest, while Jacklynn nodded and said, "Yeah, I want to know."

And with that, Brennan began telling the infamous story of Arie taking a stand against Jefferson, with Alaina adding commentary when she thought appropriate, her black eyes darting to Lennon from time to time. It was hard to relax with him there, but we tried. By the time Brennan was detailing the drunk hobos, many infecteds had slid closer to us so they could listen in too.

"Whoa," Tristan muttered once the story was over. "I can't believe you actually did that."

"It wasn't that big—" I started.

"We were on a time crunch too," Brennan added, ignoring me. His dramatics had no time for my excuses. "Lucy had some serious hypothermia problems and being trapped in a cold, damp basement was not helping."

Lucy nodded. "If Arie hadn't gotten me out when she did, I could've lost some of my fingers."

Hadley and Jacklynn's eyes both went huge. "No way," Hadley mumbled.

I shook my head, uncomfortable.

"We would've made it out earlier," Alaina said, flipping her hair theatrically, "if it weren't for our beautiful, long locks."

Jacklynn gasped. "That happens to me all the time! They always pull on my hair or drag me by it and that always hurts."

"You know, what is it with that? Everyone always goes for the hair first."

"It's really annoying," I agreed, and Lucy nodded with me.

One girl—I think her name was Kat—suddenly piped up from her spot in our circle.

"Yeah, I got so fed up, I finally just chopped all mine off." Her dark pixie cut stood as proof.

Sasha wasn't really okay with that. "That's no excuse, girl." She fluffed her lush curls. "My hair is proof it's possible to keep up."

She told us the story of how hairspray and a bottle of nail polish saved her life—I wasn't sure how much of it was true—which led Tristan to tell us about the time he survived on two water bottles, three cups of flour, and a Dr. Pepper for two and a half weeks. Apparently, Carl once hid in a claw machine while he hacked into Alexis' database from his phone; Dustin once used Rubik's cubes to outsmart his handler.

I settled back next to Sark, Hadley asleep in my lap, listening as each story sparked a new one. The rain still pounded, but nobody seemed to notice anymore. It was nice to see everyone let the walls come down slightly. We were all so different, but we were all infecteds. We had more in common than we would've ever thought.

Oddly enough, I was almost happy that I had decided to come back tonight. I didn't want to miss this moment. I remembered Erika's words from her letter:

"For me, it was a perfect moment—a gorgeous silver lining within the many clouds. Make sure you always look for those, Arie. Great moments like that often get overlooked in the storm."

And for the first time in a long time, I knew exactly what she was talking about. I guess that's one of the great things about the worst times in life: the stars never shine brighter than they do in the dark.

26

"Freak Storm of the Decade" they were calling it. Apparently, a rainstorm *that* insane, unexpected, and unexplainable hadn't happened in Colorado for at least ten years. If you walked outside, though, you almost couldn't tell. Yeah, the city was a disaster, but the weather was perfect—the sky looked like it had been painted a deep blue, without a cloud in sight. The sun shone brightly, oblivious to the utter pandemonium that had been raging just the night before.

Thankfully, the damage to our place was minimal. A light post had fallen and grazed the roof, but that was about it. We were lucky, especially compared to some broken buildings around us.

Everyone rose shortly after sunrise and went to work. Boxes were packed, rooms were cleaned, and arrangements were made. Sark was in the thick of it all, and I hardly caught a glimpse of him for hours. Between talking on the phone, ordering people around, and watching over Lennon, he had his hands full. He refused to tell anyone where we were going in case the information accidentally got back to Lennon, which was smart, though I still wasn't sure what he planned to do with Lennon once we were ready to leave. Hopefully nothing too drastic.

Of course, I was still trying to decide what *I* was doing. The more I worked, the more panicked I got. I couldn't stay with these people, especially now that Lennon knew. Sark would do his best to keep the knowledge of my existence contained, but I couldn't just rely on that. I had to wait for the right opportunity to slip away and the courage to actually do it. The 'do or don't' dilemma hung over me, like I was a French woman sentenced to the guillotine, just waiting and waiting for the blade to fall.

I was helping pack up the kitchen—to Mara, dishes are just as important as beds—when things more or less fell apart. I guess I shouldn't have been surprised: everything was hanging together by a thread anyway.

Lucy and Mara were across the counter, Alaina next to me, as we packed up huge amounts of plates. Suddenly, Lucy reached over and grabbed my hand, which was when I noticed it was shaking. I looked up from my work to see her concerned expression.

She spoke before I could ask. "Brennan told me, okay, and you don't need to be thinking that way. You're a part of us now. You're coming with us."

It stirred me that she was so concerned, but I couldn't afford to get all touchy feely now. I just gave a small grin and nodded.

She sighed. "I'm serious."

"No, I know." I tried my best to sound sincere. "I really only thought about leaving for a second. Habit, you know?"

Alaina snorted next to me, causing Lucy, Mara, and me to glance at her. She just made a face at the dishes, not acknowledging us. Her implications bothered me, but I just let it go. Alaina got weird when she was stressed.

Lucy looked at me again. "You don't need to—"

"I'd only really leave if it was literally the last option I had left," I said. "Only if something made me have to go."

"Like some crazy murderer showing up to track you?" Alaina asked, rolling her eyes. "Or Lennon finding you're alive? Oh wait…my bad."

"Alaina," Lucy snapped, as a warning, which made both Mara and me jump. It was strange to hear her angelic voice use such a harsh tone.

Alaina raised her eyebrows in surprise, but quickly rebounded. Alaina didn't let people one up her.

"What? It's not my fault Arie can't keep herself together." She flipped her hair. "I'm just saying maybe it's for the best if she leaves."

I winced in spite of myself. Mara and Lucy stared at Alaina, who just rolled her eyes again.

"Oh, don't look at me like that. We were all thinking it, I'm just the only one brave enough to say it."

She's right.

Uncomfortable silence pulsed in the air. I had no idea what to do.

"Alaina," I finally started, "I'm sorry, but I just want to protect—"

"You don't need to protect us." She glared at me. "You need to *stop* trying to protect us. You're just making it worse."

I felt my hands start shaking harder. "I have no idea how. I don't know what to—"

Alaina lifted the plate she was holding and smashed it on the floor. It broke into a million white pieces, flying everywhere, shocking me into silence

"What about us, Arie? You think the world's against you 'cause you're such a freak? What about the rest of us? What about me?"

People were starting to come into the kitchen to see what all the noise was about. I couldn't tear my eyes away from Alaina, who was just getting more livid by the second.

"Do you know how hard it is to be your friend? Have you ever thought of how you've affected me? Do you even care about that?"

"Of course I do!" I had finally found my voice. "Everything I do is for you."

"For me?" she asked in disbelief. She stepped forward so she was yelling right in my face. "You left me here! You left me here to deal and burn and die all on my own! I needed you!"

I felt anguished at the thought that I had let her down. "I—"

"You what, Arie? You freaking left! You were hanging out in La La Land while the rest of us were being gunned down. You got to hide while we lost everything. Don't tell me you're sorry because you showed up too late to a show you started in the first place."

I stepped away from her, feeling like she'd slapped me. "I didn't know." My trembling voice was barely audible. "But I came back to—"

"It doesn't matter that you came back! Even when you're here, you're not here. You shut me out 'cause that's what was 'best' for you, the 'team player.'" She folded her arms across her chest. "So, go ahead. Leave. Go live your oh so horrible life and leave me to pick up the pieces, because that's all you know how to do."

Then Brennan showed up, pushing through Peter, Dustin, Kayla, Hadley, Carl, and several others who were watching in stunned silence.

"Alaina, shut up," Brennan said, stepping in between us. "You're being—"

"Oh, get off it, Brennan," Alaina scoffed. "We all know it's the truth."

Brennan glared at her before turning to our audience. "Everyone out. Alaina seems to have lost her mind. Hopefully it will be back before she does anything else she'll regret."

Alaina then turned on Brennan and nobody needed to be told twice. They filed out of the kitchen with only Peter lingering where he was, his guarded eyes going between me and Alaina. I didn't know if me leaving the room would make the confrontation worse than me staying would.

This is so messed up. How did we get to this point? How could I possibly fix this?

You can't. I couldn't tell if I was thinking it, or the monster was telling me. *You've already done the damage. It's too late to fix it.*

Someone ran into the room, breaking up the confrontation. I was shocked to find Micah's frenzied eyes focused on me.

"Get downstairs," he ordered. "Now."

I got questioning glances from Alaina, Brennan, and Peter—they expected me to run—but I didn't pay them any mind.

"Why? What's wrong?"

Micah pushed past Peter, grabbed my arm, and yanked me forward. "Now."

"Hey!" I heard Brennan yell as we left the kitchen.

I dug my heels into the ground, attempting to pull away but to no avail. "Micah, what are you doing?"

He didn't answer. He dragged me across the room and down the stairs. My complaining must've been loud because Sark met us at the bottom. Rage in his eyes, he went to hit Micah, who ducked out of the way, jerking me along with him.

"What is he doing here?" Sark demanded.

"You should know," Micah said, a furious growl to his voice. "You let the idiot through the door!"

"What are you talking about?" I asked Micah. He still wouldn't let go of my arm.

"Norwood was just here." Micah glared at Sark. "Wasn't he?"

My eyebrows shot up as I sucked in a sharp breath and looked to Sark. Norwood was Dalton's right-hand man. If he had really been here…

Sark didn't understand who we were talking about. "He wasn't from Alexis," he said through his teeth, irked he had to explain himself. "He looked around for a minute before I kicked him out…" He trailed off, as if remembering something, then glanced at the memorial wall. I followed his gaze. It took me a moment to realize what was missing.

There was an empty space at the top—my name was gone.

Oh no.

I felt the color drain out of my face, my hands shaking as I raised them to my mouth to stifle my gasp. Tears stung my eyes, and I shook my head. "No, no, no, no." The image of my cell, the darkness, my home for eight months filled my mind. "I can't. I can't. Please, I really can't."

Micah grabbed my shoulders, looking into my eyes. "He's here now. They've got the building surrounded, but they're not going to call Dalton until they know you're here. Lindsey's on her way, but I—"

Loud footsteps sounded against the basement ceiling, heading for the stairs. Sark reacted at lightning speed, jerking the nearest door open—the storage closet—and shoving me inside, the action giving me a hundred different senses of déjà vu at once. The door clicked shut just as I heard a man swear in exclamation.

Not just any man. Norwood.

I flinched at his voice, covering my mouth with the hope I wouldn't scream.

I can't do this. I can't.

"Turns out Arie isn't the only one who just won't die," Micah said, his voice somehow calm. Micah wouldn't really be calm. Micah was terrified.

"You were dead," Norwood said. He was trying not to be scared too. "I saw you. We—"

"Murdered me? Yeah, I appreciated that. It's pretty amazing what you can live through when you have a little extra juice."

"You're like the freak?"

They didn't know Micah was infected either.

"You know, I prefer to think of it as 'special.'"

I heard Norwood took several deep breaths in an attempt to compose himself, but his voice was still shaken. "Where is she?"

"Come on, man." I could imagine Micah holding his hands halfway up, almost a surrender. "Just walk away."

"Dalton is looking for her."

"Dalton never has to know she was here."

"She's wanted for—"

"Shut up. We both know that's a load of crap Dalton says to justify himself. Why are you really here?"

A beat of silence. "I'm here for her." Norwood's authoritative tone fell a little flat.

"No." Micah was impatient. "You're here because you're scared, because you're too much of a coward to get yourself out of a bad situation after what happened to Erika. This is deeper and darker than anything you signed up for—you have the chance to walk away. Take it."

When we're dragged back to hell, remind me to say sorry. I'm sorry for every horrible thing I said to you. You're an angel, Micah.

Norwood whistled through his teeth. "You don't know him."

"Oh, I know him." Micah's tone darkened. "He murdered me, remember? He murdered me and destroyed Arie. You know she's innocent. Don't do this to her."

The silence gave me an impermissible gleam of hope. Norwood was just a guy being bullied by his boss—he didn't have the blackness to his soul that others did.

Twelve footsteps sounded. Norwood's commanding voice. "Step aside, Mr. Sark."

More silence, but I could feel Sark's rage through the door, as if the heat of it would set the building on fire.

A gun cocked. I couldn't unfreeze myself.

"Move," Norwood said.

More silence. I didn't think Norwood had it in him to actually kill Sark, but I didn't want to take the chance either.

"Oh, I get it." Norwood's voice went mocking. "You're trying to make up for the first time, right? Is that what this is? You let us walk right out the door with her."

Scuffling sounded and I knew Sark had gone for him. Sark could've easily taken him, but Norwood was a chicken at heart: he would have a gun, and he wouldn't go into a fight alone. I had counted to eleven when four guns cocked, and the scuffling stopped. Footsteps came closer to the door, giving me about six seconds. I dashed to the back of the closet and ducked behind a shelf. I was startled to see Lennon in the back corner opposite of me, tied to a shelf, watching me in curiosity.

The door opened and I shoved my fist in my mouth to keep myself quiet. Light cast itself across the ceiling. I held my breath.

"She's not here," I heard Sark say, as if the wrath in his words could vaporize Norwood on the spot. "Leave and we'll say you never came."

More footsteps. Silence. "She doesn't work that way." Norwood raised his voice, a call to me. "Arie, I count eight people here, including your comrade and Sark."

He didn't finish the threat and he didn't have to. I knew the rules.

I clenched my teeth, not realizing until too late that my tongue was in the way. Tasting blood, I stood up from my hiding place, raised my violently shaking hands in surrender, and took one slow step after another out of the closet. As procedure dictated, I kept my hands in the air as I knelt down in front of Norwood one knee at a time, my gaze glued to the ground.

It's just a dream, I tried to tell myself. *It's just an awful nightmare. Sark will wake you up.*

"And there she is," Norwood said. I watched his brown boots take three steps toward me. "Somebody's in trouble, aren't they?"

Wake me up, Sark. Please, please, please just wake me up. I can't do this.

I saw a shadow of Norwood's arm moving, hearing Micah's voice interrupt the action from behind me.

"Hey—"

"Shut it, kid," Norwood said, his tone over the top. He was scared too. "Get down there with her."

Micah walked forward, hands raised like mine, then kneeled next to me. The shadow of Norwood's arm moved across the floor again. Less than a minute went by before I heard the unmistakable sound of Dalton shouting through a phone.

Norwood's calling him. The reality of my situation started creeping up on me. *He's coming.*

A moan escaped me as I curled into a ball on the floor.

No, no, no. Please, no.

"We found her," Norwood said, his usual confidence a bit lacking. "A club back on the south side…There's a handful down here and another couple dozen locked in a room upstairs."

I started hyperventilating, deep memories beginning to resurface from where I had buried them. The sickening smell that stung my nose, the engulfing darkness that swallowed me whole, the hair-raising screech the door made when it was inched open…

Micah gently nudged me, keeping his eyes on the conversing Norwood. "Arie, I called Lindsey. She's on her way here," he said, keeping his tight voice low. He was fighting hard to keep himself in check. "But you have to stay calm. You have to."

"I can't." I forced the words through my teeth. "I can't, I can't. I can't go. Please, I really can't."

"He's going to be looking to you, Arie—you're the one that's gonna have to get us all out of here."

"I can't."

"Do you *want* to go back there?" he asked, his voice verging on desperation. "I don't. And what about everyone here? The second Dalton finds out they're all infected, he's going to drag them to hell too. You want that to happen?"

I shuddered at the thought. Alaina, Lucy, Jacklynn…*Hadley*…

Too much. This is too much. I couldn't handle it. I had to get out. Grabbing a fistful of my hair in each hand, I closed my eyes and started willing reality away from me. I couldn't stay.

"Oh, she's talking again," I heard Norwood say. "Going faster than usual…No, she'll be gone by the time you get here."

"No, Arie." Micah nudged me again, harder. "If he sees you like this then we're all going to die. You know you're our only chance. You can't leave, okay?"

"Yes I can," I mumbled. It was too late. I was already falling. Down through the clouds and the blackness and the haze.

"You can't go all zombie on me. I know that's your safe place, but not now, okay? Please Arie, stay with me."

I'm sorry. Then the cord broke. The force holding me to this earth obliterated and I was left to my own. A high ringing sounded in my ear, as if there was now a barrier between the world and me.

I was aware of Micah calling my name in the distance. A small part of my brain registered that I should answer, but I couldn't force myself to act on it. I was in my bubble now, where it was safe, where I had housed my consciousness during those brutal eight months. It was where I had learned to stay if I wanted to survive. Unfortunately, survival came at a heavy cost, but that was just the way the game was played.

I sat in my bubble, watching the small flecks of color amidst the nothingness, surveying the area like I would my home after a summer away. It was familiar, but dusty. I hadn't been here in a while.

Time didn't mean much in the bubble. I sat. I waited. Sometimes I managed to think. But mostly I just existed. There was no point in keeping time because there was no time to keep. Just one eternity melting into the next. Maybe that was how those eight months had been the longest and the shortest months of my life.

I didn't know how long it had been when I sensed the change. Something inside me churned and I just knew he was there.

The buzz of voices sounded far away. I knew there was no point in trying to make out what they were saying—it was never anything I wanted to hear. I felt a small amount of pressure under my chin, my head being pushed up. Darkness melted into light and colors and shapes. My eyes kept things blurry for me. Blurry was always better, I had discovered. More voices. Nothing worth listening to. My head fell back down into darkness.

A flash of red streaked on my right, sending burning sparks into my bubble. It hurt, but pain was different here. There was a disconnect—I felt it but I didn't really *feel* it, like a headache you can almost convince yourself isn't there.

So, you're just going to give up, huh? Figures.

I stiffened at the voice that wasn't mine. Well, it *was* mine, but it wasn't me. That wasn't right. I was supposed to be alone here.

How did you get in here?

I could see her now, her blue flesh glowing in the darkness, eyes haunting and arrogant.

She smirked. *Oh sweetie, I've always been in here. This is my kingdom.*

No. This is my safe place. This is my freaking head! Get out.

You might feel safe here, but this is where you're most vulnerable.

You're full of crap.

She laughed. *I'm just a reflection of you, princess.*

I didn't understand her—I knew she was an obvious side effect of me being the key, but I didn't know where she came from. How does something that nasty just appear in your head?

I didn't just appear, she told me. *I've been here a lot longer than you think. I just wasn't strong enough to make myself known until now. Congratulations. You're losing.*

What are you talking about?

Think about it Arie. She started pulling up mental images to prove her point. *Every time you look in the mirror and wince, every time you see your arm and feel disgusted, every time you wonder if anyone actually likes you, every time Dalton or anyone tells you that you're nothing and you agree or call yourself a monster—where do you think that comes from?*

You're making this up.

I didn't just appear when you dreamed of me or when you started growing a tattoo. I'm a part of you. You brought me to life without realizing it because you were too prideful to admit you couldn't handle this on your own. And because of your stubborn ignorance, you're going to lose everything to me.

That was it, then? If I had recognized her, if I had stopped lying to myself and realized that something was really wrong, swallowed my pride and asked for some help…I could've done something.

And now it's too late, she informed me snidely. *I'm here and there's no going back. I'd say it's my accomplishment, but we're one in the same, aren't we?*

I am nothing like you.

She laughed again. *Don't lie to yourself. I highlight the worst parts of you—of course the perfect princess Arie would hope to blame her faults on me. Your shame just makes me strong.*

You don't know what you're talking about. You don't know me.

I know you inside and out, every part of you, every secret and emotion and confession you sweep under the rug. That's what makes you the perfect toy. So, by all means, go ahead. Get Sark killed, the infecteds in chains, and yourself carted back to that prison. It's just a glorified playground for me.

I felt the stubborn instinct rise up in me to fight back. *Yeah, well I'm not going back. Sucks to be you, I guess.*

She raised a jagged eyebrow. *Really? Look at you,*

Arie. I see no loser as big as you are right now. Nobody can or will save you, and you're too weak to do anything yourself. Stay down. You're done.

I don't think so. I'm not going back. Hesitantly, I started working my way back to reality. I had to prove her wrong. *And Sark isn't going to die.*

Yeah, sure princess. We'll see.

Slowly, the image of her got less defined as I came back into the world. Back through the glass, the blackness, the clouds, and into the loud light. I became aware of my shaking hands, my pounding heart, my spinning head. The sweat beading on my face. The taste of blood in my mouth. The stinging on my cheek.

I really hated it here.

Sensations came back to me, and I realized I was sitting on leather, not the floor.

How long was I out?

I blinked, my eyes focusing, and I saw I wasn't in the club anymore. I was in a car—a stationary car parked in the garage of the club, which meant I still had a chance if I was careful. Flyers littered the front seats and dashboard, catching my eye because I was on them.

'Wanted,' they read. 'Arie Nolan.' A grainy picture of me was placed just above the accusation that I had murdered a government agent and the warning that I was dangerous.

I didn't have the time I needed to process that. A second after I noticed the flyers, I noticed the man sitting next to me in the car. Young, arrogant, scared. One of Dalton's officers.

He glanced over at me in routine, then stiffened when he saw my focused eyes. I only had a moment's jump on him, relying solely on the instinct that came over me. He went to grab me. I seized his wrist and twisted his arm the wrong way, then slammed his head against the window. It was harder than I meant to. His head went through the glass, shards going everywhere, knocking him out cold.

Oops. So much for subtlety.

I paused to listen, only hearing a few rogue glass pieces hit the pavement. It must've been safe, whatever that word meant in my messed-up life. Opening the car door, I kept my body bent as I crept out of the vehicle and around the back of it, hoping to cut through the middle of the garage.

Boy, was I wrong.

Alaina, Peter, Brennan, Kayla, Tristan, and Lucy were lined up against the wall, four guards over them, about to be loaded into the back of a moving truck. Sark and Micah were on their knees in the center—Sark's nose was bleeding—with a guard over each and Norwood a foot away. Across from them, closest to the open garage door and the free world, was the devil himself.

"Well, well," Dalton said, fury boiling in his eyes. "Look who decided to join the living."

I flinched at his voice, dropping my head, fighting the overwhelming urge to go back to my bubble.

This was an awful idea.

We stood in silence. I held my breath, afraid the simple movement of oxygen going into my body would be a cause for punishment.

When he spoke, his voice was heavily controlled. Contained. "What do you think you're doing?"

I counted to eight in my head. Then my mouth moved without permission.

"I decided to get out."

"Really? And why did you do that?"

"I don't want to go back," I told the pavement and winced, sure my actions would cause a meteor to fall from the sky and crush me.

More silence. He hadn't hit me yet. I didn't know why.

"You've been out too long," Dalton said, rage bubbling under the surface of his smooth tone. "You've been learning things that don't concern you, like entitlement and exemption—exemption from punishment. That's not for you, remember?"

Yeah, I remember.

Dalton's black shoes came closer to me. "So, you decided that staying hidden was your safest idea? Tell me, how long have you known dear Micah was still alive?"

My tongue stuck to the roof of my mouth. I just shook my head.

He laughed slightly. "You didn't know. He left you there, didn't he? Really, Arie, are you surprised?"

No. I wish I was.

"I am curious as to how you escaped," he continued, a new edge to his voice, "considering you couldn't walk. We've got to make sure that doesn't happen again, don't we?"

I shuddered. He waited for an answer. I didn't know if responding or silence would be safer.

Out of the corner of my eye, I saw someone peek around the wall from outside, behind Dalton.

Lindsey!

She held up her pointer finger. *Give me a minute. Keep stalling.* Then she was gone.

How am I supposed to stall?

Give up, the monster supplied. *It's what you do best, isn't it?*

A banging sounded against the side of the garage, where Lindsey had come from. Dalton started to turn toward the noise. I panicked.

"There was an accident," I said, pointing at the guard's head leaning out the broken car window. "He got hurt."

Dalton raised an eyebrow. "An accident?" His eyes narrowed. "It looks like someone did it on purpose and pretended it was an accident."

That was a warning tone. I couldn't feel my toes.

"That's funny." I gave him a look that was almost a glare. "That sounds a lot like the accidents that happened to me."

I took a step toward him. Adrenaline surged through me when he took one back. He was scared of me. I knew he always had been. That was why he beat me down so far in the first place.

My voice was airy, light, almost childish. "Why were there so many accidents?"

Dalton looked at me like I was crazy. I sounded like it. I probably was.

"You killed Erika Malone," he said, an automatic response. "You deserved it."

I shook my head. "I didn't kill her. You tell me I did, but I know I didn't." I tapped my finger against my head. "I remember. I can't forget."

My hands went numb. It didn't feel like I was the one talking. The words came from an essence other than myself, just using my mouth as an alternative exit.

Dalton took a big breath, going back to his scare tactics. "You are a lying little devil that—"

"I get it," I said even though I didn't. "You didn't mean to kill her. You got mad. You get violent when you get mad. You don't think." I shrugged. "Just an accident, right?"

His mouth was hanging open with slow, heavy breaths, his face beginning to turn red. "You will regret this, Arie." He came closer to me. "You know how this ends."

I know how this ends. A wave of hopelessness crashed over me, breaking through my thin charade. Any ground I had gained was lost as I dropped my gaze, whole body shaking, taking four steps away from Dalton.

"Grab them and let's go," Dalton ordered. "We're done here."

I didn't resist as Norwood grabbed my arm roughly, jerking me back toward the car.

A voice stopped us in our tracks. "Richard, you let them go. Now."

I glanced up to see a furious Lindsey walking right up to Dalton, halting a few feet in front of him. Norwood moved past me, standing next to Dalton, gun trained on Lindsey.

"Lindsey Carter," Dalton said in disgust, gesturing to me. "I can see you've turned to the dark side."

She was bravely angry for someone who had a gun on her. "I finally found the files you tried so hard to bury. You can't even imagine the hot water you're in. Keaton is ready to kill you himself."

"You told him?"

"It's been sent. Within a half hour, the entire agency will know and a watch will be put out."

Dalton cleared his throat, getting nervous. "It doesn't matter—"

"It *does* matter actually," Lindsey said, her hands balling into fists. "This is way past lying to the agency.

This is murder, kidnapping, and extortion, all with a fake government identity." She gave a small smile. "You're finished."

"No." Dalton shook his head. "Keaton won't believe you."

"Keaton doesn't have to believe me." She pointed to me. "Keaton has talked to her. Keaton knows her. Better yet, Keaton owes her. Keaton will get you nowhere."

At that, Dalton instantly turned on me, the fury making his face go bright red.

"You've talked to Keaton?" he shouted, making me cower backwards against the car. "What did I tell you about talking?" He shot the ceiling three times, his eyes wild, no longer in control. "That's it. Apparently, you need another lesson."

My body went numb, an acid pit in my stomach. "No…no, wait, please." I took a step forward, but Norwood cocked his gun, sending the message: I move and Lindsey dies. I watched in horrified helplessness as Dalton stomped over to Sark.

"No, please," I begged, my desperation clear. "I'll go back with you, no problems. I'll never try to get out again. Just leave them alone."

"I told you what would happen, Arie," he said. "The rules were always very clear. You disobey and you are punished. Considering how many violations you've racked up, I'm starting with Sark and just going down the line of your friends here."

"You can't do that." I could feel myself starting to unhinge. "You can't do that to me."

"I can do whatever I want to you! That's the point you are missing. I can do whatever is necessary because you are not worth anything more."

"You can't do this to me again!" I screamed, my whole body shaking.

"You deserve every bit of it!" His face was nearly crimson. "You're only a pathetic little brat whose idiocy cost me everything!"

My eyes widened in shock. What Lindsey had said made more sense, adding up with his behavior. Only one thing was 'everything' to Dalton.

"You put me through all this hell because you *lost your job*?"

Dalton stalked up to me, striking my face with his gun. "Don't talk to me like that! You were supposed to get me to Sark, not send me on a ludicrous hunt for months that led me nowhere. The agency cut me off while you were on a beach with the man himself and *my assistant*!" He went to hit me again. "What kind of—"

A loud cracking sounded, and Dalton dropped to the floor in a pool of blood. I put my hands over my mouth to muffle my scream. Blinking back shock, Norwood and his men began to lower their guns in surrender as Brody ran in, Deron and a group of agents following close behind.

Brody came up to me first, breathing hard. "You okay, kid?"

I couldn't tear my eyes away from Dalton, so I closed them instead, taking a few deep breaths to keep myself in check.

Do not lose it now. Do not lose it now.

Someone put their hands on my shoulders. "Arie?" Lindsey asked. "Can you hear me?"

I cleared my throat. "Can I be excused please?"

"If you need—"

I didn't wait for her to finish. I ran, not fully opening my eyes until I felt the fresh air on my face. I sprinted down the sidewalk, hearing the faint sound of someone calling my name, and felt a sick sense of freedom. The trouble was, when you've been in prison for so long, you have to learn to live with it. Sometimes, in a weird way, you learn to like it, to rely on it. Because when you've been in prison for so long, sometimes the confinement is the only thing you have.

27

It took a long time for me to get my head together. I walked forever, unable to focus on much besides the chaos going on inside of me. The fear, the triumph, the isolation, the confusion. I had no idea what I was feeling, or what I should've been feeling, or if I should've been feeling at all. I just won, right? Dalton could never try to kill Sark or lock me up ever again. Shouldn't that feel more like a victory?

For whatever reason, it didn't. It only felt like I had somehow done the wrong thing, which was absolutely ridiculous. Right?

When I finally came to myself, I realized three

things: it was dark, I was alone, and I had no idea where I was.

How long have I been going? It had to have been afternoon when I left. How could it be dark already?

I surveyed my surroundings, hoping to gain a clue. There was a gas station, a convenience store, a bank, a diner, and a few other buildings, but nothing much and nothing I recognized.

I'm lost, I realized. *But wasn't that the idea in the first place?* The plan this morning had been to run away, back to Dalton of all people. That seemed like it was months rather than hours ago. How could that have been my plan?

Sark was right. That was incredibly stupid.

A few drops of rain fell from the black sky, heightening my nerves. I decided to duck into the diner to escape whatever might be coming.

Ignoring the few people in the establishment, I went straight into the single bathroom and locked the door behind me. Then I pulled off my hood and looked in the mirror. My reflection had a few bruises and a bit of blood, but nothing I couldn't fix. Turning on the sink, I started to go to work, managing to wash the blood off, but wasn't able to do anything for the wounds underneath.

Oh well. It's good enough.

Satisfied that I looked somewhat normal, I ventured back into the diner, sliding into the booth closest to the door. Quiet eighties music played in the background, overrun by the sound of a wailing baby. A young mother was in the corner booth holding the crying child while trying to keep a four-year-old boy from running out of his seat. Two men were sitting at the counter, sipping coffee and watching a basketball game on the

TV hanging on the wall. Besides them and the lady behind the counter, the place was empty.

Okay, you need a plan. I looked out the window into the night, watching as the rain started coming down harder. *You need to figure out what the heck you're doing.*

"Excuse me," someone said, rather close to me, making me jump. I glanced up to see a plump, fifty-something waitress standing next to my table. "Can I get you anything?" she asked, her tone telling me her shift should've ended three hours ago.

I cleared my throat, hoping my voice was mostly there. "Um, no. No thanks."

The lady huffed in irritation, and I couldn't really blame her. I wouldn't want to work here with stranded teenagers who didn't have the money to order anything.

She turned to walk away, but I caught her in time.

"Is there a phone I could use?" I asked, my voice shaky.

She raised a skeptical eyebrow. "You don't have a phone?"

"It's…it's dead. Please, this is really important."

She sighed, contemplated for a minute, then reached into a pocket in her apron. Sliding an ancient flip phone on the table, she glared at me sternly.

"Three minutes. If you try and run off with it, I'm calling the cops, you hear me?"

I nodded in a jerky motion. "Yes, thank you so much."

Giving me one more glare, she turned and went behind the counter. I could feel her gaze penetrating through my soul, so I turned my back to her, bringing my legs up so I could rest my chin on my knees. Then I picked up the phone, flipped it open, and dialed the number I had memorized so long ago.

He answered halfway through the second ring, rushed and panicked. "Yeah?"

"Sark?" I kept my shaky voice down.

"Arie?" The relief hit him like a baseball bat, leaving him breathless. "Oh Arie…are you okay? Where are you?"

"Um, I don't know. Are you okay? And the infecteds?"

"Yeah, we're fine. Lindsey took the men back with her, including Lennon. Arie, where are you?"

"Is Micah okay?" I couldn't help asking. "He was…with everything…"

"He's just fine," Sark answered, his tone slightly irked but not pushing it. "He's gone, actually."

Thank goodness. "And you promise you're okay?"

"Yeah, I told you, I'm fine." He seemed almost annoyed. "Why?"

"Well, I…" *This is going to sound stupid.* "If Dalton ever found me, you were going to die like Erika because I broke the rules," I stated, like the fact of life I had believed it to be.

Sark waited for a second until he realized that was it. "Okay…well, I didn't."

"Yeah," I said thoughtfully. "I guess you didn't."

"Arie," Sark started, his voice mildly cautious. "Are you okay? Because you're talking like you're okay."

"Dalton is dead," I said, internally wincing at how I wasn't outwardly wincing. "Shouldn't I be okay?"

"Uh, yeah, I guess." Sark didn't seem convinced. "We're about ready to leave here. Tell me where you are and I'll come get you."

"I'm at a restaurant—a diner—but I don't know where."

"Can you give me anything? What does it look like? What's it called?"

"Um…" I ducked my head to the side so I could read the sign out the window. "It's called 'Nan's Place.' It's small and white and there's a black motorcycle in the front."

There was faint rustling on the other end. I heard the waitress behind me clear her throat and knew my time was up.

"Sark, I have to go. She needs her phone back."

"Okay, Arie, listen to me very carefully: do not move. You stay exactly in that spot and you don't move for anything until I get there. I mean anything. Got it?"

"Yeah."

"I'm serious, Arie."

"I know."

"Stay where people can see you." His voice echoed, as if he were in the garage now. "I'll be there soon."

"Okay."

I hung up the phone and stared at it for a moment before getting up to give it back to the lady. She was still staring at me, disapproval in her eyes as she twisted a towel in her hand.

"Thank you," I told the floor, sliding her phone to her. She nodded and I went back to sit down.

Lighten up. I knew I probably didn't look like someone she wanted to deal with, but she could at least be nice. She had no idea what my day had been like today.

Oh well. We can't have everything.

I shifted around on my seat, suddenly aware of my tired, aching body. Waiting for Sark had seemed like a good idea until I got to the *waiting* part. What if the diner closed and I had to leave? What if Sark couldn't find me? What if someone else found me first?

Like who? Sark said himself that Lindsey has everyone. There's nobody out there. I still wasn't sure that was enough to reassure me. Something didn't feel right.

Of course something doesn't feel right, I reasoned with myself. *You just faced Dalton. This is normal.*

Right. Normal.

I tapped my fingers on the table, looking around until I found a clock. It had been six minutes and forty-seven seconds since I had hung up the phone. Forty-eight. Forty-nine. Fifty.

This is impossible.

Absentmindedly, I reached over and grabbed the black container that held all of the mini jam containers. When I was a kid, my grandpa would take me to a diner like this once a month, just me and him. While we waited for our food we would make small towers out of the different jam squares. He would always 'accidentally' knock mine down, claiming that his was taller and he won. Even up until I was fifteen, right before he died, I would always laugh.

I sighed, watching as my small tower toppled over. Grandpa was never afraid of anything, in life or in death. He was a Christian, which greatly irritated my dad, and they never really got along, often tearing my mom between the two. Grandpa thought my dad needed to put away his obsessions and care for his family. Dad thought Grandpa's head was way too far up in the clouds. They were a thorn in each other's side.

Maybe if they had been better friends, Mom wouldn't have been so alone in it. She wouldn't have taken his death so hard. She and Dad would've been closer, she would've convinced him to give up the cult thing, Kieran would've stayed, and we could've been a normal family.

I wonder what Grandpa would think of his son-in-law's obsession now. Grandpa would've been on my side for sure. He was one of the people I was certain had really loved me.

I looked at the clock again. Twelve minutes. One of the men from the counter got up and left. I couldn't help but stiffen as he walked past me to get out the door.

Turning my attention back to the jams, I noticed that I was no longer alone. The little boy with black matted hair had escaped his mother and was now standing next to my table. His focused eyes kept going from my face to the jams in my hand.

I gave him a small grin, which seemed to be good enough for him. He climbed into the bench across from me, his sneakers squeaking against the plastic, then sat with his hands in his lap. I offered him the jams in my hand. He waited for a second before taking them, going to work on his own tower. I watched with amused interest as it fell over several times while he was getting it just right.

"Ronan!" the mother in the corner called, trying to turn around in the booth while holding her baby. Both the kid and I tensed up. "Ronan, where are you?"

The kid gave me a look of secret confidence before bolting back to his mom. I heard her scolding voice echo before she craned her neck around, trying to see me. I went back to my jam tower.

Another fifteen minutes went by. It had only been a half hour. This was going to drive me insane.

Eventually, Ronan made his way back over to me. He didn't hesitate as he sat across from me, ketchup now smeared in the corners of his mouth. We built up several towers, knocked them all down, and then made a giant one. I kept checking the clock, nervous anticipation building. After ten minutes, the mom came over too. She sat down next to her kid, her baby now asleep in her arms, an exhausted expression on her face. With a start, I realized she couldn't have been that much older than I was.

I shrunk back into the seat, feeling as if I was in trouble too. It was easy for me to be around kids—anyone else, not so much.

"Ronan said you needed help," she told me, her voice guarded. "Are you harassing my kid for money?"

The accusation startled me. "No, no…I mean, I…no. Absolutely not."

Her face softened slightly. "Okay then. What kind of help do you need?"

"I, uh…I didn't tell…" I looked to Ronan, who just stared back at me.

Who is this kid?

"Can you just give me some directions?" I asked, finally finding my voice.

She brushed a strand of blonde hair out of her face. "Where are you headed?"

"I came from the downtown Denver area and I'm trying to get back."

She nodded toward the window. "Did you come northbound?"

"Um…I think? Sorry, I'm kind of directionally challenged."

She pointed. "From there?"

"Yep. That road."

"If you go that way, it winds around forever." She pointed out the window to the right. "That road connects you to the highway—it's a straight shot."

"How long would it take to get there?"

She shrugged. "Maybe an hour and a half, with traffic. Not bad."

Sark should be here by now. It had been an hour since I had called him. Sark wouldn't take an hour and a half. With his speeding issue, he could shave off thirty minutes easy.

"What's the problem?" she asked, shifting the baby in her arms.

I shook my head. "Um, I…I'm just waiting for someone. They should've been here by now. And they're not. It just…worries me."

"Do you need a phone?"

"Um, yes. That would be great."

She looked to Ronan, who started digging through the petite purse that hung over her shoulder. He put a cell phone on the table and slid it to me.

"Thank you."

My fingers couldn't move fast enough; dialing took too long. A pit formed in my stomach when the first ring sounded. Then the second. Third. Too many. The monotone lady came on, informing me that the person I was trying to reach was not available.

Something is wrong. Something is very very wrong.

I tried it again. Same thing. One more time. Nothing.

Shakily, I slid the phone back to Ronan. His seemingly unblinking eyes stayed trained on me.

Maybe his phone died. His phone probably died, and he's racing to get here before I panic. That's it. Or something minor happened and he had to stay back for a little bit longer than he thought. Maybe something broke, or someone got hurt, or…

No, something big happened. I knew it. I could feel

it. Only the zombie apocalypse itself would keep Sark from getting here when he said he would.

The woman cocked her head to the side, narrowing her eyes slightly.

"You're in deep trouble, aren't you?"

I sighed, holding my head in my hands. "You have no idea."

She waited for a second, then tapped the table with her hand. "All right. Come on."

Taking care to not jostle her baby, she stood up out of the booth, gesturing for me and Ronan to follow.

"Come on. I'm taking you to Denver."

I waited for the punch line. It didn't come. "Why?"

"One troubled sister to another. I'm heading that way anyway."

She didn't wait for a response; she just walked right out the door. Ronan squeaked his way out of the booth, then stood and watched me.

Is this worth it? Risking my life in the hands of a stranger just to get to Sark and the others? I knew the answer: of course it was.

Hesitantly, I followed the girl outside into the rain, checking to see Ronan trudging along after me.

The girl had already strapped her sleeping baby in a car seat and started the car. Ronan stopped outside the vehicle, watching me until I slipped gingerly into the little beater.

"Are you in, buddy?" the girl asked, peeking in the rearview mirror to look at Ronan. He must've nodded, because she pulled out of the parking lot and onto the road.

"I'm Maisley, by the way. That's Ronan, and the sleeping bear is Banks."

"I'm Erin," I mumbled, using the fake name I

always used to say. I hadn't needed to use it in a long time.

"Well, Erin, it's nice to meet you."

"Yeah, you too. Um, why are you doing this? Really?"

She pursed her lips, adjusting the heater. "How old are you? Nineteen?"

"Eighteen."

"Eighteen." She nodded in reminiscence. "I was eighteen once too."

I decided not to press that point. It sounded a bit too personal.

Where are you Sark? What happened? I tapped my foot against the ground, trying to distract myself.

"So how old are they?" I asked, nodding toward the back.

"Banks is eight months and Ronan is almost six."

"Six?"

"Yeah, he's a small kid. Looks a lot younger than he is. He's smart though."

I thought of his deep penetrating eyes—I could feel him staring at me now, through the seat. He seemed to be on a different wavelength than the rest of us.

"I believe it. Does he ever talk?"

Maisley's mouth twisted down. "Sometimes. We're working on the whole 'confidence' thing."

I folded my arms across my chest. "He seems like a great kid."

"Yeah." She smiled. "Yeah, he is."

We spent the rest of the time listening to the quiet radio, making small talk from time to time. She seemed to understand my stress and never pressed it. Strangely enough, no stress came from being in a car with a stranger. Part of me thought that was weird, but I didn't really care. I studied every car we passed, hoping in vain I would recognize it.

You're overreacting. It's totally fine. You're going to show up and laugh at yourself because you blew this way out of proportion. It wouldn't be the first time. For some reason, I couldn't believe myself.

Maisley made great time: we arrived in forty-five minutes. I told her to pull over a block and a half down from the club, just in case.

"I can't even begin to say thank you," I said. "I'm sorry I can't pay you."

She waved her hand. "Don't worry about it. I was coming down this way anyway."

Before I could get out, I felt a hand tap my shoulder. I turned around to see Ronan leaning as far forward as his seatbelt would let him, reaching his hand out to me. In it was a small container of strawberry jam.

I couldn't help but smile. "Thanks Ronan. This is the best present I've ever gotten."

Ever so slightly, the ketchup-stained corners of his mouth turned up. Then he sat back into his seat.

"Good luck," Maisley said. "Make the right choices and all that jazz."

"Bye guys. Thanks again."

I stepped out of the car, rain seeping into my sweatshirt, then waited until Maisley had disappeared around the corner before I made my way to the dark club.

Please be okay. Please let everyone be okay.

I walked as fast as I dared around to the side door we all used. I pushed. It wouldn't open. I pushed harder. Nothing.

Oh no.

Finally, after slamming my shoulder into the door,

it gave way. I slipped through the small crack I was able to make.

The place was a disaster. Windows shattered, chairs broken, walls bashed in. Going as quietly as I could, I made my way around the room, straining my ears for any sound. Nothing. I crept to the stairs, finding blood smeared on the wall. It was then that I saw the body lying in a heap on the stairs. Neil.

I checked and found a small heartbeat, breathing a small sigh in relief. Trying my best to be careful, I dragged him into the kitchen, which was where I found Mark and Mara. They both appeared to have been shot but were still alive. Mara was barely awake.

Setting Neil down next to them, I grabbed Mara's bloody hand.

"Mara?" I whispered in a panic. "Mara, what happened?"

She couldn't open her eyes, but her eyelids fluttered at my voice. "Arie? Arie, they're gone. They're gone."

"Okay, it's okay." I ripped off two strips of her jacket, tying one around her shoulder and one around Mark's bleeding side. "It's okay. Just breathe. It's okay."

Who did this?

I tore through every drawer in the kitchen until I found a rogue emergency cell phone. Still holding Mara's hand, I dialed 911, then grabbed a marker out of a drawer.

"Three people are seriously hurt," I told the operator once they answered. "We need help now." Quickly, I gave them the address and hung up.

"You're going to be okay," I repeated to Mara over and over as I wrote names on her, Neil, and Mark's right arms. "Don't worry, it'll be okay."

Using the phone again, I dialed Lindsey's cell phone number—hopefully she could tell me what was going on.

Come on, come on, come on.

It rang. It rang. It rang. She didn't answer.

Oh no. Lindsey.

"Arie," Mara mumbled. "Arie, you have…have to…help them. Fast. Now."

Hearing sirens in the distance, I leaned down and patted her hand reassuringly. "I will. You just wait here, okay? Someone will come help you. You're going to be just fine."

I got up, did a quick double-check around the club to make sure I didn't miss anyone, then went back out into the rain, running. I ran flat out, pushing myself as far as I ever had, making it to Lindsey's office in record time.

Out of breath, I shoved the front door open. The dead ring of silence crashed into my ears. I flipped a light switch—nothing. The power had been shut off. Rain dripped off of my body as I hesitantly made my way down the darkened hallway, not able to shake the feeling I was in a horror movie.

My heart pounded as my eyes adjusted. Empty. Offices empty. Not a soul around. Besides that, there was nothing out of the ordinary. I silently kept going until I got to Lindsey's office.

This is it. If she's in here…

Taking a deep breath, I opened the door. Lindsey was nowhere to be found, but Deron was on the ground. It wasn't until I got closer that I could see the red seeping from his silver hair: he was dead.

Bile rose in my throat and I fought to keep it down.

A small square of the ceiling was illuminated a split

second before a ringing sounded, making me jump. I approached the desk to see a cell phone going off.

That's Lindsey's phone.

I stepped around Deron and cautiously picked up the phone. It was a blocked number.

Do I really have a choice here?

My finger hit the answer button without real permission and I brought the phone to my ear.

"Hello?"

"Arie," Lennon greeted, sending a chill down my spine. "You are quite predictable, you know that?"

No, no, no. I kicked Lindsey's desk as hard as I could. *Lennon escaped. He made contact. Alexis has them all.*

"If you touch them," I started, "I swear, I—"

"There's a shopping mall on the north side that's closed for the evening," Lennon interrupted, his voice dripping with the utmost arrogance. "Your friends are waiting for you to join them."

I shook my head, fiery anger battling with the sheer terror inside of me. "You're making a big mistake."

"I'm afraid the mistake was yours, but you know that. You made your choices."

"I hate you," I forced through my teeth. "And I can't wait to see you get what you deserve."

Lennon ignored me, a sense of impatience to his tone. "For old-time sake, Arie, come play the game one last time."

"No, we're done playing," I told him, my voice like ice. "The game is over. This is war. And I promise you, you will lose."

I hung up the phone and chucked it at the wall. That was it. No more hiding. No more running. This had to end now.

I turned Lindsey's office upside down until I found a gun hidden in a desk compartment. Stowing it in my jacket pocket, I grabbed a set of car keys hanging on the wall and stalked out the door.

The monster's mocking voice echoed in my head. *This is war? Seriously? I hope you realize how ridiculous you sound.*

Shut up.

The violent sky was still dumping rain when I got out to the parking lot, pressing the button on the remote a million times until I found the car that lit up.

What do you think you can do? she asked me. *You're just a damaged little girl. I mean, let's be honest, you can't actually win here.*

That's why they should be afraid of me, I told her, pulling the car out onto the street. *I'm damaged because I should've died but instead I survived.*

28

I should've been at least trying to think rationally, but I wasn't. All of the months of burying emotion helped me to stay in control. I couldn't think many actual thoughts, but at least I was in control. Mostly.

I set the navigation in the car to the mall I assumed Lennon was talking about, though I still had no idea what my plan was. I was doing exactly what he wanted. How was it going to help me win?

Doesn't matter. I have to save them. Nobody is going to die today. I tried to ignore the fact that the infecteds had been in Alexis' custody for at least an hour, maybe more. The truth was they could already be dead.

Parking the car two blocks away from the mall, I got out and half ran down the street, passing the businesses that were asleep for the night.

Every step was torment. Every step was one closer, yet one still too far away. Every step a name echoed in my empty head.

Sark's dead. Alaina's dead. Brennan's dead. Sark's dead. Hadley's dead. Jacklynn's dead. Sark's dead. Lucy's dead. Liam's dead. Sark's dead.

Sark's dead.

Sark's dead.

I stopped once I was across the street from the mall. It seemed much more sinister when vacant and black, no hustle and bustle of ordinary life, especially when I knew what was waiting for me inside.

Entry plans started going through my head. There was a parking garage underneath the mall—that was my safest and most concealed approach. I could sneak up the stairs and be inside the mall without anyone knowing.

But that's what they expect me to do. They know I'll take the option where I'll feel hidden and in control. I tapped my foot against the ground in agitation. *I need to do the opposite of what they expect...why not just walk through the front door?*

That was definitely not typical infected behavior, especially for me. In fact, I was willing to bet nobody was even watching the front door, since everyone assumed I wouldn't even consider it. Plus, they would've turned the security systems off so they could get inside in the first place.

Worth a shot.

My whole body was numb as I quickly crossed the

wide parking lot, feeling like a deer in the free pasture during open season. Picking up one of the decorative rocks from the landscaped grounds, I went right up to the main door.

Here goes nothing.

I smashed the glass with the rock, wincing as the door shattered, then braced myself for the worst. Nothing happened. Careful not to slice my hands, I gently brushed the glass pieces onto the ground until there was a large enough hole that I could climb through.

I crept soundlessly into the dim building, freezing when my shoe squeaked against the floor. I'd forgotten I was sopping wet.

Doesn't matter. Just be careful.

Hugging the wall, I held my gun at the ready and tiptoed up to the first store, which was a nail salon. A silver chain gate blocked the entrance. Nobody was inside.

One down. There were tons of stores in the mall though. Checking them all one by one would take forever, but it was the only option I really had. I followed that pattern—hugging, tiptoeing, peeking, aiming, empty—several times, taking me deeper and deeper into the mall. It wasn't until I got to a clothing store called 'SD Cove' that I saw lights. As I cautiously went closer, I could make out angry voices inside.

"Shut up!" a man yelled. A smacking sounded, followed by a muffled cry of pain that I knew so well.

Alaina.

"You tell me where she is," the man demanded. "And you tell me now."

"Not today, Porky," Alaina retorted. "Go eat yourself another sandwich."

Careful to not be seen, I reached forward and banged my gun against the bars. Ringing sounded. Silence. A few moments passed, then I saw a hand lift the gate halfway up. That was my chance.

Instinct took over my body in a way it never had before. Leaping forward, I grabbed the guard's hand and twisted it the wrong way, slammed my knee into his gut, then smashed his head into the wall. He crumpled to the ground.

I ducked smoothly underneath the silver gate. By the time everyone registered who I was, I had shot at a giant '50% off' sign hanging from the ceiling, and it crashed to the ground, landing on top of the remaining guard and putting him out.

Kinda scared at my ability, I stared at my hands in shock for a moment.

Did I really just do that? For some reason, it really freaked me out. *Where did that come from?*

Shaking the thought out of my head, I rushed to Alaina, who was on the ground, falling to my knees and helping her sit up. "Are you okay?"

"Yeah, I'm fine." She rubbed a bruise on her face before turning on me. "What the heck are you doing here?"

I ignored her, now noticing the people tied to clothing racks in the back of the store.

"Arie!" Hadley yelled, pulling on his restrained wrists. "Arie, you're okay!"

I stood up to get a better view of Hadley, Brennan, Lucy, Peter, Jacklynn, Kayla, Lindsey, and Brody, each with a measure of disbelief in their eyes.

Sark isn't here. The thought hit me like a ton of bricks. *He isn't here. He's dead.*

"Earth to Arie," Alaina said, standing up next to me.

"Are you insane? Do you have any idea—"

"Where's Sark?" I cut her off.

She took a deep breath, trying to keep her voice from cracking. "I don't know. They started with him first."

"What do you mean first? What happened?"

"Lennon, he…he came back. He brought Jefferson and a ton of guards with him and everything was insane. They grabbed everyone who they thought would know something about you—us—and took Sark away right after we got here. Everyone else…they could…they might be…"

"Help me cut these guys loose," I told her, searching the room until I found scissors at the checkout desk. We worked through the restraints as I filled them in on what I knew. "Neil, Mark, and Mara were taken in an ambulance under the names Charles, Tanner, and Trisha Cohens. They were critical, but I think they'll be okay."

"How'd you get in here?" Brennan asked, straightening the thread bracelets on his wrist once his ties had been cut.

"I broke through the front door."

He did a double take. "You what?"

"Yeah, I know."

Lindsey and Brody were the last two I cut free. Lindsey had a decent sized gash on the side of her head.

"Are you okay?" I asked her.

She just nodded. "Are *you* okay?"

I didn't answer. Hadley and Jacklynn both wrapped their arms around my waist, burying their faces in my shirt.

"Arie, you need to get out of here," Alaina told me as soon as everyone was free.

I shook my head. "I have to get to Sark. They're going to tear him to shreds."

"We can—"

"No. I'm getting him out. Besides, this has to end. Now."

It was silent for a minute as I glanced around at all of them. Then Peter stepped forward. "I'm in."

"Me too," Brennan said, and Lucy nodded.

Alaina grinned. "Well I'm not one to bow out of a fight. Let's give the psychos a taste of their own medicine." She glanced at me. "Do you have a master plan, or do we have to wing it?"

"Here's the deal," I said, talking fast, tapping my foot against the ground. "I'm willing to bet the other infecteds are alive. I don't think Jefferson was going to actually kill anyone until I got here, just to make absolute sure I got here. Once they find out I'm here, though, there's no guarantee."

"But you're the priority," Peter said, an edge to his voice. "Once they find out you're here, everyone else will take a backseat until they get you secured."

I nodded. "Exactly. Here's what's going to happen." I handed a pale Kayla the car keys. "The car is parked two blocks down. I want you to take Jacklynn and Hadley back to the club and go get the small moving truck. Dump everything out of it and bring it back here, two blocks down. Then wait for whoever can make it out."

She pursed her lips and nodded once.

I turned to Lindsey and Brody. "You two should go with them. This is going to get ugly."

"Not a chance," Lindsey responded, jerking her chin up. "We're with you."

Brody's eyes glinted darkly. "I've got a bone to pick

with the man who murdered my partner."

"Okay." I detached Jacklynn and Hadley from my body. "Go with Kayla."

Jacklynn had tears rolling down her cheeks, while Hadley kept sniffling to keep his inside.

I leaned down to look at them both head on. "I need you guys to be brave, okay? Can you do that for me?"

They both nodded and Hadley put his brave face on, taking Jacklynn's wrist as they followed Kayla obediently.

"Wait," Brennan called, and Kayla stopped. He looked at Lucy. "You go with them."

Lucy's eyebrows shot up in desperation. "No, Brennan—"

"Yeah," he said, his voice firm. He pushed her softly toward the door. "Go now."

For a second I thought she would argue, but instead she kissed Brennan on the cheek before following Kayla out of the store and out of sight.

"Now what?" Alaina asked me.

"We start looking," I said. "We find Sark and the other infecteds and get them out alive. Alaina, Peter, and Lindsey you take the left side. Brennan, Brody and I will take the right. Grab whatever you can for a weapon and stay alert."

I tossed Peter my gun and he caught it, giving me a questioning stare.

"It'll look better if I'm not armed," I explained. "When they find out I'm here, I mean."

He raised an eyebrow. "And they *are* going to find out you're here?"

I didn't have time to answer. A crackling sound went off, voices filling the air. We all froze in terror.

"Any sign of the subject?"

"That's a negative."

It was then that I realized the voices were coming from the sign victim's walkie-talkie. I walked over and carefully removed it from the carrier on his belt.

It crackled again. "Has Sark said anything?"

"That's a negative. The guy won't break."

"What about the others?"

Silence. I was so focused on the mention of Sark, I didn't register that the man who I had knocked out was supposed to respond.

"Repeat: have the infecteds given any information?"

Silence. Alaina and I exchanged glances.

"Brett? Brett, respond."

Silence. *This can't be good.*

Lennon's voice broke out over the mall's sound system. "Arie Nolan. If you are in the building, would you be so kind as to make your way to the center display on the ground floor?"

"Looks like the cat's out of the bag," Peter muttered.

I didn't move, not entirely sure what to do. Obeying him was a bad idea. Staying put was a bad idea. Standing around trying to decide what the crap to do was an even worse idea.

A few minutes passed. "Very well then," Lennon said. An excruciating howl echoed throughout the dead mall, making my mouth fall open in horror.

Sark. Sark is dying right now.

"You aren't the brave face you put on, Arie," Lennon continued. "I know that now. You show up or he dies." Then the speakers clicked off.

Alaina grabbed my shoulder the same time I took a step toward the door.

"You can't just go waltzing over there, Arie," she

started.

I shrugged her hand off. "Of course I can. What did you think I was going to do? Show up here just so I can sit and listen to Sark die?"

Her eyes narrowed. "You want to know what I think? Fine. I think you're crazy right now. I think that none of us took Dalton seriously enough, Sark's life is on the line, and now you're going all kamikaze on me 'cause you feel so screwed up."

I dropped my gaze, pressing my lips into a thin line, breathing deeply through my nose while attempting to not think.

The monster's voice rung in my head. *I told you, Arie. The fact is, you are screwed up and you can't handle this. Just because you ignore it doesn't make it go away. The harder you try, the harder you'll fall.*

Will you just stop talking?

"New plan," I said, my voice dry. "Alaina and I will find Sark and hopefully the other infecteds. The rest of you search this mall top to bottom, subduing every guard or system possible. Do anything that could cause a setback. We'll meet up at the truck Kayla should be bringing. Once we're all safe we'll figure out where to go from there." I looked up from the ground to glance at all of them. "Okay?"

There were a couple mumbled 'yeah's which was good enough for me. I turned and briskly walked out of the store, noticing Alaina yank a metal pole off a rack before following.

We went into stealth mode, using a map we'd found to navigate the mall while steering clear of the ground center display. Finding the security room was our priority—I figured they'd be keeping Sark somewhere they could shut the door. It took over twenty-five minutes of scouring every nook and cranny of the mall to find a door where we could hear men talking on the other side.

Neither of us had any idea what to expect. Alaina had her weapon ready as I put my hand on the knob, then she nodded. I shoved the door open to see three unsuspecting guards sitting at a desk. It only took a minute for Alaina and me to put them out. Then I went for the crumpled body fallen on the floor.

"Sark!" I collapsed to my knees, pulling him up onto his. He fell into me, his head hitting into my shoulder, and I could hear his faint gasping. I held his head up so I could look at him. His beaten face was hardly recognizable, his jaw hanging at an odd angle, blood dripping off his fingers.

"Arie?" he whispered, wincing, trying to open his eyes.

"Yeah." I breathed a sigh of relief as I realized he was really there. He was alive. "Yeah, it's me."

"Arie…get out," he said, his voice rough with pain and urgency. "Get out now."

"You're coming with me."

I untied his wrists and ankles and helped him attempt to sit up. It was then that I saw the extra cords connecting him to some sort of machine. The burns on his skin made more sense: they were shocking him to death. At least, they were *starting* with shocking him. Who knew what else they had planned for him.

We aren't going to find out.

After he was free, I put his arm around my shoulders and dragged us both up. I staggered under his weight but forced myself onward. He was going to survive. If nothing else, Sark would make it.

With Alaina covering me, I was able to get Sark out

of the room, heading back to the front of the mall. Without warning, something slammed into my back, and I felt a needle dig into my spine, making me lose control of everything. My body locked up, sending both Sark and me to the floor.

Momentarily paralyzed, I could only watch from the floor in helplessness as a dozen guards poured into the space around us, two apprehending Alaina, holding her arms behind her back, and another pulling a gun on Sark. Lennon appeared from behind them. He grinned and kneeled down in front of me.

"Don't touch him," I warned, trying but failing to fight my way to Sark. My body still wouldn't work.

Lennon grabbed my hair and forced me to my knees. "You should take a bit of comfort knowing that Sark remained faithful to you—him knowing your location was the only thing that has preserved him thus far. In a way I'm glad. Now you can watch him and Alaina die."

Over my dead body. I met his stare evenly and spat in his face. He grimaced, wiping the saliva off his cheek, then punched me. Blood dripped out of my nose as a tapping sounded down the hallway. Lennon stiffened and stood up, turning to reveal the guards parting for someone to walk through. With a start, I realized it was Jefferson. He who once stood straight and dignified, now looked worn and aged, hunched over a cane. His furious eyes were trained on me, making me flinch in spite of myself. There was no going back now.

"Glad you could join us," Jefferson told me, his voice frosty. "I was beginning to wonder if Lennon was wrong in his assumptions."

Lennon gritted his teeth and looked at the ground, but didn't say anything.

They were going to kill Lennon if I didn't show up.

"And to think we met this way just over a year ago," Jefferson went on, "you swearing on your grave that you had no idea what we were looking for. I'll admit that I am impressed, Arie. To keep up a believable charade for that long requires at least a whit of skill. It's too bad that it all has to come crashing down around you."

The paralysis was wearing off; I could move my hands. *Keep him talking. You've got to buy time for...for what?*

Jefferson stopped, his shoulders tensing. "Now, I'm going to ask you this once, Arie. Just once. I would choose your answer carefully."

He made a motion, and the guard pressed his gun against Sark's head.

"Arie," Jefferson stated. "Are you the key to the infecting formula?"

Even after all this time of my secret being known, I still felt the stubborn instinct rise up in me. And he knew that. Jefferson thrived on public humiliation.

I dropped my gaze, the shame weighing me down, and admission took over.

"Yes." With that one mumbled word, everything my life had been about for years was over.

Jefferson grinned. "Well, that's been coming for quite some time, hasn't it? Please do continue."

I gritted my teeth, hating where this was going, still very conscious of the gun to Sark's head.

Jefferson tapped his cane against the ground in impatience. "Arie, tell me how to access the power you possess. Now."

Keeping my eyes on the ground, I gave the whole entire truth: "I don't know."

"That won't work anymore, dear." The warning in his tone scared me, though there was nothing I could do.

"I'm telling you, I don't know." I looked up to meet his eyes. "I never have."

"Strangely enough, I don't believe you."

"You have to."

He motioned again. The man pushed the gun harder against Sark's head, making him wince, and a loud cocking sound filled the air.

"No!" I lurched forward but Lennon grabbed me by my hair. "Please, you can't…just wait."

"The time for waiting is past." Jefferson's voice was cold. "You've kept us waiting long enough."

I couldn't keep the desperation out of my voice. "You have to believe me. I don't know…I mean, there isn't anything that I…I just know as much as you do. You probably know *more* than I do—"

"I have no more patience for your lies."

"But I'm not lying!" I struggled to get out of Lennon's grip. "I know I've lied to you before, but I'm at the end now. Could my dad tell you anything?"

Jefferson pursed his lips, and I knew I had hit a nerve.

"See? The only stuff I would know would've come from him. I'm not lying."

"Then tell me why one of my men found a file in your collection mentioning things such as peak phase and breaching concerning the key."

Oh crap.

I shook my head. "I just heard the terms. I don't know what they mean, I swear."

"Uh huh." Jefferson raised an eyebrow. "And how can that be proven? How do I know you haven't breached the key and ruined our opportunity?"

An idea popped into my head. An irrationally stupid idea, but an idea nonetheless.

"I can prove it," I said. "I can prove it and give you the only piece of information I have." I nodded to Sark and Alaina. "But you have to let them go."

I didn't get the chance to plead my case. Alexis stormed in from down the hall, bringing the astonishing coldness that I remembered from my nightmares. He walked right up to me without hesitation, kicking me so hard that a fell back a few feet. I got up just in time for me to see him take a gun from the closest guard and stalk up to Sark. The man guarding him stepped out of the way just in time as Alexis shot Sark in the shoulder.

"No!" I shouted, running and diving in between them, and Sark slumped forward. My panic escalated as I felt the resemblance from my dream. We were heading toward the ending, and I could not live with that ending.

I met Alexis' glare cautiously, knowing I was crossing so many boundaries that had been set over the years.

"There is something I can show you." It took me a moment to realize that it was me talking. "I can give you what you want. But you have to let them go."

Before he could shoot anyone else, I raised my right arm, my hands shaking as I pulled the sleeve of my sweatshirt up, barely exposing the tip of the blue symbol.

Alexis moved so fast, if I blinked I would've missed it all. He yanked me up by my hair, somehow switching his gun for a knife, and carefully pierced my jacket. The sound of fabric tearing filled the silent room as he cut my sleeves off of me.

Many audible gasps sounded as my luminescent skin pattern was revealed. Alexis' thick eyebrows shot up—the most surprise I'd ever seen on his face—as he traced the smooth blade of his knife along the vine going down up my arm to my elbow.

I couldn't help but glance at Alaina, which was a mistake. Her wide eyes were filled with a mix of horror and disgust.

A whistle echoed through the mall, breaking the spell, and I didn't allow myself to think—I just reacted the way I knew I was supposed to. Digging deep for any ounce of courage that might've been left in me, I slammed my knee into Alexis' stomach and smashed my fists into his face. He staggered backwards, which was a feat in itself—the guy was a brick wall.

Alaina had gotten free too and we both dropped to the floor. A second later, bullets rained down from all sides. I glanced up to see Peter, Brennan, Lindsey, and Brody, each coming from a different corner with two big guns apiece, not stopping until they stood in front of Alaina, Sark, and me, like a human wall.

Several of the guards went down while everyone else was herded like sheep, then the gunfire momentarily stopped. For the first time in history, the infecteds were staging an uprising against Alexis—and we actually had a chance. Many of the guards were realizing that, but Alexis had the face of a grizzly bear that'd just been irritated. His eyes burned with icy fire as he glowered at us.

"Are you sure you want to fight this fight?"

Peter tossed Alaina one of his guns and she gave a spiteful smile. "You have no freaking idea."

They let the bullets go again and Alexis' men scattered, heading for any form of cover. I rushed to Sark and dragged him up off the ground, his shirt soaked through with blood.

He's lost way too much blood. He was barely conscious but was aware enough to try and walk.

"Go downstairs," Brennan shouted at me over the gunfire. "Section A of the parking garage."

I was off, Sark and I stumbling over each other as I guided him away from the confrontation and to the stairs.

"Stay with me, Sark," I kept telling him. "Please, you have to stay with me."

We were finally able to make it to the right section of the garage, where Kayla was waiting inside the miniature moving truck. She got out of the front seat, and Lucy, Jacklynn, and Hadley opened the back and jumped out. I was surprised to see Liam was with them. They all gasped when they got a good look at me and, even with the harrowing situation, I felt self-conscious.

Hadley stopped, his mouth hanging open, giant eyes on my arm. "Arie, what—"

"Not now." I couldn't handle that conversation at the moment. Or ever.

Lucy recovered fastest. She pushed the others out of the way as I loaded Sark into the back of the truck. I set him down carefully in the corner, trying to prop him up as comfortably as possible. When he was settled, I checked for a pulse. It was weak but it was there.

"Sark? Sark, can you hear me?"

His eyes didn't open, but he muttered something incoherent. I took that as his reassurance.

"Just hang on a little longer," I told him. "We're going to get you help." I slid away from him a bit so Kayla could examine him.

"When did you get here?" I asked Liam.

"I was locked in the garage," he explained, trying extremely hard to not stare at my arms. "When Kayla came for the truck, she let me out." He hesitated. "Neil, Mark, and Mara…are they…"

"Not dead." My voice was firm. "And not going to be."

One by one, everyone else caught up to us. Lindsey, Brody, Alaina, and Brennan jumped into the back with us while Peter slid into the driver's seat. Brennan shut the doors as Lucy opened the connecting window between us and Peter. Then everyone sat down and braced themselves. Within moments we were speeding down the street.

"Jefferson's been hit," Alaina shouted over the noise of the truck. "Lennon and Alexis scattered, but they'll go back for him. I'm sure they've called in; I just don't know what kind of backup they have around here."

"It can't be much," Brennan reasoned. "This was a spur of the moment thing—not much planning could've gone into it. And they wouldn't skimp on numbers when the stakes were this high. I'll bet they brought all the power they had direct access to right then."

Peter yelled through the window, glancing at us in the rearview mirror. "We have to pin 'em down, then beat it out of here."

"Wherever we go needs a hospital." Kayla scooted away from Sark, her hands covered in his blood. "I've done what I can, but if we don't get to a serious medical facility within twenty minutes…" She pursed her lips, glancing at me.

I looked to Sark helplessly, the idea swallowing me up.

He has twenty minutes to live.

"We can't do anything?"

"No. Even if I had the right supplies, I don't know

if I could save him. We'll just have to wait—"

"We can't wait."

"I can have a helicopter land five minutes from here," Lindsey piped up. "We can get Sark to a hospital far enough away quickly, and I can arrange for your other injured friends to get transferred over."

Finally, Peter just parked the truck in an alley and came into the back with us. "So what do we do?"

"Alexis needs a distraction," Brennan stated. "We took out a ton of their guards. It won't take much to keep them occupied."

There was an uncomfortable moment of silence and I knew everyone was thinking the same thing I was.

"We all know Arie is the only thing that would work," Peter said. When Alaina glared at him, he shrugged. "Sorry. It's just the truth."

I nodded. "He's right. Do we really have another option here?"

"Um, yeah, we do," Alaina snapped.

Lindsey folded her arms across her chest, eyes on me. "Arie, you can't seriously go back to them. You can think of something else."

"Like what?" I asked, exasperated. "They can't risk letting me get away again. They just can't. Alexis would chase me around that mall for hours if he had to. If I go now, he'll still be limited to the mall, I'll hopefully find out where the other infecteds are, and you'll have the chance to get Sark out of here." I met Alaina's gaze. "He's not going to die. Not like this."

She thought for a second, then nodded. "Then I'm coming with you."

"No," Liam said to Alaina. "Absolutely not. You're staying here." He looked at me. "You both should."

I shook my head. "It doesn't work like that."

Brody—who had been working on his phone—spoke up. "I've got a chopper on its way. We have an eight-minute window: we miss it, then we miss it."

Eight minutes. "Then you go now."

Lindsey started tapping her fingers against her arm. "I can have a car waiting for you, Arie. Go just as long as you have to, then get away as fast as you can. I'll even send the helicopter back for you." She took a deep anguished breath. "You just have to come back."

"Wait," Peter said, uncertainty coloring his tone. "You're going by yourself?"

I didn't answer. I gave one last glance to Sark.

Don't die on me, okay? I'll come back as long as you won't die. Please?

Lucy tossed me her jacket so I could trade it for my sleeveless one. I gave her a grateful look before stuffing my freak arms through and zipping it up. Hadley and Jacklynn both broke out of their terrified frozen states to give me another huge hug, not as hesitant to touch me once my marks were covered. I gave them a tight squeeze before breaking their hold. Brennan handed me a gun and a spare magazine. Lindsey pursed her lips, giving me a nod the same time Brody did.

Alaina stepped in front of me before I could jump out of the truck, her black eyes like lava rocks as she jerked her chin at Sark.

"Just keep in mind what would happen to him if he wakes up and you aren't there," she said, her tone edgy with warning. "Do what you have to do but save your sacrificial crap for another time."

I knew she had a point, but I couldn't make promises.

"Just make sure he wakes up," I said, a hint of pleading to my tone, knowing it wasn't what she wanted. Her lips pressed into a thin line, but she let me pass.

Taking a deep breath, I jumped out of the truck and into the frigid night. Right as I took the first step, Peter grabbed my arm and turned me to face him. I was surprised to see his forehead creased with worry, his eyes somewhat distant.

"You can't go by yourself," he said.

I jerked my arm out of his hand. "I'll be fine." Then I turned and ran down the street, back toward the mall, which was now about six blocks away, knowing I had to get there fast if I wanted to make it the playing field.

I had only gone two blocks over before I sensed someone following me. Ducking into the nearest alley, I waited until they caught up before pulling my gun on them, then breathed an angry sigh of relief when I saw it was only Peter.

"What are you doing?" I demanded, securing the gun back in my jacket. "That truck has to leave now."

He shook his head. "Relax. The truck already left."

"Why aren't you in it?"

"You can't be out here by yourself."

"Why not?"

He paced in front of me, obviously stalling for a minute, then answered. "You're injured and too emotionally invested. They need a better chance of getting out of here."

Ouch. I guess he was right. It didn't really add up with standard Peter behavior though.

I folded my arms across my chest. "Then why don't you go your own way, and I'll go mine?"

"No way." His eyes got that distant look in them, something hiding just below the surface. "I don't make the same mistake twice."

What are you talking about? Before I could ask, a car passed by the alleyway and Peter pushed me back into the shadows. We both held our breath, but nothing happened.

I didn't want to waste any more time, so I started running down the sidewalk again. Peter kept up with ease.

"So how do you want to play this?" he asked, slipping into a survival mode. "Do you have something in mind?"

Not really. "I was thinking I'd get their attention then run away like the devil's chasing me and cause some chaos in between."

He scoffed. "No wonder everyone's worried. That's the stupidest thing I've ever heard."

"You got any better ideas?"

"Uh…" He thought for a second. "I'll get back to you on that."

I rolled my eyes. "Yeah, whatever."

I led the way back to the mall, making it there in a couple minutes. I didn't know what to expect. Either the place was vacant, or we were going to walk into a trap. I couldn't decide which would be worse.

Peter and I stopped at the shattered front door, preparing our guns, before stepping inside.

The stench was the first thing that hit me, my nose automatically wrinkling in response. Then my eyes adjusted and took in the horrific scene around me.

"Whoa," Peter breathed.

The guards Alaina, Brennan, Peter, Lindsey, and Brody had injured were still here—but they were dead. A single bullet hole marked every man's forehead.

"I guess Alexis means it when he says he doesn't tolerate failure," Peter said, disgusted.

I shook my head. "That's just sick."

We wound our way carefully through the bodies, checking to see if everyone was really dead. They were. I stopped when I saw the fabric from my sweatshirt on the ground.

Peter saw it too. He looked at me curiously. "So what's with the glow in the dark tattoo? You trying to pull a rebellion on Sark?"

I sighed, kicking the fabric with my shoe. "No."

"Well, where did it come from? What does it mean?"

"I really don't know." I couldn't keep my voice even. "But it's probably nothing good."

"Does it hurt?"

I gave him an annoyed look. "A blue substance burning itself onto my skin twenty-four seven? Yeah, it hurts."

He decided to take the lead then, going through every inch of the mall, even the room we'd found Sark in. My stomach churned when I saw the big electric machine they had him hooked up to.

Please wake up, Sark. Please wake up.

Peter broke our silence. "He was really messed up, you know."

I glanced over to see him staring at the machine too. "What do you mean?"

"When I first showed up at the club." He looked at the gun in his hand now rather than me. "I wasn't one of the first, so I didn't get to see the beginning, but that didn't really matter. He…it was painful to watch, really. Even after I knew who he was." He shrugged. "Maybe that made it worse: knowing what a monster he had to be to work for Alexis and seeing him be annihilated by an infected dying."

I didn't really know how to respond to that; I just stared at him.

He met my gaze. "Honestly, I don't think he could live through that again. I don't think anybody could."

I cleared my thick throat. "Why are you telling me this?"

"I'm just asking you to be careful. You think you can save him—save all of us—by selling yourself out, but you might just destroy him all over again, not to mention some others. You think no one would care, but they would. Believe me, I was there."

Who is this guy? Suddenly, it occurred to me why Peter would be acting like this, why he would ask me to look out for myself and mean it. He lost someone like Sark did.

"Is this because of Leslie?" I asked, my voice quiet.

He flinched at the name, taking a step away from me. I'd never seen such emotion in his eyes before. As quickly as it came, though, it disappeared. He composed himself and turned around, stalking out of the room. I hesitated before following.

I guess that's my answer.

Discouraged that we hadn't found anything—and worried by what that meant—Peter and I made our way down to the parking garage. He checked out the stairwells while I poked around. When I wandered into section E, I found a door that seemed to lead to a small storage room and examined it in curiosity. To my surprise, I could hear muffled voices coming from the other side.

I tried the knob, but it was locked. Instantly, the voices went silent. I froze, sure I had just exposed myself, then someone shouted from inside the room.

"What do you want?"

I blinked in shock. "Tristan?" I yelled, putting my face close to the door.

"Arie?" His voice grew slightly louder. "Arie, is that you?"

"Yeah, hold on." I turned around. "Peter! Peter, come help me with this door."

Peter realized what I needed and brought a fire extinguisher over, using it to break off the handle. I kicked open the door to find thirty grimy faces I recognized crowded together in the tiny room.

"They're all here," Peter breathed in relief as everyone trickled out into the garage, all talking at the same time. Through the blabber of voices, I was able to gather that Alexis' men had locked the infecteds in there, saying they would be back to kill them all in time.

Tristan's eyes were wide but serious. "What happened?" he asked me. "I thought you left." At that, every voice went quiet, every eye trained on me.

I wrapped my arms around myself. "I did. I came back."

"You came back?" a girl—I think her name was Elizabeth—asked in astonishment.

I glanced at Peter nervously, who just shrugged. Then Sark's voice came into my head.

I knew if you would've been there you wouldn't have hesitated to do everything you could. As quickly as possible, I thought of every movie I'd ever seen where somebody had to give a good speech.

"Here's the deal," I started, surprised at how authoritative I sounded. "Alexis is probably somewhere in this building, but we don't know that for sure. A ton of his guards have been taken out and Jefferson himself was hit." I took a deep breath, trying to keep my voice steady. "Sark was critically injured, so Alaina, Brennan,

Lucy, Kayla, Hadley, and Jacklynn took him to a hospital. They're unharmed and safe for the time being."

I shook my head. "I'm not going to lie to you, this is scary. Alexis wants you all dead and me gifted in Christmas wrapping. As far as I'm concerned, that's not going to happen. But we do have a choice here, a chance, and I say we take it. We've done our running, hiding, and fear—I don't know about you, but I'm tired of that. Let's show Alexis that we aren't just some kids he can squash whenever he wants to. Let's take our lives back 'cause I've missed mine."

I stopped talking, the attention making me self-conscious and anxious that I had said the wrong thing.

I laid it on too thick. Too thin?

Nobody moved; nobody spoke. Thirty pairs of eyes just stared at me.

Maybe the whole thing was just incredibly stupid and I should never open my mouth again.

Finally, Tristan took a step forward, giving me a salute. "I'm with you, one hundred percent."

Daxton stepped next to him. "Same here."

After that, I received many nods and excited smiles.

Peter grinned. "I already told you I was in. Let's do this."

"So, what's the plan?" Tristan asked. Everyone looked to me expectantly, as if I could just produce great plans on the spot.

"Well, um…" *Come on, Arie, what's your plan?* "I'm going to go back into the mall to use the speaker system so Alexis will know I'm here. If Jefferson was actually shot, they've got to still be in the building. They haven't had time for anything else."

"And what's that going to do, exactly?" Peter asked.

"Get them out in the open. We can't strike if we can't see them." I paused. "I'm not saying that we can completely do them in tonight. That's reaching for the stars." I smiled. "But we can probably do some damage and send a message."

"Excellent."

"What do you want us to do?" Tristan asked.

I shifted my weight so I could tap my foot against the ground. "I'm thinking we need to subdue the rest of their guards—every single one. I want to make Alexis, Jefferson, and Lennon feel alone and exposed."

"They're used to being behind the line of fire," Tristan said, more to himself. "They won't know what to do."

I nodded. "Exactly. Let's split up into five groups. One of them will be tasked with the job of finding the hospital Neil, Mark, and Mara are staying in and making sure they're okay, then contacting the police. The other four will take different sections: two in the mall and two in the parking garage. Use whatever you can as weapons, collect as you go, and contain the unconscious guards when possible."

"I don't want to be stupid," Carl said, "but what's the police going to do?"

"Lock Alexis and his cohorts up," I answered. "Of course, it won't be long before someone comes to bust them out, but it will buy us time and let them know we aren't messing around anymore. Everyone good with that?"

I was met with many enthusiastic nods—no rejections. That was a good sign.

Once the groups were settled, I gave a few instructions to the infecteds going to find the hospital.

"All right then." I waved my hand at them. "Split up

and go."

I shouldn't have been surprised when Peter followed me, claiming he was in too far now to give up on me. I couldn't tell if I thought it was sweet or annoying.

We made our way up to one of the sound system boards. Carl was in a group posted in the mall, so he followed us and helped patch me into the speaker system before leaving to join his crew.

I blew into the small mic, hearing a crackling sound repeat through the mall.

"This is your moment," Peter said, mostly joking. "Don't ruin it."

Right. Don't ruin it.

I debated for a few seconds before speaking. "Arie here." My voice broadcasted in the air, making me wince in spite of myself. "I told you, Lennon: you made a big mistake. We aren't going to go down without a fight. Or at all."

Ah, you're so stupid.

"So I'm waiting here," I went on. "When you're ready, come and get me."

Stepping away from the mic, I looked to Peter and gave a curt nod. "That's it. Let's go."

"Where?"

"Back up to the security room. Maybe we can turn the alarm systems back on and watch the cameras or something. Alexis has got to be around here somewhere."

He nodded and we started for the room. "And what happens if we find him?" he asked me as we walked.

"No idea. Maybe a dance number. How's your pirouette?"

He snorted. "And who let you make the plans?"

"I don't hear you coming up with anything."

Peter had to break the handle on the security door to get it to open, which we thought was weird, but once we were finally able to get inside we saw why Alexis didn't want us in there. Jefferson lay unconscious, sprawled out on the floor with a bloody bandage over his left side. He was alone.

I went over to inspect the sickly Jefferson while Peter relocked the door.

He looks bad, I thought. *He could die here.* I wasn't sure how I felt about that.

Peter walked up next to me and gave one scornful glance to Jefferson, then spat on him. "He deserves it."

It was then that I noticed a small chain around Jefferson's neck, his shirt concealing what was hanging on it. Trying not to be grossed out, I held my breath and pulled the chain to reveal a small flash drive.

"What do you think is on it?" Peter asked.

"I don't know." I popped the drive out of its cap attached to the chain. "Let's find out. Isn't there a computer in here?"

Peter pressed a button on a big black box by the desk and a large screen blinked to life. I plugged the drive into the computer, sat at the desk, and held my breath.

At first, the surge of data that popped up on the screen was too overwhelming, but eventually I started to work through it. My jaw dropped when I realized what I'd found.

"Peter, do you know what this is?"

"Um, no," he said flatly. "I don't really speak computer. What is it?"

"It's…" I was at a loss for words. "It's everything. It's dates, account numbers, passwords. It tells me what files are stored on what database and how to access them. It details important locations and hideouts." I sat back in my chair. "This could change everything."

I leafed through every drawer in the room until I found another flash drive, then started copying the information onto it. Jefferson couldn't know I'd found his files. We needed the edge.

This is what you've been waiting for. This is your chance to fix everything.

Peter paced around the room while I watched the screen in fascination, my eyes concentrating on the small bar that said 'copying files.' After fifteen minutes, I was afraid Peter was going to go crazy.

"Go round up the others," I said. "Tell them we've got something important and we're getting out of here. I'll meet up with you in five minutes."

Peter gave me a skeptical look and I was nervous he was on to me, but he just sighed.

"Five minutes," he repeated. Then he left, making sure to shut the door behind him.

I waited for the last of the passwords to be copied over before ejecting the two flash drives. There wasn't enough time to copy everything, but I had gotten exactly what I needed. Carefully, I returned Jefferson's drive to its place, put mine in my pant pocket, then slipped out the door, heading for the front entrance.

I went to the center of the mall only to find Peter waiting for me, impatient agitation on his face.

"It's quiet," he told me when I got close enough to him. "I don't like it."

"Let's just go." I glanced around. "Where's everyone else?"

Before Peter could respond, a black SUV came racing through the mall and slammed right into him. He flew several feet in the air and landed in a heap on the ground.

"Peter!" I shouted, starting to move toward him. Someone grabbed me from behind, and I caught the half sweat, half expensive cologne scent of Lennon. He jammed something that looked like a TV remote into my shoulder, sending an electric current that tore through me, making me feel as if I were on fire. My body went limp and lifeless, and Lennon started to throw me into the car.

Peter reappeared and socked Lennon in the face. I fell to the ground as they got into a brawl.

My head was buzzing violently as I crawled toward Peter, tackling Lennon off of him. Lennon hit me square in the jaw, then wrapped his hands around my throat, cutting off my air. I pounded his face with my fists until he lost his grip. Peter grabbed him from behind, landing a nice blow to the back of his head, but Lennon elbowed Peter's shoulder and Peter grimaced in pain.

I moved to help Peter, but I didn't get very far— Alexis got out of the car and caught up to me. He seized me roughly by the hair and bashed my head into the ground several times before throwing me into the backseat.

You're caught, the thought echoed uselessly in the back of my battered skull. *Alexis has you.*

I was able to open my eyes and lift my head up, seeing the lighting in the car change. We were speeding through the parking garage now, almost to the outside world.

A thunderous sound exploded to my left, causing Alexis to lose control of the car, putting us on course for a giant cement pillar. The car slammed into it with full force. I flew into the windshield, glass shattering everywhere, as the airbags went off. My head smacked against something solid and the world went black.

<div style="text-align:center">~~~</div>

When I came to, I was lying on the ground, every part of my body aching. I groaned, opening my eyes to see a night sky full of twinkling stars and a bruised Sasha sitting next to me.

"Your head is bleeding," she told me. "You're going to want to be careful."

Heeding her warning, I slowly sat up, looking over my bruised and bloody body before surveying my surroundings. We were in the corner of an alley. Peter, Daxton, and Tristan were talking a few yards away.

Sasha answered before I could ask. "The police finally showed up, so I'm sure Alexis and his boys are locked up by now, just like you said, but the officers started asking us questions, so we had to disappear."

I stretched my sore arms out, trying to hide a wince. "So…it kind of worked?"

Sasha grinned, the kind of grin that let me know she didn't completely hate me anymore. "Yep. Message totally sent."

"All right," Tristan said as the boys came up to us. "We've got to get out of here. I give it six hours before handlers are all over this place."

I noticed Peter favoring his right arm—he offered his left hand to pull me up. I was able to keep myself from vomiting in response to my dizzy head. We all walked together out of the alley and into the night, and I could feel the excitement and freedom emanating from the others, but I only felt heavier. A wave of exhaustion hit as the day's entirety started to catch up with me.

"We're heading to the hospital," Tristan told us.

"We're working on getting Neil, Mark, and Mara moved to the same facility where everyone else is."

"Have you heard from them?" I asked, my voice urgent.

Daxton answered. "Neil and Mara have woken up and they'll be okay. Mark is alive, but still unconscious. We haven't heard about anyone else." I knew he was referring to Sark; he just didn't want to say it.

No, Sark, you have to wake up. You just have to.

"Then we'll meet up with you later," Peter said. "Arie and I have some things to take care of."

We do? I gave him a questioning glance, but he purposely ignored my gaze.

Tristan looked confused too, but didn't raise the question. "Okay then. See you later."

Daxton nodded and Sasha waved before the three of them turned and left. Peter grabbed my arm and started leading me the opposite direction.

"Where are we going?" I asked, somewhat annoyed. I remembered why I'd wanted to be alone now. He was messing up all my plans.

He didn't answer. He just continued to lead me for a long time, weaving around several blocks. Finally, he stopped at a corner where a car was parked. Leaning down, he found a key on the top of the front right tire.

"Where did this come from?" I asked. Again, I got no answer. I didn't really like where this was going.

He sighed. "Just get in."

"No."

Peter was careful but firm as he forced me into the passenger seat. I tried to fight it, but my body was extremely opposed to any kind of effort. He got into the driver's seat, started the car, and sped through the night.

"What are you doing?" After everything I'd seen

today, this was scaring me. "Where are we going?"

Peter must've sensed my bubbling fear because he finally gave me a response, staring straight out the windshield. "I promised Alaina I would bring you back, no matter what. No matter what you wanted or what plans you came up with. The government chick said she'd provide the car as long as I brought you back safely."

"No…no, Peter, please no," I moaned, pulling my knees up and wrapping my arms around them.

"I know you don't want—"

"It's not about what I *want*," I said bitterly. "It's about what I have to do. I can't keep doing this to you guys. I can't. Can you just respect that?"

He pressed his lips into a thin line. No answer.

"If I go back there and see them all again, I'll never be able to leave."

"That's the idea."

I shook my head, suddenly feeling dangerously unstable. "No, you don't understand!" I pushed one of my sleeves up, revealing the blue tattoo, and Peter flinched in spite of himself. "I don't know what this is," I said, my trembling voice cracking, "but I know that one day I'm going to wake up a monster that kills everyone and I can't be around you when that happens. How many more people have to die, how many more lives ruined, for everyone to get that? Huh? People love to shun me like a pariah and glare at me all day, but nobody understands how bad this is—this will take down *everyone*. And I can't control it. I can't. I've tried, but…it's not good enough."

My breathing started to speed up, my body shaking violently. Emotions were coming out—the intense, raw emotions I'd tried so hard to beat down over the past two days. Lennon coming and Alaina fighting and Dalton raging and Alexis killing and Sark dying and me losing it all over and over again: losing secrets and people and stability and things I loved but didn't deserve.

"You've had an insane day," Peter said, his voice quiet. "Emotional overload?"

That brought me out of it for a second. "What?"

He cleared his throat, the corners of his mouth turning up slightly. "That's what Leslie used to call it, right before she cried. She never cried. She felt stupid when she did. She called it an emotional overload."

That gave me a bit of relief. At least when I lost it, Peter wouldn't judge me too much. "Yeah…I might…I might need a minute."

"Go ahead." He gave a small smile. "I won't tell anyone."

I actually laughed through my formed tears. "Thank you." Then I pulled my hood over my head, wrapped my arms around my knees, and sobbed as quietly as I could until my face was raw, my throat was scratchy, and the supply of tears in the world ran dry.

29

By the time we drove to the hospital, it was almost six in the morning. 'Exhausted' couldn't really describe how I felt, 'achy' couldn't really describe my body, and 'unstable' couldn't really describe my emotional state. I was a wreck, but I didn't care.

The time it had taken to get to the hospital nearly killed me. There was no way to get an update on Sark until we got there, and that took way too many eons.

Peter pulled the car up to the front of the hospital. I opened my door before the car stopped, hastily stepping out and was off. The automatic doors didn't open fast enough as I rushed right up to the counter. The receptionist's mouth dropped open in alarm when she saw me.

"Lindsey Carter," I said, out of breath. "Where's Lindsey Carter?"

"Downstairs," she automatically answered, her eyes huge, as she pointed to the left. "The end of the hallway."

I half ran down the hallway, dodging people and tables and IV stands, stopping only to open the door to the stairs, taking them three at a time. Bursting through the door, I went down the new dim hallway.

"Where is he?" I muttered to myself.

"Arie," Peter called from behind me.

"Where is he?"

"Arie."

"No…but I…where is he?"

"Arie!" Peter caught up, snatching my arm and jerking me backwards. I turned my head, seeing through a window next to a door that I had run right past. Pulling my arm away, I barreled through the door.

"Where is he?" I demanded. Alaina, Liam, Brennan, Lindsey, and Brody were all sitting on chairs around the room, two men standing by another door. I could see a hospital bed through the small window next to it.

Sark. Before I could get inside, one of the men—a doctor—stepped to the side, blocking me. I punched him in the face and shoved him viciously out of the way. Right when my hand closed around the handle, someone grabbed me from behind. Peter wrapped both his arms around me, trapping mine, and picked me up, pulling me back away from the door.

"No!" I kicked my legs. "Let me go! Let me go now!" He put one hand over my mouth, causing me to scream muffled nonsense at the top of my lungs.

Alaina and Brennan stepped in front of me, anxious expressions on their faces, trying and failing to console me. I attempted to bite Peter's hand, but he used his thumb to hold my mouth shut. We struggled like that for a moment, and I decided to take the low road, throwing my head back against his right shoulder—the one I knew was hurt. Peter groaned and almost lost his grip on me, but my escape was unsuccessful. Then I saw a nurse coming toward me with a syringe. In a complete panic, I fought even harder to get out of Peter's iron grip, my muffled screams growing louder.

Brennan glanced at Peter before turning around, seeing what I was so afraid of. He put a hand out to stop the nurse, then he turned to me.

"Look, Arie, if you calm down then we won't have to use it," Brennan told me, his eyes pleading. "Get yourself in control and you can stay awake. Understand?"

I nodded rapidly, then closed my eyes at the dizziness it brought. I forced myself to relax, clamping my teeth and holding my breath to stop the screaming, trying to focus. Peter took his hand off my mouth and I let out a harsh breath through my teeth.

Opening my eyes, I saw Brennan wave off the nurse, who gave me a skeptical look, and the relief helped calm me further. Peter hesitated before letting me go, keeping his hands cautiously at the ready. Alaina gave me a weak grin as she looked me over, her eyebrows creasing. I looked past her, to the door, and took a step forward. My knees buckled; Alaina and Brennan caught me. The room started spinning as my head pounded, my brain feeling as though it was being grated and sautéed for tacos.

"There was a car accident," I heard Peter say. "She's

got a cracked skull and a possible concussion."

I felt that was unfair. "Peter got hit by a car," I mumbled. "He can barely use his right arm." The second I regained my footing, I tried for the door again.

Alaina stopped me, grabbing my shoulders. "Arie, you have to stop."

"No, please." My voice cracked. "Please, I have to see him."

"They don't let crazy people into the hospital room," she said, her joking tone falling flat. "Plus, you're a mess."

I tried to push past her, my hands shaking. "But Alaina—"

"Hey." She grabbed my shoulders, forcing me to look at her. "Have you looked in a mirror? You need to get yourself cleaned up. Can you imagine how badly it would scare him if he saw you like this?"

That stopped me. She had a point. "Is he awake?"

Her face fell slightly, but she tried not to show it. "No. He hasn't woken up yet." She brushed some bloody hair out of my face. "But he's going to anytime and you can't look like this when he does."

My stomach dropped. "He hasn't woken up yet?"

"No."

"At all?"

She shook her head sadly. "But he will. I know he will."

That wasn't enough for me. I trembled as I gently pushed past her, and this time she let me go. She kept a hand on my arm as I walked slowly up to the window. Sure enough, Sark was settled into the bed, his beaten face tranquil with unconsciousness. If it weren't for the oxygen tube sending air through his nose, making his chest move up and down ever so slightly, I would wonder if he was dead.

I rested my forehead on the window in defeat, noticing Lindsey in the reflection walking up to my other side cautiously.

"What happened?" I whispered.

Lindsey answered me in a hushed voice. "Alexis must've injected him with…something. We aren't sure what yet, but it needed to come out. They kept him sedated while they drained it out of him, just in case, then did a blood transfusion. The sedation wore off almost an hour ago. He should wake up anytime."

"He should?"

"He will," she clarified. "And Alaina is right. Let's get you cleaned up so when he does come around you won't have to wait." She pulled on my arm softly. "Come on."

Hesitantly, I tore my eyes away from Sark, letting Lindsey and Alaina lead me into a chair. Liam handed me a cup of water as Brennan ducked out of the room. Something caught my eye and I realized that I knew the man standing in the corner with a grave look on his face.

Keaton walked up to me, extending his hand to shake mine. I stared at it until he dropped it.

He cleared his throat. "Ms. Nolan, I want to extend to you a sincere apology from myself as well as from our agency. If I'd had any idea of Richard Dalton's corrupt actions, corrective measures would've been taken a long time ago. You should know you are now safe from him and those affiliated, and have the gratitude of the agency. Do not hesitate to ask for anything you may need, though I understand we will never be able to make it up to you."

I stared at him with glassy eyes, then realized I should respond. "Thank you."

He caught on that I didn't want to talk to him. Motioning to Brody, they both left the room. Brennan walked back in, the nurse from earlier following him and carrying a bag. I tensed up when I figured out she was coming for me.

Alaina grabbed my hand before I could freak out, giving me a small smile. "It's okay. She's here to help you."

The nurse set her bag down on the ground, then knelt in front of me, her soft chocolate eyes kind.

"Hey sweetie," she said. "I'm just here to look at your head, okay? You don't need to be afraid. I'm not going to do anything that you don't want me to."

Alaina squeezed my hand and I nodded. The nurse opened her bag, grabbing a mini flashlight and shining it in my eyes.

"Does your head hurt?" she asked.

I nodded again.

"On a scale of one to ten, how would you rate the pain in your head?"

I furrowed my eyebrows. That was probably the stupidest thing I'd heard all day. Wasn't pain just pain?

She offered numbers when I didn't. "Eight? Seven?"

I nodded.

"All right." She brought out more supplies from her bag, preparing to stitch up something on my head. "Do you want to tell me what happened to make your head hurt?"

"Um, a car crashed into cement."

"And the glass in your hair?"

"Uh…the windshield broke."

The nurse pursed her lips and went to work, basically having to stitch my whole head back together.

I just drank water, closed my eyes, and waited, making sure to blow even breaths out of my mouth to keep me calm.

"Where are Hadley and Jacklynn?" I asked Alaina. "Are they okay?"

She nodded. "They're in the cafeteria. They had a hard time, watching Sark, and it took forever to get them calmed down about you, so Kayla finally took them up there." She gave a small smile. "Hadley said to tell you he'd save you some Goldfish."

The corners of my mouth turned up. "Good."

The nurse was almost done with my inspection when she decided to take my blood pressure without telling me. She moved my sleeve and gasped at the blue marks, jumping up and backing away from me. Her reaction caused many to look at us, including Alaina who jerked her hand off of mine.

That was it. I couldn't stay there anymore. Springing out of my chair, I rushed into Sark's room. This time, though, nobody stopped me.

A solemnness enveloped me as I watched him. One slow step at a time, I went forward until I was standing right next to his bed. The monitor sounded his steady heartbeats, which was comforting to me. As long as I could hear those beeps, Sark still had a chance.

I scooted a chair up against his bed, angling it so I could look at his face. Sitting down, I brought my knees up, resting my head on them, and carefully reached my arm over the bed railing, finding his hand. It was warm. I held on to it, feeling as if I would never let go again.

"I came back," I whispered to him, my throat thick. "I came back just for you. Please get up. Please, Sark? Don't do this to me. Don't go this way."

Nobody disturbed me as I spoke softly to my

brother, silently begging the heavens to let him stay. It wasn't long before my pleading whispers turned to quiet breaths and I drifted off to sleep, still clutching his hand.

<center>~~~</center>

The nurse came in every half hour to take his vitals. I was only vaguely aware of this, and sometimes I wondered if I just dreamed her coming in. If she woke me up, I fell back asleep almost instantly. I didn't want to sleep, but I didn't really have a choice. My body refused to let me stay awake and I didn't care as long as nobody made me move.

Somewhere in the distance, I heard the nurse talking. I struggled to wake up, irritated that she was bothering me in my state—I had made it clear that I had no desire to speak to her about any of my injuries. Slowly, I started lifting my head off of my knees. Then I felt a slight amount of pressure on my hand and my eyes snapped open.

The nurse was checking the monitors, but she hadn't been talking to me. My heart leapt in my throat as I saw Sark's tired blue eyes open, watching me.

"Sark!" I gasped quietly, nearly falling out of my chair. "Sark, you…you're awake…how are…I mean, what…are you okay?"

His eyes roamed the room curiously before he responded in a weak voice. "Where are we?"

"We're in a hospital. Lindsey brought us here. Don't worry, you're safe here."

His eyebrows furrowed. "Where's Alexis?"

"He's, uh…" I tucked my hair behind my ear. "He's busy right now. But he doesn't know where you are, so

438

it's okay."

Sark let go of my hand and reached up to my face, tapping his thumb against me as if in question. I had seen it in the mirror: I had four black bruises and a torn-up cheek, while my head was ridden with stitches everywhere.

"What happened?" he asked, his forehead creasing with worry. That made me panic. He looked so pale and fragile, like even the slightest amount of stress would cause him to break.

I put my hand over his, bringing it back down to rest on the bed.

"Nothing," I said. "It's no big deal. I just…I almost…I'm *so* glad you woke up. I can't even tell you. I've been a nervous wreck for hours."

I knew the answer wasn't enough, but he seemed too tired to press it. He closed his eyes, breathing evenly, as his mouth turned up in a faint grin.

"Now you know what it's like for me," he said, "waiting for you to not die. You owe me a couple more times."

"Um, no. How about neither of us do it again and we call it even?" I asked hopefully.

His grin grew a tiny bit. "Good call."

The nurse brought in a cup of water, allowing me to take it, before leaving us alone again. I helped Sark take a few sips. He attempted to shift around, a slight grimace on his face.

"What do you need?" I asked, my hands fluttering around him helplessly. "What can I do?"

He just sighed, giving up on comfort. His hand reached out and I took it.

"Arie?" he asked, his voice straining.

I rested my head against the railing of the bed so I

could hear him better. "Yeah?"

"I am so sorry…about Dalton." His grip tightened a bit on my hand. "That…that was…bad."

"No, don't worry about it." I tried to pretend like it wasn't a big deal. "That was my fault. I should've…I mean, I guess I could've…"

Stood up for yourself? I supplied in my head. *Not allowed Dalton to walk all over you? Been there when Alexis showed up, maybe keeping Sark from being so close to death?*

"Done something," I finished quietly. "But it's fine. It's over now."

He nodded slowly, as if in approval. "Did you…you did it, didn't you? You saved me and brought me here."

"Well, it wasn't just me." I gave a small grin, hoping for a joke. "But you've saved me enough times, I figured it was my civic duty to return the favor."

He didn't think it was funny. "It was stupid," he told me. "And reckless. And dangerous."

The grin fell from my face. "I know."

His eyelids fluttered as he struggled to open them, and I braced myself for a lecture. Instead, his sincere eyes gazed into mine. "Thank you."

"Of course."

"No." Sark's eyebrows furrowed. "I mean it. I was nineteen when Alexis murdered White. I knew…I'll never regret leaving…coming to you…but since I defected, I've been scared of that day…when he would do the same to me."

He closed his eyes again and three monitor beeps sounded before I could respond.

"I thought you don't get scared," I said, my voice quiet.

"I do. That should've been it…the end for me. It

was going to be bad. It's selfish, but I'm glad you came." He sighed. "I underestimated you. I've done that too much since you came back. You're stronger than I give you credit for."

I brushed my hair behind my ear, not able to keep my mouth from smiling. "Thanks."

"No. Thank you." We were quiet for a minute before Sark let out a long breath. "I'm sorry…I'm so tired. Just so tired."

A pang of hurt went through my chest. "It's okay. Go to sleep. I bet you'll feel even better when you wake up."

I could tell he was already drifting, his body relaxing, as he nodded again.

"I'll…see you…in…awhile," he mumbled. Then he was out.

I watched him for a moment, a thousand different thoughts running through my brain. Ultimately, though, I knew what I needed to do.

Being as quiet as possible, I walked over to the door and cracked it open. Lindsey was on the other side in a second.

"What do you need?" she asked, her bandaged forehead creased with worry.

"I need a laptop and a flash drive," I answered slowly. "As soon as you can, please."

Lindsey's eyebrows arched in surprise, but she didn't ask questions. My wish was granted and soon I was back in the chair next to Sark's bed, staring at a blank computer screen.

Okay, here it goes. Make it count.

Once I finally got my fingers to start typing, they wouldn't stop. I went for hours without so much as a break. Sark's heart monitor and the rapid tapping of my fingers against the keys were the only sounds to comfort me as I worked through the first part of my new plan.

The whole experience was more emotional than I had anticipated, and I found myself drained when I was finally finished. I saved everything onto the flash drive Lindsey had given me, wrote a few keys things on my wrist, then deleted it all off the computer and shut it down. After I returned it to Lindsey, I set off to find Kayla, setting my next step in motion.

She was sitting in the hospital cafeteria, holding a cup of coffee she didn't look interested in. I sat down across from her, and she blinked in surprise.

"What are you doing here?" she asked me. "I thought you were with Sark."

I cleared my throat. "Kayla, I need you to do something for me. It's extremely important, but I trust that you'll do it right."

She straightened up. "What did you have in mind?"

Pulling one of my flash drives out of my pocket, I set it on the table in front of her, then met her gaze.

"This has the power to change everything as we know it, but you have to do this exactly as I tell you to. You have to keep it a secret until I say, and you have to follow every direction to the letter. Can I trust you to do that?"

Kayla nodded. When it came to new discoveries, she wasn't one to back down, which I was counting on.

I leaned forward and lowered the volume of my voice. "When Peter and I went back to the mall, we found Jefferson's stash of passwords to files and databases, and I copied them onto that flash drive."

Kayla's eyes widened in shock, but I kept going before she could interrupt.

"Whatever they have—whatever information on

reversal they have access to—we now have. You can get to it. The thing is, Jefferson doesn't know that we took this off of him, and the longer it is until he figures it out, the better."

"So we have to drain it slowly," Kayla guessed. "If we log onto their database and try to download everything, they'll notice and know that they've been breached."

"Exactly. You have to be smart about this or we could lose our only shot." I brushed my hair behind my ear. "Also, there are plenty of bank account numbers you could hand over to the police or flush out yourself. Either way, if we cut off their funds, it cripples them."

She nodded, picking up the flash drive in reverence. "I'll take care of it."

"Remember: keep it a secret until you can get started. After that it's up to your discretion who you tell when. This just can't get messed up."

"I understand."

Satisfied, I stood up and made my way to the stairs. I was halfway down the hallway to Sark's room when I bumped into Hadley and Jacklynn. All three of us stopped when we saw each other, then they both broke into a run. I fell to my knees right as they barreled into me. We nearly squeezed each other to death before the kids broke away.

"We were so scared for you," Jacklynn said, her lip trembling.

"I wasn't." Hadley folded his arms across his chest.

Jacklynn pushed him. "Yes you were! We were both so scared. We wanted you to come back."

"Well, I was only kind of scared," Hadley clarified. "I knew you would come back. You always come back."

Jacklynn shook her head at me. "He didn't know. Neither of us did."

"It's okay now," I said. "We're all okay."

Hadley's forehead creased with worry. "Even Sark? Because he's hurt in the hospital."

"Everyone tried to keep it from us," Jacklynn jumped in. "They wouldn't tell us what happened to Sark or if you were okay, but we overheard Alaina and other people saying that you both might die."

"Yeah, they said that." Hadley's eyes were wide. "It was so scary. And you weren't even there to tell us it's okay." He took a step closer to me so he could whisper. "Kayla tried, but don't tell her because she's not as good at it as you."

Jacklynn nodded. "We missed you."

I smiled. "I missed you too. But you don't need to be scared anymore—Sark's going to be okay."

They both gasped in unison, which was pretty adorable. "Really?"

"Yep." I grabbed each of their hands. "You guys were so so brave. Thank you."

They both grinned with pride. "You're welcome," Hadley said.

My heart ached as I looked over them, and I pulled them both into a tight hug. "You guys need to keep being brave, okay? No matter what. Can you do that for me?"

Their chins dug into my shoulders as they nodded.

I cleared my throat to keep my voice from cracking. "I love you both so much. Just keep looking out for each other. Keep being brave."

Hadley broke out of my grasp and looked at me, eyebrows furrowed. "Are you going somewhere?"

I shrugged. "I just wanted you guys to know." I gave

a small smile. "With everything that's happened in the past few days…I've thought about everyone a lot. I want you to know that I love you so much no matter what and I am so so proud of you. Will you remember that?"

They both nodded again.

I sniffed, hoping they really suspect me. "Okay, well keep going wherever you were going. Glad I ran into you."

"Bye Arie," Jacklynn said as they started walking.

"Wait!" Hadley exclaimed. He turned and ran back to me, taking a small, crumpled bag of Goldfish out of his pocket and offering it to me. "I saved these for you."

I grinned, ruffling his hair with my hand. "Thanks." I watched as they left together, both giving me a last wave before they disappeared around the corner.

Clearing my throat in an effort to compose myself, I stuffed the crumbled Goldfish in my jacket pocket and went back to Sark's room. My feet felt heavier the closer I got.

I sat in my chair, the urge to cry suddenly coming over me, and I had to force it down. Not now. There would be plenty of time to cry later, alone. I couldn't afford to lose it yet.

The nurse came back in to take Sark's vitals, explaining to me again that he would probably be asleep for a while before he would come around again, but that was normal. He was going to be okay.

My joy at the news was bittersweet. I thanked her and she left me to my responsibilities. Even though I knew it was coming, I still didn't realize how hard it would really be.

"Sark?" I asked, checking to see if he could hear me. No response. He was dead to the world. The selfish part of me wished he would wake up again, forcing me to postpone my objective. It shouldn't matter, though—this was inevitable. I had known that for a long time now.

"Sark...I'm so sorry. I'm sorry you're here. I'm sorry this happened to you. I'm sorry I put you in harm's way." My whispered voice started trembling. "I know you probably wouldn't agree with me, but...I have to leave now. And I can't come back."

My eyes were stinging with tears. "Please try to understand this. Please don't be mad at me. I love you and I can't go through this again. I can't put your life at risk just 'cause I never want to leave you. Someday the monster will take me over and I won't have control. You can't be around me then. Nobody can. But I found a way I can be useful. I found a way I can help. I'm going to work on getting rid of Alexis for you—that way he can never try to kill you or another infected ever again. Like you said, I'll do whatever it takes."

The heart monitor continued to beep steadily. I felt like it was counting the time, counting the moments, reminding me I was out of it.

"Please try to move on," I told him. "Don't try to look for me. Don't come after me. It will just make it harder. I'm going...I'm going to miss you so much."

My voice cracked, a tear rolling down my face. "I'm sorry I couldn't fix myself. I'm sorry I couldn't be better for you. I'm sorry I caused you so much pain. I promise, I never wanted it to be that way. I never did. I tried so hard and I'm sorry it was never good enough. I'm sorry I couldn't beat this. I'm sorry I let you down."

My breathing caught, and I had to put a hand over my mouth to stifle a sob. "I'm so scared, Sark. I'm so scared. I don't think I can do this, but I have to. I have to."

I wiped the tears off my face, taking several unsteady breaths. I couldn't walk out of here this way. I'd never get past the door.

"If Kayla can ever crack reversal—and I'm sure she can—I'll come back. I will. I promise."

Standing up out of my chair, I gave his hand a last soft squeeze.

"Thank you for everything," I whispered. "You're my angel. Thank you." I let out a long breath, squaring my shoulders. "Please take care of yourself. Take care of the infecteds. Find a way to save them. I know you can."

My feet seemed to be glued to the floor—it took an enormous amount of effort to take the first step away from him. A physical breaking went through my heart as I forced myself to walk out, shutting the door softly behind me.

I turned to survey the small waiting room. Lindsey and Lucy were both fast asleep in chairs. Liam, Peter, and Brennan were sitting on the floor against the far wall, Peter's arm in a sling, all of them failing to fight off the drowsiness too.

Goodbye guys. Thanks for being my family. Take care of yourselves.

Holding my breath, I quickly stepped out before they woke up. The dim lights in the hallway did little to make me feel better. Already I felt utterly alone.

One more item of business.

I went straight for the office next door, knowing that's where he'd be, and entered without knocking. Keaton was standing next to a desk, speaking in a solemn voice into his cell phone. He stopped when he saw me.

"I'm going to have to call you back," he said before clicking his phone off. Then he gestured to me. "Ms. Nolan. This is quite a surprise."

I shut the door behind me. "I need to talk to you. Confidentially."

"All right." He leaned back against the desk. "Go ahead."

I decided to get right to it. "Yesterday I found important files on Alexis' organization that I was able to steal without his knowledge."

Keaton's eyebrows shot up. "What?"

"They could really go a long way, if they're used right."

"And you're going to give me a chance to see these files," Keaton said, adding a slight command to his voice. "Am I right, Ms. Nolan?"

I nodded. "In the right time." I wrapped my arms around myself. "But that's not my point. My point is that I know where Alexis' most important locations are and I'm going to destroy them, one by one."

"You don't trust the police with that?" he asked. "Or at least us?"

"No. Can you blame me? Alexis is too powerful anyway. I give it a couple days before he's out of jail and back on the streets."

"Why don't you let me help you destroy all the locations at once?"

I shook my head. "That won't work. I have to take it slow. If they feel too threatened, they'll close off all of their databases and we'll lose access. My friend needs time to slowly leak the information we need."

There was a minute of silence. Neither of us moved.

"That's quite dangerous," Keaton finally stated.

I stared evenly at him. "But you're not going to stop

me. You owe me."

He gave a slow nod. "Yes. I'm just confused as to why you came to me with this."

"You're involved but impartial. And you can help."

"Fair enough." He folded his arms across his chest. "What do you want me to do?"

"I want you to keep up with them," I told him, pointing in the general direction of the infecteds. "I want you to give them whatever assistance they need—whatever it is, I don't care. You get it for them."

"You know I have to ask you, Ms. Nolan—" Keaton started.

I shook my head. "I will do what I have to do, one way or another."

Alone I have nothing to lose.

"And what if Alexis gains the upper hand?"

"If something happens to me, you'll know, because you'll be with the infecteds and if something happens to me, Alexis will make sure they hear about it. I know that much." I took a step toward him, pulling my new flash drive out of my pocket and gingerly offering it to him. "And if that happens, you publish this."

Keaton hesitated. "What is it?"

"Lindsey once told me that my story is the most valuable thing I'll ever have to offer, and I understand that now." I took a deep breath. "So, this is it. My story, from the beginning to today."

He seemed skeptical, so I went on before he could tell me it was a stupid idea. "I can't put it out there now. I have to buy Kayla time to get the reversal files. She needs a few weeks at least, and Alexis' organization needs to still be running for that to happen." I lifted the flash drive. "The world doesn't really know about infecteds or Alexis or the illegal aspects of it all. This comes out now and Alexis will be forced to retreat. My friend won't have a chance."

Keaton raised an eyebrow, stayed still for a moment, then took the flash drive from me. "You do realize that—"

"Yes," I interrupted impatiently. "Yes, I realize the risk; yes, I realize my friends won't be happy; and, yes, I realize it's horrendously cliché, but I need you to do it. Please."

He let out a long breath, rubbing his jaw. I waited in nervous anticipation.

"Okay," he finally answered, his voice quiet. "I'll do it."

I breathed a sigh of relief. "You swear?"

"Yes."

"Thank you." I brushed my hair behind my ear. "This never happened, okay? You never talked to me."

He gestured to the door. "I understand. Just go while you have your chance."

I gave him a small nod of appreciation before slipping out the door. My victory was hollow though. The sight of Sark's door made me remember what I was really doing, and the crushing loneliness came washing over me again. But I knew I had to continue.

I wasn't far down the hallway when a voice interrupted me.

"Don't do anything I wouldn't do."

I froze, then turned around to see Alaina leaning against the wall. The pain in her eyes didn't match the resolute expression on her face. I understood: she knew I was leaving, and she was letting me go.

I couldn't help it. I ran up to her, throwing my arms around her, hiding my face in her shoulder as a few tears escaped me. She held on to me tightly, her body shaking underneath me, and I knew she was crying too.

"Be careful," she whispered in my ear, her voice breaking. "Please be careful."

I nodded. "Take care of him. All of them. Watch over Hadley and Jacklynn for me. Please."

"I will."

She waited until I broke away from her, reluctantly letting me go. I wiped the tears from my face with the sleeve of my jacket. It was time. If I didn't leave now then I never would.

"Bye," I said, my voice barely audible.

A dry half sob came through her mouth. "Bye."

Then I walked away. The floor was scalding under my feet; the walls seemed to close in around me. Numbly, I went up the stairs and out the front door of the hospital, squinting at the bright afternoon sun.

You are alone now, I couldn't help thinking.

Pulling my hood over my head, I took the shape of my true form. I melted into the background, strategies going through my dazed mind, as people passed by me in oblivion. The feeling of duty toward my mission came over me. I would do this right. The pain of leaving would not be for nothing.

This is war.

~~~

My plan was working. There were definitely some bad days, some setbacks, some things I hadn't anticipated. But overall, it was going well.

Over the past two months, I had successfully eradicated four of Alexis' operational locations and caused hundreds of his employees to wind up in prison, all without getting caught. Of course, there were always
~~~

close calls, but I'd been lucky. Alexis had never seen me and no cops ever had direct contact with me. I was really careful. And though it was always too soon to say, I felt like I was making some progress.

That should've made me so happy. Ecstatic. The simple fact should've put a smile on my face and a spring in my step. It didn't. I pretended like I didn't know why, but I did.

Living alone on the run again left me with this uncomfortable sense of dèjá vu—as if I were reliving a different time period, after I'd run away from home and before I met Erika, my life revolving around the fear of getting caught. Granted, getting to watch part of Alexis' organization go to ruin every couple weeks was a new feature that I liked about my circumstances. It felt different.

And I was getting worse. I tried to ignore that fact, but it was true. The vines from my tattoos had grown almost to my shoulder, while the monster in my head *never* shut up. I didn't know what that meant. All I knew was that spending so much time with only her to keep me company was literally driving me insane.

That wasn't the point though. Yeah, I was getting worse and was constantly haunted by the idea of waking up a monster—whatever. The real thing I should've been focusing on was how much progress I was making. I was chipping away at the idea that infecteds could never be safe. I was helping to save my family.

Of course, that line of thinking brought on a crippling wave of homesickness that I almost couldn't handle, so I tried to avoid it, which was why all I could think about was the burning on my arms and the ticking of my clock. My brain was just a weird place to be.

It was mid-June when I was going through Salt Lake

City, on my way to California. The higher temperatures made it difficult because I had to constantly wear long sleeves, often leaving me hot, exhausted, and in a terrible mood every day.

That night I was wearing a black long sleeve shirt—not a good idea for heat stroke—and walking down a street named Mario when he found me, catching me by complete and total surprise.

"Micah? What are you doing here?" I asked when I saw him walking down the sidewalk toward me, his arrogant attitude on full display. Call it what you want—bad boy, rebel without cause, he's attractive and knew it—but to me it meant one thing: he was going to be a jerk. Which wasn't like the Micah I knew at all.

What happened to you, Micah?

He grinned. "Just checking on my favorite girl."

For some reason that made me uneasy. "How did you know I was here?"

"Come here." He grabbed my wrist and started yanking me through an empty parking lot of a strip mall. "I've got to show you something."

I ended up following him, mostly because I couldn't get my arm out of his grip. Once we were concealed in the alley between two stores, he let go of me, stepping so he was blocking my exit.

This is a bit more than jerk. This is now on the level of creepy.

"What's going on?" I asked, trying to keep my bubbling fear out of my voice.

"Actually, Arie, I'm here to grant you a wish." He bowed gracefully. "You told me once you wanted to know who my employer was."

Oh great. My hands started fidgeting. "Yes. I guess I did say that."

"Well here's some great news: my employer wants to offer you a place in his community. He says you've proven to be what he's looking for." Micah held his arms out in presentation. "Isn't that great?"

Um, no. No, not really. "And what if I had to decline his offer?"

Micah's eyes hardened as he set his jaw. "I would say that's the wrong answer."

I took a step away from him, remembering vividly the night he tried to murder me all those months ago. "And what if I said thank you, but no? Because that's what I'm going to say."

"I would say you don't understand your situation. You don't really have a choice here."

"I beg to differ."

Micah shrugged. "Suit yourself. You'll just have to tell him that to his face—he doesn't really like to be told no."

A white van drove up and parked behind Micah, further limiting my ability to make an escape. The door slid open and out stepped three people who I could easily profile: the guard, the victim, and the leader.

Well this should be fun.

The guard was the first one out, dragging along the victim who was tied up and had a bag over their head. I had to stifle a gasp when I saw the designated leader.

His shoulders didn't sit straight on his body, the effect only heightened by his severe limp, and though he could've been somewhat tall, he hunched over, his back seeming to be permanently arched. Four jagged scars deformed the left side of his face, pinching up the skin, and his green eyes never stopped moving.

"Arie Nolan," he greeted, his voice sounding like every accomplished professor's should. He clasped his gloved hands. "I have been waiting eagerly for this moment for quite some time. My name is Cyrus."

I didn't really know what to do besides try extremely hard not to stare.

"I assume Micah has told you about my hopes for you," Cyrus went on. "That you have a place in my community for—"

"I'm sorry," I interrupted, finding my voice, "but you've got the wrong girl. I'm not accepting your offer."

The man raised a misshapen eyebrow and Micah glanced at him.

"You're not accepting it?"

I shook my head. "No. I'm kinda in the middle of some personal stuff right now anyway." *Plus, I try not to associate with psychopaths on a regular basis.*

"And what is that?" Cyrus asked. "Trying to bring down the organization that threatens you and your family?"

"Um, yeah, actually." *Who the heck is this guy?* "It's pretty important, so I'm just going to keep it up for now."

His eyes seemed to see right through me. "Have you ever thought to look outside yourself, Arie? That maybe there are opportunities for you that you have not yet considered?"

Not this crap again. "Look, um, sir, I don't really have time for this. I won't just—"

He shook his head once. "I believe you are misunderstanding me. I am not a stranger approaching you for a needless venture. I am an old family friend whose cause stands to save humanity. I have been watching you for many years now—we don't approach just anyone. I'm asking you to realize your potential and join me."

My eyebrows furrowed in disgust. *He's been watching me?*

"You should take this seriously, feel honored even," Cyrus added, a small smile on the good side of his face. "I rarely make personal calls."

I took a small step to the side, gaging the space between the wall and the van. "I don't know you." *I would definitely remember you.* "And I'm not interested in saving humanity, so if you would please let me get back to work, I'd appreciate it."

Cyrus let out an impatient breath. "I don't appreciate your tone."

"My *tone*?" I asked in disbelief.

"If you knew better, dear, you'd give me more respect."

"If I knew better, I would've left five minutes ago instead of letting you waste my time." I took a step forward. "Now, if you'll excuse me, I'm—"

Micah stepped to the side, in front of me, his arms tense and ready as his somber eyes bore into mine.

"He needs you, Arie."

Unfortunately for Micah, my patience had run out four days ago. "He *needs* me? He doesn't even know me!"

"Yes, I know you." Cyrus took a step toward me, and I automatically took one back, the hair on the back of my neck standing up on end. "I know everything there is to know about Arie Nolan."

I took a breath to steady myself. This guy was really freaking me out. "Yeah? You sure about that?"

"I know that you nearly died of pneumonia when you were five years old; that when you were eight you fell out of a tree, which is why you're afraid of heights when you're unrestrained; that when you were twelve your father lost his job again, forcing your family to relocate to Saratoga Springs and start a new life. I know that you were infected at age fifteen, shortly after your mother's father passed away and before your older brother was killed in action. I know your friend Connor was a fraud for Alexis, that you consider your ex-handler your brother, that your favorite teacher in high school was Mr. Markham." His fingers started twitching. "You tell people you're allergic to peanuts to hide the fact you detest them, you have an irrational fear of dogs due to a few unfortunate instances, and you now have a new addition to your inner monologue that can be tedious, marked by the arrival of the symbols on your arms, neither of which you understand or will tell anyone about."

I listened in stunned silence, not realizing until he stopped that my mouth was hanging open.

He took several deep breaths, as if his whole speech had tired him. "Need I continue?"

This is a whole new level of stalker. You need to get out now.

"As I said," Cyrus went on when I didn't, "I've been watching. Micah was sent to test you and you've passed. You should be proud of yourself, dear. Few are worthy of our attention and even fewer make it this far."

"No," I said quietly. I cleared my throat. "I'm not interested. Leave me alone."

Cyrus shook his head again, one jerky motion. "I'm sure if you listen to the entirety of my offer, you will see it my way. This is a historic enterprise—"

"No thank you." My tone was absolute. "I'm not coming."

"Yes, I think you are."

"Look, I've done the whole kidnapping thing before, so—"

Cyrus chuckled once. "Dear, I'm not going to kidnap you. You're going to come with me."

Uh huh, over my dead body.

Cyrus nodded to the guard, who took off the victim's bag. I froze over in shock when I saw it was a beat-up Alexis. Muffled sounds came from his taped mouth, his frenzied eyes widening when he saw me.

They have Alexis tied up in a van? Can you even do that?

I took a shaky breath, my instincts telling me to get the heck out of there. "What are you doing?"

"Let's make a deal, shall we?" Cyrus gestured to Alexis. "You come with me, and I'll give you exactly what you want—the freedom of your family."

It took a few seconds for that to sink in. "No." I shook my head. "No, I didn't want to—"

"Tick tock, dear." Cyrus snapped his fingers and Micah straightened up, stepping closer to Alexis, tense and at the ready. "You have thirty seconds to decide."

"Decide what?" I asked, exasperated, hands shaking. "I wasn't going to kill him!"

"I've given you exactly what you wanted." Cyrus walked over and patted Alexis on the head, making me wince and Alexis scowl furiously. "I've done everything but decorate him with a bow. Aren't you going to take the opportunity—give him exactly what he deserves? It's the least you could do after all my trouble to get you this peace offering. Not to mention everything he's done to you and your family."

My head was spinning. "No, I..." *This is insane.* "I was going to do this the right way."

"The right way?" Cyrus repeated in surprise. "My,

we have a lot to work on, don't we? Not to worry. You're nothing that can't be fixed." He snapped his fingers again. "Micah?"

I only had time to close my eyes, but I should've closed my ears too. Footsteps and scuffling, muffled screams, squelching, breaking, snapping, gurgling.

Silence.

A thud.

Silence.

The stench of blood made its way to my nose. The only sounds I could hear were the faint buzz of distant cars and my heart pounding in my chest.

Vomiting was already a hazard, but my eyes still opened to see the body—I had to swallow down throw up and look away.

He just murdered Alexis. Murdered. Alexis.

Micah resumed his place to the right of me, a smug smile on his face, blood dripping from his fingers.

"Why…why did you do that?" I breathed, wrapping my arms around myself.

Cyrus gave me a crooked grin. "Tell me, dear, do I have your attention now?"

ACKNOWLEDGEMENTS

No novel ever writes itself, nor can one be published by just one person. Buckets of thank you's to my editing team for giving so much of their priceless time to helping me build a novel; to my bestie, Nan, for being my co-editor and rock of strength, not only in writing but in every crazy situation we find ourselves in; to Court, for continuing to show me why believing in yourself is so important; to my mom, for birthing me, raising me, not giving me away, and always putting me first, no matter how weird or difficult my need is. If it weren't for my Executive Producer and constant wingman, Padre, I would still be a girl with an idea, too terrified to write an actual book, and would've given up at least six hundred times by now. I have the most amazing family and friends, a support system that is truly invaluable—thank you. It wouldn't be right to not call out NaNoWriMo: their amazing program jumpstarted the journey that would turn my dream into a reality. And, of course, giant thank you's to those of you who read my books, check out my website, and follow me on social media. There is no feeling in the world like expressing yourself and having people support and cheer you on. I love you guys!

ARIE SURVIVED THE NIGHT...BUT CAN SHE SURVIVE THE END?

**Part one of the epic finale is available now!
Turn the page for a sneak peek.**

I darted down the darkened hallway, my eyes barely able to make out the shapes of the slick walls around me. Massive picture frames and lopsided fake plants threw lumpy shadows along my path, standing silent, like grave onlookers lined up to watch a grisly execution. I pretended not to notice them, ignoring their judgmental stares boring into my skin. There was nothing in the thick silence—my quick footsteps had been practiced into soundlessness—but I could hear the verdict the shadowed onlookers gave me like the pounding of drums before the guillotine: *guilty.*

A shiver went down my spine without my permission. I pushed it away, willing my fraying nerves to harden and mold into something strong. Indestructible.

Focus, I told myself, scolding, like my brief moment of weakness was a sign of bad behavior. *Down this hallway and take the second right. It's the second right.*

Are you sure it wasn't left? my inner unwanted consultant chimed in, her snarky voice feigning innocence. *It would be such a shame to screw this up. And by a shame, I mean I really want to see you bleed.*

It's right. I'm sure, I snapped back. Except now, I wasn't sure at all.

The uncertainty filled my head like the rising tide despite my efforts to keep it down. She fed off any and all negativity, especially in me, and I felt her rise up. I saw as the grotesque image of her formed in the corner of my head, the image of a nightmare but one that was unfortunately all too real in ways I couldn't explain: nearly a perfect reflection of me. At least, what *used* to be me. Her skin was ridden with scars and torn to expose electric blue flesh, half her hair had been ripped out, and the left side of her face was marred nearly beyond recognition. My right eye looked back at me, but her left was just a brilliant solid blue orb in the socket, and she gave me a smirk with her half-disfigured lips.

Oh, but princess, you sound less sure now.

Shut up, Vanessa. You're not helping.

Whatever you say, princess. After all, I live to serve.

I rolled my eyes at her, trying to ignore her continuous presence. Months back I had named her Vanessa, mostly because I needed something else to call her besides "Monster Me" and thought it was fitting since that was the name of the sea witch in *The Little Mermaid.* At first, she was really annoyed by the name, which was why I kept using it, but now she had embraced it. As she put it, naming her meant I was accepting that she wasn't going anywhere. I always got nauseated at the thought.

Trusting my gut, I continued down the hallway and took the second right. Sure enough, my comrade was there waiting for me, standing against the wall with a loose but alert stance.

"The system's disabled," I breathed, barely audible. "We're good to go."

Micah nodded and straightened up, not hiding the boredom in his bright green eyes that seemed to glow in the dark: radioactive, unstable, and ready to blow. "After you then."

I complied, taking the lead down the corridor. It was two lefts, stairs, and a right—I knew that—but I still found myself mentally running through the map I had memorized the day before just to triple check. Micah didn't allow for mistakes on assignments. That was easy for him until I started accompanying him. Now if anything went wrong it was usually my fault, and I paid for it.

Making my senses focus again, I concentrated on where I was. Feet against shoes, shoes against marble. Musty atmosphere. Faint tropical freshener staining the stagnant air. Micah following close behind, his pace rapid but his breathing even. The shadows that watched us, silently waiting in stoic anticipation for judgment to be passed. Left. Stairs. Right. Never making a sound. Focused on putting one foot in front of the other, leading, tensing, recoiling from what would happen when I reached my destination. The shadows shouted soundlessly at me, exposing me for what I was despite the long sleeves I wore.

A shaky breath escaped me, and I felt Micah's disapproval without even seeing his face.

Stop it, I commanded myself. *Don't think. Focus. You just have to focus.*

I stopped at the immense black double doors with gold letters immortalizing the name 'Laurent Bridges.' How nice of him to put his name on the door, like an invitation beckoning us in.

You don't want us to come in, Laurent. You want to run.

Micah lifted his arm to push me out of the way; I stepped aside on my own. He put his ear up to the door, listened for about twenty seconds, then signaled with his fingers.

Three guards in there, he told me. Piece of cake for us. Poor Laurent thought hiding out in his expensive office with a personal detail would help his situation.

Micah took out his precious knife and started working his magic on the locked handle. Though assignments often made me feel like a spy in need of dart guns, elaborate wigs, and fast cars, my comrade preferred the simplistic approach. Hands-on. For Micah, it's just about him, his weapon, and his target. Anything else—even cool gadgets—were just unnecessary annoyances. He didn't need them.

I made myself count while he worked. Counting helped in lots of situations. There was something calming about the succession, the order, the absence of chaos without the terror of dreading inevitability. Six came after five, and it would always come after five, and there was never a reason for anyone to be upset that it did. Numbers had such a deep-rooted foundation that even the universe bent around them, allowing them to exist as they were without forcing change.

Twelve. Thirteen. Fourteen. Fifteen. Six—

The handle clicked, my adrenaline spiked, and we stormed in. The look of shock on the guards' faces would've been hilarious in any other circumstance. I knocked out two of them before either could get their guns out; the third got a shot off—I ducked just in time—before Micah took him out.

We both turned to see Laurent sitting at the desk, face pale and clammy, as his entire corporate life flashed before his wide eyes.

"I'll give you anything you want," he blurted, his reedy voice shaky. "Anything. Money? New identities? A private plane anywhere you want to go. My investments. Anything."

Laurent continued to attempt a bargain, but Micah couldn't care less for the dead man's last words. He walked toward me and pressed the flat side of his knife against my cheek, too soft to actually cut me but threatening nonetheless. I stopped myself from cringing away.

"You take this one." The hair on the back of my neck stood up at the dark murder of his tone. "Let's see what you can do."

Translation: don't mess up or you die too.

I swallowed myself down, letting a coldness overtake me, numbing me from the core and distancing myself from the situation. Settling into something less Arie but not quite Vanessa, I shifted my glare to Laurent, repeating the thoughts that it was either him or me, and I was stronger, I was more powerful, and I couldn't care what happened to him. This is what I'd come to do, and once I got it over with, it would be done. Just like counting. Six would come after five, and we'd move on to seven.

My muscles tensed as I took steady steps forward, gaze zeroing in on the target, and he shrunk back into his black leather chair as I got closer. The space between us grew smaller while I climbed onto his desk, keyboards and monitors and paperweights crashing to the floor. I stopped and sat on the edge, digging my boot behind one of the wheels on his chair leg so he couldn't back away from me. He couldn't seem to look away either. Laurent Bridges stared at me, hypnotized with fear because he knew exactly why I was there.

Leaning forward, I rested my elbows on my knees and stared into Laurent's eyes like I'd been taught, like I could reach down into him and crush everything in its wake. A shudder went through him when I parted my lips to speak.

"Where is it?"

Each word was its own cold thing, my voice sharp but lifeless, like a dead snake's fangs still dripping with venom. Empty but no less dangerous. I barely even recognized my own voice because it wasn't really me. For these tasks, I had to become something else entirely.

It took Laurent twelve seconds to answer, and even then his words stuttered and faltered and tripped over each other. "I, I don't...I don't know...I don't know what you mean."

My eyebrows rose at his bold decision, and he flinched.

This'll be too easy.

Child's play, Vanessa echoed. *It's almost not even fun.*

Faster than Laurent could follow, I jerked my hand out and snatched the closest weapon to me—a long silver letter opener, sharper than was safe—and drove it into Laurent's leg. His scream ricocheted off the walls of the spacious office, and I found my mouth twisting with disgust. This man had no concept of real hurt.

"Where is it?" I asked again.

Laurent was already crying—seriously?—and blubbered something in response. Not an answer, though. Not what I asked for.

Lifting my free leg, I slammed the heel of my boot down on his good knee, just like I'd been taught, and heard a deafening cracking sound. Laurent shrieked and doubled over. I leaned forward further, clasping my hand around the letter opener, and Laurent screamed again before I even moved it.

"Laurent," I said, forcing the name off my tongue because I hated the taste of it. "Do you know who I am?"

Laurent looked at me through his tears for a moment before finally nodding.

"So then you know who sent me."

Another cry burst through his teeth, and he nodded again, miserably.

I held his gaze with a warning glare. "Where is it?"

I gave him thirty seconds to answer, which was generous—I heard Micah huff in impatience behind me—but when Laurent stayed quiet, I jerked the letter opener around, and he howled in response. Something inside me winced when I saw his hands clutch the armrests, like my soul was reminding me that I'd been the one in the chair too, screaming through number six and begging for seven. For the counting to keep going. For the pain to stop.

Please make it stop.

The thought made me slip, a lapse in the charade, and I had to shake my head to focus. That's when I saw it. Subtle, but still there: the shift of Laurent's eyes away from mine. Just for a split second. Just enough.

I straightened up and raised my voice a notch, so Micah would know I was talking to him. "It's somewhere in here. He wouldn't part with it."

A crashing sounded, then a smashing, clattering, more crashing, as the tornado that was Micah tore through the place. I didn't flinch at the chaotic symphony, but Laurent did, wet eyes wide while he watched Micah destroy the beautiful office that stood for his pride and had probably cost a fortune on its own.

"Better tell me now," I said softly, too low for Micah to hear, and Laurent's gaze snapped back to me. "Give yourself a chance."

It was getting warm in the office—uncomfortably warm. Sweat beaded down Laurent's face, his cheeks flushed, as he'd probably never been uncomfortably warm in his life. He opened his mouth, hopefully to speak, but a last crash from Micah sent the words back down his throat. I turned to look. Behind an abstract painting Micah had torn off the wall, there was a cutout nestling a small black safe.

I actually snorted, a chemical reaction between the two sides of me that were never meant to go together. "Behind a painting? Seriously?"

Micah snapped his fingers at me while he inspected the safe. "Code?"

I turned to look at Laurent, and he recoiled under my gaze. Taking a breath, I steeled myself, preparing to go deeper and darker than some flimsy little letter opener, because I was trained to do much worse.

Laurent must've finally got his head screwed on straight because he let it all out in a gust of painful breaths. "Nineteen, Ninety-one, sixteen, twelve, five, six."

That was it. Micah must've put in the code because I heard a pop and turned to see him holding up a black plastic rectangle with fancy silver embellishments. A flash drive. Neither of us knew what was on it, but we weren't supposed to. Assignments were for what, not why.

Micah pocketed the drive, then turned around to face us, jade green eyes locked on Laurent. I stood just as Micah stepped forward.

"We have it," I said, trying to bring the cold cruelty back to my voice. "Assignment complete. Let's go."

Micah shook his head and jerked his chin at Laurent. "No, *he's* the assignment. Anything else is just extra meat."

My mouth went dry. "We have what we came—"

"Arie," Micah growled, drying the rest of me up, and I actually took a stumbling step away, nearly tripping over the end of the desk. A flash of surprise went across Laurent's glazing eyes at my fear. I wasn't supposed to be scared. I wasn't supposed to care whether he lived or died.

In fact, I was supposed to kill him.

Don't miss this heart-pounding novella from the Arie's Story series!

The Kids Aren't All Right follows Leslie and her brother Peter as they navigate their high school classes and friends—until one fateful night their lives are changed forever.

Emilee King is the author of the Arie's Story survival series and the Elarian Chronicles. She loves fairy tales, superheroes, fantasy, and murder mysteries, and is constantly on the hunt for good stories. When she's not writing, you can find her reorganizing her bookshelves, eating pasta, beating the high score on Galaga, or spending time with her family. Visit her website at emileeking.com